A STORM OF BLOOD AND STONE

MYTHS OF STONE BOOK III

GALEN SURLAK-RAMSEY

A Tiny Fox Press Book

Library of Congress Catalog Card Number: 2020946529

ISBN: 978-1-946501-28-8

Tiny Fox Press and the book fox logo are all registered trademarks of Tiny Fox Press LLC

Tiny Fox Press LLC
North Port, FL

For Andy

Chapter An Unwanted Meeting

Euryale had turned a lot of people to stone over the course of her life, even a few of the gods as the Fates had seen fit, but she'd never known what it was like to be petrified herself.

Until now, that is.

Athena, Goddess of Wisdom (and at times, petty revenge), had called upon the gorgon not long ago to help find a missing hero of hers. For most, that wouldn't have been a bad thing, unless, of course, one happened to have had something to do with the assaulting, drugging, and imprisoning of said hero.

At which point being nervous would certainly be under-standable.

Or being scared witless.

Or in Euryale's case, being completely and utterly petrified because she'd done all that and more to Perseus only days ago.

"Sweetie?" Alex said softly. "Sweetie, can you hear me?"

At the sound of his voice, Euryale managed to break free of the hold fear had over her, and she looked to her husband who stood next to her throne. The subject of the conversation they'd had moments ago—the source of her abject terror—was ever-present in her mind.

"Sorry, I...I don't know what to do," Euryale eked out.

"Well, you don't *have* to go see Athena right now, do you?" he asked, his dark eyes filled with worry. "Go see her tomorrow."

Euryale glanced around the Great Hall of Olympus to see who might catch wind of their conversation before answering. There was hardly anyone left from the celebrations. Aside from her children, Aison and Cassandra (who were entertaining themselves with a ride from their pet chimera, Tickles), only a half dozen satyrs who were still cleaning remained.

"I can't," she said, shrinking in her throne and keeping her voice low. "It will only make things worse if I don't talk to her right now."

Alex pressed his lips together. "Should I come with you?" he offered. "Or do you want me to check on...our guest," he said, bobbing his head toward the doors leading outside.

"Neither," Euryale said. "He doesn't need to be disturbed, and I'm hoping Athena will be less confrontational if it's only the two of us."

"Are you sure?" Alex asked, his brow arching. "This could go badly. You might need the extra help."

"I know. And I'm sure."

"Have you ever negotiated something like this before?"

Euryale laughed, hitting light notes that put them both at ease, despite the grim situation. "No, Alex," she said. "I can honestly say I've never had to do this before."

A screech of joy from the twins interrupted the conversation, and both Euryale and Alex twisted around in time to see Tickles bowl over a couple of satyrs before bounding out a side door with Aison and Cassandra on his back, each swinging toy swords wildly in the air.

"You're on twin duty," Euryale said, rising from her throne. "Go put them in line before they destroy something of Zeus's, and we're in even more trouble. I'm going to go talk to Athena before my nerves come back, and I talk myself out of it."

Alex gave her a quick smooch on the cheek. "On it," he said. "You'll be fine, I know it. After all, you did sort of save everyone from Typhon."

"Right," Euryale said, exhaling slowly. "See you soon."

With that, the gorgon slithered out of the Great Hall and headed for Athena's home in Olympus. All the while, one question burned sharply in her mind:

How did the gods negotiate?

The answer to that eluded her at first, but it wasn't long before she realized she'd known the answer all along:

They didn't.

Arguments were settled by spear or wit, sometimes both. Hardly ever were they settled on merit or morality, no matter who was involved. This realization soured Euryale's gut even more, as Athena was easily a hundred times stronger and smarter than the gorgon could ever hope to be.

As such, there was no possible way Euryale was going to win this argument, and she was likely about to meet a painful end. Still, she had to try.

"Keep it together, Euryale," she said to herself, using two fingers from each hand to rub her temples in a vain attempt to ward off a self-induced headache. "You're one of them now. Act like it."

Euryale looked up to get a bearing of where she was, only to find herself right outside Athena's home. She stood there shocked to no end that she'd snaked her way through half of Olympus and hadn't realized it at all.

A few more seconds passed with her not moving a muscle, and then whether it was due to her own willpower or simply a nudge of the Fates, she sucked in a deep breath, rolled her shoulders back, and climbed the marble stairs leading to the front door.

She passed through the entrance without hesitation and quickly entered Athena's courtyard that now held the recent addition of a rocky fountain set in the middle of a large pool stocked with koi fish.

Euryale would've liked to stop and enjoy it for a few moments, but she knew if she paused even in the slightest, she'd lose her nerve. She traversed the courtyard in seconds and entered Athena's west wing. There, she slipped by a few satyrs who were keeping the place tidy, and after taking a couple of bends in the hall, Euryale entered Athena's planning room and came to an abrupt halt, her jaw hanging open nearly to the floor.

The room had been turned into a half-scale replica of the forge the traitor Hephaestus had used under Mount Etna, right down to every conceivable detail Euryale could remember—and another three hundred she'd forgotten. The anvil was set up perfectly, with the exact amount of scratches and wear the original had suffered, while table and smithing tools nearby had been painstakingly recreated as well. There were even carefully painted spots on the floor where Euryale's blood had spattered, thanks to a wicked strike to the back of the head with a hammer when Hephaestus had attacked her.

In the very middle of it all, Athena stood quietly and in deep concentration, wearing her usual garb of leather cuirass and bronze helm. Whatever she was thinking about, she didn't share. Athena turned toward the gorgon and flashed a warm smile. "Euryale," she said. "You're here."

"I am," she replied. "I was told you wanted to see me about something?"

Athena beckoned her over with a wave of the hand. "I did. Please, come here so we can talk."

Euryale slithered forward, trying to ignore the mounting angst in her stomach. "This is quite the setup you have."

"Thank you. I probably spent an extra half hour making sure that everything was perfect."

"You did this by memory?"

"I did," Athena said, beaming with pride. That pride, however, faded slightly as she made the following admission. "But I feel like I've missed something. Does it look right to you?"

Euryale shrugged, although she wished she hadn't. Given the approaching topic that was about to tear the two apart, she would've liked to have been able to offer some sort of insight into the current matter first. Perhaps then Athena would listen to her. "It looks right to me. But even if it isn't, it has to be close enough."

Athena shook her head and scowled. "Our complacency is what led to our near downfall," she said. "I should've seen our betrayal coming. We all should have."

"No one wants to believe their family would be the cause of so much hurt and pain," Euryale said. "Maybe you're being too hard on yourself."

"Perhaps," Athena said. "Either way, I can't help but feel this setup is missing details, details that could lead to vital clues."

"Clues to what?"

"Clues to who else is working with Typhon," she said. "Despite Dad's reassurances, I'm not convinced he's still not a danger, and if he still has spies in Olympus, we've got to find them before they can cause any more damage."

"Has Hera said anything?" Euryale asked.

"No," Athena said, shaking her head. "I doubt she will anytime soon, despite Dad's interrogations."

"Oh," Euryale said. "Where's she being kept, anyway?"

Athena burst into laughter. "Trust me, you don't want to know," she said when she finally regained her composure. "Dad isn't telling anyone, and I promise you, anyone who happens to discover where he's got her kept will be immediately branded a traitor and dealt with accordingly."

Euryale cringed, and the vipers atop her head recoiled in fear. "Then forget I asked."

"Consider it done," she said. "But take heart, if there's anyone who both Zeus and I trust near explicitly, it's you. If you hadn't been...well, you...Typhon would have already ravaged half the world by now."

"Thank you," Euryale said, blushing at the praise she felt was unwarranted. Yes, she'd fought Typhon and won, but that victory was hardly won on her own, and Typhon was hardly at the height of his power when they'd fought.

As a beat of silence settled between them, Euryale sensed she was about to be plunged into the conversation she dreaded, and with that feeling, every bit of confidence and optimism she had vanished. Worse, her internal fears turned into external expressions far too quickly for her to stop them. By the time she realized what was happening, she'd already been fumbling nervously with her hands long enough for Athena to not only take note but to say something as well.

"What's the matter, Euryale?" Athena asked. "You look like you're about to stick your head in the torrents of Chaos."

Reflexively, Euryale put her hands behind her back, which only served to heighten her anxiety and then double it again when she saw Athena raise an eyebrow. "I..." she started but ended up halting when not a single word as a follow up seemed right. After a huge breath, she managed to spit something out. "I have to talk to someone soon, and I'm worried about it, is all."

Athena laughed, her face brightening with amusement. "You? Worried about talking to someone?" she said. "You're hilarious, gorgon. What topic of conversation could you possibly be nervous about?"

Euryale shrugged. "It could go badly. I'm praying it won't."

The liveliness in Athena's eyes and voice kept strong. "If anyone should fear it going badly, it should be the other party," she said. "Come on, Euryale, you're the Goddess of Stone. No one in their right mind will challenge you if, for no other reason, they don't want to be a statue."

"I know."

"Do you?" Athena challenged, tilting her head but holding on to her grin. "I've got to say, if you don't at least try and act the part, you'll never get anywhere in your new station."

"I know...I know," Euryale said, wanting to believe Athena. But no matter how hard she tried, all she could believe was disaster loomed, and all she wanted to do was race out of there as fast as her tail would carry her.

A softer, though more serious, look grew on Athena's face. "Honestly, Euryale, we're friends. What insurmountable task has you so distraught? You took on Typhon, of all things. I can't imagine there's anything more fearsome. Well, maybe Cronus—but he's still sleeping."

"A negotiation," Euryale replied hastily. The moment those words passed her lips, she scolded herself for giving that up. Athena would want details—demand details. "I'm terrible doing such things. Not a lot of practice, you know, when you've been exiled for thousands of years."

"Alright, look," Athena said. "I know you've not always seen the wisdom of my ways, but to show my appreciation for all that you've done for us as of late, I'll help you out with this. Now come over here, and we'll practice."

"No, I—"

"Stop," Athena said, beckoning her over. "I'll have you believing in yourself before you know it. Now, get over here."

Euryale obeyed and probably would've tripped over her feet with nervousness if she'd had any.

"Right," Athena said, grabbing the gorgon by the shoulders and adjusting her position so that they were perfectly squared off with one another. "Tell me, who's causing you so much angst?"

"Why?"

"Because I need to get my mind right and slip into the part," Athena said, looking as if the answer should have been obvious. "I'm no Dionysus, but I've played a part or two before."

"Oh."

When Euryale didn't provide any other details, Athena laughed. "Is it Dad? It is, right? He can be scary. I'll grant you that, but I promise whatever you two need to hash out, he's not going to care in the least."

"Why is that?"

"Because he's obsessed with finding Typhon and any other traitor in Olympus, and you are neither."

"I know, but…" Euryale said. She wanted to explain that that wasn't it and get it all over with, but she couldn't find the words to make it happen. Everything that came to mind seemed foolish and likely to only make things worse.

"By the Fates, Euryale, you really are in a knot, aren't you?"

Euryale nodded. Her head swam. Nausea built in her stomach, and she hated every second of it. Her growing panic was nothing more than a not-so-subtle reminder of who she was, or rather, who she wasn't: a real goddess.

"Fine. We'll try something else," Athena said with a heavy sigh that cut through the gorgon's runaway thoughts. "I won't pretend to be Dad. You can practice on me. That should make things more palatable, yes?"

Euryale's eyes went wide. "What?"

"You heard me. Give me some bad news."

"I—I don't have any."

"Oh stop," Athena said, waving her hand at her. "I'm going to be embarrassed for your sake if you don't come up with some-thing."

"I don't know what to say."

"Say anything you want. Anything at all," she said. "Tell me my hair's a mess."

Euryale shrank back. "I could never. It's lovely."

Athena laughed again, hard, and buried her face in her hands as she tried to recompose herself. "You're making this impossible, gorgon," she said. "Now, seriously, tell me something."

"I…"

"Go on. Make whatever you want up," Athena said, her voice trading its playfulness for hints of harshness.

"But—"

"Now!"

"I have Perseus locked in a dungeon!" Euryale spit out faster than she could think. The gorgon froze the instant she'd finished, claws digging deep into her palms, head dipped, and snakes hiding behind her.

"There, that wasn't so hard, was it?" Athena said as she took off her helm and set it aside before shaking out her hair.

Euryale said not a word. She didn't even breathe.

Athena tilted her head. "Wait..."

"Wait...what?"

"You're serious?"

Chapter Demands

"I'm serious," Euryale said. Her voice wavered at first, and she hated how weak she sounded, but she quickly turned her fear into determination and righteous anger. She was a goddess, damn it, even if the entire notion of being one still felt surreal. People, *Olympians*, were going to respect her. More importantly, she hadn't done a damn thing wrong when it came to Perseus.

And perhaps most importantly, she had a demand to make, one that had come to her only a few seconds ago, and one she'd die before leaving it unfulfilled.

With all those thoughts, Euryale stood tall, proud, and unyielding in the face of Athena. "Your hero threatened my family and attacked me," she said evenly. "As such, I've sentenced him to imprisonment until I've decided what I want to do with him."

Athena's affect went flat, and other than a brief twitch of her finger, she remained motionless, no doubt using all of her energy to think about this unexpected news from every angle as well as to plan out her next hundred actions she'd take in response. "He attacked you physically?"

"He did."

"Because?"

"Because I wouldn't let him kill my chimera."

Athena placed her fingertips together in front of her face and tilted her head slightly downward. "I see."

Though sweat beaded on the back of her neck, Euryale kept strong, knowing she owed not only herself that much, but her family as well. It was a tough stance to take while staring down the Goddess of Wisdom and War, but the longer she took it, the easier it became. "I'm assuming you would like his release."

Athena nodded slightly, and a small, genuine smile graced her face. "I think that would be for the best, wouldn't you agree? As your Alex can attest to, I defend my champions."

"I know," Euryale said. "But before I do, I need assurances that this will end well."

"End well?" Athena echoed. "If you mean you want the matter to be considered settled, then yes, it will end well, assuming Perseus hasn't been permanently harmed."

"He hasn't," Euryale replied, "but I also had something else in mind."

Athena sighed and shook her head. "What more could you possibly want other than to keep this cordial?"

Before the words graced her tongue, the fury behind them caught Euryale by surprise, and she let slip a growl. "I want my sister back."

Athena's gray eyes narrowed, ever so slight. "Medusa?"

"No, Stheno," Euryale corrected. "You turned her into a whale, remember?"

Athena chuckled as if recalling nostalgic times she'd nearly forgotten. "I'm sorry, Euryale," she said. "But your sister is not part of these negotiations. She got what she deserved. Both of you should be grateful that's all I did to her. It could've been much worse."

"What I could do to Perseus would be a lot worse than what's happening to him now, too," Euryale countered. "What do you think Ares would do to him had he stabbed him in the leg? Or your father, Zeus, for that matter? I think you'll agree, me keeping Perseus chained and isolated is a mercy he's lucky to be granted."

"I think," Athena said, pointing a finger at Euryale, "that you're lucky I've entertained this idea of yours as long as I have."

Euryale's tail rattled at the challenge, her soul tapping into a primal strength that made her feel as if she could harness all of Chaos if she set her mind to it. "And I think a prisoner exchange is more than fair. If I were you, I'd consider that point one more time."

"Fairness? Is that what you're after?" Athena asked. "If so, it's only fair that your sister pay for her crimes."

"As should Perseus."

Athena set her jaw, and deep wrinkles formed in the middle of her brow, which led Euryale to wonder if she needed to strike first in order to survive the upcoming fight.

"Euryale," Athena said evenly. "We don't have time for your pettiness. In case you've forgotten, we need to focus on Typhon."

"You're wrong," Euryale said. "There's plenty of time for this, because all that needs to happen for it to be over is for you to release my sister."

"Are you insane? Me? Wrong?" Athena scoffed, pointing to herself. "I'm never wrong."

"There's a first time for everything," Euryale said. "And if you think my offer isn't a fair one, I have to seriously question how deserving you are of being called the Goddess of Wisdom."

Yes, her response was a touch on the nasty side, and yes, it did little to help matters, but Euryale would be damned to exile if she hadn't taken extra delight in seeing those words dig under the goddess's skin.

Athena, whose fair complexion was now red, scowled at Euryale and spoke with soft words full of command. "I am never wrong, gorgon, and if you walk out of here and don't release my hero, I promise you your house will be in ruins faster than you can curse what fate you've dealt yourself."

Euryale, refusing to leave her sister condemned for the rest of time, glared back with a headful of hissing vipers. "You're wrong," she said evenly. "When I leave here, the only thing I'm going to regret is not standing up to you sooner."

Chapter The Prisoner

With one hand gripping a rocky overhang, Zeus, dangling miles above the earth, studied the area around him.

His eyes carefully swept every inch of every cloud, scouring for any sign of anyone foolish enough to have followed him. Once he was convinced no one joined him in the sky, his gaze drifted to the rocky, snowy slopes below where he repeated the process. This took a few seconds longer, as numerous crags in the terrain and small holes where animals had burrowed required extra attention, but in the end, he was convinced he was alone. Sure, his giant eagle sentries would have long ago alerted him to an intruder, but Zeus was as clever and careful as they came when the situation demanded it.

And did the situation ever demand it.

Grunting, the God of Thunder, Ruler of Olympus, yanked himself up and over the edge. His body, clothed in only his flowing chiton, relished the frigid air, and his nose delighted at how pure the world smelled at such unfathomable heights.

As much as Zeus wanted to take a seat and let his feet dangle over the world and relax, he knew he couldn't. Business had to be attended to. Business that involved the interrogation of a traitor.

And by the Fates, he was going to get answers this time, or the world would be witness to his fury like never before.

Zeus broke into a light trot, his bare feet hardly making a sound against the steep mountainside. Powerful legs with muscles that dwarfed those of Heracles careened him up to ledges forty, fifty, even a hundred feet away, while fingers that could peel the armor off the kraken as easily as they could split open a pomegranate, drove into the otherwise unyielding rock as needed to help him scale his way to the top.

Finally, after another invigorating one-mile climb (that ended with him setting a new personal record which clocked in at twenty-one-and-a-third seconds), Zeus popped over another overhang and came face to face with a pair of giant eagles who flanked the entrance to the opening of a dark tunnel.

Their chests, wider than a pair of oxen, held a beautiful array of plumage, while wings that could lift dragons were folded neatly on their backs. The two birds stared at the approaching god with brilliant yellow eyes, eyes that Zeus knew could spy any movement, pierce any illusion, and spot any would-be intruder a hundred miles away. And should any illusionist, intruder, or generally stupid being happen by without the god at their side, they'd be met with talons more dreadful than spears and beaks sharper and stronger than any ax forged by Hephaestus.

"Polyxeinus, Tecton," Zeus said, giving an approving nod to each. "Things are well, I take it?"

Polyxeinus, the eagle on the left, screeched, and then Tecton did the same, although his held a higher, more energetic pitch than the other.

"No, I haven't forgotten," Zeus said with a hearty laugh. From a pouch that hung off his belt, a pouch that happened to be fifty times bigger on the inside than the outside, Zeus pulled out two blue marlins and tossed one to each bird. They promptly tore into them with such speed and viciousness, a school of sharks worked into a feeding frenzy could not have devoured them faster.

"Happy?" Zeus asked.

Tecton wiggled his tail feathers and squawked with approval, while Polyxeinus, ever the pig with an insatiable appetite, looked at Zeus for more.

"You're worse than Aldora," Zeus said, shaking his head. "And she had a never-ending supply of liver."

Zeus continued forward, scratching each of his eagles behind the head a few times before entering the tunnel. The path through the mountain snaked through the rock for a couple of hundred yards before opening up into a rounded, cozy cave.

Well, cozy was relative. Bats, no doubt, would have enjoyed its spaciousness and numerous places to perch on the ceiling if it weren't for the frosty air and the distinct lack of flying insects to dine on. The eight-foot-tall flesh-eating bull who was currently lounging on a large bed of straw certainly enjoyed being spoiled by the God of Thunder in exchange for guard duty. The goddess, however, who was chained, wrapped in a net, and stuck in a cramped, adamantine cage clearly wasn't enjoying the accom-modations whatsoever.

"Well, woman," Zeus said as he approached his wife. "Are you ready to talk?"

Despite her imprisonment, Hera's words dripped with venom. "I have nothing more to say to you. Not now. Not ever."

"Tell me who else is working with you and Typhon!" he bellow-ed, storming up to the cage. "Tell me or I'll feed you to Crios, one limb at a time!"

Hera broke into a fit of laughter. "We both know your bull likes me more than he likes you," she finally said. "Your threat is hollow."

Zeus snorted, and though he had to concede her point, he had no intention of playing games. "Woman, my patience wears thin," he said. "I showed you mercy the first time you rebelled against me after you promised never to do so again. What makes you think I'll be merciful this time around?"

"As if you have any grounds to judge me for broken promises," she spat. "How many harlots have you run off with? How many children have you sired out of wedlock?"

"None of that holds a candle to you betraying all of us!" he bellowed. "By the Fates, you could have killed everyone!"

"I had nothing to do with Typhon!" she shot back. The goddess caught herself before launching into a full tirade, and as she calmed, a new emotion, regret, quickly took hold. Her posture fell, and her usually sharp features softened. "With the Fates as my witness, I had no idea Hephaestus was working with that monster."

"You expect me to believe that Hephaestus outwitted you? That he moved in ways that even your eyes could not see?"

"He had nothing to do with it," she countered. "Typhon did. That titan outwitted us all. All I wanted—" Hera's words caught in her throat, and it took her a hard swallow and the shedding of a few tears before she spoke again. "It doesn't matter."

Zeus, at the sight of his wife's anguish, backed from the cage and lowered his voice. "Tell me."

Fresh tears found Hera's cheeks, and the goddess averted her gaze to her husband out of shame. She spent a few moments breathing slow and deep as she recomposed herself, and when she returned to the conversation, her eyes flashed with anger. "All I wanted was for you to feel half the pain I felt every day," she said. "To know what it was like to be humiliated in front of everyone, to finally have to show me some courtesy and respect. That's all I've ever wanted, to be treated with dignity, but instead, all I ever got from you were lies and disgrace."

Though her accusations struck a painful chord in his heart, Zeus quickly hardened himself. "Perhaps if you'd acted in a way deserving of respect, I would have," he said. "Your nagging, your constant second-guessing, your refusal to want anything to do with me other than hound my every decision is more than enough to drive any husband away. Don't you dare act as if you're the innocent, wounded party in all of this. There's not an Olympian alive who'd say otherwise."

"Think what you like," Hera said, dismissing his words with a snort. "None of them side with you, except out of fear. Take that fear away, and they'd have a plot to take your throne before the day ended."

"Your desperate attempts to cause trouble will get you nowhere."

"Desperate? Hardly," Hera shot back. "I can hear it in your voice. You know I'm right. In fact, I'm confident one schemes against you as we speak."

The certainty in his wife's voice gave Zeus pause. He knew all the gods, save one or two, could be incredibly ambitious and jealous, and that combination always led to trouble. Always. And while he refused to believe that any of them would accuse him of wrongdoing when it came to Hera, he did fear that should he be seen as weak, a second attempt at usurping the throne might soon come to pass. "Who?"

"Oh, so many to choose from," Hera purred. "They've all had desires to rule the world, haven't they, your brothers especially."

"They have their sovereign realms," Zeus countered, now feeling as if his gut reaction had been correct. The goddess was trying to sow seeds of distrust for no other reason than petty revenge.

"True, but that still leaves the rest, and I, for one, wouldn't put it past your newest Olympian to seize the opportunity."

Zeus erupted into thunderous laughter. "The gorgon? You've gone mad. She wants nothing to do with my throne. Besides, she had her chance with Typhon and turned it down."

"Did she because she didn't want it? Or did she because she had higher ambitions than to serve beneath him?"

"She doesn't want it," Zeus said with finality.

Hera smirked. "You see? Even now with all that's transpired, you still have no idea what happens inside your kingdom."

"As if you do, woman, locked away where no one will ever come," he retorted.

"I know I stripped her curse a moment before she died," Hera replied. "I know Aphrodite brought her body to Nyx, and I know Cronus restored her. So, ask yourself, dear husband, what price did Euryale pay for such a favor? Or perhaps a better way to phrase it would be, since she had nothing to pay with, what sort of deed did Cronus demand of her?"

Hera's words seeped into Zeus's mind, and he hated that he hadn't thought of her insinuations first, even if they would likely prove untrue. That said, he didn't have an answer as to why Cronus would help Euryale, especially since that help would prevent Typhon's successful return, and both the titan and Nyx were not fond of Zeus whatsoever. Cronus and Nyx would be more than happy to see Zeus's rule come to a violent end.

Did the titan strive to set Euryale against him? Possibly. Unlikely? As far as he knew, yes, it would be unlikely, but possible. And if Hera's theory proved true, Zeus knew he'd have to act swiftly.

"I know that look, husband," Hera said, chuckling. "Perhaps it's time you and the gorgon had a little talk of your own."

Chapter Declaration of War

As she snaked her way back home, Euryale kept her arms folded across her chest and dug her nails into her skin. Her tail rattled behind her, and more than one hapless satyr or dryad who wandered the streets of Olympus nearly became a permanent fixture when they inadvertently crossed in front of her path, and she had to slow. In the back of her mind, the gorgon didn't want to lash out at them, but the more she brooded over Athena's stub-bornness, the more Euryale needed an outlet, and ripping into her own arms would only take her so far.

Euryale halted, lowered her hands, and took a deep breath. She had to concentrate. Torturing herself would get her nowhere and certainly wouldn't see Stheno restored. She needed clarity. She needed focus. She needed to see that arrogant bitch of a goddess humbled.

"Threaten me, will you?" Euryale hissed, not at all bothering to keep her voice low. "We'll see about that."

Euryale sharpened her claws against one another and resumed her trek home, faster and more determined than ever. Her abode rested at the top of a large hill on the southeast side of Olympus. It was far from the monumental estate Zeus and Hera enjoyed, with towers that could swallow small countries with ease and swimming pools that could hold a score of armadas in the shallow end. That said, her new home on Olympus was not without its perks: three dozen rooms for servant quarters (not that she had any at the moment), a personal movie theater which could seat every Super Bowl attendee (Alex's request), and a vineyard in the back that grew the most delicious grapes anyone shy of Dionysus could ever hope to cultivate. The cherry-red ones were her favorite.

What Euryale did not have, or rather, what she never knew she had, were a pair of eight-inch howitzers standing on either side of the steps that led to her home, barrels pointed skyward. Each of the massive artillery pieces sat atop a tank chassis, and stacked nearby were about three dozen shells.

Thoughts of her troubles with Athena vanished with this new mystery, and Euryale quickly hurried inside, hoping Alex would be able to shed some light on what was going on.

"Alex?" she called out once she was in their inner courtyard. "Alex, where are you?"

Pop.

Pop.

Euryale eased to a halt at the unexpected pair of sounds, the likes of which she'd never heard before. The vipers on her head tasted the air and recoiled. There was a soapy, metallic scent floating about.

Pop. Pop.

Another brief pause, and then whatever was making the noise rattled off like a machine gun.

Pop-Pop-Pop-Pop-Pop-Pop-Pop-Pop-Pop-Pop-Pop-Pop!

"Alex!" Euryale yelled, chasing after the noise. Her search led her through the dining hall and through their kitchen that was in dire need of tidying, and eventually she darted out a side door to where the start of her vineyard lay.

"I got you!" Cassandra yelled, shooting free of a cluster of grapevines. The twin was covered head to toe in bright yellow paint, and she clutched a paintball marker firmly in her little hands while wearing a plastic mask on her head.

"Nuh-uh!" Aison shouted. The little gorgon, dressed like his sister, darted out of another cluster, sporting a couple dozen bright, gooey splats across his body.

Euryale watched, stunned, trying to make sense of it all as her twins sprayed a hundred shots at each other in under a few seconds. They squealed with delight, running back and forth, trying to duck, dodge, and dive out of the way of the wanton spray of paint.

The firefight lasted a few more seconds until Aison caught sight of his mother watching. "Oh, hi, Mom!"

Cassandra glanced at her mother and waved but went right back to shooting her brother as fast as she could. A heartbeat later, the two sprinted away, disappearing into the vineyard, popping off shots and laughing the entire time.

It was at that point that Euryale snapped out of her semi-daze. "Hey! Get back here, you two! What in the Fates is going on?"

"They're having a paintball war."

Euryale pivoted right as Alex trotted up to her. He, too, sported a paintball marker, mask, and a few splats. "Why are they having a paintball war? And why do we have giant cannons outside our house?"

Alex chuckled as he glanced over her shoulder. "You noticed, huh?"

"They were hard to miss."

"Well, the answer to both is Uncle Ares brought them."

"*Uncle* Ares brought them."

Alex nodded. "That's what the kids are calling him since he gave them their presents."

"Those presents better not be that artillery."

Alex balked.

"They are?" Euryale said, arching her brow. The initial surprise lasted about a millisecond, and then the stress of the day and meeting with Athena quickly caught up to her. Her fingers dug into the sides of her face, and she groaned. "Alex, how could you possibly let him give our kids those things?"

"I didn't!"

"They're outside out house, Alex!" Euryale shot back. "They're outside with live shells just waiting to go off! Why would you ever think I'd be okay with that?"

Alex's usually light demeanor faded. "Hey, now, I'm not stupid."

"You—" Euryale caught herself before she lost it completely. Her head dropped, and she rested her chin on a pair of pressed-together fingertips. "I know," she said softly. "I know. Today is not going well, is all. I'm sorry I snapped."

Alex pulled her in and kissed her forehead, which ended up leaving a smear of paint across her cheek. The transfer of goo was enough to defuse the situation, and they both shared a laugh. "Ares brought the artillery over about an hour ago," he said, keeping his voice low and calm. "I figured, well, maybe if things went bad with Athena, it might not be a good idea to insult him by rejecting his gift to the kids."

"Oh..."

"It did go bad, right?"

Euryale nodded. "Understatement of the year."

"Figured," he said before squeezing her. "Anyway, I convinced him maybe the kids ought to start small first, you know, which would give us time to figure out what to do with the cannons. He liked that reasoning, and at first, wanted to come back with heavy machine guns. I talked him down to paintball."

Euryale titled her head up so she could look directly into her husband's serene, adoring eyes and smiled. "You talked Ares down to paintball?"

"Yeah," Alex replied, his chest puffing with pride. "Impressed?"

"Alex, you always impress me."

The two stood there for a few quiet moments, embracing, but the peace didn't last long. In the stillness, Euryale's mind quickly returned to her troubles with Athena. She couldn't understand why the goddess wouldn't grant her sister's freedom, especially after all Euryale had done for her. And the more those thoughts turned in her head, over and over, the more she could feel her temperature rise and her muscles tighten.

Euryale toyed with her fangs with the tip of her tongue, fantasizing about how good it would feel to sink them into Athena's neck and pump her full of venom. If she shut her eyes, she could hear the goddess's screams and feel her hands push against the gorgon's body in a vain attempt to break her hold. The old, coppery scent of what would be the Olympian's blood would fill the air, driving her serpents atop her head into a frenzy, and then, when Euryale tired of it all, she'd petrify the goddess and put her on display.

Where? That was yet to be decided, but probably outside her home to serve as a warning to all that she was no one to be trifled with.

"Honey?" Alex said, tapping her gently on the shoulder. "What's wrong?"

"Huh?"

"You're rattling."

Euryale twisted in place and looked at her tail, which indeed was rattling. "I'm done being walked over," she said. "I know I've said it before, but I mean it, Alex. I'm done, and if Athena doesn't come around and accept my perfectly reasonable demands, it'll be the last mistake she ever makes. I'm not giving her Perseus back for nothing in return."

"So...wait...She just wanted her hero freed?" Alex asked, obviously trying to put together the pieces that seemed plain as day. "Like, that would've been the end of it?"

"No, that wouldn't have been the end of it," Euryale spat. "She'd know, they'd all know, I was still their plaything—that we were all their playthings."

Alex cringed, albeit only momentarily. He quickly recomposed himself, but Euryale could easily tell it was all an act. "This sounds bad," he said.

"I told you the conversation didn't go well."

"Yeah...yeah, you did," he said. "What did you want in return?"

"Stheno."

Alex's mouth twisted. "Stheno. Your sister, Stheno? The one she turned into a whale? The one she squashed me with?"

Euryale nodded and blew out a sharp puff of air from her nose. "Yes. She says her punishment is to last for eternity, and I'll be damned by the Fates if I'm going to let that happen."

"But what can you do? What can we do? She's Athena, Goddess of Wisdom *and* War," Alex pointed out, his face growing three shades paler as he spoke, and then six more when he added one last thing. "She's also the favored daughter of Zeus. I mean... like... Zeus! The ruler of Olympus!"

"I know who she is, Alex."

"But...Zeus! This isn't Ares we're talking about, and he was scary enough," Alex said. "He's not a mindless brute we can trick, and say what you will about his extramarital affairs, but this is the guy who took down Typhon and Cronus!"

"I don't care, Alex!" Euryale screamed, driving an elongated claw into his chest. "She's my sister! My sister, damn it! I will not sit here in Olympus, living a life she couldn't even dream of and pretend everything's just peachy!"

"But you're talking about going to war," Alex protested. "I understand where you're coming from—"

"No, Alex, you don't. You don't understand a damn thing."

"Sweetie—"

Euryale narrowed her eyes, and she jabbed him in the chest again. "Don't you dare 'sweetie' me on this," she said. She sucked in a breath, but it did nothing to help alleviate the unbearable tension throughout her body. As such, all the gorgon could do was grab a pair of unlucky vipers atop her head and yank them hard before spinning around and slithering off so she didn't shred her husband to ribbons.

"Euryale, wait!" Alex called out as he tried running after her.

He didn't get far. Euryale twisted in place and pointed finger at him, which alone was enough to stop him dead in his tracts. "You will never understand, Alex," she said, tears of anger and sorrow glistening in her eyes. "Never. You hear me? You will never, ever understand what this is like."

To his credit, Alex nodded, and though he wore a pained look upon his face, he stayed standing tall, and the tone in his voice was nothing but gentle. "I would if you'd tell me."

Euryale snorted and forced a smile before clearing her eyes. "I tried, Alex," she said. "I tried."

With that, the gorgon stormed off.

At the top of the tallest spire in her estate, Euryale wrestled her chimera.

She grabbed Tickles, the family pet, by its horns and tried driving it to the ground. The monster bleated playfully before bucking her in the chest and sending her sprawling across the hay-lined floor.

"Am I crazy?" she asked the monster as she picked herself up. When Tickles chirped, she threw up her hands in frustration. "Well? Am I?"

Tickles's only reply was a prompt pounce that Euryale narrowly avoided. She slipped to the chimera's side and grasped the mane on his lion head, trying to guide it by her body while simultaneously trying to throw it off balance by wrapping her tail around his waist and pulling him over.

Tickles, however, reared back before she could fully anchor herself onto him, and with a heavy swipe of his right paw, claws sheathed, he swatted Euryale across the face.

The gorgon spun with the blow, the metallic taste of blood filling her mouth. As quick as she noticed it, she ignored it, instead choosing to focus her energy, her rage, on her thoughts.

"Why? Why do they still hate me?" she asked, throwing herself at the chimera. "Why am I not good enough?"

Tickles met the charge head-on, and the two wrapped themselves around each other. Across the floor they rolled, trading strikes that would've snapped the bones of any mortal but only left bruises on each other.

"And Alex! Of all people in this world who should be at my side..." her voice cut off as she choked on her words. Though she now had the lion head of Tickles in a firm lock, her heart wasn't in the sparring match, not with that thought now running rampant.

Her grip weakened, and Tickles slipped free. But instead of continuing the fight, Tickles walked around in front of her and nuzzled the gorgon gently.

"I don't know what to do," she admitted, stroking the top of his goat head. Tears fell now from her cheeks unabated. "A goddess would. A real one, that is," she admitted. "But what am I? An imposter at best. Someone not even her own husband will stand behind."

A cough interrupted her monologue, a cough she knew all too well.

Euryale steadied herself and cleared her eyes before turning around to face Alex. Her husband stood at the top of the stairs that led into the room. He fidgeted with his hands that were held at his side, and he flashed her an awkward smile.

"Do you have a moment?" he asked.

For a brief second, Euryale thought about kicking him out. She didn't need complications or another fight. She needed someone to support her, and as pessimistic as she was that she'd never get it given how this day had gone, she dared to believe—after all, if there was one thing true about her Alex, it was that he never, ever gave up on her.

"I do," she finally said.

Alex approached her with slow, careful steps. "You're right," he said. "I don't know what you're going through, but I don't have to, either. I married you for better or worse. So, however you want to handle all this, I'll be at your side, forever."

Euryale stood there, statuesque, for a few heartbeats before throwing herself at him and wrapping her arms around his neck. She squeezed him tight, quietly crying with relief as she buried her face in his neck. One of his hands snaked across her lower back while the other gently caressed the back of her head. The gorgon stood there, sinking into his loving embrace for a lifetime before she realized she should probably say something.

"Promise?" she said, leaning her head back and smiling through her tears.

"I promise," he replied. He then toyed with one of her snakes for a moment before adding another thought. "You know, you might not have to actually go to war with her."

"I'm not giving Stheno up."

"I know. I know," he said. "I mean, if you maybe found a way to reverse the spell yourself, you wouldn't need to use Perseus as a bargaining chip. That would show her up at the same time, you know."

Euryale's gaze drifted to the side as she thought about what he'd said. It had a lot of merit, and there would be an unparalleled satisfaction she'd get while seeing Athena's curse come undone by her very hand. That said, however, practicality seemed to get in the way. "But how?"

"Hera is the undisputed queen of curses, is she not?" Alex said. "And didn't Jessica find her secret lab?"

"She did."

"Then I'd wager a woman as clever as you could find whatever she needs in that lab to counter whatever spell Athena cast on her sister."

A devilish grin spread across the gorgon's face, and for the first time that day, Euryale felt as if things might actually work out in her favor. "That's a really good idea," she said. "A really, *really* good idea."

"Thought you'd like that," Alex said, kissing her softly.

"Very much."

"What do you need me to do, then, to help?"

Euryale thought about his question. There was probably a laundry list of things he could do, but one task in particular stuck out that he had to do. "Get some food as well as some chain and a spear," she said. "Then go run around the underworld, like you're on your way to check on Perseus, or better yet, like you're going to move him."

"You want me to keep Athena busy following me, you mean."

Euryale nodded. "Absolutely. Think you can manage that?"

Alex laughed. "Euryale, my love, if there's one thing I've learned how to do over the past year, it's how to keep her attention."

Chapter Schemes

"Look! Look! That's her! That's really her!"

The unexpected voice, deep but full of enthusiasm, snapped Euryale back to the then and there. She'd been so lost in thought, trying to stay one step ahead of whatever Athena was planning (but likely still a thousand behind), that she hadn't even realized she was at the foot of Hera's estate. While that itself was a bit of a shock, what she hadn't been expecting at all were the two cyclopes who stood at the base of the steps, wearing bronze helms and clutching highly polished decorative shields and spears.

Right as she stopped, the one on the right nudged the one of the left with his elbow. "Told you she was taller."

"Told you she was prettier," the other whispered, nudging him back.

Euryale couldn't help but blush from the unexpected comment. For thousands of years, her looks had driven men and women to their deaths, literally, and the last thing she'd ever expected from anyone other than Alex was to be called pretty.

"Thanks?" Euryale said, stammering over her reply. "And hello?"

"Sorry," the right one said. "Kyros and I were just talking about you."

"Nothing bad," Kyros quickly added. "We wanted to meet you at your coronation, but you know, Zeus wouldn't allow it."

"He wouldn't?" Euryale asked, feeling like she was missing a lot to this conversation. "Why?"

The cyclops hiked a thumb toward Hera's abode. "Guard duty till this mess gets sorted out, but at least I got Pelagon here to keep me company. Not a bad guy to be stuck with, all things considered."

"Oh, I see, well, that's something at least," Euryale said.

Before the gorgon realized what was happening, Pelagon tossed his spear to the side and darted over to Euryale, his large feet thundering against the cobblestone road as he came. The moment he reached her, he fumbled around as his hand dove into a leather pouch hanging off his waist before he whipped out a smartphone. It wasn't one of the prized Olympi-phones Hermes had made for the Olympians, but it was still one of the messenger god's creations. While it could only do some of the things an Olympi-phone could, and wasn't quite as indestructible, it was still eons ahead of anything the mortals could dream of coming up with.

"You don't mind, do you?" Pelagon said, leaning his shoulder against Euryale's and making a face as he stuck the phone out for a selfie.

Before he could hit the button, Euryale backed out of the shot reflexively. "What's going on?"

Kyros smacked his face with an open palm. "Knock it off, Pel," he said, shaking his head. "You can't run up to celebrities like that. It's creepy."

"Yeah, but…she doesn't mind, right?" he replied, eyes looking to Euryale for confirmation. "And the kids! I'll never hear the end of it if they found out I ran right into her and didn't get a picture!"

"Why do you want a picture with me?" Euryale asked. "I'm hardly anything special around here. This is Olympus of all places."

The two cyclopes exchanged confused looks before they each grinned like awestruck schoolboys. "You don't need to be modest around us, Goddess of Stone," Kyros said. "There's not a soul in this city who's not infatuated with you, and rightly so. Freed Athena. Stopped Hera. Took down Typhon. By the Fates, we should be groveling at your feet for the next thousand years."

Pelagon chuckled nervously. "But you're not going to make us do that, right?"

Euryale sighed and flashed them a sweet smile. "No, I'm not," she said. "I'm not the sort who needs that from others."

Kyros clapped his hands together, fire and excitement gleaming in his ginormous hazel eye. "Of course, you aren't!" he boomed. He then hunched over and dropped his voice to a playful whisper. "And between you and me, you're my favorite Olympian. Just don't tell the big man that, right? He can be a little touchy about those things."

"I won't. Promise." Euryale then turned to see Pelagon fidgeting with his phone, lines of anxiety spread across his brow. "Come get a picture if you'd still like. I don't want you to think I'm rude."

The cyclops beamed like a kid given free rein in a candy store. He bounded over, struck a pose, snapped a picture, and then snapped a couple dozen more before he finally had enough self-awareness to realize he was getting carried away.

"Sorry," he said, straightening and stuffing the phone away.

"You're fine," Euryale said, patting one of his massive arms. "Now if you'll excuse me, I have matters to attend to."

"Of course!" the cyclopes said in unison. They hurried back to their post, but the moment Euryale made for the stairs to go into Hera's estate, Kyros nervously cleared his throat and spoke. "Begging your eternal pardon, your highness," he said. "But I'm afraid this area is off-limits."

Euryale stopped on the second step from the bottom. "You're kidding, right?"

"Wish we were," Pelagon said. "But we're not. No one's allowed in or out. Zeus's orders. I'm sure you understand."

"I assure you, I don't."

"The big guy's still on the lookout for any other traitors and whatnot," he explained.

Euryale pressed her lips together into a thin line as every muscle in her body tensed in frustration. "I'm sure he'd be fine with me going inside for a moment," she finally said after a slow, deep breath. "By your own words, I'm the reason there's even an Olympus to defend."

Again, the cyclopes glanced at each other. Kyros's pained expression grew worse, while Pelagon seemed to carry more regret than Sisyphus did once he caught Zeus's wrath. "Please don't hate us," the cyclops begged. "But he was very explicit. No exceptions. There's nothing we can do."

"There most certainly is something you can do: you can step aside," Euryale retorted.

"No, honest, we can't."

Euryale, sick and tired of nothing working out, growled while flicking her claws for both to see. "I'm not asking."

"We're not budging," Pelagon replied. The one-eyed giant drew in a deep breath and his face held a calm resignation, one that only found itself on the faces of those doomed to hold an impossible line at all costs. "You do what you have to do, goddess, and so will we."

"Dad! Are you even listening to me?"

Zeus was not listening to her. Or at least, he was trying not to. Working with his eagles inside his giant aviary was supposed to be a relaxing pursuit, and for the last half hour, instead of enjoying their company, he'd had to put up with Athena's ridiculous request to settle some minor spat between her and Euryale.

"I will lodge formal grievances if this isn't settled immediately," Athena went on, no doubt knowing how much the judiciary process would get under his skin.

Zeus scratched the back of one of his birds' necks, a gargantuan red-and-black feathered creature named Memneus who had piercing blue eyes and a swaggering attitude that de-manded constant servitude from all those around it—Zeus being the only exception.

"You test my patience, daughter," he finally replied. "Let it drop so we can tend to more important matters."

"More important matters? She's making a mockery of my judgments."

"She locked up someone who attacked her family and now wants a favor for a favor," Zeus countered with a groan of exaspera-tion. "That's hardly a mockery. I might ask the same if I were in her position."

Athena snorted, her face an ugly scowl. "And if you were in mine, you'd chain her to a slab to have her liver torn out for the rest of eternity!"

"For a mortal, perhaps," he said. "She's no mortal."

"Neither was Prometheus!"

Zeus huffed. She was right on that point, sadly, but ultimately, she still compared olives to figs. "Euryale is one of us. Prometheus was not."

Athena narrowed her gray eyes and folded her arms over her chest. "You think I'm wrong as well, then. Is that it?"

Zeus inadvertently rolled his eyes and grumbled, which did exactly what he was afraid it would once it happened: anger Athena even further. It had been a long, long time since the Goddess of Wisdom had lost her bearing to this degree—specifically, back when she, Hera, and Aphrodite fought over a golden apple—so in that sense, Zeus figured, his daughter was due for another overreaction. Why the Fates had ordained it had to happen now of all times, he had no idea.

And truth be told, he didn't feel she was wrong, not completely at least. But Zeus couldn't be bothered to play mediator since he had much bigger concerns to deal with. Concerns that all led back to his traitorous wife, Hera; the Father of Monsters, Typhon; and now, the elder titan Cronus. They all threatened his kingdom in some way, and in some way, they all seemed related.

How Euryale fit in with nightmare, he had yet to discern, but he did know one thing for sure: If a full-blown war erupted between his daughter and the gorgon, dealing with anything else that involved Cronus or Typhon could prove impossible. Such a war might also mask the truth about Euryale's loyalties, should Hera be right as well.

"I need you to let this matter drop," he finally said. "There are...other considerations you are not privy to."

Athena straightened, her face almost aghast at the notion there was information out there that she was unaware of. "What do you mean there are considerations I'm not privy to?"

"Exactly what I said."

Athena studied her father for a few seconds, and though he didn't show it, Zeus hated every second of it. While it was true she was indeed his favored daughter, the light of his life, and the source of all his pride when it came to things he'd made, she could also be his biggest headache, putting even Hera to shame. Her mind, unequaled, would often pick apart his thoughts and analyze them to their fullest before he was even aware of them himself. "You don't trust me," she said with a snort. "Me. Your own daughter."

Zeus walked over to her and put both of his hands on her shoulders and gave them a deep squeeze. "If there is anyone I trust explicitly, it's you."

"You hesitated."

"I'm being pragmatic," he countered.

"That's one theory."

"What's another?"

"That you're scared," she said. "That with Hera and Heph's betrayal, you're afraid even your own daughter might turn against you, not to mention everyone else. Which means you're going to do what you always do when you get nervous, shut me out and go at it alone."

"Bah," Zeus growled, letting her go and shooing her away. "What do you know?"

"That's precisely my point! What do I know?" Athena asked, throwing her hands up in frustration. "According to you, nothing!"

"Well, isn't that interesting," said a new voice to the conversation. "And here I thought I was the only one who'd dare utter such a thing. I wonder, Athena, are you going to threaten him as well?"

The two gods spun in place to find Euryale approach. She kept her hands clasped behind her back as she came, and the vipers atop her head reared, nervously tasting the air. Even her tail rattled every now and again, and though Zeus couldn't believe it—or maybe he could, given Hera's charge against her—Euryale looked ready for a fight.

If that were true, who else did she have on her side? Her father, no doubt, possibly Ares as well. And if Ares, Aphrodite? Alex's aid to Persephone might also mean Hades would side with her—especially since the ruler of Hades might want to expand his rule. To top off the list, Zeus considered Apollo, as the God of the Sun had always been exceedingly friendly to both Alex and Euryale, not to mention he'd tried to usurp the throne before but obviously failed.

All of that flashed through his mind in under a second before he grunted at himself and pushed those thoughts away. His wife was playing mind games, something she was exceptionally good at. He didn't want to act without proof, and her whispers were anything but.

"You're much more foolish than I'd ever thought you'd be," Athena said.

"No, you mean I'm much more willing to stand up for myself than you'd thought I'd be," the gorgon countered.

"Enough, both of you," Zeus said, leveling his finger at the pair. "What have you come for, Euryale? And if the answer is to try and get me to settle this spat you two are involved in, I've already told my daughter that I'm not getting involved."

"That's fine," Euryale said, catching him completely off guard. "I've come to ask for a minor favor completely unrelated."

Zeus arched an eyebrow. "Which would be?"

"I'd like you to tell the guards outside Hera's abode that I'm to be allowed in."

Athena shot forward. "Absolutely not! You're only going there to rifle through her library and find a way to undo my spell."

"And when I do, you can have your hero back," Euryale replied evenly.

The Goddess of Wisdom whipped around to face her father who was considering the request. "You can't do this," she protested. "You said you weren't getting involved."

"I'm not," he replied. Before she went to protest even further, he raised his hand, bidding her to quiet. "But I'm afraid, Euryale, I won't be letting you in, either."

"I want my sister back."

"I am aware," he said. "We'll deal with that later."

"No," Euryale said, in a low, even manner. "We're going to deal with it now."

The cords in Zeus's neck bulged, and the tips of his fingers crackled with energy. Hera aside, he couldn't remember the last time anyone had challenged him so blatantly. That said, however, he could understand why she was behaving so rashly, and thus, instead of letting the encounter grow even worse, he tried to de-escalate the situation while at the same time getting what he needed out of her.

"Euryale, I can relate to your...frustrations," he said. "And I know what it's like to have to fight an insurmountable adversary to rescue loved ones."

The harshness in Euryale's face and posture softened, as did her tone. "Cronus."

Zeus nodded. "He nearly killed everyone a long time ago, as you know," he said. "But since we're talking about him now, I have a question that's been lingering in the back of my mind I'd like you to answer."

Euryale shifted. It was a slight movement, one that perhaps no one but Zeus would've picked up thanks to his unmatched eyesight, but it was there. "What would that be?"

"Why did he bring you back from the dead?"

Another shift, greater this time, but still incredibly minute. Had Athena seen it that time? Possibly. He didn't want to divert his attention away from Euryale for even an instant to check.

"I'm afraid I don't know what you mean," Euryale confessed. "Aphrodite's the one who spoke to Nyx. I had nothing to do with it."

"The titan said nothing to you, then?" he asked. "Or Nyx, for that matter?"

Euryale shook her head. "Nothing I haven't already said a thousand times over. Nyx took pity on me for being a mother and apparently wasn't too fond of her nephew, Typhon, misbehaving."

Zeus waited a few seconds before asking one last question, wanting to make sure he was studying every possible facet of her body when she answered. "I ask only because a favor from Cronus can carry a burden even Atlas could not rest upon his shoulders," he said. "And if that's the case for you, given all that you've done for us, I'd hate for you to have to deal with that alone."

"As I said before, I never spoke to Cronus," Euryale replied, her affect unnaturally flat. "Aphrodite will tell you the same. He was asleep the entire time."

Zeus stroked his beard, though it was all for show at this point. He'd already planned out his next dozen possible moves if the conversation had gone the way that it had. "Very well," he finally said. "Thank you for indulging my curiosity."

"Thankful enough to grant me access to Hera's library?"

Athena tutted. "Are you honestly going to test the patience of both of us?"

"It's not your matter to decide," Zeus rebuked. Though he still kept his eyes on the gorgon, he could easily imagine the outrage that Athena had on display. Face crass. Arms crossed. And there it was, the tap-tap-tapping of her foot echoing in his ears.

"She's right, however," he said. "No one goes in there. If I start making exceptions for you, I'll not hear the end of it from others, and it will be a nightmare trying to discern who's trying to help and who's trying to destroy."

"Exactly," Athena added. "Now run along, Euryale, and in the meantime, perhaps you should think about returning my hero."

Euryale's claws grew threefold, and her eyes darkened. Zeus, knowing she was one stray thought from launching herself at both of them, quickly gave her the peace offering she so desperately desired—an offering he hoped she'd take. Not so much for her sake, but for his. He needed her defenses lowered.

"I'll bring you her tomes on curses," he said. "You're free to read them in your home, for one day, provided you share them with no one. Fair enough?"

Euryale drew back the corners of her mouth into a devilish grin as she tipped her head toward the ruler of Olympus. "Fair enough," she said. She then shot Athena the smuggest of looks. "I'll only need half that, anyway."

Athena's skin flushed, and when she reached out—to either sling a curse of her own or simply to use that hand to get into the gorgon's face, Zeus didn't know—the God of Thunder quickly grabbed her by the wrist. Stunned at his intervention, she said and did nothing else until Euryale had left.

"There had better be a damn good reason you're tolerating her," she said. "I don't care what she did for us with Typhon. She's not Chaos. She can't treat me however she likes and think that's okay."

"I know," Zeus said.

"Then..." Athena's voice trailed and after a split second—which was about three times as long as Zeus would've thought it would've taken—she laughed at herself. "I'm such a fool. You think she's lying about Cronus. You think he wants a favor of her."

"The thought had crossed my mind," he said. "Or rather, Hera planted it."

Athena's face soured, understandably so. "She could be trying to sow strife."

"Possibly," Zeus admitted. "But that doesn't mean she's wrong, either."

"What are you going to do then?"

"Only what I must to get to the truth," he said. His eyes lifted from staring at the ground. "I need you to do something, however."

"And what would that be?"

"I want to speak with her alone after she's had time to think about things," he said. "Can you keep Alex busy for a few hours without him growing suspicious?"

Athena laughed as if she'd been dealt the most curious and pleasant of coincidences. "I think I can manage that," she said. "He's been trying to subtly get my attention for a while now."

"He has?"

Athena nodded. "To follow him somewhere, likely to distract me with a wild goose chase for Perseus while Euryale tries to save her sister. I can't imagine what else it would be."

"Even better," Zeus said with a short nod. "I'll call you when I'm done. Till then, I don't want him anywhere near his home. Understood?"

"Understood," she said before turning around and leaving.

Once Athena was gone, Zeus sat on a nearby marble bench, trying to decide how aggressive he wanted to be with Euryale. He hadn't come close to making up his mind when Memneus made a short flight and landed on a thick branch next to him. The giant eagle cocked his head before letting loose a sharp squawk.

"Don't look at me like that," Zeus said. "I know what I'm doing."

Memneus squawked again.

"No, I won't make things worse," the god added, brow furrowing, mouth frowning. When the eagle said and did nothing, Zeus stood with a defiant grunt and started to leave.

When he was only a pace from the exit, he looked over his shoulder at the ever-watchful eagle, pointed his finger, and reiterated his point one last time. "I know what I'm doing. You'll see."

Chapter The Bath

Someone, or something, was following her.

Though Euryale never saw whoever kept a close trail, the taste that lingered in the air alerted her to their presence, and it was one that she felt as if she'd never come across before. It tasted like... forgotten dreams mired in the shadowy edge of Chaos, which might not make a lot of sense to some, but to the gorgon, it was completely accurate. If she thought about it a little more, there were notes of emptiness and fear, which further heightened her unease.

Not many things in this world would stalk a gorgon, and given her recent fame and appointment as an Olympian, those who would were likely beings not to be taken lightly.

As she made her way home, she tried to catch a glimpse of whoever it was by stopping in random places or taking a convoluted path that saw her backtrack more than once, but all of her attempts proved in vain.

Eventually, Euryale had to entertain the idea that stress was getting to her, and it was all a figment of her imagination. Her anxieties, worries, and fears didn't want to go along with it, but her mind, completely exhausted, refused to give it up. She needed some rest, even if that rest was going to be in a state of pure denial.

As such, when Euryale made it home, she headed straight for the wine cellar, grabbed the nearest full-bodied red, and made for the bathhouse, leaving a trail of silk garments behind in her wake.

The bathhouse itself was one of her favorite places of her new home. Back when she lived on her island in exile, she'd had a small pool fed by a hot spring that she enjoyed, but its aesthetic appeal was scant at best, as it was little more than a rocky hole in the ground. Her new spot, however, was as ornate as any other room or temple in Olympus, complete with a large frieze running across the top, a sunken tub large enough to hold Leviathan sitting in the middle, and a slew of windows on three of the four walls that let inside both fresh air and the short, scratchy calls of the red-legged partridges who'd taken a liking to the gorgon's vineyard.

"By the Fates, this feels good," she said as she lowered herself into the wide basin and relished the heat from the waters within. She leaned back against tub's edge, outstretching her arms to either side. There, she sat, drank, and enjoyed the quiet stillness the room provided.

It didn't take long for her eyelids to grow heavy and her consciousness to slip away. A moment before she drifted off, she at least had the awareness to carefully set her glass and wine bottle aside. The sleep that followed was heavy, and though she had no idea how long had passed when she finally woke, she was so groggy that had she not seen her husband standing a few feet away, leaning against a marble column, she was certain she would have gone back to sleep for a hundred years without a second thought.

"Something the matter?" she asked.

"No, why would there be?"

Euryale forced a smile and shook her head before yawning and stretching her arms high above. "You know how dreadful this day has been," she said. "I guess I figured things would still get worse."

"Oh, well, relax," he said. "Everything's fine."

"Have you been standing there long?"

"Long enough to watch you sleep and fall in love with you all over again."

Euryale blushed and couldn't help but slip a little bit deeper into the water. "You're too much," she said before throwing him a wry grin. "But I hadn't realized you'd fallen out of love with me."

"Didn't you get the memo?" Alex teased.

"I'm afraid I must've missed that one," she said. Her eyes then drifted to a small leather sack that had been propped up against the marble column Alex leaned against. "What's that?"

"Oh," Alex said, glancing down. "That's for you, but..."

"But what?" Her mouth twisted to the side, and she ended up biting her lower lip. She knew that tone in his voice, that tone that held the wariest of edges. "I thought you said nothing was wrong."

"I did! And there's not!" Alex quickly replied, stumbling over himself in the most adorable of ways. "It's just, well, something's been on my mind for a while now, and I'd really like to know, and I don't want it to be a fight, and you know I'll always give you your space, and—"

Euryale laughed before shooting her husband a deadpan look. "You might as well come out with it now, because there's no way you're going to walk this back."

"I was hoping maybe you'd tell me a little more about what happened when you died, is all," he said with a shrug as his gaze found the floor. "I mean, I know what it was like being with Kharon and all. You know, been there, done that. But Nyx? Cronus? I've got to know more."

Euryale groaned as she rubbed her temples with her fingers. Though she couldn't blame her husband for wanting to indulge his curiosity, and she did want to tell him the specifics eventually, she still wasn't sure it was in his best interest to know. After all, he had plausible deniability if any Olympian came and wanted answers. Then of course, there was the little fact that Alex was a terrible liar, especially when it came to dealing with the gods. They'd know something was up the minute he opened his mouth, and then not only would she be in danger, but Alex and her children would be as well.

"What?" he asked, cutting into her thoughts.

"Can we not talk about it now? Please?"

Alex frowned, and he ended up crossing his arms over his chest. "When then?" he asked. "Shouldn't I get to know?"

"I already got grilled over it once today," she explained. "I really don't want to get into it with you. There's...There's a lot to unpack, Alex. You've got to believe me that if I don't want to discuss the matter, it's not because I'm hiding anything from you."

"Kind of seems like you are hiding something from me."

"You know what I mean, Alex," Euryale said.

"I do, but that doesn't change the fact that you're still keeping me in the dark," he pushed. "I thought we could trust each other."

"We can," she said, shocked. "Why would you even suggest otherwise?"

Alex shrugged again. "I don't want to be the guy who gets blindsided, is all. I mean, how many times do you think Aphrodite said the same thing to Hephaestus and look where they ended up."

"Don't you even dare suggest I'd ever do anything like that behind your back," she growled.

"Then stop acting like it," he replied. "What would you think if you were me?"

"I'd trust you had good reasons, that's what I'd think!" Euryale snatched up her bottle, poured a glass, and downed it in one shot. "I can't believe you're being like this, Alex. Why does everyone all of a sudden want to know what it's like being dead?"

"Who else wants to know?"

"Zeus."

"Did you tell him?"

Euryale shot him an incredulous look. "You think I'd tell him something I wouldn't tell you?"

"No..."

"No, but what?" she said, frustration clear in her tone. To make things worse, as if they couldn't be already, her headache, once thought gone, quickly made a reappearance. "Tell me the truth, Alex. Do you think I'm doing something I shouldn't be?"

"No, but I think I'm your husband, and I deserve to be treated as such."

For whatever reason, his words struck a chord in Euryale. Perhaps because in and of themselves, they were true, but perhaps it was also because at some level, she still couldn't believe she was married and had been for over a year now. Either way, it pained her to argue any further. "I can't keep doing this, Alex," she said, half choking on her words. "I'm losing my mind here. I promise I'll tell you eventually. Just not now."

"Then when?"

"I don't know, Alex. Eventually. I promise."

Alex drew in a slow lungful of air and exhaled. His features softened, and he ended up forcing a smile. "Okay, okay," he said. "But I'm going to hold you to that. You have to tell me. Eventually. Not never. Eventually. Preferably before I hit my ten-thousandth birthday."

"Thank you," she said. She ran her fingers through her vipers, concentrating on the way their scales felt against her skin, an act that often helped her calm down. At that point, she decided to change the subject. "Mind telling me what's in the sack?"

Alex grinned and arched his eyebrows a couple of times. "Something special."

"Oh?"

Alex nodded before reaching into it and pulling out a small copper pendant in the shape of an eagle claw on a simple chain. He twirled it a few times on his fingers as he sauntered over to his wife. "Know what this is?"

"A necklace?"

"Not any necklace, my dearest," he said. "I bumped into Zeus on the way back. He wanted me to give it to you."

Euryale reflexively pulled away, and she eyed the pendant with suspicion. "Why?"

Alex didn't answer, at least directly. Instead, he continued to walk until he was standing behind her. Once there, his clothes hit the floor, and he dropped into the tub behind her. "You'll see."

Euryale tensed as he slipped the pendant over her head. The chain was cool against her skin, and the moment the pendant settled in the middle of her chest, a warm, tingly sensation emanated from it. A sharp pain, like the digging of a heft needle, hit her on both sides of her hips. She winced in response and immediately tried to tear the necklace free, but Alex was quick to catch her by the wrists and hold her back.

"Give it a second," he whispered in her ear. "It should only take a moment."

"What should?" she replied, grimacing further. The muscles in her tail contracted, painfully so, and it soon became excruciating. She fought against her husband's iron grip, but somehow either she had grown weaker, or he had grown stronger, and she was unable to wrestle free.

"Alex," she cried out. "Get it off me."

Her words had barely passed her lips when all the pain suddenly melted away. Relief washed over her body, and she fell back against his embrace with a sigh. For a moment, she thought he'd ripped that awful piece of jewelry away from her, but that notion only lasted a fleeting instant. It still hung off her neck, and to her shock and utter delight, she noticed she no longer sported a massive, serpentine tail, but rather she once again had her long, supple legs that were the envy of any woman, save perhaps Aphrodite.

"They're back," she whispered, as if the slightest acknowledgment of their existence would make them disappear.

"Thank the Fates," Alex said with a chuckle. "I was going to feel really bad if that didn't do what he said it would. I mean, all that build up and nothing? Talk about embarrassing."

Euryale kicked a foot out of the water and brought it close for inspection. It was as small and as cute as she'd ever remembered. All of her toes wiggled exactly as they should, and when she lightly tickled the arch of her foot, she couldn't help but jerk it away and laugh. "I can't believe I have these back," she said. "I mean, I honestly thought I'd be stuck with that tail forever."

"You like?"

"Are you kidding me? I love!" she exclaimed. "I actually feel normal again, even if I still have the snakes."

Alex slid his hands around her midsection and pulled her in close as he lightly kissed her cheek and sides of her neck. After every brush of his lips against her skin, ecstasy seemed to follow. Her heart quickened in tempo, and her breathing increased. "You know," he whispered softly into her ear. "Feet aren't the only thing you have again."

Euryale's body warmed to his suggestion, but as she reached back and ran her fingers through his thick hair, she couldn't help but feel a little playful as well. After all, half the fun was in the chase. "I know," she said. "I'm quite fond of my knees. Maybe I should give them a run, you know? Make sure they work and all."

"Mm-hmm, knees," Alex replied, still kissing her soft and slow. "I like your knees too. And your shoulders. And your breasts."

Euryale rocked her lower half a couple of times, being sure to press it firmly against his groin, taking pleasure in his growing arousal before slowly turning around. She straddled his waist and lifted herself slightly out of the water so that not only didn't she sit on him, but her husband got a good, close-up view of her chest, glistening with water. "Oh, you like them, do you?" she said, stroking the top of his head. "I'd never noticed."

"Perhaps we should fix that," he said. His mouth found the underside of her jaw, and she tilted her head up to encourage him to travel further down, which he gladly did.

"Perhaps."

Alex's hands swept down her body and under her bottom. With a heave, he lifted her into the air and carried her out of the bath. Euryale had barely managed to cinch her legs around his waist before he crushed her back against a column.

The air flew from her lungs, which only seemed to drive her husband into a further state of frenzy. The foreplay felt carnal, his hands clenching her body, and her nails carving deep lines across his skin. And the more he ravished her body like a wild animal, the more she fed off his energy and ravished his.

When he finally entered her, she arched her back and gasped. Gods, had it been that long since they'd been together? Or had she just missed it so?

The two toppled over onto the floor, not slowing in the least. Alex built himself into a steady rhythm while clasping her hands in his and stretching her arms over her head. She struggled against his grip, dying to touch him, but loving the control he exerted over her. It wasn't long after that when Alex grabbed her by the waist, flipped her around, and took her from behind, at which point, her nails clawed at the marble floor, and she gasped in delight.

The intensity built from there even more, and by the time their escapades finished, the two lay there, panting, spent, and awash in a sea of bliss. Alex was on his back, while Euryale rested her head against his chest, face glowing. Sweat covered them both, and the gorgon had the distinct feeling walking might be difficult come the morning.

A small price to pay, she felt, and certainly no worse than what he'd suffered thanks to her nails and a few overzealous vipers.

"You've never been like that before," she whispered, reaching up and caressing his cheek.

"You didn't seem to mind."

Euryale tilted her head and looked deep in his eyes. "Not one bit."

She settled back down and nuzzled her head against his neck. His arms wrapped around her back and squeezed, and the love she felt in them made her wish she could freeze that moment in time for all eternity.

"So...Cronus?" he asked, half-joking.

"Wants me to rule Olympus," she replied with a heavy sigh. The words had come so naturally, so quickly, it took her a second to realize what she'd said. Immediately, she jerked up, eyes fearful, and covered her mouth. "Oh, gods, Alex," she said. "You can't say a word."

"But—"

"Not a word," she reiterated, voice dropping to a harsh whisper. "If they found out, there's no telling what they'd do to us."

"I think they're going to find out once you take the throne," Alex said with a nervous laugh.

Euryale shook her head. "I don't want the throne. I never did."

"Is Cronus aware of that?"

Euryale's shoulders fell, and then her whole body seemed to crumple under the weight of the impossible predicament she'd gotten herself in. "No," she said. "He made it quite clear it didn't matter what I wanted, and frankly, I'm terrified what will happen if I cross him."

"If?"

"When."

Alex played with his fingers. She could tell his thoughts were churning like the sea caught in a violent storm, but he didn't share what those thoughts were, only what he thought should be done. "You've got to tell Zeus."

"I can't. He won't understand."

"He'll understand," Alex said, sounding as if he were saying it for as much his sake as hers. "I mean, unless you really want the throne..."

"No, I..." Euryale rolled away and buried her face in her hands. "I wish it were that simple, but I'm afraid whatever I do, I'll put everyone I know and love in danger."

"Yeah, but still...they've got to know. Right?"

"No, they don't," she replied before settling into the familiar, safe, dark space her hands over her eyes provided her. After several moments of silence, and after she felt strong enough to continue without becoming a complete wreck, Euryale looked up. To her surprise, she found that no one else occupied the room with her.

"Alex?" she called out. "Alex, where are you?"

For a brief second, terror gripped her heart as she feared Alex had gone to see Zeus on her behalf. That thought vanished, however, when she heard his voice call to her from far off in the house.

"Euryale? Where are you?"

Euryale, confused, could only take to her feet and give a short reply. "I'm still in here. Where are you?"

A few seconds later, Alex appeared in the doorway, wearing mud across his body and excitement across his face. "You should've been there," he said, laughing and leaning up against the threshold to the bathhouse. "I had Athena spinning in circles for at least a couple of hours before she got fed up."

"A-Athena?"

Alex cocked his head. "Yeah, why?" He then perked and smiled. "Oh, hey! You got your legs back! When did that happen?"

Chapter Confessions

Rats clawed at her insides.

Or at least, that's what it felt like. Euryale staggered, wailing and clutching her stomach, as the world spun around her. The floor suddenly disappeared beneath her, and she lost her balance and toppled backward into the bath.

Under the hot waters she went, thrashing about underwater in a complete state of panic. She had to get out of there. Had to leave the bath, her home, her everything. Had to go where there was nothing and no one for thousands of miles.

The moment she broke the surface, Alex grabbed her by the arms and yanked her out. "Oh my god," he said, terror striking his face. "Are you okay?"

Euryale flew backward, all the while fending off additional grasps that never came. Her eyes burned with anguish, and it was hard to see anything in the blur of shadows in color. "Stay away from me," she said, driving toward the exit.

"Euryale—"

"I said, stay away!" she yelled. Her foot found her robes, and she quickly scooped them up and hastily threw them over her body to cover up as best she could. She then raced up the flight of stairs that led to the main floor of her home. Twice her feet slipped, and she nearly came crashing down, but she managed to catch herself each time on the rough stone walls.

When she reached the inner courtyard, she could hear Alex calling out to her, trying to catch up, but instead of slowing down or even answering him, she fled faster than she'd thought possible. She didn't know where she was going, only that she still had to find somewhere safe, somewhere she could melt away.

With every step she took, she could feel *his* fingers caressing her body and his lips finding hers. She could smell the stormy scent of his body, taste the salt of his skin on her tongue. Euryale dragged her claws time and again down her neck and chest, leaving grievous wounds in the process, but the pain did nothing to rid herself of the horrors going through her mind.

Someone had been with her, on her, inside her. Someone who wasn't Alex.

Euryale fell to her knees as a tidal wave of shame and anguish crushed her spirit. Sharp pain exploded up her legs as bone struck rock, which was the only thing that spurred her back into action. The physical agony gave her something to concentrate on, something she could concentrate on.

"Euryale!"

The gorgon stood and gritted her teeth, Alex's voice feeling like rusty hooks tearing through her head. She didn't dare look back, afraid she couldn't ever see him again without having to relive the past hour over and over.

"Leave me alone!" she bellowed, her voice no doubt staggering all who happened to be in the great city.

On she ran, darting through her kitchen and dining hall, slamming oak doors behind her. She had no rhyme or reason where she was headed until she was about to fly out a side gate and realized she had a place she could go, a place where no one would ever follow her. A safe place, a place she called home.

Euryale spun on the balls of her feet and bolted toward the house's stables where her and Alex's ponies stayed. She found them in their stalls, casually nibbling on some nearby hay, their chariot parked only a few yards away.

Quickly, she freed them both and pulled them in place. Her hands shook violently as she got their bridles, fit their harness, and attached them to their yokes. More than once the leather straps slipped from her grasp, or her fingers lacked the dexterity to work the buckles. Thoughts of Alex finding her here only added to her panic, but those fears never came.

Once Euryale managed to ready the chariot, she wasted not a moment climbing inside the carriage. A flick of the reins sent the ponies bolting out of the stables and then into the air.

She never looked back, not even when she heard the gods call to her.

Athena cringed, her grip tightening so hard on her spear that she nearly broke the shaft.

She knew that wail, and even if half of Olympus separated her from Euryale, she'd never mistake the sound of the gorgon's cries. Those, however, were different than the lonely cries Euryale had once made on her island or the bursts of anger she'd always been infamous for. No, this time something horrifying struck Euryale's soul, and as furious as Athena was over the Perseus affair, she feared something dreadful had happened to the gorgon's children.

Athena shook her head to rid herself of the shriek lingering in her ears before racing out of her home. Her sandaled feet made long strides, picking up speed every second, and soon all of Olympus blurred. She bounded through the Asphodel Gardens, covering the three-hundred-yard width in less than a dozen heartbeats before effortlessly leaping over a wide stream. When she landed on the other side, another Olympian landed right next to her, one with bulging muscles, glistening sweat, and an elated war face everyone knew.

"Ha! I knew this day would come!" Ares roared. "Typhon has finally stopped cowering and sent war to our doorstep!"

Athena shook her head in disbelief, then scolded herself for doing so. It was always war with her brother. Always. But as the two broke into a run toward Alex's and Euryale's home, her brother's point couldn't be completely dismissed. Perhaps Typhon was behind this. A full-scale assault? Probably not. But an assassin? Certainly. And as for the Father of Monsters, Euryale was a prime target for revenge...or worse, her family.

A minute later, the two Olympians reached the gorgon's estate, Ares singing songs of war while Athena's vision sharpened and hearing heightened to keep her ready for whatever lay ahead.

Athena heard a door slam to their right, likely coming from the inner courtyard. She grabbed Ares by the arm, but he quickly shrugged her off.

"I heard!" he cried out with glee before bounding forward with a speed and lust for blood she could never hope to match.

"This is her home, Ares!" she yelled to him. "And there are children here! Try not to destroy everything!"

"Bah! What do you know? They each have their own guns I personally gave them. Guns they no doubt long to use to level everything around!"

"Just don't, okay?" Athena said, trying not to get drawn into an argument. She then bolted through the main welcoming area, slowing only a moment to ensure that nothing looked out of the ordinary. If her brother ended up giving in to his desires for wanton violence, she wanted to have a snapshot of as much of the area as possible for a later postmortem.

She did the same when she crossed the inner courtyard, and then through the kitchen and dining area, following the sounds of someone fleeing. Or maybe it was her following Ares who was following another. It was hard to tell, especially since whoever she was chasing seemed to be fleeing through the estate at random.

Eventually, she found herself toward the back of the home, about halfway between the vineyard (which for some reason was covered in tiny blobs of paint) and the stables (which suffered a lot of the same damage). Ares stood nearby, crouched and grinning.

"They're close," he said, sniffing the air.

"Who? Alex? Euryale?"

"Yes," he said. "But hopefully our foe, too."

The stable doors burst open, and Athena barely caught her brother's arm before he hurled his spear and skewered Euryale in the chest. The gorgon, with eyes wide and white-knuckled fingers gripping the reins to her chariot, shot into the sky.

"Euryale!" Athena called out. "Come back!"

Ares spun, taking a half step in a few random directions. "She's running from someone," he said. "We must find them and crush them before they get away."

A door leading into the servant quarters shot open and out spilled Alex. He was still covered in mud on the quote-unquote chase he'd led her on, but instead of the misguided amusement he'd worn on his face not even an hour ago when he thought he was being clever, now all he wore was confusion and worry.

His eyes found Athena's and quickly narrowed. "What did you do to her?"

"Alex," Athena said as evenly as she could, given his insubordinate tone. "I didn't do anything to her. We quite literally just arrived."

"Then why did she tear out of here like that?"

"You tell me, Alex."

Euryale's husband shrugged and threw up his hands with a helpless look on his face. "I have no idea," he said. "I came home. She was in the bath, took one look at me and ran, screaming."

"Madness, perhaps?" asked a new, soft voice. "Induced by some creature that's hidden from our eyes."

Athena glanced over her shoulder to see Artemis trotting up to join the three of them. The goddess wore her usual attire of a silky, white chiton fastened with gold clasps with her crescent-moon circlet neatly resting atop her head of brown hair. However, she also had her chlamys, a dark hunting cloak, drawn about her shoulders, and kept a bow and arrow in hand.

"I get the feeling whatever pursuit you were on led you here," Athena noted, pointing to the ensemble.

The Goddess of the Hunt nodded. "Something's been slinking around Olympus," she said. "I don't know what it is, but I intend on finding it and killing it."

"There wasn't any creature," Alex said, shaking his head. "She was scared of me."

Athena cocked her head at the unexpected development. "Of you?"

Alex ran his fingers through his hair once more. "Yeah, of me. And she wasn't crazy. She was scared out of her mind."

"That sounds like insanity to me," Artemis interjected.

Athena held up a hand, stopping Alex's protest before it even began. "Perhaps, but perhaps not. I think we need to see the scene of the crime before we speculate any further."

Ares grunted and drove a fist into an empty palm. "Bah! We need to capture whatever monster Artemis is tracking, and as we tear it limb from limb, we need to find out where it came from so we can strike at our foe with the full fury of the gods!"

Athena hummed to herself, trying to decide what to do, but also knowing that every second she spent thinking things through might be one she didn't have to spare. "Ares, scout the perimeter," she said. "We need to make sure there aren't any surprises whilst Artemis and I look around."

"Scout?" Ares scoffed. "My skill should not be wasted in such pathetic tasks."

"You have my permission to beat into submission anyone you find who shouldn't be here as much as you like."

Her brother's eyes brightened, second only to the enormous grin that spread across his face. "It shall be done!"

While Ares ran off, Athena then turned to Alex. "Your children, has anything happened to them?"

"I don't know," Alex stammered, face losing all of its color. "I would assume they're fine."

"Don't assume," she said. "Find them. And when you do, take them to my temple."

"But—"

"No buts, Alex," she ordered. "Something happened to your wife, something I fear might be bigger than any dispute between her and me, given Artemis's words. If that's the case, not only do we need to preserve any evidence here, but they need to be safe."

Alex nodded. "Okay," he said. "They should be in their room, assuming they haven't freaked out with their mom running off like that."

"Good. Now go."

Once Alex left, Athena motioned with her head for Artemis to follow, and the two made for the bathhouse. Along the way, they were careful not to disturb anything and tried to take note of everything, but Athena had so many unanswered questions, she wasn't sure what she should be looking for whatsoever.

"You know something," Artemis said as they drew near their goal.

"I have a suspicion," she admitted.

"One that doesn't involve my hunt."

Athena shook her head. "I don't know," she said. "I don't want to taint your opinion inadvertently. So, I'd rather not speculate in front of you."

"My opinion?"

Athena nodded. "There is no better tracker to have ever lived than you, my sweet Artemis," she said. "I need you to tell me what you see once we reach the epicenter of this event."

The goddess opened her mouth as if to say something else, but ultimately nodded and briskly walked in step with Athena. Once they reached the stairs leading into the bathhouse, they slowed, being careful not to disturb a thing. To the untrained eye, even the stairs were devoid of anything, but to Artemis, Athena knew, a tracker without equal, there was a wealth of knowledge.

What the Goddess of the Hunt saw, she didn't say, at least, not at first. It wasn't until after the two had stood quietly about a dozen paces from the edge of the sunken tub that Artemis finally shared some of her thoughts. "Euryale came here alone," she said. "Relaxed and wanting to soak. Aside from the obvious wine bottle and glass, her path was lazy."

"You could see her come in?" Athena asked, genuinely impressed. She'd picked up on the wine in an instant, and even saw a number of places on the floor where water had pooled. But traces of Euryale's entry? Even with Artemis's motion to the floor, Athena was at a loss as to where they were.

"She picked up some dust from the wine cellar."

Athena laughed and clapped her half-sister on the shoulder. "Plain as Apollo riding through the sky to you, I'm sure."

"Even more so."

"What happened next?"

Artemis pointed to the bath and then nodded her head to the stairs. "She bathed, likely fell asleep—her arms rubbed some of the dirt away from the floor—until someone else joined her."

"Was that someone Alex?"

"Someone mimicking Alex," she said. "Same stride. Same foot size. Came without worry, but definitely not Alex. You can easily see the muddy trail Alex left coming and going. It would be very strange that he came in, engaged with Euryale, left, and came back muddy."

"Agreed," Athena said. "Could it be this mystery intruder you've been hunting?"

Artemis shook her head. "I don't see any signs of whoever it is here, nor on the stairs," she explained. "Even though I don't know who or what it is, only that its tracks felt more watchful."

"Watchful?"

"Measured. Careful. Someone trying to see as much as they could without being seen themselves."

"I see," Athena replied, not liking where this was going. "We'll have to deal with that later. What happened next?"

Artemis blushed, which told Athena exactly what was about to be said as well as lent credit to the scenario she was building in her head. "The gorgon was intimate with whoever came," the goddess went on. "Everywhere."

"Everywhere?"

Artemis went around the room and pointed to a dozen different places. "There, there, there, and so on. I'd say that's everywhere. Then whoever came left while she lay on her back. Soon after, I assume, she rose, and Alex entered, at which point she ran out, screaming."

"Any idea where she went?"

"Game that flees with such reckless abandon usually won't stop until exhausted or somewhere it knows is safe," Artemis said. "And if Olympus is no longer that place, I'm at a loss for where she might head."

"I'm not," Athena said, shaking her head. "She's going home. Back to her island. The one place no one could ever harm her, even if she did live in exile."

"But Medusa—"

"Was not her," Athena finished. "Trust me on this. She's going there. This thing, however, bothers me. Its tracks led you to this estate?"

Artemis nodded. "Circling it, but yes."

"I'm not yet sure what that means, but it's nothing we should ignore. That said, I need a favor that will take you elsewhere."

"Where would that be?"

"Euryale's island," she replied. "I'll need you to win back her trust."

"Me?" she asked, clearly surprised. "She knows you more than me. You should go."

"I can't," Athena said. "We're...having a disagreement already."

"Then send another," Artemis replied. "Harmonia, even. She's the Goddess of Concord, after all."

"True, but you have a heart, too, and more importantly, you'll be here for this phone call."

Artemis dropped her brow. "Phone call? To whom?"

"Father," Athena replied, taking out her Olympi-phone.

"What does he have to do with all of this?"

"Everything, I fear, and I want a witness to what he says." Athena swiped past the picture on her lock screen, a snowy owl perched on a stump with a frozen lake and full moon in the background, and called Zeus. It took a few rings before her father answered. Though she couldn't see much of where he was, the warm glow coming from off the screen made her think he was lounging in front of his fireplace.

"Athena," he said with a merry cheer that soured her stomach. "To what do I owe the honor of this call?"

"What did you do?"

Zeus chuckled and tilted his head. "Whatever do you mean?"

"I mean, what did you do to Euryale!" Athena yelled before turning her phone so she could pan it around the bathhouse. "Tell me!"

"I did what I had to," he said. "Precisely what I said I would."

"No, you did what you wanted to. *Again.*"

Zeus's face hardened, and lightning crackled in his eyes. "I am your father, Athena," he said. "You'd do best to remember that."

"Something I'm completely ashamed of at the moment," Athena said. "Pray tell, *Father*, was it worth it?"

"Cronus wants her to steal my throne, so I'd say it was very much worth knowing who's after me."

Athena snorted with disgust and felt bile rise in her throat. "She doesn't want the throne," she scoffed. "She never has. Never will."

"She said as much, but—"

"No buts, *Father*!" Athena yelled with such force Zeus snapped back and cut himself off. She cursed under her breath in the momentary silence and rubbed her temples. "You have no idea what you've done," she said, dropping her tone so it was only a degree below irate. "No idea whatsoever."

The shock at being berated by his daughter wore off a split second later. "I know exactly what I did," he said. "Not that I have to justify my actions to you, but I gave her a chance to tell me, twice even, and instead, she chose to keep her secret—a secret that could spell the end of us all."

"She would've told us eventually," Athena said, crossing her arms. "Now, it's likely you've made her our enemy."

"To her own end."

"To yours!" Athena retorted. "Her father alone is no one to be trifled with."

"I can handle the Old Man."

"Can you? What about the others?" she asked. "Everyone in Olympus loves her, especially after ferreting out Hera, thwarting Hephaestus, and putting a stop to Typhon! Who do you think they will rally behind? One who risked her own existence to save those who mistreated her, or a brutish ruler who thinks it's okay to defile one of our own? She's an Olympian, remember? And even if she weren't, that's no excuse to..." Athena halted her rant and groaned out of frustration, balling her fists at her side. "I can't believe you did this."

Zeus's face turned hard as stone. "You think they won't understand or say they wouldn't have done the same?"

Athena pressed her lips together so she didn't say anything else that would make things worse. "Meet me at the acropolis at noon tomorrow," she said. "I'll call everyone together, and you can make your case to them there. Then we'll see which of us is right."

CHAPTER THE ISLAND

Euryale flew for hours, rocking in her chariot, numb in body and mind.

By the time the tiny, barren island she'd once called home, which was stuck on the western edge of the world, crested the horizon, the sun had nearly set. Its golden rays reflected off the sea, giving it a bright sheen but also casting long shadows across the island's bay where a myriad of mismatched, ancient ships whose crew had long perished, still lay at anchor.

The sight of those ships put a smile on her face. Those were things she knew. Real things. Not illusions she couldn't see weren't true.

Euryale set the chariot down near a trireme that listed sharply to one side. Its sail had long disintegrated, and most of the deck had rotted away, but despite the decrepit look, that one was her favorite. It was the first ship that had found her island thousands of years ago. Though the soldiers who came with it had proven to be arrogant and hostile—and were dealt with accordingly—she'd always liked to sit atop the cliffs, stare at the vessel, and dream about what it would be like to roam the world, free of exile, and see what it was like.

She didn't have to wonder anymore, sadly, because horror lingered everywhere.

The thought, born from nowhere, stabbed Euryale's heart, and she squeezed out a few tears before hurrying up a rocky footpath. It snaked its way up a sharp incline before coming to rest near the mouth of a cave. Several statues flanked it on either side, their faces forever twisted in anguish, and beyond them, her old fire pit made of rough stone still stood, and it even had coals inside.

She thought about lighting it and watching the flames dance for the next several hours, or weeks even, or maybe she'd simply find her old bed and see how long she could sleep. Maybe when she woke, she'd find this all to be a dreadful nightmare.

But no, that wasn't going to happen. And she couldn't sleep, not with her skin starting to crawl once more and his stench still on her.

The gorgon dashed into her cave where walls protected her, and she raced all the way to the back. There, Euryale squeezed through a narrow crack, scraping her back and shoulders in the process. After a few feet, it widened into a small, but passable, tunnel. Light had no place there, but Euryale moved through it with ease, her vision quickly shifting to detect even the smallest variations of heat.

And where she was headed, there was a lot to be had.

The tunnel descended only a few dozen yards before making a hairpin turn and opening up into a cavern whose only item of note was the hot spring that filled nearly two-thirds of it.

For the second time that day, Euryale tossed her clothes, only this time, they couldn't tear from her body fast enough. They'd scarcely hit the floor when she jumped into the scalding water. Her skin turned bright red, practically cooking, but she didn't stop at a mere soaking. At the edge of the pool were a half dozen pumice stones. She grabbed the largest and roughest of the group and scraped it over her body twice as hard as she would have ever dared before.

Layers of skin sloughed with each stroke, the burning pain that accompanied it at first was simply a welcome distraction, but that distraction quickly turned into a euphoric feeling when she realized that beneath her old skin was a new body, a new her—a creature that had not been defiled and never would be.

An hour passed, maybe two, before she finished. Slowly, Euryale exited the now scarlet-tainted pool and grimaced with each move of her broken body. But before she left, she felt something tap her chest. A glance showed what it was: the copper pendant still hanging from her neck.

"Stop following me!" she screamed, ripping it from her body and hurling it into the water.

The moment it left her hand, her legs gave out. Euryale crashed to the floor, nearly cracking her skull open on a rocky outcropping. She was about to curse her existence when she realized she no longer sported a pair of legs, but rather once again, she had her serpentine tail coiled around her.

"Am I ever glad to see you," she said, sitting up and admiring the tail. She ran her hands across its scales, loving how perfectly they glided across each other and how much strength the muscles underneath had. Most of all, she loved how much more of a monster it made her, a monster no one would want or even dare to touch.

Euryale left the hot spring, pushing through the crack once more, though this time finding it more difficult than before thanks to her serpentine lower half. Still, a small price to pay for something so empowering. When she returned to her cave, she gathered some nearby deadwood and set it alight in her fire pit. The flames quickly illuminated the walls with their orange glow and filled the air with a pleasing aroma.

She stood in front of it for a while, basking in the warmth with her hands outstretched, delighting in the occasional pop of wood that sent embers flying. When exhaustion took hold, mental and physical, she snaked to her former bed and curled atop it and tried to sleep.

Euryale must have lain there for an hour, maybe two, but sleep eluded her. Tension plagued her body, and her mind focused on every detail the world had around her, watching, listening, and waiting for her tormentor to come.

A couple of her vipers stiffened. Their tongues licked the air with nervous energy, and soon the others joined. Euryale sat up and focused. That taste she'd noted earlier in Olympus was back in the air. Faint and hard to discern due to the persistent smell of salt water, but there.

Light from the sun had long gone, and only a half moon provided any sort of light to her barren island. It was easy for the gorgon to slip out of her cave and stick to the shadows. She glided along the terrain, her senses heightened as they'd never been before. She felt every bump in the ground, every sharp point to even the smallest of rocks, against her scales. She could hear the moss grow on boulders far away, and spy the tiniest bits of smoke that still lingered in the air from her fire.

Her pupils narrowed to slits, the fear she had giving way to anger. She would find whoever this intruder was and take great pleasure peeling the flesh from his wretched body for the next thousand years. How dare he even think about putting a single foot upon her island.

Euryale paused near a jagged boulder she used to climb to watch the sunrise. She could taste the intruder even more now and to such a degree that she could pinpoint his location, not even fifty yards away and off to the side where a sharp cliff fell into the sea.

Was he still climbing it? Euryale didn't know. Possibly, but he could simply be skirting along the top, trying to find the best angle at which to approach her cave. But this was her island, her home, her fortress. She knew every nook, every cranny, every spot one could hide or ambush, and she was going to have no trouble turning this predator into prey.

Euryale darted off, keeping low to the ground as her tail propelled her along. She flanked the trespasser's position, pausing every now and then to ensure that yes, she still knew exactly where he was. When she reached a wide, flat ledge, she melded into the dark, her body contouring against a rocky wall, and watched the footpath a few dozen yards away.

She didn't have to wait long.

A cloaked figure, hunched and carrying a short bow with a black arrow notched and ready, cautiously made his way toward her. His head constantly swept the area, no doubt looking for any sign of danger. A few times, he would take to the shadows as well, blending in to such a degree that to anyone else, he would've disappeared from view.

Whoever this was, sadly for him, had never stalked a gorgon before.

The heat from his body, even with the cloak, burned in Euryale's vision like a bonfire at midnight. But to the man's credit, he held still for a quarter-hour before breaking out of the shadows and creeping to his next spot.

Euryale watched, muscles tight, breath held, rattle held firmly in place. Three feet from his goal, the gorgon struck. She lunged out of the shadows with the speed of a black mamba. She hit the poor man so hard that his ribs shattered, and his spine broke three times over before his bow had a chance to leave his hand. The gorgon kept up her momentum and drove him into a nearby oak tree where he came to a sudden halt with a satisfying crunch.

With one hand, Euryale pinned him to the oak by the neck, her claws digging deep into his skin, and with the other, she tore away the hood. The intruder was someone she'd never seen before. He had dark, weathered skin that was broken up by countless scars. Gray symbols, the likes of which Euryale hadn't seen before either, were painted on his cheeks and forehead, while his mouth and lips had turned crimson where blood bubbled out.

"Who sent you?" Euryale hissed, bringing her face close to his.

The man coughed, sending droplets of blood everywhere, and smiled. "Your days are numbered, gorgon. Yours. Your husband's. Your children's, unless you let me go and never return to Olympus."

"The only thing in question right now is how fast and free of pain you want to die," she growled. "Now, who was it? Athena? Typhon? Cronus?"

"It doesn't matter," he spat. "Everyone hates you. Everyone will use you."

"Answer me!"

"Everyone will have their way with you—"

Euryale screamed and ripped the man's throat out. His body fell to the ground with a quiet thump, and she stared at it for a few seconds with her teeth clenched. As good as what she'd done had felt, on some level, she regretted the rash act, if for no other reason than she would've liked to torture something useful out of him. Medusa was always good at that. Stheno, even more so.

Thoughts of her sisters drowned Euryale in a sea of grief. Images of waking up to the horrifying discovery of Medusa's headless body resurfaced, and the only thing that managed to replace it was what happened right after, when she and Stheno made vows to look after each other until the end of time. While Stheno could say she'd lived up to the promise, could Euryale, given how her sister languished alone?

Euryale didn't know.

She didn't want to know, either.

A new scent drew her attention, crisp and energetic. Euryale twisted, claws ready, and was shocked to find Artemis a few paces away. The goddess's bow was kept low in her grasp, though she did have an arrow notched.

"It seems you've done my work already," Artemis said, nodding to the body at Euryale's tail.

"Or I've stopped your assassin," Euryale replied with a growl.

Artemis took no offense at the charge. Instead, she calmly took the arrow from her string and returned it to the quiver hanging from her hip. "We're not enemies, Euryale," she said. "I don't wish to make you one, either."

"Funny how you Olympians say such things but are so quick to reverse yourselves when the moment suits you," Euryale spat. She could feel the rage building in her soul, the fire running through her veins, and the lust for vengeance clawing at her self-control. And with an Olympian before her, a daughter of Zeus, no less, how tempting it was to unleash her fury on the goddess.

"You'd best leave before I add you to my collection," the gorgon said, gesturing back to her cave where her statues stood. "This is your one and only chance."

Artemis held up a hand and replied with a soft voice. "I know what he did to you," she said. "And my heart breaks for yours even thinking about bringing it up."

"You have no idea what he did to me!" Euryale bellowed. "Don't you dare come here and offer your worthless sympathies. I am not some helpless thing to be pitied!"

To the gorgon's surprise, Artemis didn't argue. She simply nodded and set her bow at her feet. "You're right. I have no idea, only guesses. But I can see the wounds he gave your spirit, that wonderful soul who fought for those who cast her out when she had every right to side against them."

"Maybe I should have."

"It would be tempting, now more than ever, if you could go back and choose a different path to follow," Artemis replied, beginning a slow approach. The goddess only managed a couple of steps before Euryale's eyes turned black.

"Hear me out, please," Artemis said, extending an open hand. "I know you're feeling alone and vulnerable—"

"I am not vulnerable!"

"That's not what I meant," she said, still as calm as ever. "What I'm trying to say is that I'm here to help you, and more importantly, I'm not the only one who wants to."

Euryale laughed mockingly. "You want to help me?"

"I do."

"Why? You barely know me."

"I know both strength and splendor are inside of you, unlike any other," she replied. "But moreover, if I turn my back and ignore all that's been done, how am I any better than he is, especially when I'm in a position to make a difference?"

Euryale eyed the goddess with skepticism. Deep down, she still felt Artemis couldn't be trusted, but there was a small part of her that dared to believe that maybe there was some truth to her words.

"Give me your oaths then," the gorgon said. "Oaths that bind you to me. Oaths that promise you'll seek the justice I deserve. Make those oaths, and I'll entertain your words; otherwise, whatever you say will be worthless to my ears."

Artemis nodded, and as she placed her hand over her heart, she began to walk and give Euryale exactly what she wanted. "By the River Styx, I swear that I abhor how Zeus defiled you and will never defend his actions. Furthermore, I swear I shall fight to see justice done on your behalf and shall not relent until it's been served or you desire it no more."

Euryale's throat tightened. She could scarcely believe the goddess's vows, nor the strength in her tone that drove it. Before she knew it, Artemis had her embraced, at which point the gorgon sank into her arms.

"I hope you've got more than Alex in mind when you said others would help," Euryale said with a pained laugh. "I'm not sure he'll be enough."

"There will be others," Artemis said, still keeping her close. "Who, I'm not sure. But others. Athena is calling a special council tomorrow, and then we'll see who sides with whom."

"Athena? I would've guessed she'd defend her father to the end."

Artemis pulled back and gave the gorgon a loving smile. She reached and brushed the tears off Euryale's cheeks before replying. "No, Euryale," she said softly. "She's leading the charge against him."

Euryale's jaw dropped. "She is?"

"She is," Artemis replied. "You'll have to testify, though, tomorrow at noon. Will you?"

The world blurred, and colors grew vibrant and surreal. Euryale stood, detached from her body, trying to figure out what to say or do. She had to do something, didn't she? But could she?

A gentle hand squeezed her shoulder. "Euryale, can you tell them what happened?"

"I don't know," she said, choking on her words. She couldn't even talk when it was just her and Artemis, a goddess who'd sworn to stay at her side. How could she stand in front of the entire pantheon with their eyes questioning her, judging her?

"Perhaps there's one more thing we can do to bolster your unparalleled bravery," Artemis said.

"I'm hardly brave," Euryale said, managing a forced laugh. "I'm terrified."

"It's not bravery if you're not scared," Artemis said. She then reached into the leather pouch hanging off her belt and handed the gorgon a small, glass globe that held flecks of silver and gold inside. "Take this, a gift from Athena."

"What is it?"

"If you break it over your sister's head, she'll be restored to her former self," Artemis said. "Though Athena is giving you this freely, I would be remiss in my duties as a mediator if I didn't add that if you were to free Perseus, the act would be much appreciated."

Euryale cried, laughed, and cried some more. "Of course," she managed to blubber out. "I'll draw you a map to where he is."

Chapter Stheno

The moment she flipped her phone on, Euryale grimaced. She'd forgotten that she'd put it to sleep when she went for her bath, and now that she'd remembered to check it, she was horrified at the dozen messages waiting for her, all from Alex.

Using one hand to steer the chariot back to the world of mortals, Euryale sucked in a breath to steady herself and then used her other hand to dial her husband. He answered before the first ring had finished.

"Euryale?" he said. "Please tell me that's you."

"It's me," she replied, her voice surprisingly weak. "I'm okay."

"What happened? Where are you, and why did you run off like that?"

Euryale froze at the question, unable to formulate any sort of reply. She knew what she should say, what she had to say to make him understand, to bring to light what she wanted nothing more than to cast into the deepest pits of darkness to be forgotten forever. But she couldn't. Thinking about what Zeus had done, even in the abstract, was painful enough. To speak of it, however, made it all far too real. And what if Alex didn't believe her? Certainly, he would, but maybe she was deluding herself on that, too. Or worse, what if he blamed her and thought she knew exactly what she was doing?

Gods, even she wondered at that last bit. Not in totality, but partially?

On some level, she'd felt the encounter seemed off, that "Alex" wasn't acting as he normally did. Maybe she knew all along it wasn't him. Maybe she wanted to be with someone else. Pain erupted across her midsection, and she doubled over, wrapping an arm around her stomach. No. No...she didn't want that at all, she told herself. She never wanted it.

"Honey?"

Alex's voice pulled her out of the spiral she was in. "Sorry," she said, trying to regain her composure. "I'll explain later. I promise. Where are the kids?"

"They're with me," he said.

"Are they scared?"

"No," he said. "I haven't told them anything."

"Good," she said, sighing with relief. The last thing Euryale needed was her own children ashamed of her.

"Talk to me," Alex pressed. "You can tell me anything. You know you can."

"I know. I know," she replied as she started to nervously rock back and forth. "Just keep them safe for now."

"From who?"

"Someone tried to kill me," she explained. When Alex gasped, she quickly filled in the details. "He didn't stand a chance. You don't need to worry about that."

"That's a hard thing not to worry about. Who was he?"

"Artemis thinks he was sent by Typhon," she replied. "He's the only one who makes sense, after all, which is why I need you to make sure the kids don't wander off. Not until we put an end to him for good."

Alex exhaled sharply. "Christ. That really can't be good."

"It's not. But Tickles will protect them, I'm sure," she said. "So, keep him around."

"I wonder if we could borrow Cerberus, too," Alex said. "Or maybe get a couple of guard hydras? They breed those, right? If not, man, oh man, we need to corner that market immediately before someone steals the idea."

"Alex!"

"Sorry, you know I can get a little carried away when things go wonky."

Euryale smiled, feeling her numbed heart warm. "I know, Alex. It's okay." She paused for a half breath, but she quickly feared he'd start to pry again, so she opted to end the conversation as quickly as she could. "I have to go," she lied. "I'll call you soon."

"What are you going to do?"

"I'll call soon," she repeated before hastily ending the call. She spent a few seconds staring at the phone, second-guessing everything she'd said and done. She should've told him everything. Alex deserved that much, but...but she was too much of a coward. And now? How could she? It would go even worse than before. After all, it wasn't exactly a topic one could bring up with, "Hi, honey, I forgot to mention one little thing when we talked five seconds ago..."

Euryale buried her face in her hands where it was warm and safe. She hated how weak, small, and most of all, alone she felt in all of this. The gorgon took in a slow, deep breath and straightened, refocusing on the task she'd set out to do. No, she wasn't alone, at least, not for much longer. She'd have her sister back soon enough, and Stheno had always granted her strength like no other.

Euryale slumped in the chariot. Alex deserved better, and she should be drawing her strength from him as much as from her sister. She pulled out her phone and dialed him again before she could think herself out of it.

"Euryale?" Alex said once he answered. "Something wrong?"

"No, well, yes," she stammered. "But I'm going to free Stheno. I'd like you there when I do. Bring the kids. They should meet her right away, too."

"How?" he asked, sounding astonished at the very notion. "I mean, of course, I'll come. Except, you kind of took the chariot and all, but I'll think of something. She's still at the aquarium, right?"

"She is," Euryale replied. "Grab a chariot from Apollo and meet me at the ticket counter. I'll be there in a few hours."

"Okay," he said. "See you soon. Love you."

"Love you, too."

Noka Marine Aquarium.

The entire complex spanned nearly a half mile in each direction, not including the myriad of hotels and resorts that had sprung up next to it over the past year. True, the entire complex had pulled in its fair share of guests over the years and had even made a decent profit for its owners throughout that time. The penguin exhibit on the south side was often heralded as one of the best in the world—their secret being an exceptional lighting engineer who'd managed to make the small, flightless birds look extra cute.

However, with the addition of a killer whale who'd not only been found in the middle of a nearby city—alive, no less—but had also survived a fall from so high she should've burned up on re-entry, the aquarium still had a waiting list for Stheno's show that extended out for the next three years. Everyone and their mother (and their mother's mother) wanted to see this immortal marine mammal do her tricks. They also probably wanted to see if she'd fly again.

"Mommy!" the twins shouted, tearing free of their father's grasp and running full steam toward Euryale. The gorgon barely had time to brace herself for the hit when Aison stuck himself to her hip, and Cassandra launched herself into her arms.

"Daddy says we're going to see our aunt!" Cassandra said, eyes full of excitement.

"I didn't even know we had an aunt!" Aison added. "Except for Miss Persephone. But she's not a real aunt."

Cassandra scowled and smacked her brother on the head. "She is too!"

"Is not!"

"Is too!"

"Okay, okay, let's not get into that," Euryale said, squeezing them both tightly, stopping the argument before it escalated into the next world war.

"Should I buy tickets?" Alex asked, looking at the row of booths that stood a few dozen yards away. His face soured as he did, and for a good cause, too. The line was enormous.

Euryale shook her head. "No."

"No?"

"I'm not giving money to the people who jailed my sister," she said.

"But they didn't really know she was, well, not a whale," Alex replied.

"Which is the only thing keeping me from tearing off their limbs and feeding them to their children." Euryale stiffened and flashed a smile to her semi-horrified children. "Mommy's exaggerating. No one is getting torn apart."

The twins exchanged glances. Cassandra elbowed her brother and whispered, "I don't think she is."

To which Aison whispered back, "I kinda wanna see her do it. Do you think it'll be like the movies?"

"No one is torn apart," Euryale reiterated. She then took them both by the hand and slithered for the entrance.

"What if they want to see our tickets?" Alex asked, trotting a few steps to catch up. "Maybe I should buy some anyway."

Euryale grinned, having flashbacks to a particular encounter she'd had with a ticket agent at an airport not long ago. "I can be persuasive, don't worry."

And she was. Quite.

Much to her delight (and the disappointment of Aison), the teen manning the turnstile decided not to stop the gorgon whatsoever when she simply pushed her way past not only the line, but his position as well. Euryale gave him full marks for a smart choice on that one. After all, was he seriously going to risk petrification or worse to enforce some silly thing like making sure she had a particular piece of paper? Of course not.

Once through the entrance, she grabbed a park map and gave it a look while people bustled by, and the sounds of excitement filled the air. Long ago, Euryale would've never thought anyone, let alone the crowds at large, wouldn't run away screaming the moment they laid eyes on her monstrous form. And while some people did stare a little longer than they should, most people, young and old, gave her and her family nothing more than a passing glance. With the Olympians' return over a year ago, the world truly had grown used to all things mythological.

It took Euryale a few moments to find exactly where she needed to go to find her sister, mainly because the twins were hellbent on either terrorizing the park visitors for fun or disappearing completely to do gods knew what. And given everything she was dealing with already, she didn't need any more added stress.

"Hey!" Alex shouted. "If you two don't settle down right this instant, no cotton candy for either of you."

Aison and Cassandra didn't move a muscle, each hanging off a statue of a jumping dolphin. "Cotton candy?" they asked in unison.

"Yes, cotton candy. The treat of the gods. The candy of the divine. It is the most amazing, to-die-for confection that has ever existed."

Aison's face scrunched. "What's con...con..."

"Confection. And you'll never know what that is if you don't behave," Alex said, giving them each the dad finger of doom.

The twins, again acting as one, stood as tall and pleasant as any child from the 1950s, with their hands clasped neatly in front of them and faces smiling bright. It was all an act, an act they'd learned to perfect, but one couldn't say it wasn't effective.

"We have discussed the matter," Cassandra said, "and we've come to an afford."

"It's *aboard*," Aison whispered.

"I believe the word you're looking for is 'accord,'" Alex said with a chuckle.

"Right, an accord," Cassandra corrected. "We have decided that we want some of this cotton candy."

"Thought you might," Alex said, grinning. He then turned to his wife, who was watching all of this play out with amusement. "Shall you lead the way then?"

"I shall."

The gorgon then struck out for the whale encounter, which was situated on the other side of the park, nestled between the stingray lagoon and the penguin palace. The kids managed to hold their near-insatiable curiosity and desire to explore for a solid nine minutes, which not only was a full two minutes more than Euryale had expected, but did set a new record for best behavior without mother's intervention while somewhere new. Cotton candy, it seemed, was a fantastic motivator.

When they finally reached where she wanted to be, Euryale checked a nearby, brightly colored board with a cartoon whale leaping through a red hoop for the showtimes. The next one wasn't scheduled for another twenty-two minutes.

The gorgon then spent a half second looking the place over. The whale encounter was a large stadium that formed a semi-circle around a massive tank of water, complete with islands and a custom backdrop of a pacific island scene. A huge line swarmed the entrance, filled with guests idly waiting to be let in, all the while tackling the heat with hats, comments about the weather, and over-priced, ice-cold beverages.

Euryale hurried through the crowd, her husband and children following in her wake. This close to her sister, Euryale didn't wait to be acknowledged or even seen in some cases. She simply pushed people aside. She was surprised at how, with each passing second, she grew not only more eager to see Stheno, but more willing to tear into any hapless bystander—figuratively and literally—who stood in her way.

A young woman, at best fresh out of high school, with curly red hair and skin covered in more freckles than not, held up her hand when Euryale reach the front of the line. "We'll be seating soon," she said. "Please wait here with your passes ready."

Euryale continued on with a grunt, not bothering to even acknowledge her presence. She grabbed the thin rope that stretched from the wall to a post in the ground and with one jerk, snapped it clean.

"Hey! You can't—"

Alex leaned close to the girl as they passed. "Best to let this one go," he said. "Trust me on this."

The girl took his advice, sort of. Though she didn't challenge Euryale directly, as the gorgon entered into the stadium, she caught the woman grabbing a radio and talking to someone.

Euryale stopped once inside and pressed her hands against the eight-foot-tall, thick glass of the aquarium tank as she peered inside. The crystal-clear blue water held nothing, but she did see a wide channel on the other side that presumably allowed the stars of the show to come and go.

"This way," she said, hurrying.

After hurrying through a closed gate, slithering onto the stage, and shoving aside a couple more shocked stagehands who had the audacity to stand there dumbfounded, Euryale found a door nestled between two, giant screens that took her to the rear tanks.

She redoubled her pace. Though she was ecstatic at finally seeing Stheno again, her hands grew jittery. What if she was mad at her for never coming to visit? Or worse, somehow blamed her for being cast here by Athena? Or what if Stheno just decided to lash out at everyone around her for no other reason than to quell the anger that had no doubt been building for over a year now? She was, after all, always the most violent and brutal of the three sisters. Even Euryale would admit to that.

Maybe bringing Alex and the kids wasn't such a good idea after all.

"What?" Alex asked when she glanced over her shoulder.

Euryale paused halfway down the narrow hall. She had to speak a little louder than normal, thanks to a noisy water pump a few feet away. "She might be cranky," she said. "I need you to be on your toes."

"Cranky?"

"Yeah."

Alex shrugged. "I'd probably be cranky, too, being stuck as a whale for this long."

"I know, but when you get cranky, you want an éclair."

"Yeah, so?"

"When she gets cranky, she wants to kill a few dozen people. Maybe a hundred."

Alex's eyebrows shot up, and he backtracked a few steps. "Oooh."

"That also means you should let me do the talking," she added.

"I'm about to let you do all this on your own," Alex said. "Kids want to feed the stingrays, anyway. You two can meet us there when she's out of bloodbath mode."

Aison, who was holding a giant stack of cotton candy taller than the tower of Babel in each hand, drew them both close to his chest. "I'm not feeding them my candy cotton!"

Cassandra, carrying the same, wiped a bit of sticky, colored goo from her mouth and seconded the sentiment. "Me either!"

"Cotton candy," Alex whispered.

"Or my cotton candy!" Aison added.

The comments of the twins put Euryale at ease, or at least, at ease enough to continue down the hall before pushing through a door. This led her out to a large pool with a catwalk that ran across its middle and two sloped entry points at opposite ends. To her relief, the pool happened to be occupied by a pair of killer whales. They swam leisurely in the water, and for the moment, it didn't seem as if either was interested in the gorgon.

"Do you suppose she's one of them?" Alex asked. "Maybe we should've asked who the crown jewel of this place was before we stormed the palace."

"We'll see in a moment," Euryale said, slithering forward. She went along the pool's edge, letting her tail flick into the water, trying to draw the whales' attention as she went to one of the entry points.

She was about halfway there when a door flew open on the other side of area, and a couple of security guys dressed in crisp black-and-brown uniforms and menacingly clutching handheld radios barged in.

"Hey! You four!" the bigger and older of the two yelled while pointing a finger. "You can't be in here! I don't care who you are!"

Euryale ignored them and kept moving, which seemed to fluster the duo.

"I mean it!" the guard yelled, still approaching, but clearly not sure of himself. "We've got contacts, you know! Up high. Like in Olympus high. There's a whole temple to Poseidon not even a block away. He's going to be pissed if you don't leave right this instant."

Euryale felt her jaw tighten and a growl slip from her lips. The faint outline of scales appeared on her skin, and as her fangs elongated, she forced herself to remember they were only doing their job. As such, she could at least give them a chance. "Alex," she said. "Deal with them, please."

"On it," he said, hastily making his way across the catwalk.

Euryale smiled, not at her husband's quick action, but at the fact that one of the whales had come to see her. With every foot of ground she covered, it was right next to her, shadowing her every step.

This creature had to be Stheno. It had to be.

Euryale dipped into the entry point, and the moment her body sank into not even an inch of water, the whale lunged forward, sending a cold, salty spray everywhere and beaching itself next to the gorgon in the process.

Euryale felt her throat tighten, and tears of joy form in her eyes. She reached out and placed a hand against the massive creature's head. The smooth, slippery, and rubbery skin sent a tingle up the gorgon's arm.

"Stheno?" she asked.

The whale answered by thrashing about, thoroughly soaking the gorgon even more than she already was.

"I'm here," Euryale said, caressing her sister. "Everything's about to change for the better. I promise. Give me a moment."

The whale stilled, and it tracked every movement Euryale made with its eye. The gorgon reached into her pouch and pulled out the glass sphere Artemis had given her. She then looked at it briefly before smashing it across the whale's head.

The silver and gold flecks sprayed across the whale's body, glowing fiercely the moment they came in contact with her skin. Light shot out in all directions from each spot, and within seconds that light burned so brightly across the entire whale's body that Euryale was forced to shield her eyes and look away. A loud droning sound built in the air, and after a few seconds, the light faded. The world quieted, and Euryale dared a look.

Standing a few feet away, awestruck, was Stheno. Bronze skin covered a slender frame that only a fool would think was weak. While she, too, carried a nest of vipers atop her head as Euryale did, every last one of Stheno's was scarlet in color with bands of black, all hissing and coiled, ready to strike.

"Euryale!" her sister cried out, wrapping the gorgon in a hug tight enough to crush diamond. "I knew you'd come for me."

"Of course I would," Euryale replied, her words wheezing out. "I'm sorry it took so long."

Stheno's claws dug into Euryale's back, painfully so.

"It did take a while," she said, drawing blood. The gorgon lifted her head off Euryale's shoulder before glaring at the men Alex was trying to usher out the door as quickly as he could. "And for that, I'm going to enjoy making them pay for every stupid trick they made me do."

The gorgon lunged forward, roaring with such ferocity that even Scylla would have heeded Stheno's every command. Euryale, knowing her sister's fury, managed to react fast enough by latching hold of her arms and coiling her tail around her legs so that they both fell to the floor.

The act only enraged Stheno further. The gorgon struggled against her sister's vicelike embrace, clawing at the ground, yelling obscenities that would make even the most hardened drill instructor blush, and trying to drag herself toward her former captors. "I'll kill you all!" she roared. "You hear me? I'm going to flay you alive and put your children's children on spits for all to see!"

Euryale, still locked on Stheno, took her attention off her sister long enough to shout out to the security guys who, for some stupid reason, hadn't run off yet. "What are you waiting for?" she yelled. "Get out of here!"

A shove from Alex helped put the two men in gear, and off they ran.

"Run, you cowards!" Stheno yelled, still struggling, still fighting. She elbowed Euryale in the gut and even slapped her across the face, but the gorgon held on.

"Stop!" Euryale pleaded. "This isn't the time!"

"Of course it's the time!" she fired back. "Do you know what they did to me? You of all people should be at my side, gouging eyes and ripping hearts!"

"I do," Euryale said, ignoring the next few blows her sister gave as well as the previous. "And if I were in your place, I'd want the same."

Stheno hissed, as did every viper atop her head. "Then let me go. We promised to be at each other's side forever."

"We did, and I always will be," Euryale said, praying to the Fates this fight would end soon and peacefully. "There are more important things going on than this. I swear."

At first, Stheno didn't react, and Euryale kept a tight grip on her as she seethed, snorting like a rabid bull. But as time marched on, Stheno slowly calmed, and eventually, she simply huffed and relaxed.

"More important things?"

Euryale nodded and loosened her hold. "Much more important."

"Fine," Stheno said with a huff. She then shot Euryale a half grin. "Medusa was right about you, you know."

"How's that?"

"She always said leave it to you to spoil a good time."

Chapter Whale Riding

"She doesn't look very scary," Cassandra said, bumping her brother with her shoulder after introductions had been made.

"Not scary at all," Aison replied with a nod. Though his mother had promised them all that Stheno was the most vicious of the gorgons, he was having a hard time believing it. No one, he knew, could possibly be more frightful than his mother, especially after he tested some of his homemade Greek fire in his bedroom a couple of months ago and got caught. Besides, Aunt Stheno was rather naked, too, which for the twins meant funny and not at all deadly.

"You don't think I'm scary?" Stheno asked, cutting into the twin's thoughts.

Aison shook his head. "Nope."

His aunt's fiery eyes gleamed and turned predatory. She flashed a demonic grin and beckoned them both over with the curling of a single claw. "Come here, if you would," she purred.

"Why?" they asked in unison, eyeing her skeptically. Fear didn't grip them, but they weren't fond of tricks, either, which is what both thought they were being set up for.

"I have a secret to tell you," she whispered.

The twins shrugged and took a few steps forward. Stheno held her smile as they came, and when they were within arm's reach, she lunged at them with her face twisted, fangs barred, and a primal scream.

Neither of the children jumped, but Aison did place his hands on his hips and gave an approving nod. "The important thing is you tried," he said. "Right, Mommy?"

Euryale burst into laughter. She put a hand on her son's head and toyed with his serpents. "That's right. You should always try."

Stheno dropped to a squat and rested her arms casually on her knees. "I guess I'm not as terrifying as I'd thought."

"Mommy's way worse," Aison said. "Don't feel bad."

"Especially when you play rodeo with the chimera in the kitchen," Cassandra added. "Don't do that."

"Or make a mud fort in the living room."

"Or reenact the Trojan War in the wine cellar."

"I'll remember all of that," Stheno replied, rising. She then directed her attention back to her sister. "I can't believe I'm an aunt," she said. "Who would've thought? I'm not even sure what I'm supposed to do. Take them on their first pillage? Show them which bones break best? Finer points to dismemberment? Archery? Spear work? What?"

"No, no, none of that will be necessary," Euryale said, chuckling nervously, as she wasn't sure if her sister was joking or not. "I need your help with something other than the children."

"Ruining Athena? Toppling Olympus? Gutting all of mankind?" Stheno said with eager anticipation. She rubbed her hands together and sucked in a quick breath, clearly excited at the possibilities of any of those and more. "I'm ready to get started on all of that."

"No, well..." Euryale sighed, and her shoulders fell. Aison wasn't sure why, but he couldn't shake the feeling that this was one of those mommy-daddy conversations he and Cassandra were often not allowed to listen to. That feeling turned to reality when his mother gave him and Cassandra a shooing of the hand. "You two go play quietly somewhere else," she said. "We need to talk in private."

"But—"

"Now!" she barked.

Aison jumped and scampered back. When his heart slowed to a mere thousand beats a minute, he glanced at Stheno with eyes as wide the Mediterranean Sea. "Told you she was scarier."

Cassandra grabbed him by the arm and tugged. "Come on," she said, "I've got an idea what we can do."

"What?"

"I'll tell you in a second," she said as they hurried off.

"And stay where your father and I can see you!" Euryale called after them.

"We will!" Aison promised while simultaneously crossing a few serpents on his head. The Fates wouldn't punish you for breaking a promise with your vipers crossed. Everyone knew that. And while he didn't intend on running off, there was no harm in edging his nets. No, that wasn't it. Edging his...bets, that was it. Edging his bets, which is what Daddy would say when he'd behave a certain way to keep Mommy happy, like making sure he cleaned the kitchen when he wasn't sure whose turn it was.

After Cassandra had led him to the other end of the holding tank, she stopped and glanced back the way they'd come. Euryale, Stheno, and Alex stood in a tight group, having a quiet and hushed conversation. Aison could only pick up on some of it, and it sounded as if Euryale was telling his new aunt the story of how she met Alex, which Aison was now glad to be free of.

He really didn't want to hear all the mushy, gushy, kissy parts, anyway. He'd heard it once already, which, as far as he was concerned, was more than enough to last the rest of his life.

"Okay, here's what we're going to do," Cassandra said, raising a pair of excited fists. "Remember those pictures we saw coming up here?"

"With the penguins?"

"No, the whales, silly," she said. "There aren't any penguins here."

"We could go grab some," Aison replied, thinking his penguin suggestion was already much better.

"And do what with them?" she asked. "They're way too small to ride."

Aison perked, immediately tossing his let's-see-if-we-can-feed-one-to-the-whale idea. "Wait. You want to ride the whale?"

Cassandra's face brightened, and she started to bounce on the balls of her feet. "Yes!"

"Mom will never let us, and she's right there," Aison rightfully pointed out.

"She's not even paying attention," Cassandra replied. "Watch."

Aison bit his lip, trying to keep from laughing, as his sister first started making faces at their parents and ended up with faking a heart attack (a world-class performance as far as Aison was concerned), all of which elicited exactly zero response from any of the adults.

"We should get a rope," Aison said, helping his sister to her feet. "But it'll have to be like ...four feet long to lasso him with."

"I bet we need at least eleven."

Aison's eyes bulged. He'd never heard of such a monstrous piece of rope before. "Eleven?"

Cassandra nodded. "And we'll probably have to bribe him, too, so he gets close enough."

Aison's eyes darted around backstage. There wasn't much to work with, aside from a few empty buckets and a mop someone had left propped up against the corner. "I'm not giving him my cotton candy," he said, clutching the last bit he had left close to his chest.

"He probably doesn't even know what it is."

"Maybe we could get some fish. They eat fish, right?"

Cassandra nodded again. "Yeah, but it probably can't be cooked."

"They eat sushi?" Aison asked, proud of himself he knew what that word meant, and just as smug that his sister probably didn't.

"No, tapioca head," she replied. "I mean like, they have to eat it whole. Like, right from the tank."

Aison huffed, slightly irritated that apparently Cassandra did in fact know what sushi was, and thus his one-up on her turned out to be a big nothing. But as quick as that came, he turned his attention back to figuring out how to capitalize on this once-in-a-lifetime opportunity and ride the killer whale. "I bet they have some fish around here somewhere we could use," he said. "You watch Mom. I'll get the snacks."

"Okay. Hurry."

Aison watched his parents for a few seconds to be sure that they were indeed still busy talking adulty stuff before ducking out of the backstage area. Once through the door that led to the hall they'd initially come through, he continued down it until he reached a side passage which he promptly took.

This short stint led him to another door, which in turn led him to a storeroom full of cleaning supplies as well as an entire wall full of gadgets and tools that looked like they'd be really, *really* fun to test on all sorts of things. The one with the big jagged blade definitely had promise, and he wondered how fast it could chop through the coffee table in their living room. He figured maybe to the count of five. Three, if Cassandra was counting and cheating by going fast. Regardless, there was only one way to find out.

He started to reach for it when the vipers atop his head grew uneasy. Since his mother had always told them never to ignore a nervous snake, he instinctively crouched. There was an odd taste to the air. It tasted like...like when he'd have nightmares about their room being messy and no matter how much he and Cassandra tried to clean it before their parents got home, it only got worse.

"Cass?" he said, hunching down even further before darting to the corner. His stomach knotted as the taste grew stronger. If he had a tail as Mommy did, he was sure it would've been rattling now, but alas, he wasn't as awesome or strong as she. One day, he thought. Maybe he could get one from the big fat guy that came around in the winter giving presents. Sparta? Spanta? He decided he should probably learn the guy's name before putting in a request for a tail.

Aison refocused on the there and then. What would his mother do with this situation? Not hide in a storage closet, that was for sure. She conquered titans! She pitted herself against the gods! She insisted Dad take Tickles for a walk every night! And if she could do all that, he could face whatever silly taste was in the air, with or without a tail.

The little gorgon eased toward the door with unparalleled determination before cracking it open. He only moved it an inch, enough so he could see what was going on down the hall. At first, there was nothing but an empty corridor to look at. He was going to press forward when the snakes atop his head grew even more agitated, so he kept still, not out of fear, he told himself, but out of necessity.

Not even two heartbeats later, a cloaked figure slipped by his vantage point, heading toward the backstage where everyone else was. Though Aison only saw him for a fleeting second due to being down a side hall, he was certain he saw whoever it was carrying a bow and arrow.

Quietly, Aison eased from his hiding spot and trotted lightly down the hall, making less noise than a feather dropping onto a pillow. He reached the corner to the main hall, and practicing his stealth skills (something his dad had impressed upon him as necessary if he ever wanted to join a monster hunt when he grew up), he dared a quick, silent peek.

At the end of the hall, maybe twenty yards away, the figure stood crouched near the door. Aison watched him carefully open the door a few inches. At first, he didn't know why, but all that changed the moment the figure raised his bow.

Aison dashed forward, operating on pure instinct, as the figure drew back the arrow. Aison screamed, trying to sound as fearsome as his mother, and launched himself at whoever this bad, bad person was.

Right as he hit, the arrow flew.

Chapter The Trial

She felt the air grow warmer a split second before Aison screamed.

Euryale twisted, half expecting to see one of her children missing an arm. Or worse, holding onto someone else's missing arm. Instead, what she saw was her son firmly latched onto the back of a cloaked figure, and what she heard right after was the whizz of an arrow as it zipped by.

Aison fought valiantly, his tiny fangs and claws tearing into the attacker, but in the end, clearly, he was no match for his opponent. The assassin reached back and grabbed him by the neck and threw him over his shoulder. Aison slammed into the ground, and the air blew from his lungs when he hit.

Euryale, already charging the attacker, bellowed. The assassin staggered away, clutching his ears with both hands. Before the gorgon could take advantage of the situation and pounce, her sister, Stheno, beat her to it. Claws flew, and fangs ripped. Before five seconds had passed, Euryale had scooped Aison up in her arms while his aunt gleefully ripped the last appendage from the man's bloody stump of a body.

"Are you okay?" Euryale asked.

Aison nodded. "I'm okay."

"And why wouldn't he be?" Stheno said, panting, smiling, and covered in blood and gore. She then reached down and lifted the corpse by the head and tossed it to their feet the same way a cat would when bringing home a present. "I left the head intact, so you could bring it home."

"Stheno!" Euryale chided.

"What?" she replied, genuinely shocked. "I know as far as the rules go, he was my kill, but I think we can let that slide. Your son did all the work, flushing him out like that."

"We're not collecting heads."

"It's a head," she pointed out. "Singular. And he has to start sometime. Might as well be now."

"I said no."

Stheno shrugged. "Tell you what," she said. "I'll hold on to it so that when you change your mind, you won't feel bad about leaving it behind."

"I'm not changing my mind."

Stheno laughed. "You always say that."

At that point, Alex, who'd been off to the side of the exchange, suddenly snapped to attention as if a thought he should've had long ago struck him. He looked over his shoulder, and his face drained of color. "Cassandra?"

The unsettling tremor in her husband's voice put the fear of Chaos in her heart, and that fear only doubled when he broke into a full sprint. She spun around to see where he was going, and it only took an instant to realize what had happened. At the other end of the pool, Cassandra lay sprawled out on her side, mouth open, with an arrow sticking out of her back.

Athena trotted up the steps to the acropolis, and though she felt in her heart of hearts that what she was doing was right, she hated how uncertain she was of the outcome. Merely thinking about her father's actions made her queasy. For centuries, if not millennia, she'd wished he'd rein in his lust and decide to live by a moral code that wasn't simply might is right.

Sadly, she knew—or rather, now decided to admit—he would never change. Not unless he faced serious consequences and not merely a beratement by his wife, which clearly never did a damn thing. And if he wasn't reined in now, he likely never would be, and then things would only grow worse.

Would Euryale be the last he'd defile if nothing changed? Athena snorted. She'd sooner bet on Ares trading spears for flowers or the Fates burning their tapestry than bet on that. Who'd be next, she wondered. Artemis? Aphrodite? Demeter?

Athena paused, halfway up the marble steps to the acropolis. Would it be her? The Goddess of Wisdom shook her head, trying to tell herself that would never be, but a week ago, the thought of Zeus forcing himself upon a gorgon would've seemed so laughable, she'd never have thought it to be true even if Apollo had given the prophecy himself.

Athena shook her head and cursed. Life would be a thousand times easier for everyone if Zeus would stop dropping his robes at every opportunity. At the very least, perhaps Hera wouldn't have tried to usurp the throne, and they could've avoided everything with Typhon that followed.

Hopefully, the others would see it this way. Athena figured she at least had Artemis and Apollo on her side, even if she hadn't spoken with the God of the Sun yet. A few others she could likely persuade, but would Zeus's brothers, Poseidon and Hades, condemn his actions? Or would they side with their brother out of a sense of loyalty no matter what? Or simply out of a guilty conscience? It wasn't as if either of those two hadn't done the same.

In the end, however, Athena knew if she couldn't sway at least one of the two, all of her efforts would likely be in vain. Worse, even if she was Zeus's favored daughter, there would be repercussions, swift and severe, for dragging her father through a public trial.

As such, for the first time in…well, forever, Athena doubted not only her abilities but her wisdom. Was this a hill she was ready to die on? To protect a monster of her own making?

She didn't get a chance to consider every facet of the question, sadly. By the time she'd passed through the giant colonnades of the acropolis, she'd only considered twelve dozen serious consequences that would befall her should she fail, all of which would make life painful for the next eon.

Athena stopped a few paces inside the massive structure as the chatter she'd heard on the way up the hill gave way to an uncomfortable silence. Eight sets of eyes belonging to eight other Olympians stared back at her, and the expression each god wore was one of ambivalence.

The Goddess of Wisdom spent half an instant to recount those attending, and to her dismay, there were indeed eight gods and goddesses, and not a single one of them was Euryale.

"Athena!" Zeus boomed with life and energy, jumping up from a bench and beckoning her over with a giant wave of his hand. "Come. Join us. You'll be glad to know that this matter of yours is settled, and we've decided on a course of action to prevent any of your admittedly justifiable concerns to rest."

Athena tilted her head at the unexpected declaration. "Did I miss something?" she asked. "Surely, you're not talking about what you did to Euryale."

"What other matter would I be talking about?" he replied, waving her over yet again. "Now come. Sit."

Athena made her way over to the group and sat on a marble bench next to Dionysus, who, predictably, offered her a full goblet of wine. She hesitated in taking it, but given the looks of apathy on everyone's face, save Artemis who seemed pained, Athena accepted the drink. She had a distinct feeling she was going to want it. Or need it. Probably both.

"What did you tell them?" she asked after taking a sip. "I doubt it was the truth."

Zeus chuckled. "Oh, sweet daughter of mine," he said. "Why so pessimistic? I told you from the start I did nothing wrong and have no need to hide. But by all means, give them your account."

Athena cursed under her breath. He wasn't lying or bluffing. He wanted her to speak, no doubt to make a fool of herself in front of them all. Punishment, in essence, for going against him. Punishment that wasn't nearly as severe as he'd done to others, gods included, who'd dare challenge his rule, but it was punishment that was effective nevertheless, because he knew, above all else, that Athena loathed the possibility of ever being wrong.

Still, the Goddess of Wisdom wasn't without options, and she knew how to put pressure on the Olympians, too. Before she spoke, she counted to five in her head, letting the silence linger so each of them would hang on her every word. She only needed three.

"He raped her," she said, making eye contact with each one. "He raped her so that he could satisfy his urges, urges that nearly cost us everything already. Don't let him trick you into thinking it was for some noble cause like the pursuit of truth. He violated one us, and if there aren't consequences, he'll do it again, and again, and again until Olympus is in ruin."

Poseidon, who leaned on his trident a few paces behind Zeus, was the first to speak. "From what we've understood, she's in league with Cronus," he said. "Or rather, was tasked by Cronus to take the throne. Is that true?"

Athena reluctantly nodded, as there was no point in hiding that aspect to the story. "It is. But she would've told us that if given a chance."

"From what we've also come to understand, she was given two chances," her uncle went on. "Is that also true?"

"It is, but—"

"Then there are no buts," Poseidon said as if he were lecturing a toddler. "She was given opportunity and paid the consequence. It's not as if he chained her to a slab to have her liver ripped out for the next thousand years. I'd say that's far worse, wouldn't you? Or should we ask Alex how he truly feels about how you treated him instead?"

Athena narrowed her eyes as murmurs of agreement rippled through the gods. "That was different," she said.

Poseidon smirked. "Was it? You've certainly done far worse than that throughout the ages as well," he said. "Was the gorgons' curse different? Or Medusa's execution? What about your dealings with Arachne? The poor girl only wanted to weave tapestries to the best of her ability, and because she did it better than you, you turned her into a spider—a spider who, I might add, as long as we're talking about long-term consequences, harbored a deep grudge that proved most troublesome."

The goddess felt her skin warm and her mouth dry. She had no defense to any of that, and she hated how vulnerable she became because of it. She didn't feel vulnerable because the others would bring judgment upon her. She felt that way because to make them see what Zeus had done was egregious, she'd have to admit something she couldn't bring herself to do. She'd have to admit she was wrong to a great many things.

"I'm not the one on trial here," Athena said, hoping she could turn this around and spare her ego. "Regardless of...your inabilities to see the nuance in my dealings with others, Dad raped Euryale, and there's no telling what she'll do when it comes to revenge."

"Then she'll be responsible for her own undoing," Hades said. "Not that I care either way. It all seems like a waste of time if you ask me, which, no one ever does."

"This is serious, Uncle!" Athena shot back at him.

"No, it's not," Zeus said, finally cutting in. "Just because you say I forced myself upon her, doesn't make it so. She quite enjoyed every second, and if you doubt me, ask yourself this: If I've committed such a heinous act, why isn't Euryale here to say so?"

The Goddess of Wisdom nervously threw a glance behind her, hoping that somehow the act would summon the gorgon. But, of course, it didn't. So, when she turned back around, Athena set her jaw and cursed the day she ever let Euryale off that island. Where was that ungrateful monster? Here she was, sticking her neck out, trying to ward off a civil war, and the gorgon didn't even have the common courtesy to show up and present her case. And since she didn't do that, what sort of answer could Athena give to Zeus? None, sadly.

"I don't know," she reluctantly admitted.

"Then my point stands on its own merit," Zeus said with a triumphant nod.

Athena's temper flared at the smugness in his voice. She did, however, have enough remaining self-control to realize she needed support, and fast, if this meeting wasn't going to go completely to Hades. Her gray eyes darted to the other gods, and she started to call them all out by name as she locked her gaze on each one. "And what of you, Dionysus? What would you say if it were your wife and not Euryale?" she asked. "Or Hades, what if Persephone had been broken? And do I even need to ask you, Demeter, what words would flow from your mouth if your daughter came to you with such news?"

To Athena's utter shock and dismay, not a one supported her. Worse, when Apollo spoke, his words became the death knell to everything she was trying to achieve. "The future is clear to me on this," he said. "From a certain point of view, what happened to Euryale is indeed unfortunate, but our future would be much darker had it not happened."

"Unfortunate?" Athena yelled, her hands tightening on her spear and her rational side barely keeping her rage from using said weapon to skewer the god. "This goes beyond unfortunate, Apollo! It's sick and twisted that none of you are willing to hold ourselves accountable with even an ounce of what we hold the mortals to. How then are we ever superior?"

Zeus, face burning red, went to speak, but Apollo beat him to it, managing to hold up a quick hand that kept Zeus's words at bay.

"Again, Athena," Apollo said with a slow calm. "I understand how unfair this feels, and perhaps it is. But the world isn't always fair, and it certainly can be cruel. Sometimes, for the greater good, we all must endure even the harshest of atrocities."

"So, you do think it's an atrocity," she said, crossing her arms. "You proved my point."

Apollo shook his head. "I think one could see it as such from a limited view, yes, but a moment of unpleasantness that avoids thousands of years of torment is not an atrocity when compared to what could be."

The fury in Zeus's eyes faded, and the Ruler of Olympus settled back with an air of satisfaction about him. "There, you see, Athena? Even Apollo has foreseen my choice was the right one," he said. "As such, I'm calling an end to this discussion. However, before the matter is dropped completely, I want to assure you that as I said before, we can easily put to rest any fears you have about what she may or may not do."

Athena tutted. "And what, pray tell, did you have in mind?"

"She will take binding oaths swearing loyalty to Olympus."

Athena's jaw hung for several seconds before she snapped out of her shock and laughed. "You honestly think she's going to do that after what you did to her?"

"Yes," he said. "You were wrong about who supported you. You will be wrong about this, as well. She will understand what had to be done and will be glad that her actions will also be forgiven without consequence."

"And if I'm not wrong, and she refuses, what then?"

"Then Euryale will be the author of her own destruction," he said.

Athena's eyes scanned the others once more, hoping, praying to the Fates, she'd find support. She found none other than Artemis. Though the Goddess of the Hunt stood quietly with her in spirit, Athena didn't want to out her sister. She couldn't shake the feeling that if Zeus didn't know what Artemis truly felt on the matter, that would be a good thing.

"This is immoral and wrong," Athena said. "When it erupts in your face, I want you to remember that I never backed down."

"Noted," Zeus said. He then chuckled to himself as a new thought came to him. "If you would indulge me on one thing before we put the matter to rest," he said. "What's your end game to all of this?"

"What do you mean?"

"What did you expect me to do, assuming I had committed some sort of horrible crime? Say I'm sorry? Pay reparations to Euryale? Be cast into exile? What?"

Athena felt the knots form in her stomach. She'd thought about this, of course, but sadly, with everyone clearly against her, she hadn't come up with a good way to address this point, and worse, it likely didn't matter. Still, she couldn't not answer. Everyone knew she'd already thought this through.

"I think," she said slowly. "At the very least, until we come up with an appropriate response, you need to abdicate the throne. Such reckless behavior threatens us all."

Zeus smirked. "And having no one to oversee Olympus is a good thing in your mind? Or would you rather start a war for the throne so we're further weakened when Typhon makes his return or Cronus rises from his slumber?"

"Neither," she replied. "I'll take on the responsibility, even if it's temporary. I am the Goddess of Wisdom, after all. Of all the options, it is the soundest."

Zeus erupted into a bellowing laughter, slapping his knees with both hands with such force that lightning shot out in all directions. "And there it is for all of you to see," he said, grinning at his fellow gods. "She doesn't actually care what happened to the gorgon. She only wants the throne. Nothing more."

"I only want it because you've forced my hand," Athena said evenly. Gods, how she hated being thought so little of, as if she were that petty.

"Ah, I don't blame your ambition, child," he replied, face still cheerful. "Like father, like daughter, after all."

Athena clenched her jaw, but then the lively ring of an Olympi-phone interrupted the proceedings. Reflexively, everyone there checked theirs to see if they happened to be the one getting a call.

"Alex?" Apollo said, answering his phone once he realized his was the one making all the noise. Alex's panicked voice came through, and though Athena couldn't make out what he was saying to the god, when the brightness to her half-brother's face dimmed, she feared the worst. After a few more moments and a brief exchange over the phone, Apollo hung up and filled everyone in. "It's his daughter, Cassandra," he said. "Someone put an arrow through her back."

Chapter A Mother's Love

Euryale sat next to a bed inside Olympus's asclepeion, which was on the northern end of Apollo's temple. There she held her daughter's tiny hand. She'd never felt more powerless in all her life. All she could do was watch an ever-creeping rot spread across Cassandra's back, down her arms, and up her neck, while Apollo and his son, Asclepius, tried everything they could to stop it from claiming the child's life.

"It's going to be all right, sweetie," Euryale said, gently patting Cassandra's head with a wet cloth. Her daughter's skin burned like fire, and as troubling as that was, it was her breathing that scared Euryale the most—shallow, raspy. Sometimes non-existent.

Cassandra managed to open her eyes halfway. "I'm sorry, Mom. I'm sorry we tried to ride the whale."

"It's okay," Euryale said, forcing out a weak smile. "You didn't do anything wrong." She glanced over her shoulder to Aison, who hid in a corner with his head ducked low, watching everything with a look of guilt only borne by the damned upon his face. "You didn't do anything wrong, either."

Despite his mother's reassurance, Aison shrank into the corner even more, practically folding himself into the shadows. "I should've stopped him," he whispered. "I should've..."

"Stop that right now," she said, harsher than she intended. The gorgon exhaled slowly and softened her tone. "You were very brave."

Apollo walked around to the head of the bed and placed two fingers on the side of Cassandra's neck. He left them there for a few seconds before checking her wrists and the back of a heel. He didn't say what he was thinking, but Euryale didn't have to ask. Things were dire, even if the arrow had been removed and the wound sutured.

"How long has it been?" Apollo asked, directing his question to Asclepius.

"Twelve minutes and sixteen seconds," the God of Medicine replied, leaning on his staff and toying with a thick, curly beard. "The restoration spell seems to have worked even less than the previous attempt, which was barely successful."

"Something is better than nothing," said Apollo. "How much longer until you can try again?"

Asclepius sighed heavily. "Not for another half hour, I'm afraid," he answered. "I've spent all the energy stored with this wood. But even if I'm successful, without a proper antidote, even if she survives—"

Euryale shot out of her chair, claws digging deep into the edge of the bed. "*IF* she survives?"

Aison dropped to the ground, curling into a tiny ball and pressing his face into his elbow. Stheno rushed to comfort him, which gave Euryale a moment to steady herself so that when she spoke again, her words, though still full of anger, were at least not as loud.

"You will never speak like that about my daughter again," Euryale said. "Do you understand?"

For the moment, the gorgon wondered if Asclepius, or even Apollo, would square off against her for talking down to the god in such a fashion. To their credit—or rather, to their exceptional understanding—neither did.

"You have my sincerest apologies, Euryale," Asclepius replied, his hazel eyes filled with compassion. "Those were ill-chosen words. I'm only trying to help, but at the same time, I want you to understand what's going on. Lies and misconceptions help no one."

"I…" Euryale's throat closed, and she had to clear her eyes and shake her head before she could speak again. "I understand exactly what's going on, and I sorely wish I didn't."

Alex took to his feet and paced. "There's got to be something we can still do," he said. "I mean, you turned me to stone, and you flat out died, and that all worked out."

"It's not that simple," Asclepius replied.

"Why?"

Asclepius looked to his father for help, and Apollo gave him a nod before directing a question to Euryale. "Perhaps we should discuss this outside? The details may be…troubling to younger ears."

Euryale shook her head as new tears streamed down her face. "I am never leaving her side. Not even for a moment. Just tell us. It's not as if she doesn't know I'm worried to death."

"As you wish," Apollo said. "This poison, whatever it is, isn't merely attacking her body. It's attacking her soul. If we don't find a way to stop it, there will be nothing left to bring back. She won't even wind up at the shores with Kharon. She'll simply cease to be."

"But you can neutralize it," Euryale said, her voice little more than a begging whisper.

"With enough time to research it and find a cure, absolutely," Apollo said.

Euryale swallowed hard. Her eyes, cloudy, settled on her near-lifeless daughter. She watched Cassandra's chest rise and fall, rise and fall…and then, nothing.

The next moment stretched for an eternity, and the world around Euryale became a muted blur of shadow and color, with only her motionless daughter held in clear focus.

"Cassandra?" she whispered, touching her shoulder with a shaky hand.

Cassandra tensed and gasped before settling back into her shaky rhythm of shallow breathing.

"The apnea will grow worse as things progress," Apollo said. "It also means we have far less time than is ideal."

Stheno put Aison in his father's arms and sat in a chair at her sister's side. There, Stheno leaned over and slid an arm across Euryale's shoulder to give a warm hug. Euryale leaned into the embrace and smiled as Stheno's bronze vipers brushed against her cheek.

"How much time do you need?" Stheno asked.

"Every bit we can get," Apollo said. "But..."

"But you don't know how to get it," Euryale finished.

Apollo nodded solemnly.

At that point, Euryale broke down, unable to hide under the façade of strength she'd erected, not that she had much of one left. Stheno cradled her head as she sobbed and waves of anguish ripped through her soul.

"Why couldn't it have been me?" she asked, heart tearing. "I would suffer this fate a thousand times to spare her from it—I'd suffer it a thousand times just to even give her a chance."

Euryale felt Stheno stiffen, and when the gorgon looked up at her, she could see an idea gleaming in her eyes.

"We...we can give her all the time we need," Stheno said. "Or rather, you can."

"I can? How?"

Stheno didn't reply, verbally at least. All she did was point two fingers at her eyes before redirecting them at Cassandra.

"No," Alex said. "You can't."

"She most certainly can," Stheno replied.

"She'll kill her!"

"She'll petrify her," Stheno corrected. "It can be reversed."

"Last I heard, only Hera knows how to do that. And I'm going to go out on a limb and say she's not too keen on helping any of us for anything."

Apollo nodded gravely. "This is true. Hera has been and still is, the only master when it comes to restoring flesh from stone."

Alex turned to his wife with a pale face. "Listen to him," he said, pointing a finger at Apollo. "You can't do this. We'll find another way to save her."

Euryale barely heard it all. She had her daughter's hand firmly clasped in both of hers, as if Cassandra would slip away forever should she let go for even an instant. Eventually, long after the room quieted, the gorgon quietly addressed them all, her stare never leaving her child. "I'd like you all to leave."

Apollo was the first to respond. He clasped her shoulder and squeezed. "We'll be in the next room, trying to brew another cure."

He left with Asclepius following quietly behind, and when they were gone, Euryale looked at Alex. "You too."

"No," Alex said, shaking his head. His eyes glistened, and his voice cracked. "You're not going to do this."

"Alex, please," she said softly and evenly. "I can't take a fight right now."

"Then don't you dare start one."

"Alex, please," Euryale said once again, her voice growing darker and stronger. "I need you to listen to me very carefully. I love you with every fiber of my being, and I love our children even more. But you have to go. Right now. If you don't, I'm going to lose my mind, and when I do, there's no telling what will happen."

Alex balked, and Stheno stood and flicked open her bronze claws. "Listen to your wife, Alex," she growled. "I'll make you leave if I must."

"Daddy?"

Alex, staring down Stheno, stroked the top of his son's head as Aison clutched him tightly around the neck. "Come on, kiddo," he finally said. "Let's go see if we can help Apollo figure something out."

With that, Alex grunted, shook his head, and carried their son out of the room.

"I'll leave if you wish," Stheno said, "but I want you to know, you don't have to do this alone."

Euryale shook her head. "No. I do."

"Why do you think that?"

"Because no one needs to see the monster I am—that I'm going to be."

Stheno nodded weakly and toyed with the chiton she now wore. She didn't say anything else, but she did place a soft kiss on her sister's forehead before leaving the room.

Euryale sat with watery eyes for far longer than she thought she would, all the while trying to say something to her daughter. Finally, she found the only words that she could muster, and even then, only barely.

"Sweetie," she said, stroking the top of her head. "Mommy loves you very much."

Chapter Confessions

Euryale usually loved her new living room. It had a cozy fireplace that was perfect for snuggling, not that she had had a chance to use it for such purpose yet, but still, she could dream. It also sported a pair of couches, a love seat, four leather recliners, and a long coffee table with masterful scrolling. Granted, said coffee table had a few crayon marks, recent additions thanks to the twins testing out their avant-garde artistic techniques, but it was still one of her favorite pieces in her new home, despite the recent colored-wax flourishes.

At the moment, however, none of that mattered. She, Stheno, and Alex each occupied a different seat around a crackling fire, and no one had said much of anything since she'd left Cassandra's room. Euryale hadn't thought of anything either, opting to retreat into a mental fog that shielded her from what she'd done.

That changed when Alex finally spoke.

"What now?" he asked.

Euryale cringed at the sound of his voice, which felt colder and more distant than she had ever thought it could be. As she leaned back in one of the recliners, she wondered if this was going to be the end of their marriage. He hated her at this point for what she'd done. He had to. Or at least, he wanted to leave. It was a gut-wrenching realization, and though she felt she'd had no choice in turning Cassandra to stone, she understood where he was coming from.

Not only did she understand; on some level, if he hadn't reacted the way he did, she might've hated him, too. For what sort of father wouldn't be livid if his wife petrified their child? Only one who cared nothing for his daughter—and that wasn't the man she'd fallen in love with.

"We find a cure. That's what we do," Euryale whispered. "Same as always."

"And what about Hera?" Alex snapped. "Do you have a plan for winning her over?"

Euryale shook her head.

"You might not, dear sister, but I do," Stheno said, drawing back her lips so her fangs gleamed in the light from the fireplace.

Alex rolled his eyes. "Oh, this should be good. Let me guess, torture her? Maybe start with filleting her toes or crushing her bones one at a time? I'm sure that'll work."

Stheno licked her lips and rubbed her hands together with anticipation. "Mmmm, no, that's not what I was thinking," she said. "But I love where you're going with it."

"I wasn't being serious."

"I know, but I was."

"No one is torturing anyone," Euryale said.

"Yet," Stheno tacked on.

"What about Cronus?" Alex asked. "He helped you once. Maybe he'll do it again."

Euryale shook her head and buried her face in her hands. "He's not an option, Alex."

"Pretty sure he is."

"He's not, Alex!" she snapped. "We'll be lucky if he simply kills us all for bothering him again. Is that what you want?"

"Yeah, that's what I want," Alex tutted.

The gorgon sighed and rubbed her temples. "I'm sorry. I shouldn't have said that, but I swear, Alex, if I even thought there was a one-in-a-million chance going to him again would help, I'd take it."

"Then what do we do?" Stheno asked.

"We'll have to scour the world and find an antidote," she replied. "While we do that, Alex is going to have to figure out how to handle Hera."

Alex snorted. "Right, I'll go back to being the lapdog you get to order about."

Euryale straightened, shocked and confused. "Why would you say that?"

"Why would I?" He then shook his head and muttered to himself before taking to his feet and starting for the door. "It doesn't matter. Forget it. I'm going to go check on Aison. You know, since he's still alive and whatnot. Probably best we make sure he stays that way."

Her husband's words ripped through Euryale's gut. "Alex, please—"

"No!" he barked. "There's no 'Alex, please' here. My wishes are not some stupid afterthought—*I* am not some stupid afterthought."

"You're not an afterthought," she said. "You never have been."

"Sorry, but when the rubber meets the road, people's true character comes out," he said, his face turning three shades of crimson. "Look, don't pretend we're married with a meaningful relationship if this is how it's going to be. You yell at me. You tell me to go away. You don't explain a damn thing. You make me toy with Athena? The goddess could squash me into oblivion. And, and, and then—and *then*—you petrify our daughter without giving a damn what I have to say about it."

"I do give a damn," Euryale said, wilting under the assault. Gods, if he only knew. If she could only somehow find the strength to speak the unspeakable, maybe he'd understand. Or maybe he wouldn't.

"Yeah, well, actions speak louder than words," Alex said with a huff. His eyes then found Stheno's as she glared at him with unmatched hate. "What? You think you can scare me? I've fought a gorgon already and came out on top."

"You never fought me," Stheno hissed. "Euryale was always the nice one."

Alex tensed, not out of fear, Euryale could tell, but out of the anticipation of a full-on brawl. "The only reason I'm even remotely tolerating any of your crap right now is because you're her sister."

"And the only reason you're not lying in a pool of your own blood, torn to ribbons, is because she still loves you," Stheno countered. "I will say, however, that little fact isn't going to keep you safe for much longer. I'll have your entrails stretched from here to the Parthenon if you keep that up."

"Whatever," Alex said, waving her off. "I'm going to get Aison—make sure he knows at least one parent isn't going to hurt him."

Euryale burst into tears. "That's not fair."

"What's not fair is cutting me out of everything," Alex snapped back. "You know what, actually? Since everything went to crap after you joined the gods, maybe you should rely on them from now on. I'll go tell Athena you want her help. Or check that, let's go right to the top. Zeus is a pretty powerful guy. I'm sure he'll make everything right."

Euryale flew out of her chair, eyes large, voice full of panic. "No! Not Zeus!"

The room seemed to freeze, and the only thing that broke the deathly silence was the sound of her heart pounding against her ribcage. Alex, with one hand on the doorknob, looked at his wife with genuine concern. "What's going on?" he asked softly.

"You...you can't go to him," she replied. As she spoke, Euryale felt her soul wither. The room seemed larger, her sister seemed farther, and her husband seemed more of a stranger than he ever was before.

"Euryale," he said, drawing her attention after gods knew how long. The gorgon looked up, not realizing she'd been staring at the marble floor, to find Alex standing in front of her, holding her hands. "Tell me."

"I—I can't."

Alex brushed his hand against her cheek, and she recoiled.

"Euryale," he whispered. "You either trust me, or you don't."

Euryale shook her head, though she knew his words were true. She stared at her hands and rubbed them over and over one another, desperately trying to find her words.

"I didn't mean to, I swear," she blubbered. "I was in the bath, drinking—"

Alex retreated a step. "Didn't mean to what?"

Euryale looked up, and the mix of fear and betrayal in his face nearly stole her breath and life away. "He came while you were away. He came, and we..."

"No..."

"I swear, Alex, I didn't want to," she cried. "I'd never—"

"No, tell me this is some sick, twisted joke," he said, stepping back again. His feet found a nearby end table, and he nearly lost his balance running into it.

Euryale's heart tore in two. She collapsed to the floor, bawling, and wrapped her arms around her sides, trying to find some measure of comfort. "I didn't know it was him," she said, rocking. "I swear, Alex. I had no idea. He looked exactly like you. I swear, Alex, to the Fates, on our children's souls, I'd never betray you. You're my everything."

"He...he tricked you?" Alex asked.

"No. He raped her," Stheno corrected, her voice full of more venom than all the creatures on earth had combined. "Call it what it is."

Euryale recoiled even further at the word. She didn't want to think about it, think about how helpless it made her feel, how useless and worthless. All she wanted to do was curl into a little ball and have the world fade away.

"Please believe me," she said finally. "Gods, Alex, if you don't, you can kill me now. I can't suffer that kind of torment."

Alex was at his wife's side in a flash, holding her tight. But the moment he did, she was back in the bathhouse with Zeus as he pulled her close and kissed her naked skin.

Euryale screamed in terror and rage, tearing out of her husband's arms, spinning across the floor and ending up cowered near the fireplace. One hand kept her steady on the ground, while the other had a shaky grasp on the fire poker.

"It's okay," Alex said, voice wavering, hands in the air. "I'm sorry. I shouldn't have done that. I should've have said any of that. I...I didn't know."

For what felt like eons, nothing further was said and no one moved.

And then Stheno was kneeling at her side, close, but not touching. "Euryale? Look at me."

The gorgon tried, but the best she managed was to turn toward her. Her focus, still out to infinity, kept her safe, so she saw nothing at all.

"Can you at least hear me?" Stheno asked.

Euryale could, but did she want to? She wanted nothing but oblivion.

"We vowed to look after each other until the end of time, remember?" she said.

Euryale nodded, her mind nearly reaching total absence at this point. "Right."

"I'm not going anywhere." She paused and threw a glance to Alex. "He's not either."

Euryale drifted. Words she didn't care to follow flowed from her husband and her sister as her thoughts ran in a thousand messy directions. Eventually, she spoke six little words that summed it all up. "I don't know what to do."

Stheno gently grasped her hand. "I do."

Euryale refocused. Her sister had inched forward. Her bronze skin glowed like a bar of metal cast into the heart of a forge, and her eyes yearned for revenge.

"We make him pay," she said. "We make them all pay."

Euryale laughed, finding the notion utterly ridiculous. "How?" she asked. "How could we ever even dream of challenging Zeus?"

"I don't care how," she said. "We'll find a way. You're stronger than they are, and they know it."

"No, I'm not."

In a flash, Stheno grabbed her face so that she and Euryale were staring at each other only an inch apart, one in shock, the other in unbridled fury. "Don't you dare say you're not," Stheno sneered. "You defeated Typhon! You destroyed his minions, stood up to Hera, and have the backing of Cronus! By the Fates, Euryale, you above all others can bring every last one of them to their knees!"

Despite her sister's swift and intense reply, fear still claimed Euryale's heart. "I'm not sure I can."

Stheno dug her claws into her sister's cheeks, drawing blood. "You can, and you will," she growled. "Do you want Zeus to go free?"

"No."

"Do you want him to think of you as something he can take whenever he wants?"

Euryale shook her head. "No."

"Do you want him to think he can do it to others? To Cassandra?"

Fire, righteous and vengeful, erupted in the gorgon's heart, instantly shattering the hold her fear and shame had upon her. "No," she answered with a strength that would cower a titan.

Stheno let go and sat back with a wicked smile. "You're damn right, no," she said. "Now, let's go save your daughter and burn this whole place to the ground."

Euryale cleared her eyes one last time with her fingers as she let her sister's words churn in her mind. Her gaze drifted down to her hands, to her claws which were now three inches long, sharp, and gleaming. She could feel her fangs lengthen in her mouth, digging into her tongue and lips, and as the room took on a reddish hue, she knew her eyes had turned black as the Abyss.

"I'm going to kill him," she said, tail rattling and vipers hissing. "Slowly and painfully."

Stheno nodded. "Yes..."

"And when I'm done with him, I'm going to kill every last one of them that stood at his side."

"Yes! We're going to kill them all!" Stheno cackled, pulling her sister upright. "Every last one."

"Every last one of them," Euryale repeated.

"We need to tell your dad," Alex said.

Stheno snorted. "If you can find him."

"What?"

"You heard me. If you can find him, the stupid old bastard."

"She's right," Euryale said with as much spite as her sister. "There's no telling where he is or what he's chasing."

"Or whether he'd even give it up to begin with if you did catch up to him," Stheno finished. "We're on our own."

"But he's your dad," Alex said. "That's like part of his job. Crack skulls when you need it most."

Euryale's tail rattled as long-dormant memories stirred. "A job he hasn't always taken to heart, despite what he did with you."

Stheno folded her arms over her chest. "That's being generous."

"Okay, well, he's out. I guess," Alex said, exhaling sharply. "What do we do about Cassandra, then?"

Euryale narrowed her eyes, not because she held any anger or spite to her husband, but because sheer determination drove her every action, and nothing was going to stop her. "Find Hera. Get her to tell you how to reverse what I've done," she said. "I don't care how you have to do it. Just make it happen."

"And the poison?"

"We could try hemalander," Stheno offered. "Or rather, Apollo could."

"What's that?" Alex asked, looking lost.

"A flower of legends," Euryale filled in. "Legends inside of legends, more like it. It's said to be the most poisonous substance ever to exist."

"And that helps us how, again?"

"The plant is also supposed to be the most powerful agent when it comes to cures, too," Stheno explained. "That said, I don't even know where to start looking for it."

Euryale turned her sister's idea over a few times in her head. It had merit, if the thing were real. It wouldn't be the first time a myth spun by the gods wasn't true, and this was an old, old myth indeed. That said, despite Apollo's promise that he'd find something to save her daughter, in her heart of hearts, Euryale feared he was wrong. Moreover, she couldn't sit by and do nothing, especially when an idea on where to find this legendary plant had just popped into her mind.

"I know where to go," she said.

Alex's eyes filled with hope. "You do?"

Euryale nodded. "Achlys."

Stheno gasped, but Alex, her dear, sweet, clueless Alex, simply cocked his head. "Who?"

"The Goddess of Death and Misery," Stheno filled in. "Daughter of Nyx."

Euryale nodded again. "If there's anyone this side of creation who knows where to find the deadliest plant in existence, it's her."

"She doesn't sound like the nicest deity around," Alex said.

"She's not."

"What if she doesn't want to help?"

"Then I'll feed her to Scylla one piece at a time until she changes her mind."

Stheno snaked an arm across Euryale's shoulders and gave her a squeeze. "Have I told you how much I love you lately?"

"No," she replied, giving her a one-armed hug back.

"Well, I do," Stheno replied. "Any idea where Achlys might be? Last I heard she wasn't the easiest goddess to find."

Euryale shook her head. "No, but Hera procured flowers from her a long time ago. We can start by paying her home a visit."

Chapter Find Her

Having already gone to the gorgon's home and not finding her there, Zeus stormed back to the asclepeion with Apollo and Athena in tow, intent on obtaining Euryale's oaths once and for all. As far as he was concerned, he'd given her plenty of space to deal with the tragedy of this morning, and if they were all to move forward and handle matters that threatened everyone—not to mention, find her child a cure—he needed to know without a doubt where her loyalties were.

That said, Zeus, Ruler of Olympus, God of Thunder, and arguably one of the hardest-headed deities to ever exist, was not prepared for what he found when he entered the room. Whereas Apollo and Asclepius had always kept the individual wards of their healing temples in immaculate condition, this one looked to be at the crux of a hundred-year war. Not a single piece of glassware remained intact, their shards scattered across the floor in every direction. Likewise, herbs and balms had been flung against walls or ground into the stone floor, and the linens had been thoroughly shredded. In the center of all of that, the small statue of a child sat upright in bed.

Cassandra's head twisted over her shoulder, and she held her hands up defensively. Tiny legs kicked at something unseen hanging in the air, while her face, once soft and full of love and life, contorted into an eternal scream of terror.

"Dad?"

Zeus turned at the weak sound of Athena's voice. Though his daughter was addressing him, her gray eyes never left the small girl. "What is it?" he asked.

"You can't go after Euryale," she said, shaking her head. "She's suffered enough."

Zeus, much to Athena's surprise, he was sure, didn't argue. Instead, he quietly made his way around the room to place himself in front of the girl. "Do you suppose the gorgon destroyed the room as well?"

Athena laughed, choking on grief, and cleared her eyes. "Most assuredly. What would you do if you had to do what she did?"

Zeus nodded solemnly. He dropped a hand on Cassandra's petrified head, felt the unnatural smoothness to the stone, as well as every minuscule contour of the unmoving vipers atop her scalp. "Much worse," he admitted. "Much, much worse."

"Then leave her alone, please," Athena begged.

Zeus steeled himself. What had to be done was often at odds with what one wanted to be done. This was a fact any ruler would attest to. Still, he wasn't completely without heart. Perhaps there was another way, he thought.

"Apollo?" he asked, turning to the god. "Do you have any insights you'd like to share?"

"If you run Euryale down like a wild beast and force her submission, I think you'll forever damage your standings with a great many gods," he said. "Demeter and Persephone for certain. I loathe to speak for anyone else, and I probably shouldn't for them either out of courtesy, but the future seems clear regarding those two, and their pull with Hades is considerable."

"Is that all you see?"

Apollo shook his head and folded his arms over his chest. "Her oaths still need to be made, regardless of what she's suffered here," he said as if the reply poisoned his soul. "Of this, I'm certain."

Athena furrowed her brow. "You can't be serious."

"I stand by what I said before. Avoiding a tumultuous week or even year is not worth eons of misery," he said.

Zeus hardened both his face and his resolve. "Then we proceed as before. We find Euryale and have her swear herself to Olympus."

Apollo held up a finger. "If I may," he said. "Offering to put every resource we can spare at her command to help save her daughter may be the difference between a successful meeting and a disastrous one."

"She'll have it once she's made her oaths."

"No," Athena protested. "She'll have it before."

Zeus held his daughter's gaze for a few seconds before looking back to Cassandra. His thoughts were torn between knowing what a parent would do to protect a child and knowing what a ruler must do to protect his kingdom.

"I want her found and brought to me," he finally said. "And you have my word, I will be cordial and patient, provided she acts the same. But I will not risk my reign nor the safety of all who live here should the gorgon not cooperate fully. She has one chance. If you find her before I do, you'd do well to remind her of that."

Chapter Hera's Place: The Sequel

"I bet I can kill two before you kill one," Stheno said, shooting her sister a devilish grin as they looked upon the cyclopes who still stood guard outside Hera's estate.

Euryale ducked back around the corner, and though she still had every intention of cutting Zeus's legs out from under him, she couldn't help but remember how fond the cyclopes were of her. "We're not killing them," she said.

"Ah, right," Stheno said. "We probably need as much time as we can get searching the place. We'll kill them on the way out, let their blood flow from here to Zeus's temple."

"We're not killing them."

Stheno set her jaw and sharped one claw against another. "They're with him, Euryale."

"I know."

"Zeus," she went on. "The god who—"

"I know!" Euryale snapped, squaring off with and ready to tear into her sister. It wouldn't be the first time the two had come to blows, and in all likelihood, it wouldn't be the last, either.

Stheno glared, and for a brief moment, Euryale thought she might strike first. "I thought you wanted justice."

"I do, and I'll get it," Euryale growled. "But not them. They've done nothing."

"Yet."

"Don't even think about it," Euryale said, pointing a finger. "They were kind to me. Genuinely nice to me. I will not be a monster."

"Is that what you think I am, then? A monster wanting to shed all the blood I can?"

"No," Euryale said, though deep down, she felt partially otherwise.

"This is war, Euryale. This is self-preservation. This is striking them before they strike us."

"It will only make things worse."

"How?" Stheno argued. "We've set ourselves against Zeus already, have we not? I promise their loyalty to him far outweighs their fondness of you. If we're going to unseat their master and take the throne, they're going to have to be dealt with. We can either do it on our terms or theirs."

Euryale groaned, hating all the inevitable consequences that were barreling toward her. "Why can't you trust me on this?"

"Why can't you trust me?"

"Slaughtering everyone in a quest for power is not the way."

"It's justice," Stheno said, not batting an eye. "Justice that only comes from toppling Zeus, and that's not going to happen without having to deal with everything he can toss at us, faithful gods and servants included. The power is, admittedly, a nice spoil we'll collect once this ends."

"You don't know how loyal they are," she said. "They might side with us later, especially if they know some of the other Olympians are."

Stheno crossed her arms and huffed. "Fine," she said. "But they're going to come after you, after us, the moment Zeus tells them to. You know it, and I know it."

Euryale sighed heavily and nodded, conceding the point. That said, she still clung to the hope it might not come to that. "We can deal with them then if they do," she said. "There's something else, however, you haven't considered."

"What's that?"

"If we're taking the throne, it would be stupid for us to kill everyone," she said. "So, if for no other reason than selfish practicality, let's leave a few of the servants alive, yes?"

"You're capable of so much more than slinking through the shadows, afraid of a couple of giants."

"I know. That doesn't change me wanting to spare them."

Stheno lolled her head to the side with an exaggerated groan as her eyes rolled back. "This is so unfair," she said. "The Fates give you all this power, and you waste it. You know what I would've done by now?"

"I already know," Euryale replied.

Stheno shook her head and shooed a hand at her sister. "I can't think about this anymore," she said. "Let's get back to finding Achlys. And since you don't want to do the easy, fun, and sensible thing that lets us by the guards, how do you propose we get inside?"

"I haven't gotten that far," Euryale admitted. "But there has to be another way in. Let's see what we can find."

Stheno reluctantly followed, and the two skirted around the outer walls, using the orchard that grew nearby for concealment. Unfortunately, every portion of wall they saw stood smooth and tall, and worst of all, not a single foot remained unwatched.

They did spy a side entrance, but the door stood inside a recess that had its gate closed and was no doubt locked. And who knew what lay on the other side. Surely Zeus wasn't so sloppy as to leave such an obvious entrance open to any would-be burglar.

When they reached the very back of the estate, where the walls met a sheer cliff, Stheno stopped and grinned. "There we go," she said.

"There we go, what?" Euryale asked. She'd felt queasy the moment they drew within a few dozen yards of the edge, and she hadn't bothered to get near it.

"Come. Look," Stheno replied, pointing to something on the backside of the estate that Euryale couldn't see.

"Tell me."

"There's no point in telling you if you're going to have to come here anyway," Stheno said, laughing. "Now get over this acrophobia of yours and get over here—or we do it my way and go in through the front."

Euryale muttered some curses under her breath and slithered forward, keeping one hand pressed against the wall for extra comfort, which amounted to little, if anything at all. The closer she drew to the edge, the more wind whipped her face, and the dizzier she felt.

"Are you sure you're the one who flew a chimera into battle? Because it looks like you're about to have a heart attack," Stheno teased.

"This is a lot higher up than that," Euryale countered. She paused a few feet away to steady her nerves, and once she felt better in control, she eased up to her sister. "What am I looking at?"

"That," the red-snaked gorgon said, pointing upward.

Euryale had to lean over the edge to follow her sister's finger—an act that nearly cost her her balance and sanity—but it only took a split second to see what had grabbed Stheno's attention. While Hera's estate had indeed been built on a hill with one side overlooking a sheer drop, there was a set of tiny ledges that jutted out of the back wall of whatever building had been erected there. Near the top of that building sat a solitary window, open and inviting.

"Easy enough," Stheno said, pressing her body against the wall and sliding on to the nearest ledge. "If I can do it, so can you."

With her heart thundering in her chest, Euryale tried to move forward, but her body refused. All she could do was stand there, petrified, eyes vacantly staring out into the clouds beyond. She had no idea exactly how far the drop was, but since they were on Olympus, a shooting star would probably fall from lower heights.

"Don't make me open the front door for you," Stheno called back, now about halfway to the window.

"You wouldn't."

"Shall we see?"

"Fine…I'm coming," Euryale said. She breathed deep a few times and repeated those words again for her own sake. "I'm coming."

Euryale tore her eyes away from the drop and instead focused everything she had on the actual climb. As she eased around the wall's corner and onto the first ledge, she reminded herself that she had scaled much more demanding places before.

"I can do this," she whispered, pushing herself along with her serpentine tail. She reached out with her fingers, digging them into small holds, and used her lower half to press her up on to the next ledge. Her tail anchored where it could on the occasional rocky outcropping, and though those points were tenuous at best, they were still better than nothing.

"Almost there, Euryale," Stheno called back.

The gorgon paused and glanced up to see her sister, who was now inside, leaning back out the window with a bright smile on her face. "What's in there?"

"Storeroom." Stheno disappeared for a moment before returning. "Bed linens mainly."

"No rope?"

"I'm afraid not," she replied, holding her smile. "The Fates aren't going to grace you that much today."

Euryale nodded and went back to her climb. A few minutes and one terrifying slip later, the gorgon pushed herself up and through the window. She fell to the floor with a heavy sigh before rolling on her back with a burst of laughter. "The ground has never felt so good," she admitted.

"Can I ask you something?" Stheno said as she helped her sister up.

"Of course."

"How tall do you think the fires will be?" When Euryale cocked her head, Stheno expanded. "Of Olympus. When we burn it."

Euryale smiled. "I haven't the smallest of clues. Not big enough for you, I'm guessing."

"I hope they're so big, the light pierces Chaos," she said. "And as it burns, I want a host to sing for us."

"Sing for us?"

Stheno nodded. "To spread the news across all of creation that the Olympians have fallen."

Euryale's smile faded. While her anger burned as hot as ever against Zeus, some of the gods she still felt favorable toward. Persephone, for certain. Aphrodite, as odd as that still seemed. Even—

"Let's boil Athena," Stheno said, cutting into her thoughts.

"No."

Stheno cocked her head. "No?"

"No."

"She cursed the three of us," Stheno said, blinking twice and stepping back. "She killed our sister. Cursed me into oblivion."

"I know, but..." Euryale sighed as she clasped her hands in front of her face. "She's changing."

"So?"

"And she also gave you back to me," Euryale added. "And convinced Artemis to help us as well."

Stheno huffed, disgusted, and gestured at her body. "And that's supposed to make up for this? We did nothing wrong!"

"I know," Euryale said, hating how much this conversation tore her in two.

"Do you?" Stheno challenged. "Do you, really? Or are you starting to cower and make excuses for those who tormented us? Who destroyed our lives and raped our sister?"

"I'm not making excuses!" Euryale yelled. Her rebuke carried such power that it was the first time in her life she ever saw her sister shrink at something she'd said.

It surprised even her.

"You have every right to be upset," Euryale said after spending a moment to de-escalate herself. "I'd be lying if I said I hadn't wanted revenge on the goddess who heaped thousands upon thousands of years of torment and misery upon us. But I was shown mercy when I didn't deserve it. I have to do the same to others."

"Athena? Showed you mercy?" her sister scoffed. "Never on my life will I believe that."

"No. Not her. I meant Alex when I tried to kill Jessica," Euryale clarified. "And then Jessica did as well when she refused to kill me after I killed him, even though I'd broken her heart. And if mortals can do such things, how can I ever be their equal, let alone claim divinity, if I can't do the same?"

Stheno dropped her brow and sneered. "I can't believe I'm hearing this," she said, folding her arms over her chest. "Who's next? Are you going to forgive Zeus, too?"

"No," Euryale said, not hesitating in the least.

"You promise?"

"I will never, ever, forgive him."

"Good." The next few moments were spent in a tense silence, which Stheno broke first. "Since we've finished that, where do we go now?"

"Hera's library," Euryale replied. "That's the most natural place to start looking for where Achlys might be."

"I imagine. Where is it?"

Euryale laughed and shrugged. "No idea. I've never been here before."

Stheno shook her head and laughed, too. "This is a brilliant start to our conquests," she said. "I thought you at least had an idea where to go in all of this."

"I do," Euryale replied. "We're looking for the place with all the scrolls."

Stheno rolled her eyes, and the conversation ended there. Quietly, Euryale went up to the door at the other end of the storeroom and pressed her ear against it. When she couldn't hear anything, and her vipers only tasted the unique scent of cotton lingering in the air, she opened the door and slipped down the hall on the other side, Stheno following right behind.

The hall had a few rooms on each side, each one holding more stores that were of no interest to the gorgon. Every dozen yards or so, Euryale would pause, listen, and taste the air. It didn't take long for her to pick up on the cyclopes roaming the place, and given the uniqueness of each one she could sense, there had to be at least a half dozen.

She amended that to ten when they found the stairs and reached the bottom. Heavy footsteps drew their attention a moment later, and the two sisters quickly ducked into a side room that ended up being a private study. A lavish desk took up most of the space, and shelves filled with books and scrolls had been built against three of the four walls. The other wall, the one on the opposite side of the room, held a pair of arched windows, six feet tall, that looked out onto the inner courtyard, which for the moment was empty.

"Oh, what do we have here?" Stheno purred once the footsteps passed, and she noticed a gorgeous eight-foot dory on display in one of the corners. She hurried over to the spear, face awash in delight, and snatched it from its stand.

The gorgon ran her fingers along its flawless cornel shaft and shuddered. "You are much too fine a weapon to be trapped inside a stuffy place like this," she said. "Much, much too fine."

"Would you like me to get you two a room?" Euryale teased.

Stheno tilted her head. "A room? What for?"

"Nothing," Euryale said, stifling a laugh. "It's a modern expression for being overly lustful for someone, or in this case, something."

"Overly lustful? My dear, sweet sister. I could never be lustful enough when it comes to this," she replied. Stheno dropped the spear point low so she could inspect the head properly. She ran a finger lightly along the edge, drawing blood, much to her pleasure. "Adamantine head sharpened to perfection," she said with a blissful sigh. "You and I are going to have a wonderful life together."

Euryale cleared her throat. "If you're done admiring your new toy, we still have a map to find."

Stheno whipped the dory through the air, made a few quick thrusts at imaginary targets to her front and on her sides, and spun it over her head a few times in a blur of motion. "Now I'm done," she said, driving its sauroter into the ground. "For now."

"Good, then you can help me search this place," Euryale said as she began rifling through the shelves at her side. "It shouldn't be too hard, I don't think. Jessica said Hera was meticulously organized. All that we need to do is find wherever—"

Euryale cut herself off as a new scent drifted into the room. Strong. Feral. Close. When the light clacking of hoof on stone hit their ears, they both flattened themselves the wall, each flanking the door on opposite sides.

There they waited, Euryale holding her breath and hoping whoever it was would pass by like the others, while Stheno crouched, her spear ready and her body swaying like a cobra ready to strike.

The door opened lazily, and in stepped a satyr, carrying a duster in his hands and fatigue on his shoulders. Before the poor creature had a chance to even blink, Stheno drove forward, using the shaft of her spear to pin him against the wall by the throat.

"Don't kill him!" Euryale hissed.

"That all depends on how willing he is to help us," Stheno replied, bringing her smiling face an inch away from her prey's.

"I would if I could," the satyr squeaked. "But I can't! Oh, gods, believe me, I honestly can't!"

"Oh, I think you can," Stheno said, patting the top of his head. "All we need to do is find the right motivation for you. Have you ever eaten hot coals?"

"You don't understand. Zeus is going to know you've been here if he doesn't already," he whimpered. "Anything you do to me, he'll make a hundred times worse if he even thinks for one second I've helped you."

"He's useless," Stheno grunted, throwing a glance over her shoulder at Euryale. "Let's eat him. Or better yet, let's test my new spear on him."

Euryale held up her hand, bidding her sister to wait. Though she stayed what would've undoubtedly been a painful execution, Euryale wasn't sure how long it would last. "Satyr," she said, drawing close. "Do you know who I am?"

"Of course. Euryale, Goddess of Stone. Everyone knows you. I helped your friend, Jessica, when Zeus needed waking, for what that's worth." When both gorgons narrowed their eyes, and Euryale rattled her tail at the god's name, the satyr's eyes bulged. "I didn't mean anything by that!"

Euryale raised a claw and pressed it against the satyr's lips. "Shhh," she said. "Do you know who my children are?"

The satyr nodded as sweat dripped from his forehead. "I do."

"Do you know what I'd do to protect them?"

"I can only imagine."

Euryale slipped her claw underneath his chin and pierced his skin. "You have no idea," she said. "Now then, I'm going to ask something one time and one time only, and if you don't answer, I'm going to let my sister have her way with you."

What little color remained in the satyr's face drained completely. "You don't understand. Zeus! He's worse than Hera!"

Euryale flicked her claw, slicing his chin open. "Yes or no only from here on out," she said. "My child's life is at stake, do you understand?"

The satyr nodded.

"If you aren't helping me, you're killing my one and only daughter. Do you understand?"

The satyr hesitated but managed to nod again before the gorgon's patience ran out.

"Good," Euryale said. "I need a map to Achlys. A map Hera has somewhere. Do you know where it is?"

Unlike the previous times, this time the terrified servant froze. The muscles in Stheno's arm tensed as her spear pushed heavily against his airway. She was probably only a hair away from crushing his windpipe, dying for permission to finish him off.

"Take me to this map, and I promise I'll let you go," Euryale said. "You can run off to Zeus and tell him you found us wherever it is. That way, you can play the good, obedient servant, and I get what I need to save my sweet Cassandra."

The satyr didn't waste a single moment taking her up on the offer. He pointed a shaky finger toward the western side of Hera's estate. "She keeps her maps in a depository above her bedroom. If she has a map to Achlys, that's where it'll be."

Stheno cocked her head. "If?"

"I don't know if she has one. By the Fates, I swear I'm not lying!"

Euryale leaned in even closer than she was already. Her eyes turned black, and the tone in her voice darkened even more so. "For your sake, I hope you're telling the truth."

"I am! I am!"

"Good. Now take us there, and let's avoid meeting anyone along the way."

Chapter Maps

"You should let me take Aison."

Alex, standing on a plateau, turned his attention from the mountain that loomed above to face the goddess. "Say again?"

"Your son," Artemis said. "I fear he won't be safe in Olympus for much longer. I can hide him in the wilds where no one will find him."

"No one? Not even me?"

"Yes, even you. Because if you can find him, so can Zeus, and I promise, his restraint will not last forever," she explained.

Alex made a face, one that wallowed in unease. "I don't know. I feel like Euryale should know about this."

"She will, when we can see her again," Artemis said. "But we tempt disaster the longer we wait to protect your son."

Alex spent several moments deep in thought, turning her suggestion over from every angle he could think of. In the end, he came down to the simple notion of better safe than sorry. "Okay," he said. "Take him. But grab Tickles, too, if you can. Aison will want him around, and it'll make him feel better about it all. Oh, and maybe not tell the little guy it's because Zeus wants to kill us all? That's probably not something a kid needs to deal with."

Artemis smiled and gave a reassuring nod. "He'll think it's nothing more than a game, I promise."

"Perfect."

The goddess directed Alex's attention to the peak of the mountain. "Up there is where you'll find Hera."

Alex squinted. "Are you sure? Looks pretty desolate."

"I'm sure," the goddess nodded and pointed to a couple of places on a rocky wall nearby. "You can see where Dad's sandals left scuff marks recently there and there. The other day, he also came back with a bit of Hera's hair on his shoulder—hair that had been recently thawed. And of course, the wildlife below has thinned, no doubt thanks to the eagles' bellies needing to be filled."

"Eagles? What eagles?"

"Polyxeinus and Tecton. Two of his favorite birds he's placed as sentries near the top."

"I get the feeling they don't eat carrots," Alex said.

"Cattle is more to their liking," she said. "By the dozen, in fact."

Alex grimaced, suddenly having flashbacks to Mister Lion eating him over and over and over again. "Don't suppose you have any suggestions on how to get by those two?"

"I do, in fact," Artemis said, unfastening her cloak and handing it to him. "Wear this. It should keep you hidden from their eyes."

"Should?"

"I haven't tested it when it comes to those two," she admitted. "And though Dad thinks their eyesight is infallible, he's wrong. For a long time, I've had the feeling I might one day need to slip by his watchful eyes, as well as his eagles'. This cloak was fashioned to do precisely that."

"What about when I talk to Hera?" he asked. "Won't they know I'm there then?"

The goddess shook her head as she handed him a small leather pouch. "You'll find sleeping dust inside," she explained. "Blow a pinch on each, and they'll nod off for a short while."

"How long is a while?"

"Long enough that you ought to be able to get the answers you seek," she replied. "But I wouldn't tarry while there. I may have command of the wilds and all its creatures, but Zeus's birds are notoriously resilient."

Alex glanced in the bag after he took it and noted there was about a tablespoon's worth of glittering gold powder inside. He quickly closed it up and stuffed it in the pocket of his pants, and as he did, an unsettling feeling churned in his gut.

"Is something the matter?" she asked.

"No, well, yeah, well. Maybe. It just feels like there's a lot that's been going on behind the scenes lately. You know, trouble in paradise and all."

"You wouldn't be wrong in those feelings," she said with a nod. "Be careful who you share those with and any favors you chase. With Zeus's rule challenged, every last Olympian will vie for the throne at some point or another."

"Including you."

"I would take it if I had a shot that was clear and true," Artemis said. "But I am no queen. I'd rather explore the wilds and hunt through all the night, neither of which one can do well while sitting on a throne."

"I see," Alex replied as he threw the cloak over his shoulders and clasped the bronze pin to fasten it together. "You have my undying thanks, regardless, for your aid, and despite your warnings, I feel indebted to you."

The glint of a hunter's moon shined in her eyes, and the corners of her thin lips drew back. "My sweet Alex," she said. "You are most certainly indebted to me. You and your wife."

Alex chuckled nervously. "I thought you pledged yourself to her side? To seek justice and what not?"

"I did, but I never stipulated that aid would come free," she replied. When Alex shifted on his feet a few times, she put a hand on his shoulder and squeezed. "Easy, Alex. I have nothing sinister in mind." She paused to laugh brightly, throwing back her head and letting her hair toss in the icy wind. "In fact, I've got nothing in mind. Only that one day, Alex, one day I will call on the both of you, and I expect my generosity here not to be forgotten."

Stheno kept a tight grip on the back of the satyr's neck as he pushed a nondescript stone on a wall, two rooms over from where they'd run into him. While there was no need to literally keep him at arm's reach due to both his utter fear and Stheno's unmatched speed should he run, the gorgon simply loved toying with prey. Euryale would've wished differently, but some things, she knew, never changed.

"There'd best not be a cyclops on the other side of this," Stheno said. "It'll be the last thing you ever see."

"They're all patrolling the grounds and the gates."

"Are you certain?"

"Very," he replied. "The cyclopes aren't interested in snooping around, anyway. Hera might be gone, but there are still plenty of traps she's left behind—traps even Zeus is wary of."

With a light scraping sound, a portion of the wall sank back a couple of feet before sliding to the side, revealing a hidden passage lit by oil lamps. They followed the passage for a few dozen yards before running down a flight of stairs, which led to an underground network of tunnels. This network didn't seem as complex as the maze Euryale had chased Alex and Jessica through the prior year, but not by much. As they pressed on with the satyr as a guide, Euryale guessed half of Olympus could fit down there.

"Why such an elaborate system?" she finally asked.

"Lets her keep an eye on her guests unseen and without having to resort to spells and scrying," he explained. "I've heard she also keeps those who displease her the most down here as well, but that's only a rumor."

"You've never looked around?"

The satyr laughed nervously. "Fates, no. I stick to the tunnels I'm allowed, and that's it. I'm no fool."

Euryale conceded the point without further comment. After pressing on through the tunnels for several more minutes, they reached a narrow spiral staircase which they took. At the top, the satyr pulled on a bronze lever, which opened up the wall and allowed them access to the depository.

The room itself was circular with a high domed ceiling and shelves crammed together. On those shelves, tightly packed, sat scrolls, trinkets, fine jewelry, weapons, artifacts, and elaborate mechanical contraptions, the likes of which Euryale had never seen. Incense burned from small iron pots which hung from columns, filling the air with aromas of frankincense, myrrh, and one other burning resin she couldn't quite place. That third incense, whatever it was, drove her vipers into a tasting frenzy that quickly irritated the gorgon.

Light for the room was provided by twelve windows—large but barred—which had been placed at regular intervals around the entire room. The view from each one provided a fantastic way to keep an eye on what was happening on the estate grounds, and Euryale wondered if the thin film she noticed that covered the glass meant those on the outside couldn't see in.

Probably, if not definitely.

"I wonder how often she'd stand here and watch over everyone," Stheno said, leaning against one of the windows and cupping her hands over her eyes so she could look out.

"Enough to drive her mad," Euryale said as she slowly made her way through the shelves, looking at the contents of each one. After passing a few and not seeing what she needed, she turned to the satyr. "Where are the maps?"

The satyr froze, and his eyes bulged. For a few seconds, it looked like he had forgotten how to breathe. Euryale was about to say something when he broke into a full run and raced to the window a couple of yards away from her.

"Oh, no...Oh no, oh no, oh no," he said over and over.

"What?"

"Memneus is here," he said, pointing a shaky finger out at the sky.

Euryale's brow furrowed, and Stheno could only offer a shrug when she looked to her for clarification. "Who?" Euryale asked.

"Memneus!" the satyr repeated, voice cracking. "Zeus's favorite eagle!" He then dropped his gaze, rocked on his hooves, and began clapping his hands together. "Okay, okay. Okay," he said. "He knows you're here, but we can still make this work." The satyr's eyes snapped up and found Euryale's. "You've got to let me go."

"We need that map," she countered.

"I told you where it is!" he shouted back. "You promised! You promised you'd let me go!"

"Quiet!" Stheno hissed.

The satyr did, but only for a moment. He retreated, rubbing his temples a few times before muttering to himself. Then his back found one of the shelves, and he jumped like a bull getting hit with a branding iron. He yelped and bolted forward, smashing into more shelves and driving himself into a further state of panic as he drove for the exit with reckless abandon.

Stheno growled and ran after him, hunched like a tigress about to make a kill. Euryale sprang into action as well, racing through the depository on her elongated tail. Right before she got to the satyr, Stheno pounced. The gorgon struck the satyr across the side of the chest, her claws sinking into his shoulder and face. A moment later, Euryale tackled her sister and coiled around her legs and waist. Stheno roared and lashed out, striking Euryale in the cheek and spraying her blood across a shelf full of trinkets.

"Run!" Euryale barked as she fought to hold her sister back. "Now!"

The satyr snapped out of his momentary daze before fleeing through a large oak door.

"Why did you let him go?" Stheno groaned, throwing her hands up in frustration.

"Because I said I would," she replied, uncoiling.

A scowl formed on her sister's face, one that seemed genuinely spiteful. "I'm getting a little sick of you trying to play nice," she spat. "He was only a satyr."

"One that was helping us," Euryale pointed.

"One who's about to bring Zeus's wrath upon us!" Stheno shot back. "You can't make nice with everyone, Euryale. Even Medusa understood that." Stheno paused, took a deep breath, and held up a finger. "I shouldn't have said that," she said. "But Euryale, you've got to realize, these gods don't care about us at all, and every chance you take with them or their servants is a chance we fall back into ruin. I don't want that for me, you, or your children."

"I know," Euryale replied. "But I refuse to be like them, thinking anyone beneath me is something to be used and discarded on a whim."

A heavy sigh was the prelude to Stheno shaking her head. "Let's find that map and get out of here."

Euryale nodded and raced to the section of the depository the satyr had pointed out before. There she found hundreds of tightly bound scrolls stacked upon each other and quickly began sifting through them all and reading the hand-scrawled notes that labeled each one. Many were of places she knew, even more were of places she'd never heard of. Not a one, however, pointed out where Achlys lived, or even mentioned the goddess or her realm of death and decay.

"Any luck?" she asked Stheno, tossing yet another scroll.

"No," she replied with a grunt. "It doesn't help that there's no rhyme or reason to how she has these arranged, either. She's got plans of her skyscraper mixed with maps of China and water parks in Inland."

"I think that's England," Euryale replied.

"And then I found one about her wedding temple tucked in a pile of zoos," Stheno went on, rolling her eyes. "What sense does that make?"

Euryale chuckled. "What sense does it make to keep that one in the first place? Of all the spots in the world, you'd think she'd want to forget that one the most."

"Her *and* Zeus."

The two gorgons froze.

"Achlys was the one who fashioned the poison she used on Zeus way back when, yes?" Stheno asked.

Euryale nodded. "He'd be the last one she'd want to know her whereabouts."

Stheno laughed and spun in place, flinging through the scrolls she'd tossed. Euryale was at her side a split second later, helping her dig. "What did it look like?" she asked in a panic.

"I don't know! A scroll!"

"They're all scrolls!"

Stheno didn't reply but instead raised herself up over the pile and circled it like a hawk eyeing a fully stocked pond. A moment later, she leaped across the entire thing. "Ha!" she yelled, snatching up a scroll. "Got you!"

"Hurry!" Euryale said, flying to her sister's side. "Unroll it."

A flick of Stheno's claws was all it took to cut through the leather strap that bound the scroll, and she had it fully unrolled before the tie hit the floor. The map itself wasn't much, a sketch of a bog, somewhere in eastern Europe. Near the top was a tiny figure of a hut, and off to the side were the most peculiar of instructions.

"Never say no," Euryale said, reading the list from top to bottom. "Mind your manners. Don't fall asleep." The gorgon looked up to find Stheno equally as puzzled. "What do you make of that?"

Before Stheno could answer, Zeus's thunderous voice filled the air. "Euryale," he boomed. "Where are you?"

Euryale narrowed her eyes and rattled her tail as she went to the window. In the center of the courtyard, she saw Zeus. With one hand, he firmly held on to the labrys Hephaestus had forged out of all the melted artifacts, and with the other, he was ordering a dozen cyclopes to search the grounds as the satyr stood next to him, pointing a finger in their direction.

"They're coming," Euryale growled. "And he brought that stupid ax."

Chapter Eagles

Alex slipped.

His hands clawed at the unyielding rock face, and his feet found no purchase. He dropped at least twenty feet before he slowed his fall, and not without losing a few layers of skin in the process. His fingertips managed to dig into an inch-wide ledge right after, and Alex collapsed against the face of the cliff, exhaling sharply.

His frosty breath hung in the air, and he watched it drift for a few seconds while he steadied himself. This wasn't the first time he'd fallen on his way up, and thankfully, it hadn't become his end, either. And as terrifying as the last few seconds had been, and as dire as the circumstances were surrounding his family and the reason for his ascent, a part of Alex found himself enjoying it all. Or at least, enjoying the purpose it gave him.

He was a hero, after all, and as Odysseus and Heracles had once put it to him, could a potter be truly called a potter without clay to work? Or a king be a called a king without land to rule? Or in Alex's case, a hero be called a hero without adversity?

Apparently not, for Alex couldn't deny that having this quest, for lack of a better word, was filling a need in his soul like no other. He only wished that the stakes didn't involve his kids.

Alex expanded his chest and focused on how the chilled air felt as it entered his body. Invigorated by it, he began his climb once more. He chose a new route this time, a much wider one that ascended not nearly as fast, but it was one that he could make with relative ease. He really should've brought an ice ax and spiked boots. Why he didn't think of that before he started eluded him. A combination of being short on time and hubris, most likely.

Within five minutes, he'd made up the ground he'd lost, and five more after that, he found a narrow crag on the mountain that offered plenty of handholds. Spirits bolstered, Alex redoubled his efforts, not stopping once until he reached the top, except to admire the view of the world when he needed to plot a tricky jump.

When he'd pulled himself up and over the last edge, he found himself staring at a pair of monstrous birds who sat perched on a couple of tall boulders only a dozen feet away. They ruffled their feathers the moment he came into view, and their vibrant eyes seemed to take in everything around them—everything, that is, except for Alex himself.

Alex held his breath. Though it seemed that thus far Artemis's cloak shielded him from their sight as she'd promised, he wasn't about to test the theory that they couldn't locate him on sound, especially with the enormous beaks and talons they sported. Cripes, he thought, it was no wonder these two were on guard. They looked vicious enough to send even Ares running.

After a few seconds spent in total stillness, Alex eased forward, carefully transferring his weight from one foot to the other. The ground there, thankfully, was bare rock, and he didn't have to worry about the crunch of snow underfoot. When the eagles failed to react to his measured advance, he took another step, and then another and another.

His lungs started to burn when he was within a couple of paces, but he didn't dare exhale. Instead, he kept up his cautious pace until he was right between them, at which point he stopped and readied the pouch Artemis had given him.

Quieter than a shadow, he reached in and took a pinch of dust. He tried to let loose a tiny puff of air from his mouth to blow it on the first bird's head, but instead, with his lungs screaming for air, what came out was an explosive exhale. The powder flew from his fingers, covering the eagle's head and promptly knocking him out, but the entire ordeal was more than enough to send the other into a frenzy.

"Shit!" Alex yelled, losing his bearing and scrambling sideways. Talons grazed his head as the enormous raptor launched itself at him.

The bird cried out as it spun around and searched for Alex. A moment later, it spread its wings and tried to shoot into the sky. It would've easily done so if Alex hadn't honed his giant-creature fighting skills to near perfection while on Elysium, and thus, his reflexes were second to none.

"Oh no, you don't," Alex said, leaping into the air. With one hand, he grabbed the eagle's head by the beak and twisted it sideways, and with the other, he clamped down on a wing, causing them both to drop like a rock. Feathers and blood flew as the two crashed to the ground and fought.

The eagle sank its talons into Alex's chest, tearing deep into muscle and bone. Had Alex not been a veteran lion wrestler as well, he'd likely have succumbed to those wounds in an instant. Instead, he gritted his teeth and accepted the strike long enough to pull out a little more powder and throw it into the bird's face.

The eagle screeched again, shook its head, and went limp. Alex waited a few seconds before releasing his hold and taking to his feet. He brushed himself off, which did little other than smear more of his blood everywhere, some of it onto Artemis's cloak. He grimaced when he noticed how much of his own gore clung to it and hoped it didn't stain. He had no idea how pristine she expected it to be when he returned it, but he definitely felt a trip to whatever dry cleaners Olympus had before he saw her again would be a good thing.

At that point, Alex continued, leaving the sleeping guards where they were and ducking into the tunnel. Along the way, he drew the hood back over his head, thinking it wise in case there were more guards ahead. Said tunnel ended up being longer than he'd anticipated, but he found the cave with Hera soon enough. That also meant, however, that he found the bull, Crios, sleeping nearby. The giant animal snorted and flicked his tail when Alex entered, a reaction that stopped his heart and rooted him in his tracks.

He did have the presence of mind to quickly dump the rest of the powder he had on its head. The amount he had left wasn't even half of what he'd put on the birds, but it seemed to be enough—for now. The beast settled down with a huff.

Hera, who remained chained, wrapped, and stuck in a cage, did not. The goddess rose as much as her restraints would allow, and Alex watched her study the entrance for a few seconds before she grinned.

"I know you're there, Artemis," she said. "I know your dust's smell like I know my own perfume."

Alex thought about remaining quiet but decided against it. He needed to talk to her no matter who she thought had come, and no matter how big the bull was who shared the cave with her. He could only hope the animal would stay asleep throughout the whole ordeal.

"It's not Artemis. It's me," Alex said, lowering his hood.

"Alex," Hera said with a sickeningly sweet tone. "To what do I owe the honor of such a risky visit?"

"I need your help," he said, glancing at the bull and taking a few quick steps away from it.

Hera cackled. "What makes you think I'd ever give it to you?"

Alex had expected such a reply, and part of him even expected worse. That said, he wasn't about to let it get to him. "It would seem to me, Queen Hera," he said, gesturing at her prison, "that you need all the friends you can get, despite the power you have."

"Alex, playing to my vanity will get you nowhere," she said. "In fact, I'm insulted you even think you can hide a single thing from me."

"I don't know what you mean."

"Of course, you do," she said. "My intuition proved true yet again. Cronus has demanded something of your wife, something Zeus isn't happy with, and now you need me to make things right."

Alex's brow shot upward, though he desperately wished otherwise a moment later. Even in his relatively short time spent with the Olympians, he knew Hera was without equal when it came to exploiting weakness. Perhaps if he could still remain strong, or at least, not desperate, he could salvage the conversation. "Cassandra's been poisoned," he said. "Apollo needs help in saving her."

"A pity."

"That's my daughter," Alex said, marching up to her as his temperature rose, and his hands trembled.

"Is that supposed to make me care more or less?" Hera asked, her tone even colder than her last reply.

Alex shot a hand through the cage, grabbed her by the hair, and pulled. "The last enemy I had in chains, I almost tossed into River Acheron," he said, low and even. "I'll have no qualms about doing that with you."

Despite having her head slammed against the bars, Hera glared. "Threaten me again, and I'll have more coals heaped upon your head, and your children's children's children's heads than there are stars in the sky."

"Bold words for someone imprisoned."

"I won't be forever," she said. "And if you think Typhon or Arachne can forever hold a grudge, you're going to quickly learn why everyone—and I mean everyone—fears my wrath."

Alex let the goddess go, shoving her head forward in the process. He paced for a few moments, rage building, trying to come up with some tact that would work. But what? She was immune to physical threats and blackmail, and he certainly had nothing she wanted, but she was the only one with everything he needed.

Alex straightened, and despite his best efforts to carry a flat affect, a smile spread across his face. "Do you know why I came to you?"

"Your first mistake is to think I'd even care."

"It's not because I'm looking for a cure," Alex said, ignoring the jab. He paused a moment, waiting for Hera's reaction. She inclined her head slightly, which was enough of a signal that he had her attention. "We have that part handled. The reason I came here was I'm looking for a way to turn stone back to flesh. I understand that you're the only one who can do such a thing."

Hera studied him for a couple of minutes, minutes Alex felt he didn't have. He wasn't sure which of the sleeping animals would wake first, but he knew the last thing he wanted to be was around when that happened.

"Your wife petrified your daughter, didn't she?"

Alex nodded.

"Then I'll gladly stay in this cage ten thousand years so she's reminded every day of the horror she inflicted on her own child," Hera sneered. "I will never help that vile monster."

"I'll admit, I came to you first because you were the closest and obviously knew what you were doing," he said. "But if you won't help, then you can rot in here alone, and I'll find someone else."

"There is no one else."

Alex shook his head. "You're bluffing."

Hera smirked. "Am I?"

She wasn't, and that was precisely the reaction he was going for. "Then I suppose when Euryale returns, I'll tell her that first. And once that's done, I'll tell her where you are, because there's no force in all of creation that'll keep her from coming up here and turning you to stone."

A vein on the side of her head popped to the surface of her skin as her face hardened and her mouth twisted into a snarl.

"And since you're the only one who could ever reverse it, I suppose that will make you a permanent statue for the rest of time," Alex added. Though it was clear he didn't need to paint her the complete picture, rubbing the obvious in her face felt damn good.

If looks could kill, the Queen of Olympus would've slain Alex ten times over by then. "Okay, Alex," she hissed, "I'll help, but not before you run an errand for me."

Alex held up a finger. "Ah, ah, ah. Statue."

"Errand first," she said. "Or I tell Zeus you were here and are in league with Cronus. I promise I'll see him again long before your wife can get to me."

Alex folded his arms over his chest, weighing her counteroffer. He knew deep down that he'd hate whatever it was, and that it would likely cause untold troubles for him and his wife later on. But with Hera being his daughter's only realistic hope at this point for ever getting her life back, Alex knew his decision was an automatic one.

"Fine," he said. "What did you have in mind?"

CHAPTER INTO THE BOG

After taking the map, the two gorgons hurried out of the depository room the way they'd come, but not before Stheno made sure to fling the main door wide open.

Within moments, they raced through the underground tunnels, intent on finding an exit that was as far from Zeus and his cyclopes as possible. To their dismay, however, progress felt slow, if not non-existent. Without their satyr guide, they were unsure which way to go as each hall looked the same: narrow and featureless.

"How can this place go on forever with no rooms and no way out?" Stheno said with an exasperating groan once they reached yet another intersection—another intersection that gave a severe case of déjà vu at that.

"I don't know," Euryale admitted. "We must be missing something. I swear we've been here before."

"If we are, we'd best gather our wits, because I'd wager Zeus will be searching these tunnels soon enough. I doubt they'll remain hidden for long."

Stheno tapped her claws on the stone wall for a few moments before her face suddenly brightened. "Wrong turns at whatever branch must send you back to the middle," she said. "Father used to tell of such mazes designed to drive people mad. We simply need to keep track of which turns lead us here and which do not."

"I'm not sure if we have that sort of time," Euryale admitted. "The satyr led us through a hefty walk."

"I know, but there's something else we can rely on," Stheno said, not losing any of her enthusiasm.

"What's that?"

"Satyr blood."

"Satyr blood?"

Stheno nodded. "You sliced his chin when we first took him captive, remember?"

Hope flowed through Euryale, and her sister's infectious smile found its way to her as well. "I do," Euryale replied. "And it's been plenty long enough for that scent to filter through the air."

"Exactly."

Euryale tilted her head up and sampled the air with all of her vipers. She found the trail in under two seconds. "This way, I think?"

Stheno did the same, her snakes extending their tongues to the fullest in a slow, deliberate manner. "Agreed. Faint, but definitely coming from the left."

Off the two went, hurrying down the hall until they reached a branch in the shape of a Y. There, the two picked up on the scent once more, this time coming from the right, and off they went again. The process repeated a dozen more times, each one at a new intersection with the scent growing stronger and stronger. Ten minutes later, they found their way back to where they'd originally pounced on the satyr.

"And here you thought spilling blood wouldn't be helpful," Stheno teased as they entered the study.

"As if you needed it to be helpful," Euryale teased back.

"Never said I did."

Euryale rolled her eyes before she quietly hurried over to the door leading out to the hall. Once there, she pressed her ear against it, listening for guards.

"I think it's clear," she whispered. "I bet we can climb out the back, slip through the orchard, and be long gone before they realize we're not here anymore."

"Assuming Zeus's eagle doesn't spot us," Stheno countered.

Euryale frowned. Her sister was right. If he was circling the grounds, there's no way they wouldn't be spotted the very second they started down the wall. But that assumed, of course, the bird was still there.

Euryale snaked her way over to one of the windows on the far wall. She kept to the side to shield herself as much as possible from those who might still be in the courtyard and dared a peek. Zeus was gone, as were most of the cyclopes. Apollo, however, now stood in the center, several yards away from his chariot while talking to a cyclops.

"Great," Euryale said, flopping against the wall with a heavy sigh. "Apollo's here, too."

"Zeus must be calling everyone to come join the hunt."

"All the more reason we need to get out of here right this second," Euryale said. She dared another glance, hoping that maybe he'd suddenly up and leave. To her horror, the moment she looked out the window, Apollo made a lazy turn where he stood and looked right at her.

"Damn it," Euryale said, flattening herself against the wall once more. "He saw me."

Stheno crouched, spear ready, looking like she was torn between running and fighting. "Are you sure?"

"He looked right at me."

"But are you sure he saw you?"

Euryale tensed, shut her eyes momentarily, and made one last glance. To her utter shock, Apollo had turned back around and was still talking with the one-eyed giant. "No, thank the Fates, he's—"

Euryale stopped midsentence. Apollo stretched and scratched the back of his head, only—

"What?" Stheno asked.

"He's scratching his head, but not."

"What do you mean 'but not'?"

"I mean, he's scratching the air behind his head," she said, watching, perplexed. "It's like he's…" Euryale tilted her head for a half second before jerking back. "He's calling us down."

"Why?"

"Like I have any idea," Euryale said, shaking her head. "But that's what he's doing, and he doesn't want the cyclops to see."

"Could be a trap."

"It's not."

"How do you know?"

"I know," Euryale said, heading for the door and bidding her sister to follow with a wave of her hand. "Come on."

Stheno started for the exit, but her steps were cautious. "How do you know?"

"He's always helped us," Euryale replied. "Besides, why make an elaborate trap when he could sound the alarm instead?"

Her sister exhaled sharply and rubbed her hands together. "Gods, I hope you're right."

With that, the two left the room, and with all the haste they could muster without sounding like a stampede of rabid bulls, they raced through the halls, down a flight of stairs, and reached the door leading to the inner courtyard in less than a half minute.

Euryale cracked the door open, but when she saw nothing, her brow dropped. "He's gone?"

"Gone? Let me see."

Euryale moved so her sister could take a look. Once she did, Stheno huffed and opened the door further. A split second later, she grabbed Euryale by the wrist and yanked her through. "Fates love us," she said, laughing. "We're free. Look!"

The gorgon directed her eyes at where Stheno had her finger pointed. A dozen yards away, a little to the side, stood Apollo's chariot. With speed to rival Hermes, the sisters leaped on the carriage with Euryale taking the reins.

A single snap of leather sent them rocketing into the sky and headed for Achlys's domain.

Apollo's chariot turned out to be much, much faster than the one Euryale and Alex had. Maybe it had something to do with the fact that his was pulled by four equines with enough combined muscle to make Ares jealous, whereas theirs only had a couple of adorable ponies. Or maybe it was the fact that the carriage itself exuded power unlike any Euryale had ever felt before. Simply touching its rails sent a warm, vibrating sensation up her arm that was equal parts ecstasy and terror, and it made the gorgon wonder what Apollo was capable of. Perhaps there was much, much more to the God of the Sun and Giver of Prophecy than he was letting on—that anyone, the other Olympians included, even knew.

As they neared their destination, a bog near the eastern border of the Czech Republic, Euryale felt the need to gloat. "I told you they weren't all bad."

Stheno, who'd been lost in thought for the past half hour, dropped her brow. "Who?"

"The Olympians," she answered.

"Says you."

"Says we have a chariot."

Stheno went to object, but whatever words she had in mind never popped out of her open mouth. Instead, the gorgon huffed at it all. "Fine," she said. "We'll keep him as a pet."

"A pet?"

"Mm-hm. He's cute enough to be one, too. And it might come in handy to have a dog who can see the future."

With a terrible cry, the horses pulling the chariot banked sharply and reared, nearly toppling the carriage and throwing the two out. Euryale struggled with the reigns to keep the animals from tearing off to Fates knew where, but even with putting every ounce of strength she had into it, the best she could do was keep them moving in a tight circle.

"You were saying about a chariot?" Stheno asked once things returned to a more normal state.

Euryale tugged on the leather one last time, finally managing to put a halt to their travel. Though they were now stopped, Euryale didn't answer. Instead, she scoured everything around them. To their backs, Lysá hora reached into the sky, its powdered slopes providing plenty of fun and adventure to hikers and skiers alike. Ahead of them, however, nestled in the valley of the mountainous terrain, was a small bog, shrouded in fog and shadow. Though the gorgon could see nothing, it only took a moment to realize what had spooked the horses. The sickly sweet scent of decay was so strong, she nearly retched.

"I think we're walking," Euryale said with reluctance.

"One of us is, at least," Stheno replied as she hopped off the chariot.

No further comments were made, and the gorgons entered the bog, side by side. With every step made, every yard slithered, the muck grew worse, and the air continually thickened. They'd traveled not even a quarter mile before the fog cut visibility in half, and it wasn't much farther when they couldn't even see beyond a dozen feet.

Miles came and went, and the two had nothing to show for it other than aching muscles and grime-covered skin and scale. Stheno's steps looked heavy and awkward in the muck as if she wore shoes made of lead. Though Euryale fared a little better thanks to her giant tail, she, too, felt her body's strength being taxed to its limits as the bog seemed to be trying to do everything it could to stop them.

"It feels like a hydra is sitting on my chest," Stheno wheezed, stopping a moment to find her breath.

"Or two," Euryale replied. "I wish I knew how much farther we had to go."

"As do I. What's the map say?"

Euryale sighed, letting her frustration loose in the process. "Nothing of use."

"Then what? We wander around here blind, hoping to stumble on a goddess who doesn't want to be found?"

"I'm up for suggestions," she replied.

"What we need is—*that*," Stheno said, pointed off to the side.

Euryale twisted and saw almost completely shrouded in gloom a gnarled tree with bare limbs and bark like soot. The two struggled to reach it; once there, the gorgon hoped this might mark a turn in their fortunes.

"I can't see the top," she said, craning her head. "Can you?"

Stheno shook her head. "Not at all. With luck, it'll reach above this fog, and we can see where we're going."

"You want to climb it, or should I?"

"I'll go," her sister replied as she drove her spear into the muck and hoisted herself up the first limb. "I'm lighter than you."

"Let me know when you find something."

Euryale watched her sister climb. She did so with speed and grace, not faltering in the slightest, even when she had to jump from one branch to catch another. It didn't take long for her to disappear above, swallowed by the thick fog that continued to choke the air from her lungs.

A massive yawn escaped the gorgon at that thought. She stretched and yawned again, not realizing how tired she'd become until that very moment when she had nothing to do but stand and wait.

Euryale lightly slapped her cheeks a few times to try and perk up, but it didn't help much, if at all. Her eyelids drooped over and over as she fought to keep them up. Her head nodded in the process, and all she wanted to do was catch a nap for a quarter century or two.

"Can you see the top yet?" she called out.

The reply felt as if it took eons to come, and when it did, it sounded distant and weak. "No. Not yet."

Euryale groaned and tried moving around to keep herself awake. Mentally, it helped, but her body protested every movement with achy pains. A few minutes later, the gorgon propped herself against the tree for a touch of respite.

The bark, hard and rough, crunched under her weight and felt surprisingly good. Euryale shifted back and forth, letting the tree scratch her back directly between her shoulder blades.

"Oh, I need you at home," Euryale said, sinking into a state of relaxation.

She wiggled a little more, her mind relishing the bit of self-pampering, and she closed her eyes. Consciousness slipped away in seconds.

CHAPTER ATHENA AND ARTEMIS

Aison lagged.

The little gorgon's mood had been subdued at best since Artemis had taken him into her care. Though she'd only been around the child for scant bits at a time prior to that, every memory she had of him was one filled with bright smiles and plenty of laughter—a dash or two of frustrated parent, too. He hadn't said much of anything in the last half hour, and so, as they walked through Athena's abode, the Goddess of the Hunt took it upon herself to speak to the young boy to see what was on his mind.

"I'll give you an obol if you share your thoughts," she said, stopping halfway in a hall filled with busts and armor.

Aison came to a halt as well, but his eyes kept their focus on the floor. "Nothing."

Artemis knelt beside him. "That doesn't sound like nothing."

"I don't care what it sounds like. It's nothing."

There was an unexpected fire in his voice, an anger that longed to get out. "Are you mad at someone?"

Aison didn't answer.

"Are you worried about Cassandra?" she asked, hoping the obvious answer would be enough to get him to speak. She hated seeing him struggle alone with such torment, but she could do nothing if he didn't open up. Not that there seemed much chance of that. He had no reason to trust her as they were mostly strangers. But sometimes, confiding in a stranger was exactly what someone needed.

"A little," he finally said. "Dad says she's going to be okay, but..."

Artemis waited a few seconds, hoping he'd finish the sentence on his own, but he never did, so she prompted him further. "But what?"

"But he's lying. I know he is. I heard them talking. They don't know what to do."

"Things change," she said, gently holding his shoulders and turning him to face her. "I promise. I can't count all the times I've been faced with a problem I didn't know the answer to. But that's why it's important to never give up, to search and struggle, because we're always much, much more capable of things than we think we are."

Aison recoiled, slipping from her grasp. "No, we're not."

"Why do you say that?"

"Because—" The rest of his sentence choked in his throat, and he tried to run.

He was quick, even for a boy twice his age, but Artemis was quicker. One didn't rule as Goddess of the Hunt without the sharpest of reflexes. She grabbed him by the wrist and pulled him close. He fought, trying to pry open her fingers, all the while keeping his face turned away.

"Aison," she whispered. "Aison, it's okay to be scared."

"I'm not scared!"

"Okay," she said, playing along. "You're not scared. Tell me what you wanted to say."

Aison tugged a couple more times, each one weaker than the previous, but never succeeded in slipping out of her grip. Once he stopped, his shoulders fell, and the words he spoke were barely a murmur. "We can't do anything, thanks to me."

"What do you mean?"

"I mean, I should've stopped him from hurting Cassandra!" he yelled, eyes fierce and tiny claws growing from his fingers. "I should've, but I didn't! I couldn't!"

"No, Aison. No. None of this is your fault."

"It is! And when she's gone, everyone's going to hate me!"

"I will never hate you," she said. "And your parents will never hate you even more. I promise."

Creases formed across his brow, and he shook his head. "Yes, they will. They don't want someone like me, someone broken."

"Broken?" Artemis echoed, not expecting the response at all. How could he think he was broken? That thought only stayed with her a moment. It didn't matter how. The goddess lifted his chin so she could look into his eyes. "Aison, where, pray tell, is the shame in being broken?"

The little gorgon's face blanked. "What do you mean? It's bad. It's always bad."

"Quite the opposite," Artemis said. "Being broken simply means finding where your limits are."

"Mom never broke. Neither did Dad. Only me."

"No, they most certainly did," she said with a knowing smile. "They broke, but that only let them know where they needed to get better, stronger, smarter, faster. Breaking is nothing more than the signaling of a choice. It's a choice where you can remain defeated, or you can realize that by simply refusing to give up, you prove to the world how unstoppable you are."

Aison sniffed and wiped his nose before using both hands to rub his eyes clear. "I want to get better."

"I know you do. And you will."

"Will you teach me?" he asked.

"It would be my pleasure, Master Aison," Artemis said with a bow.

"Master Aison?"

Artemis laughed and tussled the vipers on his head. "Never mind," she said. "It's a little something the mortals used to call each other from time to time. I like the way it sounds, don't you?"

"I'd rather be a hero."

"Well, Master Aison," Artemis said, pushing herself up off her knee. "That's a title you'll have to earn one day. Think you can?"

"Mm-hm."

"I don't doubt that one bit," she said. "Now come, let's see what Athena has in store for us. Well, for me, at least."

Artemis took the young gorgon by the hand and led him down the hall. It ended up being only a short walk until they reached Athena's library. As always, the walls were packed with shelves filled with tomes and scrolls, but the floor space had been cleared away. Where freestanding bookcases had once stood, hundreds of small tables now took their place, and on each of those tables sat a chessboard.

"Hosting a tournament?" Artemis asked, throwing her half-sister a grin. "Is picking a fight with Father not entertaining enough?"

Athena, concentrating on one of the boards nearby, looked up from the game she studied. There wasn't a hint of amusement on her face, something that troubled Artemis to no end. "No, and no," Athena answered. "I'm not that lucky."

"Then what is all this about?"

Athena opened her mouth to answer, but her eyes fell upon Aison, and she directed her next words at him instead. "Go find a book to read," she said, motioning at the shelves behind them. "Artemis and I need to talk in private."

"No," he said.

Athena straightened as did Artemis. Athena spoke first. "Did you say no?"

"I said no," he replied defiantly.

"Why?"

"That's what Mommy said before," he said. "Right before...at the aquarium."

Though it was clear to them both that he was trying to be strong, the flutter in his voice belied the show, and Artemis squeezed his shoulder. "I think, perhaps, under the circumstances, we shouldn't drive him away."

"Nothing's going to—" Athena cut herself off and sighed before forcing a smile. "You're right. I'm sorry. I'm tired."

"Think nothing of it," said Artemis. "So, what are these boards about?"

"Games I once played with Dad," she said.

"Because?"

"Because I'm trying to better understand how he thinks."

"About chess?"

"About strategy."

Athena's answer wasn't one Artemis would've guessed in a thousand years. Athena, Goddess of War, could manage more campaigns than there were stars in the sky and never grow weary. The reason, then, for what she was doing, eluded the goddess. "I don't follow."

Athena eased her way around the table, her fingertips gracing its smooth marble surface. When she reached the other side, only a few paces from Artemis, Athena asked one question. "Why are you here?"

"You asked me to come," Artemis said.

"No, that's not what I meant," Athena said, giving a pained laugh. "By the Moirae, I can't even form a question properly anymore."

"Given what's going on with Euryale," Artemis said, carefully picking her words so as not to upset Aison, "I think you're entitled to misspeak once or twice."

"No, I'm not. And that's exactly what I mean. Why are you following me when...Dad might have objections? I'm thinking, perhaps, you shouldn't."

Artemis reflexively tightened her grip on Aison, far more than she ever should have, for the boy yelped, and she quickly released him. "Apologies, Master Aison," she said before returning to the conversation with her sister. "As for why? How could you even ask? It's the right thing to do. It's the only thing to do."

Athena clasped her hands together in front of her mouth and nodded thoughtfully. "It is, but I could be leading us both to destruction."

"You think things with Dad will get worse?"

"I know they will, as much as I'd like to pretend otherwise."

Stunned, Artemis didn't know what to say. Never in her life had she ever seen such worry on any of the gods before, and certainly not Athena. No, not only worry, she corrected. Worry and self-doubt.

"Athena, listen to me," she said. "If there's anyone in Olympus who can keep things from getting worse, it's you."

"I wish I had your confidence," Athena admitted, shaking her head. "And I only bring this up because if I make a mistake, there's no reason for us both to bear his wrath. I would not hold it against you if you decided not to stay the course."

"How dare you say such a thing," Artemis scolded, skin flushed. "I would never abandon you like that. And even if I wanted to, I can't. I've made my oaths, and I intend to see them through. Justice must prevail."

"I don't want you to follow me because you think I'm something I'm not, is all."

Artemis snorted. "Sister, I've known you for eons. I know all your embarrassing secrets and dirty little stories. If there's anyone who knows what you are and what you are not, it is I."

"I'm supposed to be the Goddess of Wisdom," Athena said. "I'm not supposed to make mistakes. Yet I've made many, especially as of late."

"Being the Goddess of Wisdom doesn't mean you don't err," Artemis countered. "It means you're wise enough to acknowledge when you do and do better next time. What other Olympian can claim the same? They never change, never learn from the past—though I suppose Aphrodite has shown a little promise lately, yes? Are you going to give her your title now?"

Athena remained silent for several moments. Her gaze drifted to a chessboard, and she picked up one of the pawns and toyed with it in her hand. Eventually, the toying stopped. "I wonder how many mistakes I've made, though. How many I loathe to acknowledge."

"Don't we all," Artemis said. "Don't we all."

Chapter Achlys

A sharp pain stabbed through her fingers. Euryale jerked awake to find herself in the muck, slumped against the tree, with a skeletal creature firmly latched on to her hand.

The thing was about the size of a thirty-pound dog with four legs sporting claws and a skull that looked like it belonged more on a dragon than a canine. The moment it saw the gorgon wake, it let go of her hand and jumped back in surprise, only to launch itself at her neck a split second later.

"Stheno!" Euryale yelled, diving to the side with her arms up to try and block the attack.

The monster clamped down on her forearm, its teeth piercing flesh and digging into bone. Euryale howled and channeled her pain into anger. She grabbed the creature by the back of its neck and drove forward, using it as a battering ram against the tree.

The creature shattered on impact, sending fragments of bone in all directions. Euryale ripped its skull free of her arm and spent the next few seconds driving it into the tree as well. The damn thing was resilient but not indestructible. On the third hit, it, too, shattered.

Sensing that danger still loomed, Euryale spun around as three more similar creatures pulled themselves out of the black mud. They staggered at first, like marionettes being brought to life by a demented puppeteer, but they quickly found their footing and coordination.

Euryale didn't wait to see what they'd do. She bellowed, loud and fierce, before pouncing on the nearest one, which happened to be larger, but thinner, than the one she'd destroyed moments ago. It met her charge by leaping at her face with an open maw of broken teeth.

The gorgon caught it under the chin with her right hand, and using its momentum against it, spun it in a circle and launched it at the next monster. The two collided, breaking limbs in the process.

An instant before she tore into the third, Stheno dove on top of it, coming seemingly out of nowhere. Her sister dug her claws into the spaces of its rib cage and flung the bones, laughing all the while. "Finally!" she cried out, ripping it apart further. "And here I thought this day would be dull!"

The fourth backed away, keeping its head low, its eye sockets fixated on the two sisters, before lifting its head to the sky and baying mournfully.

Stheno shot forward, grabbing it by the neck, narrowly avoiding the snapping of teeth in the process.

"What are you going to do now, I wonder," she said, holding it up in the air. The thing struggled vainly against her grip before reaching up with its back claws and tearing a set of deep gouges in her flesh.

"Stone for you, yes?" Stheno purred. Her eyes narrowed, but nothing happened. Surprise splashed over her face, and she grunted in disgust, at which point she grabbed the creature's rear legs and tore them from their sockets. "Not immune to that, are you?"

The skeletal beast answered with more thrashing and snapping, to which Stheno began plucking its bones off its body one at a time. Euryale watched her sister play with the thing, pulling off the front legs before tossing the body. As soon as it hit the mud, the ground rumbled, and countless dozens broke free of the muck.

"More? More, Euryale! More! They want more of us!" Stheno laughed, scooping up her spear and charging headlong into the fray.

Euryale followed, and together the two decimated the undead monsters' ranks. Blood, bone, and scale flew, and with each wound Euryale suffered at the jaws of one of the monsters, each slash across her chest and face she took from a claw or hooked tail, she further sank into an uncontrolled rage.

Her world turned into a familiar blur of chaos. The snapping of bone filled her ears, and the taste of blood—hers and her sister's—lingered all around. Shadows slammed into her, latching onto her arms and tail, only to be beaten back by nothing but her sheer ferocity. She would not fall here. She would not allow these abominations to keep her from finding Achlys, from getting an antidote to save her sweet Cassandra. She'd sooner carve out her own heart before she let any of that come to pass.

Gradually, the attacks lessened in number and strength. As they did, she left that world of madness. Her vision sharpened, and everything faded back into view.

"You've come a long way," Stheno said, smiling and panting a few feet away. Her sister was covered in wounds from scalp to toe, and her blood lay caked across her body. In one hand, she held the remains of the last monster, which she dropped to the ground and then drove her spear through its skull. "That said," she added. "By my count, I killed twice as many."

"It's not a contest."

"Says the one who lost."

Stheno's reply had an edgy, confrontational tone to it, but before Euryale could respond, the bog heaved one last time upward, sending mud and water spraying in all directions. From the eruption rose a massive amalgam of rotted flesh and bone. Its head spanned a dozen feet at its narrowest point, and it had teeth the size of a giant. Fiery red orbs filled its eye sockets, and skeletal, bat-like wings shot out from its shoulders nearly a hundred yards in each direction.

"You should not have come here, interloper," the monster said, bringing its head low. "You have no power here."

Stheno backed and threw a glance at her sister. "Perhaps we ought to take this one together."

Euryale narrowed her eyes and shook her head, not at her sister, but at the thing that dared threaten her. "Take us to Achlys," she said. "I will not ask twice."

"Or what?"

"Or die."

A rolling, thunderous laughter poured from its mouth. It then reared back and tried to swat Euryale where she stood.

The gorgon held her ground. Her eyes turned to midnight, and her curse flowed.

"Impossib—" the monster shrieked.

He never finished the word. His body hardened, cracking as it did. For a few seconds he stood there, petrified, with his head turned to the side and his claws outstretched. Then the weight of his new form took over. The cracks spread and turned into fissures before he crumbled and sank back into the swamp.

Still seething, Euryale took several deep breaths, all the while staring at the remains of the petrified thing.

"I can't believe you did that," Stheno said, groaning and crossing her arms over her chest. "Even thousands of years later, you're still the one favored by the Fates."

Her sister's words caught Euryale by such surprise, her anger vanished, and she couldn't help but laugh. "What are you talking about?"

"That!" Stheno said, gesturing to the petrified remains. "You get to do all that!"

"So?"

"So? It's not fair! I swear, once we're done here, that's going to be the first thing we change."

"Fair? Whoever said life is fair, my cute little gorgon," chimed a new, sweet voice from behind.

Euryale twisted around as a figure broke through the fog and into the light, a figure that had to be Achlys herself.

The gorgon had always heard tales regarding the primordial Goddess of Death and Misery growing up, but not a single one of them did her justice when it came to offering an accurate description. As she hobbled toward them through the fog, a constant drip ran from her nose while blood seeped from sunken, pale cheeks. Her eyes looked clouded over, vacant and empty, and her torso, barely clothed with scraps of dirty rags, caved in on itself as if she'd been starving for a thousand years and had somehow lived to tell the tale. Mats of grime infested her ratty hair that fell in clumps to muddy shoulders, and her knees and elbows were so swollen, it had to be excruciating for her to even think about bending them.

Despite all of this, Achlys grinned as if she hadn't a care in the world. "Euryale. Stheno," she said, cackling between their names. "I've been dying to meet you."

Of the two sisters, Euryale spoke first. "You have? Why?"

The goddess, who barely stood to each gorgon's chest, reached up and grabbed them both by the shoulder. "Why? Because I'm always dying!" she laughed. "Isn't it grand? Now come here and let me get a good look at you both."

Achlys dug her long, dirt-encrusted nails into Euryale's cheeks and pulled her head down so that the two were face to face. "Such pretty, pretty fangs you've got, dearie," she said. "Have you killed a lot of men with them lately, or do you simply turn them all to stone now?"

"Lately, I haven't done much of either," Euryale said. "I'm trying to keep it that way."

Achlys threw the gorgon back as if she'd just been scorched. "You are? Why, dearie, why? Such gifts. Such raw power. All to be wasted? Say you're having some fun with me, love, and this is your play at humor. Please say such a thing and make an old goddess happy."

Euryale shook her head. "I don't like killing anyone."

"How dreadful! Are you bored with it already?" she asked, frowning. The corners of her mouth turned back up as she nodded to herself and tapped Euryale on the nose with a finger. "I could teach you, will teach you! Better ways to gut a man, ways to tear apart his family, see his wife boiled, and his children gnawing at their own entrails. Ways you've never thought of before. What a lovely time you'll have then, yes, yes."

"I only want to live in peace," Euryale said.

"How you tease!" Achlys replied, pointing a playful finger at the gorgon. "You think I was born only an eon ago? As if a fearsome creature such as yourself would come see sweet, little old me about peace." She laughed again and shuffled over to Stheno. As she had with Euryale, Achlys grabbed the gorgon by the cheeks and pulled her head low. "And what about you, red one? Are you going to tell me, too, that you want to waste your Fate-given talents petting puppies and planting precious little flowers till the end of time?"

Stheno flashed the goddess a predatory smile and gently took the goddess's hands in hers. "I want you to make me the deadliest thing you can," she said. "I want empires shredded by my claws, and the gods to tremble at the sight of my spear."

"Oooo, I knew I was going to like you," Achlys said, clutching her sides with a deep belly laugh. "Athena, such a fool. Thought it was a curse to turn you into what you are but look at you! Who could want more? Took on a titan, I hear. Took him on and sent him running."

The enthusiasm in Stheno's face faded, and she pressed her lips into a thin line before replying. "That wasn't me," she reluctantly admitted. "That was her."

"Her? Are you certain?"

"Much to my frustration, I'm certain," Stheno said before tossing her sister a quick smile. "No offense."

"I can't believe it! Your claws are so much sharper than hers, and your vipers! Oh, I love the color of each one! Bright red. Full of venom second to none. I've got a nose for that, you know, sweet thing."

"I do! Make me strong, stronger than ever," Stheno said, squeezing the goddess's hands eagerly.

Achlys retreated a few steps, tilting her head and eying the gorgon, all the while gnawing on her fingertips. "Decisions, decisions," she mumbled. "Always decisions."

It was at that point that Euryale jumped back in the conversation. Enough time had been lost already. "We came to you for something else," she said. "Something personal."

Achlys hobbled over to her and stood on her tiptoes, grinning. "Oh, this sounds like something I'd be interested in," she said. "What's so special about little old me that you'd come all this way? It's not my secrets you're after, is it? Wanting to steal them, perhaps?"

Euryale shook her head. "No, we're—"

"No? NO!" Achlys wailed and recoiled, swatting the air all around. "No. No. No! Such an awful, awful word, I never want to hear! Do you understand? Never! Never, ever, ever! It makes me so...so angry, and you. I like you. With all the great plans we'll make, we mustn't be angry with each other. Promise me you won't make me angry. Promise me now, will you?"

"I promise," Euryale said, tensing every muscle in her body. "I only meant that the reason we came was to seek help for my daughter. She's been poisoned, but lives, for now. We need to find some hemalander."

The Goddess of Misery relaxed, and then hunched over with a devious look upon her face. A tiny sparkle formed in her otherwise lifeless eyes, and she clasped her hands together and rocked back and forth as she spoke. "Hemalander? That's a lovely flower. Very lovely indeed, and I can help you find it, dearie dear. I most certainly can. Want to use it to make an even better poison, yes? One that can kill that nasty little brood of yours once and for all. Put her in the grave where she belongs."

"No!"

Achlys reared back again, her face twisting in anger. "No? You dare say no to my gifts?"

"You dare threaten my child?" Euryale shot back, rising up on her tail. "I've come to save her! Not kill her!"

Confusion marred the goddess's face as if the words Euryale spoke were the words of a madwoman. "Save? Whatever for? Everything dies. Everything. Men. Women. Gods. Gorgons." Achlys stopped and giggled. "Your sister died well. Such a shame you missed seeing her body fall to the ground, headless. I can still picture every twitch she made."

"I will not suffer your words any longer, goddess," Euryale growled.

Achlys hushed, like a toddler being reprimanded but not caring in the least. She then inched toward Euryale and stood on her tiptoes so she could whisper in the gorgon's ear. "Do you know who else dies? Daughters of gorgons. Wait till you see how their little lips quiver those last...few...breaths..."

"Quiet!" Euryale yelled.

"Quiet? No, no. Not quiet. I'll never be quiet, just like she'll never live, and there's nothing at all you can do about it. Nothing, nothing, nothing. Can you picture it now, I wonder? The small grave you'll dig? The frail body you'll lower into its depths? What words will you run to for comfort, I wonder, when the worms feast on her corpse."

With a dreadful bellow, Euryale lunged at the goddess, claws and fangs eager to strike, but the blow never landed. Achlys vanished into a fine mist, and the gorgon struck nothing but air.

"Such a fight, dearie," the goddess cackled, instantly re-materializing behind her. "How angry can you get, I wonder?"

Euryale growled, spinning as she did, only to catch a slap across the face. The goddess's nails burned like fire as they tore through her skin, and in the blink of an eye, Euryale could feel the wounds already festering. Her strength gave out a moment later, and she fell to the ground, barely managing to catch herself with her hands before her head hit the muck.

"I'll kill you!" Stheno screamed, sprinting forward. The gorgon drove the tip of her dory straight for the goddess's chest. Long before the broad, adamantine head could pierce her skin, Achlys twisted, unnaturally so, and the weapon slid by harmlessly. Stheno whipped the spear around, trying to score a hit with the spike on the bottom end, but again, the goddess ducked out of the way with ease.

"Fast, but not fast enough, I'm afraid," Achlys chided, darting forward and giving Stheno a set of wounds across her forearm.

Stheno howled in pain, falling back into a defensive crouch. Euryale pushed herself up and attacked. She rammed into the goddess from behind, wrapping her arms around Achlys's chest so that her fingers could reach for her neck. In a flash, Euryale sank her claws into the leathery flesh. Dark coagulated blood oozed forth, carrying with it a putrid smell that made the gorgon's eyes water.

"I told you to stop," Euryale spat, ripping out the goddess's throat and shoving her body forward.

Stheno seized the moment and lined her spear up perfectly so that when Achlys stumbled forward, she impaled her on the tip of the adamantium head. The spear pierced the goddess's dark heart and shot out her back with ease.

For a few moments, no one moved, and Achlys hung limply on the weapon's shaft. Then Stheno grabbed her matted hair and yanked her head back. "For all your bluster, you died far too easily," she said before spitting in her face.

Achlys's lips curled upward as her head rolled from side to side. "I don't think this is quite as over as you thought it would be."

CHAPTER BARGAINS

Stheno roared and tore her claws through the air, intent on ripping the smirk right off Achlys's face.

The blow, as before, never connected. Achlys turned to mist. For a few tense moments, Euryale and Stheno scanned every inch around them, looking for the goddess, before going back to back to fend off wherever the next attack came from.

To Euryale's ever-building fear, all that she saw was the gloom of the bog on all sides, and all she could hear were the sounds of their heavy breathing.

"What are you going to do now?" Achlys whispered, her head suddenly appearing next to Euryale's.

"Stop toying with me!" Euryale yelled as she lashed out, but the goddess was gone as quickly as she came.

Nails stabbed her skin across her back and shoulders, each one cramping her muscles and sending waves of agony through her body. Euryale gritted her teeth and shook her head, trying to regain her strength and not to succumb to her wounds.

"Down, down, down you go," Achlys sang, her voice coming from all around. "Forever will your daughter know, her little bitty mommy tried, but no matter what, she only died."

Stheno's hands went under Euryale's shoulders as she helped keep her sister upright. "She's not better than us," she said. Stheno lifted her head and raised her voice. "You hear me? You're not better than us! You have no idea who you're dealing with."

Mist condensed behind Stheno, and before Euryale could think about saying a word or reacting, Achlys was on Stheno's back, legs wrapped around her waist, her spidery fingers clutching her throat. Stheno froze, eyes filled with terror the likes of which Euryale had never seen before.

"And who am I dealing with, pray tell, little gorgon?" Achlys said as she pressed her cold, sticky cheek against the side of Stheno's face.

"It only took one of us to send Typhon to the Abyss," Stheno said, regaining her defiant stance. "What do you think two of us can do?"

Achlys's body shook with delight as she laughed. "Typhon? A waste of a monster if there ever was one. First war he gets in, he loses, and ends up spending how many eons trapped under a mountain?"

"She's blessed by Cronus, too," Stheno said.

"Cronus?" Achlys repeated, her eyes drifting to meet Euryale's. "Are you now?"

"I am."

"Ha! Cronus! I love it," she said as she stroked the side of Stheno's face. "I'll tell you a secret, gorgon. I don't care if that old wretch of a titan gave you all of his power. I can wither his body with a single spit from my mouth. His command of time will never, ever, ever, ever, ever save him from the clutch of death. I come for everyone. Anyone."

The goddess continued to ramble, and Euryale, realizing this fight was not one she could win through sheer strength alone, studied her adversary. It was clear now that Achlys was a far more terrible foe than the stories about her had depicted, but that didn't mean she wasn't without weakness. After all, for as much as she loved sowing death and misery, life still flourished. Something had to keep the goddess in check.

"Then why do you hide here, if you're so dreadful?" Euryale asked.

"I hide from nothing and no one," Achlys replied.

"I'd wager the Fates would disagree."

Achlys shot Euryale a wry grin. "Want to see how afraid I am of such a funny little trio of siblings? Listen to this: I swear by the River Styx I'll never put as much as a scratch on your precious sister's body from this moment forth."

"No!" Euryale cried, lunging with her arms outstretched.

Achlys used her feet to kick off Stheno's back while slicing her nails across the gorgon's throat. Stheno's neck ripped open, pus and blood pouring forth and black rot spreading across her skin.

"Euryale..." Stheno gurgled. She staggered a moment and collapsed in a heap.

Euryale scooped her sister up and cradled her body. "I've got you," she said. "You'll be right as the blue sea before you know it."

Achlys hobbled over to the pair, rubbing her hands together and licking her lips with a sore-encrusted tongue. "Will she, now? I'm surprised you would lie to her so."

Stheno reached up with a shaky hand and grabbed Euryale by the back of the head, drawing her close. "Thank you," she said with a shaky voice. "Thank you for setting me free."

With her eyes clouded by tears, Euryale shook her head, refusing to entertain where her sister was going with this. "Quiet," she scolded. "You're not allowed to give up. You're immortal, damn it. Start acting like it."

"Immortal? Is that what you think?" Achlys said, taking Euryale by the shoulder. "Who's been filling your head with such silly nonsense, dearie?"

Euryale shrugged the goddess off, keeping her eyes fixed on her sister. Her skin burned like fire, and her breathing sounded raspy and uneven. "Don't you dare listen to her," the gorgon said.

"We've still got a city to burn, remember? A god to topple. You wouldn't want to miss out on that, would you?"

Achlys straightened. "A city to burn, you say? Now, there's the first sensible thing you've said this whole time. Pray tell, dearie, what city?"

"Olympus."

"Olympus? Olympus!" she shouted, jumping up, hands reaching for the heavens. "I love it! But...but there are so many gods there," she muttered, shaking her head. "So many. They'll not like you setting fire to the place. Especially Zeus. He'll likely stop you. Sweet talk you, even. Make you his lover, caress your body till you forget all about your troubles."

Achlys had scarcely finished her sentence when Euryale spun around and attacked one last time. She howled, driving a shoulder into the goddess's chest. Her hands pinned Achlys's wrists to the ground. An instant later, the gorgon sank her fangs into her neck and her vipers struck time and again.

As Euryale ravaged her body, the goddess lay there, giggling. "Such wonderful fury," she said, dancing her fingertips down Euryale's spine. "Such burning hatred for Zeus! I could only dream of finding one like you, my sweet harbinger of death. Tell me, dearie, what did he do to earn such ire?"

Euryale reared at the unexpected question. "He..." the gorgon paused, hating how hard it was to get the words out. She took a deep breath to finish. "He raped me in my own bathhouse."

To the gorgon's surprise, the cachectic woman didn't laugh or bathe in her misery. She did, however, offer her a vengeful smile. "Made you feel small and worthless, no doubt," she said. "Still channeling that anger at yourself, though, yes, dearie?"

"No." But as soon as she spoke, Euryale shook her head, knowing it was a lie. "More than I'd like to admit."

"And you want to kill him now? Make him pay for his terrible crimes?"

"Yes."

"And all those who stand with him?"

"Yes."

Achlys wheezed and grinned broadly, as if trying to force out a sinister laugh that shriveled lungs hadn't a prayer to expel. "I like you, gorgon. Your sister even more, and your desires the most," she said. "So, I make you this offer, dearie. I'll tell you where to find this flower you seek. I'll even steal the poison that now snuffs the life of your sister, but I want something in return."

Euryale grabbed the old goddess's hands tight. "Anything."

"Anything?" she repeated. "Oh, even I'm not that cruel to hold you to that. But what I do want from you is a written confession of everything you plan on doing."

Euryale let go and furrowed her brow, not following the request whatsoever. "A confession? Why?"

"Because I'm going to send it to Zeus himself," she said. "And the war born from the two of you will be terrible, terrible indeed."

"But my daughter!"

"Might not make it if Zeus has his way with you," she chuckled. "So if you fail in this quest of yours, what sweeter suffering could there ever be for a mother to know she had the cure in hand her daughter so desperately needed, only to be killed by the god who ravaged her."

Stheno coughed, drawing Euryale's attention. "Don't. You don't need me," she said. "Find it on your own."

Euryale looked down at her sister, cleared her eyes, and traded her pain for determination. "No," she said, shaking her head. "I need you, and together no one will stop us."

"Lovely, dearie. Lovely," Achlys said as she placed her hand on Stheno's forehead. "This will only take a moment, and then we'll get to writing this letter of yours."

The black lines of rot that marred Stheno's neck withered and withdrew as pus formed on the goddess's fingers and ran up her arm. Euryale gagged at the fetid substance, but Achlys reveled in it. Once all the poison was removed from Stheno's body, Achlys tore some cloth from the rags she wore and used it as a makeshift bandage.

"There you go, sweet thing," she said, patting Stheno's head. "That body of yours ought to heal now. You'll be back to killing in no time."

Stheno swatted the goddess's hand away and rolled to the side to take to her feet. "Don't you dare touch me."

"Are you going to stop me?" Achlys chuckled while shuffling around the pair. "Let's not play silly games. I want to like you. Use you. Watch you grow and bring forth a plague like no other." The goddess paused and leaned her head forward as she pointed a gnarled finger at the pair. "But I'll not tolerate the rude. I can find others who share my love, use you as a warning to everyone else. A long time has it been since I've made an example out of someone. Might be time to do it again."

Stheno growled, and Euryale caught her by the shoulder and pulled her back. "You've made your point," she said. "Where do we find this flower?"

"You're as smart as you are deadly, gorgon," Achlys said with a nod of approval. "We're going to do such wonderful things together. Such wonderful things."

"Please, tell us where to find it already."

Achlys brought her fingers under her chin and tapped them together, turning unspoken thoughts in her mind. "A long time ago, I saw one growing on a rocky outcropping overlooking the River of Chaos," she finally said. "I'll draw you a map after you write your letter."

"The River of Chaos?" Euryale repeated, scarcely believing what she'd heard. "Beyond Nyx's realm? A place that tears reality apart a thousand times in a blink of an eye?"

Achlys chuckled. "At the edge, but yes, that's the place."

"How are we ever supposed to survive there?"

The goddess grinned and shrugged. "That's your problem, dearie. Not mine. Not mine at all."

"If you won't help, who will?"

"Perhaps Mother will," Achlys said. "But then again, she's still irked about Aphrodite being so blasé about coming to her home, uninvited. I suppose there's only one way to find out."

Chapter About That Vault

A few yards outside of Aphrodite's abode, Alex paced with his stomach in knots. He hated every ounce of the deal he'd struck with Hera. Not only because it involved a massive amount of risk to himself, his wife, and his children, but also because he couldn't shake the feeling that Hera's dirty work could end in disaster if he wasn't careful, despite her promises.

After all, her reputation for being vindictive till the end of time was well earned.

But any second thoughts about it all mattered not. He'd struck his deal and now could only pray the Fates would show him some kindness.

"You can do this, Alex," he muttered. "Aphrodite is...sort of your wife's friend now. They're practically BFFs. She'll hardly think anything of you popping by. Right? So...just go. Just go. Just. GO."

Alex didn't. He stared at the front door, rooted in place, and swore up a storm before throwing his hands up in the air in frustration. "GAH! This is so stupid."

After hammering a fist into an open palm at least a dozen times, Alex forced himself up the stairs. He was a hero, damn it, one who battled cyclopes, wrestled immortal lions, and hung on to a wheel of fire for the fun of it. Well, maybe that last part wasn't entirely true. He hadn't had any fun doing that, but he had done it, regardless. Those memories would forever be scorched into his mind. Talking to Aphrodite should be simple. Hell, they could probably bond a little over their mutually shared experience of being horribly disfigured.

"Hello?" Alex called out as he wrapped loudly on the door several times. "Aphrodite? Are you there?"

No answer.

Alex tried again, and again he was met with silence. He tried pressing his ear against the door, hoping that something would come of it, but that effort also proved to be a fruitless endeavor. So, he knocked one more time and tried the door.

It opened without protest, revealing the entryway to Aphrodite's estate. Alex wasn't sure what to expect in terms of what would be on the other side. He hadn't even given it any thought. That said, however, what lay before him turned out to be exactly Aphrodite. All of it.

Extravagant pink silk hung from the ceiling while a myriad of sculptures lined the walls, with a particularly large and impressive piece front and center inside the circular room. The figure, Aphrodite herself no less, wearing a single piece of sheer cloth, stood in the middle of a crystal-clear pool, arms raised with her hands behind her head as if fixing her hair, while she smiled and looked down at something not depicted a few feet away.

But it wasn't simply the art that screamed this place belonged to the Goddess of Love. The air held a sweet, enticing fragrance that sparked memories of a first love in Alex, and the light music of a far-off lyre carried in the air. Even the marble used for the floors and columns was tailored to her persona, as not a single inch seemed short of perfect smoothness and, in a strange way, softness, too.

Alex shook his head, snapping himself out of the trance he'd stuck himself in admiring it all. He didn't dare step foot inside without her permission, and a part of him wondered how much goodwill he'd already used up by simply pushing the door open. He hammered on the door again and tried calling for her one last time.

"Hello? Aphrodite?" he said, hands cupping around his mouth. "I really need to see you. I tried calling, but your phone was off. And...um...the door was open. I swear."

A few beats passed, and then he heard a door slam somewhere in the back of her home. Alex tensed, and a few seconds later, the goddess stormed into the entry room from the other side, hastily brushing messy hair with an ivory comb.

"What is it, Alex?" she snapped. But before he could answer, she glanced down at her disheveled chiton and huffed as she smoothed it out. "It better be important. I'm not exactly in the mood to entertain guests."

"It's important," Alex replied. "It's about the kids."

Ares joined them right as he finished, bounding into the room with unbridled enthusiasm. Though he was as naked as a newborn, on his skin, he wore a sheen of sweat and countless fine scratches across his chest and shoulders. "Something's wrong with the littles?" he asked, sounding genuinely concerned.

"It's Cassandra." Alex swallowed, only now realizing how hard this conversation was going to be and how helpless and terrified it made him feel.

Ares growled and clenched his fists together. "Ends of Chaos! She's disappointed with the howitzer I gave her, isn't she? I knew I should've given her a bigger gun."

"No," Alex said, finding some relief in how predictable Ares's thoughts were.

"No?" he said, brow furrowing. "Something even bigger? A tank maybe. No, a hundred tanks! A battleship! By the Fates! Why didn't I think of that before? What little girl wouldn't want to fling three-thousand-pound shells and watch her enemies blow away like chaff? I'm such a fool!"

"Cassandra, she's...dying. Or...petrified. Or both I guess," he sputtered.

Aphrodite's eyes grew, and she stumbled over her words as much as Alex had. "What? When? How? Why?"

Speaking on the facts, somehow, helped Alex simply go about the motions of relaying things. Facts were cold, easy to handle. Emotions, feelings, not so much. "We went to the aquarium to free Stheno. Someone tried to kill Euryale but ended up poisoning Cassandra instead," he said. "Apollo tried to cure her, but he said he couldn't. The poison was acting too fast, so Euryale petrified her to buy us more time."

"Oh, Alex," Aphrodite said, hurrying over to him and giving him a hug. "I can't even begin to imagine. You have my word. We'll see you two through all of this. It's the least we can do."

Ares strode over to the pair and clasped Alex's shoulder with an iron grip. "Yes, Alex, we will find this cowardly assassin and slowly tear him apart over the next thousand years."

"That part might be a little hard."

"No, actually, it is quite easy and enjoyable," Ares said, chuckling. "I suspect you'll pick up the finer points of torture in no time at all, especially with the need for vengeance coursing through your veins. A hero of your strength will be able to rip sinews as easily as you could parchment."

Alex laughed again at the unexpected, but once again, typical Ares response.

"That's not what I meant," he said, shaking his head. "I meant, Stheno already tore him to pieces. Literally."

Ares perked. "Stheno? Euryale's sister?"

"Yeah. The same. I told you, we went to get her at the aquarium."

"But you mean she's no longer a whale. She's a gorgon?"

"Well, not sporting the uber tail like Euryale right now, but yeah, she's a gorgon," Alex said. He then let loose a long whistle. "And holy hell, that girl is vicious. I mean, Euryale stopped her before she could bathe in the blood of every park-goer there, but I'll be damned if Stheno didn't try her hardest not to top the slaughter charts."

Ares arched his eyebrows and squeezed Alex's shoulder again. "I wish to hear more about this gorgon."

"Ares!" Aphrodite cut in.

"What?" he said, throwing up his hands. "Do you not wish to know more about this creature of bloodshed? She sounds as if she's more of an instrument of death and destruction than even Euryale—when she gets worked up, that is. Otherwise, she is a little docile, no offense, Alex."

"No, *dear*, I'm not interested."

Ares continued, lost in his own thoughts and oblivious to the continued sour look upon his lover's face. "I wonder if her beauty matches her ferocity," he mused, rubbing his chin. "Tell me, little Alex, would she stop the heart of any male who gazed upon her?"

"Uh, she's a gorgon? So, yeah. That's pretty much a given."

"You should introduce us later. Perhaps I could gift her a spear or ax to—"

Aphrodite ended it with a slap to Ares's face. "Enough!"

The slap not only got the God of War to quit his obvious lusts, but it helped Alex get his mind back to the most important task of his life: saving his daughter. "Aphrodite, I know we've had our issues in the past," he said, fumbling along as he tried to pick the best words he could. "And I know this is going to be the most monumental favor ever, but you're literally my only hope at this point. I'll do whatever you want to make this happen."

Aphrodite chuckled as she folded her arms over her chest. "Anything, Alex?" she asked with an equal mix of seduction and deviousness. "That's quite the promise."

"I know."

"Are you sure? Athena might take issue with that. Or more importantly, your wife."

Alex sucked in a breath reflexively. "I'm sure," he said. "Athena can't help right now anyway. And Euryale is desperate to save Cassandra, too."

Aphrodite huffed and shook her head. "I see. So what you're telling me is that once again, even after all I did for you and your wife, you still went to my bloody sister for help before coming to me."

"No! I mean, in a sense, Athena approached Euryale first, so technically yes," Alex said, holding his hands up defensively before rambling on like a madman. "Well, no, that's not right, either. Euryale and Athena got into a fight, and then Athena sent Artemis to talk to my wife about helping, so we never actually spoke to Athena, but I did try her phone. It went to voicemail—but that's only because, well...Gods, this is such a mess."

"Slow down, Alex. You're going to give yourself a coronary."

"I know. I'm sorry. This might be the worst couple of days in my life."

"Fine. I can understand how that might be," Aphrodite said. "As such, in my infinite graciousness, I'll ignore you granting me second fiddle—*again*. What do you need from me?"

"I need you to let me in Zeus's vault."

Ares gasped.

Aphrodite did, too, and if she'd had eyebrows, they would've hit the ceiling. But alas, she was far, far from healed, and thus didn't. But even with the horrid scarring that froze most of her face, Alex had no doubts this was as shocked as the goddess had even been before.

"You want in Dad's vault?" she said, each word spoken slowly and in utter disbelief. "And you're serious. You're not joking. You actually want in Dad's vault."

"Yes."

"And since you're not asking Dad, I'm going to assume that he wouldn't be happy with you going in there."

"Probably not," Alex replied. "Okay. Well, definitely not."

Aphrodite clasped her gnarled hands together before exhaling sharply. "Then tell me why, exactly, I should even dream about letting you in there, because aside from the fact that I'm not going to betray him, ever, even if I did, he'd find out. And once he did, he'd know exactly who let you in. And I don't know about your plans for the future, but mine don't include facing his wrath."

"I need to save Cassandra," Alex said, wishing he could say more but knowing he couldn't. The goddess would never let him in if she knew about Hera. "That's all I can say."

"Will say," she corrected.

Alex sighed with resignation. "Will say."

"You don't trust me," she said, shaking her head, sorrow in her voice and disgust on her face. "If that's all there is to this, why don't you go ask Dad for whatever's in there? In fact, isn't he helping? The two of you have always seemed to get along."

Alex sneered out of reflex. "Used to."

"Which means?" When Alex balked, Aphrodite tilted her head toward him and frowned. "I'll find out, you know, the moment I pick up my phone. Now tell me. What's going on?"

Chapter Scrying

Zeus read the letter.

Again.

That marked the fourth time his eyes scanned the parchment, and with each pass they made, his skin burned brighter and brighter. Thunderheads gathered over his temple, and Athena, who stood nearby, had no doubt that even the mortals on the other side of the planet could feel the electricity building in the air.

"Not a friendly note, I take it," she said, wondering if she should inch back in case she needed to dash out of his inner courtyard if it started to rain lightning.

His face hardened, and he seemed to grow at least four feet in stature. "This is your fault," he said, clenching a fist toward her.

"*My* fault?" Athena said, genuinely shocked. "I don't even know what this is."

Zeus flung the scroll at his daughter. "See for yourself."

The Goddess of Wisdom snatched it out of the air, but before she looked to see what was on it, she glanced to Apollo, who could only shrug. At that point, she turned her attention to the letter. With exceptionally beautiful penmanship, it read:

Euryale, wife to Alexander, sister of Stheno, mother of Aison and Cassandra, and daughter of Phorcys, to Zeus, current ruler of Olympus. I am writing to inform you that due to your assaults and abuses to not only myself, but others, your reign is coming to an end. You can abdicate the throne peacefully, or I will remove you by force and burn Olympus to the ground. The choice is yours.

P.S. Achlys sends her regards.

Athena carefully refolded the letter, and Zeus arched his eyebrows in response. "No comment?"

An unsettling feeling formed in Athena's gut. It wasn't that she didn't have a comment. She had several. Hundreds, even. Most were true. Those that weren't were simply her opinion on the state of affairs as well as what she thought of her father. None of them, if spoken aloud, would bring anything but strife and misery, and she longed to find a way to buy more time.

And she could if she conducted herself as she always had, turning at least a partially blind eye to Zeus and not holding him accountable. The problem at this point was that she knew this was a defining moment for her character.

"Well?" Zeus asked, his tone making it clear that his patience was a single pause away from ending.

Athena, taking to heart the bravery Aphrodite had shown standing up to Hera, committed herself to the righteous path and straightened. "This is not my fault," she said. "Don't you dare pin this on me."

"You said we should give her a chance!" Zeus shouted, storming up to his daughter and pointing a finger in her face. "And now look what she does! She runs to Achlys and threatens us all! They're both probably on their way to wake Cronus this very instant!"

"YOU RAPED HER!" Athena fired back, slapping his hand away. "How thick-headed can you be? None of this would've happened—absolutely none of it—if..."

Athena choked, guilt and shame strangling her words.

"You'd best speak carefully from here on out, daughter," Zeus said evenly. "And whatever you say, it had better be an apology."

"You're right," she said, laughing through the pain. "I should apologize. This is my fault. It's all my fault."

Zeus's temper faded threefold, and though the God of Thunder seemed somewhat placated, Apollo looked as confused as ever.

Athena took a moment to wipe away her tears, which didn't matter because new ones instantly replaced those that were lost down her cheeks. "It's my fault," she repeated, voice wavering as she fought to get the words out from her torn heart. "It's my fault because I never stood up to you before. I turned a blind eye to who you are, hoping, praying, fooling myself you'd ever change. And the only one who ever held you accountable up till now, we locked away. So, yes. It's my fault. But as the Fates are my witness, I'm going to do everything in my power to right my wrongs."

"Well then, this is what it's come to: my own daughter turns against me," Zeus said. "Perhaps you're not as wise as you've led everyone to believe."

Over the next two seconds, Athena considered all her options. She had to leave to set things right, and she also knew Zeus would never allow it, especially since that meant him paying for his crimes. He'd likely strike her down the moment she ran. Lethally? Probably not. At least, not at first. Though there were a total of three exits she could try for, only one was viable. But she'd need to dodge lightning for a few seconds to reach it.

Her dad's first throw would be a little high and to the right. It always was when he flung one in haste. She could spin under that easily enough. The second would be trickier, as he'd steady his aim, no doubt. If she reversed herself fast enough, she'd have a good shot at making the door. Any throws after the first two would be made in frustration—a feint to the left would counter the third strike, and the same feint two strides later would defeat the fourth. She might not even need to worry about any after the second if

Apollo cried out in protest. That could easily distract her father enough for her to escape unscathed.

All she needed to really tip the odds in her favor was a distraction. It didn't even have to be a grand one, or a good one for that matter. A split second would be all she needed.

"I think you're going to find I'm a lot wiser than you realize. In fact—" She cut herself off, feigned surprise, and looked over Zeus's shoulder. "Hera?"

Zeus took the bait.

The instant he glanced behind him, Athena sprinted away. After two strides, she reversed herself with a spin. Lightning ripped by her cheek, missing by a hair and singeing her skin. She never made it another pace. A second bolt slammed into her back, square between her shoulder blades, sending her sprawling to the ground.

Zeus strode over to his daughter's body, tendrils of smoke rising and curling in the air from her scorched clothes. Apollo raced over and knelt. After a quick exam, he sighed with relief. "She lives."

"Of course she lives," Zeus said with a snort. "I wasn't trying to kill her."

Gently, Apollo slipped his arms under her neck and beneath her knees and carefully picked her up. "I'll bring her to my temple and see to her wounds."

"You'll tend to her in jail and nowhere else," Zeus said with a tone that dared the god to offer any sort of challenge.

It was a challenge Apollo had no intention of making. "As you wish."

Though Zeus nodded in response, his face still bore a healthy dose of skepticism. "You think I was wrong?"

"I think these events need to be handled with the utmost care," he said. "Going after Euryale is one thing. Attacking your own daughter—"

"She sides with the gorgon!"

Apollo raised his hands defensively, as much as carrying the fallen Athena would allow. "I only meant, this is going to put the others on edge. If you want to show them your rule is just and not one resting solely on fear, I simply wish to remind you that tact is needed."

Zeus crossed his arms over his massive chest and studied the god, trying to get a feel for how trustworthy he was. On the surface, certainly, Apollo's advice was sound, but then again, so was Athena's, and look what happened with her. It didn't take him long for a new thought to come to him, or rather, a question—a question that demanded an answer. "Tell me, Apollo, God of Prophecy," he said. "Why didn't you see any of this coming?"

"I did," he said, matter-of-factly and to Zeus's complete surprise. "But had I told you beforehand and you'd confronted her, she never would've made this admission to your face."

"And what does the future tell you now?"

Apollo shook his head. "Only chaos, though I don't understand why."

Zeus made a fist and popped his knuckles as he let Apollo's words sink into his mind. At this point, he felt the god was telling the truth, and while Apollo's ability to speak to future events wasn't always one that could be relied on, visions of chaos were never a good omen.

"That doesn't sit well with me," he finally said. "After I jail Athena, we must scry the whereabouts of Euryale."

"I'll need something she recently touched in order to do that," he said. "Something personal."

Zeus smiled and pointed to the scroll. "I believe we have that covered already."

Apollo put Athena back down before taking the letter and examining every inch. Once he was done, he rolled it up and gave an approving nod. "It should work, but we can't wait long before scrying. Her presence on the letter won't last much more than an hour."

"Plenty of time," Zeus said. With a sigh, he then scooped up his daughter up and slung her over his shoulder. "Now go and prepare. I'll join you shortly."

The two parted ways. Apollo headed for his giant scrying pool inside his temple, while Zeus went to the back of his own temple and down a flight of circular stairs. These led him a full three hundred yards down into the depths of Mount Olympus, far from prying eyes and sensitive ears.

Initially, Zeus kept his thoughts on the superficial level, merely focusing on the mechanics of the task at hand. But as he drew near the jail cells, his heart grew heavy with sorrow, and with every step he took, Athena's weight against his shoulders felt even more unbearable than the one he'd taken before. When he finally reached her cell, a bare ten-by-ten square with granite walls and adamantine shackles, he quickly set her down, anticipating a relief that never came.

"That's called a conscience," Athena said as he locked the shackles around her ankles.

"Despite what you may think, I'm not immune to regret," Zeus replied.

"Then let me go and set things right," Athena said. "It's not too late."

"You're right. It's not too late," he said as he took to his feet and towered over her. "We still have time to stop the gorgon."

"She's not the enemy!"

"She made herself the enemy," Zeus said evenly. For a moment, he looked down at his daughter, wondering where he'd gone wrong in her upbringing. "I wish it didn't have to come to this," he said, voice full of remorse. "I've always tried to give you anything and everything you wanted, even at the expense of others and myself."

"You? Sacrifice for another?" Athena scoffed. "When?"

"You could start by asking your sister," he said. "Aphrodite's jealousy of you wasn't misplaced, and I must own up to that shortcoming of mine. But despite that, she always knew that ruling the gods was never easy, and with that responsibility came the undeniable fact that I have to deal with ugly, messy solutions from time to time. No one else. Me, and me alone. Case and point, all that's happening now."

Zeus turned to leave, but he stopped when Athena shot up and tugged against her chains. "You talk about messy solutions as if you weren't the cause of the problem to begin with," she said. "Why can't you see this? Why *won't* you see this?"

With a low grumble, Zeus shook his head and faced her one last time. "We've been over this before," he said. "We must all be able to trust one another. There is no other way, and Euryale had two chances to tell us what we needed to know. Instead, she chose herself over us, over Olympus, and sealed her own fate. If I've done anything wrong—and perhaps I have—it's that I've grown soft over the eons. I let Hera go unchecked to where she grew bold enough to try and usurp the throne, and now I've let you be filled with such hubris, you think your wisdom is greater than anyone else's expertise. You have a brilliant mind, Athena, and I am still proud to be your father, but there's a lot for you to still learn, and those are lessons I'll personally oversee once I've dealt with Euryale."

With that, Zeus left, cutting whatever conversation and objections Athena wanted to raise on the subject short. As he climbed the stairs, his spirits lifted, and his determination grew, reinforcing the idea in his mind that now, finally, he was getting things back to how they should be. Olympus would once again be the grand city it had always been known for, and thankfully, the damage it had suffered could and would be fixed in short order.

As Zeus made his way through the city, headed for Apollo's temple, raw power flowed through every fiber of his being, long-dormant energy that he hadn't realized he'd lost—or missed for that matter. Indeed, he'd grown soft and complacent, chasing pleasures of the flesh while neglecting to ensure order and discipline within Olympus itself.

Not that he wouldn't pursue the fairer sex when this was over—or even during, for that matter—but gone were the days where men and women, gods and gorgons, would challenge his authority. Euryale would serve as warning to the world that it would be foolish for anyone to go to war against him. And when he had her strung up, broken for all to see, he'd then turn his attention to Typhon, and slay that titan once and for all.

Zeus grunted.

He never should've chained that monster under Mount Etna to begin with. And that, admittedly, was another mistake he'd made: succumbing to the pleas of a desperate mother to spare her child. Gaia, primal goddess of the Earth and indeed all life, including the titans, had begged Zeus to spare her son. And though Zeus had loathed granting such a request after the devastation Typhon had wreaked, when the tears started flowing, Zeus, like many men in a similar position, felt powerless to wage war against them.

That one error, that one simple action framed as mercy, became a travesty as time wore on.

The past couldn't be changed, he knew. He could only focus on the present and his plans for the future.

But what of Alex? he wondered.

There stood a man Zeus had no plans for. He'd instantly grown fond of the hero when they'd first met during the wedding celebrations. And Alex had also shown himself as a shrewd negotiator that day when it came to dealing with Hera by not giving in to her baseless accusations. Zeus wanted to give him the benefit of the doubt.

Perhaps Euryale acted without his knowledge. His gut said Alex hadn't a clue, but he had to admit maybe that was his foolish hope for the hero. He would have to have a talk with the man, possibly interrogate him a little more forcefully than Alex would like, but either way, Zeus made a resolve to himself that he'd keep his mind and options open on the matter.

For now, at least.

Twenty minutes into his walk, he strode into Apollo's scrying room with a renewed sense of purpose and vigor. The pool in the center held waters as dark as Nyx's raven hair and as still as a dead man's breath. It was contained by rounded walls of silver, purfled with gold and platinum, and it rested on a raised pedestal of black marble. Twelve columns stood evenly spaced around and held aloft a domed ceiling large enough to house two mora of Spartan men without trouble. Four thymiaterions, all lining the back wall, burned saffron, giving the air a pleasant, sweet fragrance.

"Everything is set if you want to start," Apollo said. The god stood on the opposite side of the pool with Euryale's letter in hand.

"More so than ever," Zeus replied, quickly stepping over to him.

"Before we do, would you indulge my curiosity?"

Zeus tilted his head. "About Athena?"

Apollo nodded. "About Athena."

"And will you indulge my curiosity as to why this matters to you at this moment?" Zeus countered, his tone holding a sharp edge to it.

Apollo nodded again. "I only ask because others will want to know where she is, and I feel that I should know how you want to handle this before I'm forced to answer questions."

Zeus smiled and laughed at himself. "Forgive me, then, for being on edge," he said, shaking his head. "She's locked away and in good health. We even spoke before I left her."

"About?"

To that question, Zeus initially pressed his lips together into a fine line, but in the end, he realized it was a natural question, and it wasn't as if Apollo hadn't been privy to much already. "The same," he replied. "She still sides with the gorgon."

"I see," Apollo replied. "I'd hoped things would have turned out differently."

"In regard to her or me?"

"In regard to all of us," Apollo said. He then quickly added right as Zeus was about to reply. "I do not like the strife. It should never have had a home in Olympus. And yes, I understand no decision comes easy here. Sacrifices must be made."

"Indeed," Zeus said, hints of skepticism in his voice.

"If I may remind you," Apollo said, clearly sensing the tension that was forming between them. "I've made my oaths to you already, binding ones at that. I've long since learned my lesson on challenging your reign."

Those words helped Zeus relax. Yes, Apollo had tried to overthrow him long ago, and to some degree, Zeus understood why. They were all young. They all wanted power, and indeed, Zeus had shown weakness and recklessness. It was only natural then that some would seize the moment. But when he proved to be the victor, as Apollo had stated, the God of Prophecy had made oaths to never challenge the throne as long as Zeus sat upon it. He was no threat. "You have made vows, and I appreciate your support," Zeus said. "Now then, unless you have another matter of dire consequence, I want to see what Euryale is planning."

Chapter From Death to Dark

"Will she be hard to find?" Stheno asked, leaning forward in the chariot, eyes trying to pierce the eternal gloom before them.

"I don't know," Euryale replied. The pair were racing across the open, shadowy waters that led to Nyx's domain with their chariot, and she had a sinking feeling that the meeting with this goddess would be even less cordial than the one they'd had with Achlys.

"Do you think she'll help?"

"I don't know that, either," Euryale said. "I hope, but..." The gorgon's heart sank as the consequences of failure weighed on her soul.

Stheno slipped her arm across Euryale's shoulders. "We're getting that flower," she said. "You'll see."

"I know."

Stheno laughed and squeezed her. "You're a terrible liar when it comes to speaking with me. Always have been."

The moment of levity put a smile on Euryale's face. She bumped her hip into her sister and pulled away. "I am a wonderful liar, thank you very much. I learned from the best."

"Learned? Learned! Are you kidding me?" Stheno replied, looking more shocked than one of Medusa's victims. "Remember when you tried testing the stickiness of your homemade Greek fire and burned down our stables?"

"I do, and it was for science. I had to know if I got the mixture right."

"Science. That's the story you're going with now."

"You're the one always saying we don't push ourselves enough. So yes, I'm going with it was for science."

Stheno smirked. "Does that science also include you trying to blame your little mishap on me?"

Euryale threw her sister a sheepish look. "That...well, that was also for science."

"Remember that part earlier when I said you're a terrible liar?" Stheno asked. "Case in point: this conversation."

"I'm not lying," Euryale said, pulling on the reins to correct their course as their horses decided to veer. "I'm merely clarifying misunderstood intentions. Nothing more."

"Well, don't let me stop you from digging your own grave," Stheno said. "Go on. Explain to your dumb older sister how any of that was for science."

"I was testing the hypothesis that the powers of an adorable ten-year-old daughter were strong enough to float a minor bend of the truth when it came to having Dad believe what happened, despite evidence pointing to the contrary."

"Minor?"

"I wouldn't call it major, that's for certain," Euryale replied. "I barely had any soot on me."

"Regardless of what you'd call it, it's a good thing Dad didn't fall for any of it," Stheno said. "Because if I'd ended up taking the blame, by the time I got done with you, you'd be begging to swim the River Acheron."

"Still doesn't make me a bad liar," Euryale said, doubling down, even though she knew it was a lost cause. She couldn't lie worth a damn when it came to Stheno. She always saw right through her. But it was fun to have the banter, nonetheless.

"You keep believing that. I don't want you to get better, anyway," Stheno said. "Makes life easier."

The conversation died as the faintest outline of something appeared in the distant gloom. Though Euryale had never traveled to Nyx's home on her own, her first and only trip being made while she was dead, her gut told her this was where she wanted to be. Thus, she made another slight course correction and drove the chariot toward the mass.

As they made their way toward it, Stheno's anticipation at meeting Nyx grew even stronger. She clutched the sides of the chariot, her nails digging deep into the sides, and she leaned forward to such a degree, it seemed as if the only reason she didn't fall out was due to an intervention of the Fates.

"Could you lean back a little?" Euryale asked with a flutter in her voice. She reached out and tugged her sister's shoulder. "I'm on edge enough as it is."

Stheno shrugged her off. "You're lucky I'm not leaping out of this."

"I don't think you realize exactly who we're going to see," Euryale said.

Stheno laughed. "On the contrary. I know exactly who we're going to see."

The gorgon shook her head, and as memories of Nyx resurfaced, she could feel her gut tighten. "No, I mean, Nyx is—" Euryale sighed. "Nyx is like nothing I can describe. She's like the most beautiful nightmare you could never hope to dream on your own."

Stheno let loose an impressive whistle. "All the more reason why I want to meet her—why I have to meet her."

Euryale stiffened at the unexpected reply. "Have to meet her?"

The gorgon nodded and kept her gaze out to the approaching island. Her voice grew soft, but the tone to her words felt heavy. "I don't want us to be like this anymore," she said. "Meeting Achlys only drove that home."

"Like what?"

"This," she said, gesturing to her body. "Weak and disregarded."

"We're hardly weak."

"We are when it matters the most," Stheno said, her shoulders falling. "We couldn't stop Poseidon from defiling Medusa. We couldn't stand up to Athena when she punished us all for standing up to him or protect Medusa from Perseus. And today with Achlys? We might as well have been mice picking a fight with a lion."

Euryale couldn't argue Stheno's point. Even if Typhon had made her curse more terrible, and even if Cronus had hardened it further, others could still best her—break her.

"I don't think anyone can stand up to Achlys," she finally said, as much for her own sake as Stheno's. "Even Cronus."

Stheno snorted with disgust. "I refuse to accept that."

"If we do, it will be to our own downfall. Some things will never change."

"And things will always remain the same unless we try to make things different," she countered. "Why are you being like this? We used to dream about rising to power and crushing our foes beneath our heels."

Euryale thought about her sister's words as she brought the chariot down. She landed it on a large open cliff that spanned several dozen yards. Far beneath them and obscured by darkness, waves crashed loudly with unbridled fury, a constant sound the gorgon was able to lose herself in for a while.

"I'm terrible enough as it is," she finally said, even if that was only a partial answer. "The world doesn't need a monster like me walking around with limitless power."

Stheno laughed with disbelief. "No, Euryale. That's exactly what this world needs," she said. "It needs the strong to take charge, and that can be us! You and me! The River of Chaos is said to grant powers we couldn't even begin to imagine—"

"Assuming they don't rip you apart, first," Euryale said with a smirk. "You conveniently left that part out."

"But if we could harness that power..." Stheno's voice trailed, and she sighed longingly. "Think about it, Euryale. What if we could take it, even a little bit. We'd be like the eldest gods, Aion and Nyx, Erebus and the Moirae. Respected. Feared. Utterly unstoppable. By the Fates, you'd never have to worry about your children ever again. Or Alex. Or me..."

"I know," Euryale said as she slipped off the chariot. The ground felt cold against her tail, and there was a bitterness to the air that she hadn't remembered when she was here before. What that meant, she didn't know, but for some reason, the scent triggered a moment of insight. "Honestly, it terrifies me that we could ever be that strong."

"Terrifies?" Stheno repeated. "Why?"

"Imagine the damage we can do," Euryale said. "The lives and families we might tear apart if we're careless or cruel. I don't think I can handle that responsibility."

Stheno made a sweeping gesture. "Look around. This place, the earth, Hades, all of it is cruel and rips people apart already. It doesn't respect kindness. It doesn't grant mercy to the weak. Men. Animals. Gods. Nature. It's the same for everyone. The strong rule, and the weak only survive as much as they're tolerated."

"Believe me. I know all of that already."

"Then don't get cold feet on me," Stheno said. "Or a cold tail, as the case may be. You and I, we're going to save Cassandra. We're going to chop down Zeus at the knees, and we're going to set this world right. You and I."

A soft, refined voice joined the conversation, one that came from everywhere and nowhere and chilled Euryale's soul to the core. "That's a lot of boasting, pet. Pray tell, how will you accomplish such things after I've shattered your mind and put you both in eternal chains?"

Euryale slowly turned to find Nyx standing a few paces away. Her black eyes seemed to stare straight through the gorgon, and the robes she wore felt ten times darker than they had the last time Euryale had seen her. The goddess, with her flawless creamy skin and high cheekbones, still could command every living being with her unparalleled beauty alone, but the air around her felt sinister, and the gloomy mist swirling around her body and head seemed as if it carried a legion of nightmares.

"I need your help," Euryale said, managing to scramble forward with a combination of nerves and desperation.

Nyx pursed her lips and dropped her brow. "Oh, pet," she said, raising her hand. "Where are your manners?"

Euryale froze as fast as her heart stopped beating in her chest. "Please."

"Not even a thank you," Nyx said with the utter look of disappointment in her eyes. "I suppose I am the foolish one, then, thinking you might not be like the others who simply take, take, take."

"I didn't—"

"Quiet!" said Nyx as her black wings shot open. Though Euryale remained statuesque, Stheno did not. She shifted her weight a few times on her legs, and her hands tightened on her spear. Neither action was lost on the goddess.

"Feeling inadequate, Stheno?" Nyx said, folding her wings back and casually strolling up to her. "Are you going to strike me down with that paltry spear of yours?"

"No, she's not," Euryale said.

Nyx held up a finger. "She's capable of answering on her own."

"I'm capable of a lot more than that," Stheno said, hardening her face and growling.

"Are you, now? How charming," she replied. "Why don't we continue this somewhere better suited for conversation?"

Before either gorgon could reply, the ground shifted and turned to liquid before coiling up each one's body.

Wind assaulted Euryale from all sides, blasting her face and thundering in her ears. Somewhere in the chaos she heard Stheno yell, and then both she and Stheno ended up at the top of a large dune with a pale desert stretching as far as the eye could see in every direction. Twinkling stars shined down from above, while Nyx still stood a few feet away, casually scanning the area.

"Too dry?" Nyx asked, mostly to herself as she placed her arms on her hips and frowned. "Too dry."

The scene swirled and dissolved, and Euryale fought to keep her balance in an ever-changing blur of color that surrounded her. Then, with a pop, she dropped into the seat of a large, high-backed chair made of cherry. Sprawled out in front of her on a table large enough to cover a small country was a feast composed of meats, cheeses, bread, and fruits. Candles on the table and braziers lining the walls provided illumination to the hall they were in, a hall that had countless tapestries and banners hanging from the arched ceiling and twice as many exits filled with fog.

Nyx, who sat across from Euryale, nodded approvingly. "Much better, wouldn't you agree? I'm feeling peckish, as it were." When Euryale said nothing, Nyx gave a quiet laugh. "You may answer, pet. I'm finished."

"Yes, this is better," she said.

Nyx motioned to the food. "Take what you like. I won't eat it all."

Stheno caught Euryale's eye, and the two hesitated, but Stheno acted first. She reached over and tore off a roasted turkey leg. Going by the juices coming from it, the thing tasted delicious. Going by the heavenly look in Stheno's eyes when she took a bite, the leg actually tasted divine. "Gods, this is good," she said after chewing and swallowing. She stopped and straightened, however, when a thought dawned on her. "What do we owe you for your hospitality?"

"Manners, gorgon," she replied, taking a sip of wine from a nearby goblet. "You owe me your manners." Nyx glared at Euryale. "And you still owe me your undying gratitude."

"Thank you," Euryale said. "I do owe you more than I can repay for being restored."

Nyx raised her goblet and nodded. "There, pet. Was that so hard? Perhaps if you'd done so before you'd left the first time, this wouldn't be your last meal."

Euryale sucked in a breath and felt herself shrink in the chair. But as quick as that feeling came, she pushed it away. Stheno was right. The feeling of being helpless and disregarded as anyone of note was not anything she wanted to bear any longer. "This will not be our last meal," Euryale said, voice strong and posture stronger.

Nyx tilted her head. "Are you challenging me?"

"No," Euryale said. "But heaping misery upon one's guests is hardly polite behavior."

"Guest?" Nyx repeated, sounding amused. "Is that what you are now? Here I thought you were trespassers. I seem to have forgotten I sent you an invitation."

"No, but we did bring you a gift."

Nyx leaned back in her chair and crossed her legs as she gently placed her hands in her lap. "Did you, now? It's not another dead gorgon, is it?"

"We brought conversation," Euryale replied.

"You think that interests me?"

The gorgon nodded. "I do," she said. "Power doesn't impress you, nor abilities, nor artifacts. You can create anything you want, but gracious company and stimulating talk are not things anyone can craft. They have to be given freely by others, lest they are nothing more than hollow gestures."

"And how much time, pet, do you plan on gracing me with this company and talk of yours? Your thoughts call to me, thoughts of a daughter you're desperate to save. What can you possibly do to entertain me while you long to be somewhere else?"

Euryale drew in a long, deep breath, knowing Nyx was right. Every second she sat there, she fought against every fiber of her being that screamed at her to get moving, to find the flower, and get back to Olympus. "I'll stay as long as you'll have me," Euryale said. "That would be the polite thing to do."

"It would be, wouldn't it?" Nyx said. "And if we find each other agreeable, who knows how many hours will stretch into how many days or even years. Eons, even. I will admit, gorgon, I'm curious if there's anything you could teach me. Skeptical, but curious, nevertheless. Perhaps we'll find uncharted waters given enough time. Why don't you start by telling me about yourself?"

"Where I'm from?"

Nyx chuckled, sounding almost embarrassed for the gorgon. "No, dear pet," she said. "I'm not interested in your biography. I know it already, even the parts you've yet to live. I want to know what you are, or perhaps a better way to phrase it is I want to know who you think you are."

"I'm afraid I don't follow."

Nyx sighed, dabbed her lips with a napkin, and placed her hands on the table. "This is going to be a tedious conversation if I have to explain every exchange," she said. "That hardly makes for a stimulating time, wouldn't you agree?"

"Agreed," Euryale replied as she coiled her tail beneath her. The gorgon didn't dare ask for further clarification as to what the goddess wanted. The subject had to be one of importance to Nyx, for why else would she ask about it? And at the same time, Nyx didn't want a rote answer, one given to anyone, anywhere. So what did that mean? What could a goddess as omnipotent as she, quite literally the eldest of all the gods, want from her that she could give?

"I'm someone desperately trying her best to save her daughter," Euryale said. When Nyx raised an eyebrow, ever so slightly, Euryale continued. "I'm someone who's had more than she ever wanted thrust upon her shoulders."

"And?"

Euryale hesitated. Nyx wanted more than the superficial. She wanted to go deeper than the Abyss. "I'm someone who's petrified of being what people think I am."

Nyx hummed a moment to herself before replying. "Interesting. What do you think others see you as?"

"A god," Euryale confessed.

"It's in your title, is it not? Goddess of Stone, I believe the honors were," Nyx said. "A goddess with a seat in Olympus, no less. That's hardly a title thrown to swine."

Euryale felt the sting of tears in her eyes, and she tried to laugh them away. There was no stopping where this conversation was headed. "What powers do words give, anyway?"

"Tremendous," Nyx replied, not missing a beat. "The words you listen to are robbing you of all your strength, for example."

"What do you mean?"

"Those awful words you torture yourself with, allow your mind to be forever preoccupied thinking about, have chained you far greater than adamantine links forged by Hephaestus himself." Nyx paused a moment and swirled the wine in her goblet. After she took another sip, she set it down and stared through Euryale's soul. "Tell me, pet, how did it feel when you cast those chains of doubt aside?"

"When?"

"You know when."

"When I acted without question?"

"When you acted in accordance with who you are," Nyx clarified. Euryale balked, and Nyx gave her a nudge. "You stood up to Hera, did you not? Challenged Typhon? Even when broken and defiled, you set yourself against Zeus. How did that feel, going from meek to unstoppable in the blink of an eye?"

"It felt good," Euryale said, the words rolling off her tongue with ease.

"Is that all? I would think stronger emotions would have been elicited."

"And frightening."

Nyx settled back in her chair, shifting once to get comfortable. "Frightening? How intriguing. Do tell."

"I don't want to fail."

"Fail taking power?" Nyx replied. "Not likely. Not if you set your heart to it, daughter of Phorcys, she who is blessed by Cronus and now called the Goddess of Stone."

"No, not fail at taking it. Fail at using it," Euryale clarified. "Fail at controlling it and watching those I love pay the price—or worse, not caring at all when they do."

"You have a fire in you, pet, a wonderful, glorious fire that has the power to shape the world around you, and despite having a heart of gold, you're convinced it's blacker than the wings I bear," Nyx said, much to the gorgon's surprise. "I have to wonder: why are you so certain you're destined for failure?"

"I don't know."

Anger flashed in Nyx's eyes, and the feathers on her wings ruffled. "That, pet, is not true."

Euryale dropped her gaze, toyed with her hands in her lap. The answer was there, skirting her conscious thoughts, but her mind wouldn't let it in. To do so, she knew, would be to entertain her worst fears.

"Take your time, pet," Nyx said, her voice soft and encouraging.

Memories of her father flashed through her mind. Some of them warmed her heart. Most did not. They weren't memories she hadn't known before, but they were memories that she realized, for the first time, had had a profoundly negative effect. And they were numerous.

"Power corrupts, makes people abuse and abandon those they shouldn't," she said. "I don't want to be someone like that. Someone who can never be content."

"Your sister craves power," Nyx pointed out. "Do you think she will abandon you?"

"That's not a fair question," Euryale said, recoiling.

"Why? Because it's not easy?" Nyx said, tilting her head and looking at the gorgon as if she were a curiosity she'd never seen before. "I thought we were getting to know one another, and we've come so far. I must say, I'm enjoying this heart-to-heart you're indulging me with."

"I..."

"Don't hold back, pet," Nyx coaxed. "That's not you. Yes or no. Will she abandon you for her own gain?"

"I would never," Stheno cut in, slamming a fist on to the table. "How dare you suggest such a thing."

Nyx drew back the corner of her mouth and arched an eyebrow. "Your sister has spoken, pet. Now I'm curious as to whether you'd rather avoid confrontation or be honest with someone who means a great deal to you?"

Euryale narrowed her eyes and glared, hating the predicament she was in. "Why do you care?"

"I'm genuinely interested to see which direction you'll take at the crossroads," she said. "There's no going back, whichever way you travel."

Euryale's eyes drifted to the side and lost their focus. Her mind blanked for who knew how long, but when she eventually snapped herself back into the moment, both Nyx and Stheno were staring at her, waiting for her reply. "She likes to think she wouldn't," she finally said. "But she would. Eventually. Everyone who craves power does, eventually."

CHAPTER INTERVIEW WITH A GODDESS

Stheno dropped her jaw, and she felt her heart split in two. "How could you say that?"

"I'm sorry," Euryale said, shaking her head and avoiding looking at her.

"Don't apologize, she set you up," Stheno said, pointing her finger at Nyx. "She's toying with you, with us, for her own sick, selfish—"

Nyx snapped her fingers, and thick braids of copper rope wrapped themselves around Stheno's wrists and neck and pinned her against her chair. "Shhhh," the goddess said, placing a finger against her lips. "Childish outbursts have no place at this table. You'll have your chance to speak, provided I needn't deal with your behavior again."

Stheno glared as her heart hammered away. Her claws dug into the armrests, and though she didn't say a thing, she entertained fantasy after fantasy of how it would feel to slice Nyx's face to ribbons.

"Before I get to your sister," Nyx said, looking back to Euryale. "Indulge me in one other question. What of your dark side? I want to know more about it."

"That's a big question," Euryale said, clearing her eyes. "I don't even know where to begin."

"It is," Nyx said, acknowledging the point with a nod. "I'll spare you the gauntlet, for now, pet, since you've been so forthcoming. I'd like to know who you're jealous of the most. Not the girls with pretty hair or anything of the like. That's too obvious. Who has what you so desperately want, that you'd cast aside all your morals to be like? There has to be someone out there, otherwise, you wouldn't have such a terrible fear of misusing powers gained."

"Who am I jealous of?" Euryale said, repeating the question for her own benefit.

Nyx, however, seemed to misunderstand. "You're not going to pretend you aren't, are you?"

Euryale laughed. "I'm jealous," she said. "By the Fates, am I ever jealous."

"Of?"

"Those who had parents who didn't treat them as an afterthought, and all those who don't have to struggle as much as I do. Those who live their lives in peace, whose houses are in order without the world trying to constantly tear them down. Those who have families that only know love and laughter."

Nyx smirked. "Such beings do not exist. You're jealous of shadows."

"Am I?" Euryale retorted.

"There are countless billions of souls who would swap places with you in an instant, goddess—to be free of the shackles of mortal life and able to provide the most basic sustenance for their children without having to devote a second thought."

"I never said I had it the worst."

"Even the kings and queens of the earth struggle, as do the gods," Nyx went on. "Achlys spares no one, and one day, neither will Cronus. No one is free of strife and sorrow. Why should you be any different?"

"What of you, then? Who threatens your life? Heaps worry and angst upon your head? No one, that's who. You, Nyx, will never know what it's like to be me. So, spare me your sermon."

Nyx leaned her head forward and made a steeple with her forefingers as she clasped her hands together and rested her chin upon it. "It seems, dear gorgon, we have come to uncharted waters, to my utmost delight."

"Which means what?"

"Which means, I'd like you to teach me," she said before nodding toward Stheno. "However, I have a minor conversation to finish with her first."

"Are you going to loosen these bindings, or is this going to be more lecture while I sit still?" Stheno said.

"You've behaved well enough, I think, to set you free," Nyx said. The goddess snapped her fingers, and the copper restraints fell away, leaving deep abrasions where they'd dug into Stheno's wrists and neck. "Now, if memory serves, you're insistent on your sister's worries being misplaced, are you not?"

"Quite."

"Oh, the games we play, even now," Nyx sighed with a knowing smile. "Tell me, is your sister right not to fulfill her total potential? To grow her abilities and rule far beyond what she could ever imagine?"

"Yes, she's wrong," Stheno said. "That's hardly a secret thought of mine."

"And why do you suppose she does that?"

"Because she doesn't understand that without spear, the quill is useless."

"I see," Nyx replied. She then drummed her fingertips on the table, her nails seeming to clack louder and louder against the surface with each repetition. After a few moments of neither speaking, she asked another question. "If I were to tell you I could easily make one of two things happen, Euryale on the throne or Cassandra made well, which would you pick?"

Stheno glared at the goddess. "I would never trade her daughter's life for her ruling the world."

"Oh, I know," Nyx said as she leaned forward. "Honestly, that question was simply a lead for the next."

"Which would be?"

Nyx flashed a devilish grin, and the twinkle of mischief shined in her eyes. "What if she weren't the one who overthrew Zeus, but you?"

"What do you mean?"

"Exactly what I said," Nyx replied. "That's a future I could make happen as easily as any other. The Olympians, even if they all stood together and were a thousand times stronger than they are now, could not abate my wrath should I set my face against them. You could rule, Stheno, if I desired such a thing—you, who understands that indeed the spear is needed as much as the quill."

Stheno felt her face blank, and as she tried to figure out whether or not Nyx was serious or if this were hypothetical, Euryale jumped in. "She can't," she said. "Cronus wants me on the throne."

"That's where you're wrong, dear pet," Nyx said, keeping her gaze on Stheno. "He merely likes the idea of a gorgon on the throne, and as you can see, there is more than one to choose from now."

Stheno set her jaw in response. It had to be a trick, all of it. Another trick by another deity having her fun with them. "I'm not going to dignify that with a response."

"Manners, gorgon, manners," Nyx said, raising a finger. "If not for your own sake, then for your sister's, or more importantly, Cassandra's."

Stheno pressed her lips together as her vipers drew back, longing to strike. Her spear, which lay at her feet, called to her, promising revenge with a simple throw. And at this range, she wouldn't miss. But that was wishful thinking, she knew. She had to be stronger. Had to be smarter, more powerful. She had to wield Chaos itself if she were going to be taken seriously by Nyx, and sadly, that was a day she hadn't reached yet. "I want my niece restored," she said evenly. "And I do not appreciate you suggesting otherwise."

Nyx chuckled before sipping her wine. "You try, pet, you try," she said. "I'll grant you that. But where Euryale keeps her jealously close to her heart, hidden from all, you, gorgon, wear it as plain as the vipers on your head. You've said it yourself. You're jealous of her strength. I believe your exact words were, 'This is so unfair. The Fates give you all this power, and you waste it.' Feel free to correct me if I misquoted you."

"That's not what I meant."

"Let's not let lies become us, pet."

Stheno stood, eyes narrowing, claws digging into the table, fighting every fiber of her being not to impale the goddess with the spear at her feet. "I'm. Not. Lying."

Nyx calmly dabbed her lips with her napkin before easing to her feet. "A wager, then, to put a cap on a—unique—conversation. You prove me wrong, and I'll deliver the flower to you myself, but should you—"

"Done."

Nyx cocked her head. "You don't want to hear the rest?"

"I don't need to," Stheno said. "I'm not afraid."

"And that is why Euryale's fear will be realized."

Stheno fell, catching herself on her hands and knees. A second later, her stomach emptied. When her world stopped spinning, she realized she'd nearly flattened out on a floor made from immaculately cut obsidian bricks in the middle of a long hall that seemed to stretch out to infinity in either direction.

A light fog blanketed the floor at ankle height, and both the smell and taste of copper hung in the air. Sconces made from wood and iron lined the walls, spaced at regular intervals of a couple of dozen yards, and an arched ceiling loomed over her by at least thirty feet.

The gorgon scowled as she pushed herself up and took to her feet, and then wiped her mouth with the back of her hand before trying to rid herself of the taste of bile with a spit.

"Hardly noble behavior, pet," Nyx said, coming up from behind. "It's no wonder you're hardly taken seriously."

"I'm serious enough to hold your attention," Stheno said. "And by all means, turn your back if you think I'm not."

Nyx chuckled, and as she walked on by, she reached out and played with the vipers on Stheno's head. "You hold my amusement, pet, nothing more," she said, presenting her back to the gorgon as she headed down the hall. After she got a few yards, she glanced over her shoulder and used a hand to bid her follow. "Are you coming? We have a flower to collect. Or are you going to stand there like a child and throw a temper tantrum?"

Stheno shook her head and rolled her eyes before starting forward. "I know what you're trying to do," she said. "I'm not stupid."

"And what am I trying to do?"

"Work me up, so I'll lose this wager of yours."

"I don't need to do anything but let you be you," Nyx replied.

The ground shifted beneath the gorgon's feet, and the hall they walked down dissolved, giving way to a forest full of bare trees clothed in gnarled, yellow bark. With every step they took, the wood groaned, and the twisted limbs bent back.

"Even the trees want nothing to do with you," Nyx remarked, motioning toward them. "Funny, isn't it?"

"Or maybe it's you they abhor," Stheno countered.

The Goddess of Night shrugged. "Perhaps. But unlike you, I won't let it bother me. I know my place in the world." Nyx paused and took in everything that surrounded the pair. "Did you know Ceto once walked this place?"

Stheno felt her body stiffen at the mention of her mother's name. She tried to keep a flat affect, but no doubt failed. "No, I didn't."

"She came here, not long after the three of you were born, trying to find the River of Chaos," Nyx went on, gesturing to someplace far off and unseen. "She traveled, desperately wanting to wash the stench of disgrace from her body as no amount of scrubbing could make her feel whole again; that's a stench your sister is all too familiar with, as of late, if I'm not mistaken."

Stheno's hands tightened at her sides. She'd never known much about her mother, only that she and Phorcys were her parents, both being primordial deities of the sea. Despite her lack of a relationship with her, what Nyx insinuated could not go unanswered. "Are you saying our father raped our mother?"

Nyx broke into deep, dark laughter, and once she calmed pity filled her eyes and a sickly sweet smile spread across her face. "No, pet," she said. "She peered into your future and was so ashamed at what she saw—a needy, utterly dependent daughter who'd never amount to anything worthwhile—she dove into Chaos, only to be torn apart by the unfathomable forces contained within."

"You lie."

Nyx's face lost any trace of levity, and she cocked her head. "I have no reason to lie. I'm not the one who can't face the truth. You are."

For the first time since she could remember, Stheno felt tears sting her eyes. "I'm going to kill you," she said, quickly turning that sorrow into anger.

"Promises, promises," Nyx said, walking off.

Stheno wiped her eyes and charged. Three strides into her run, the world rippled around her, and she found herself in a massive circular library. Shelves stretched for what had to be miles in the air all around, each one crammed with scrolls and heavy leather-bound tomes. Dark shades, numbering in the hundreds, if not thousands, floated by, tending to the collection, while Nyx sat casually at a nearby oak table with her feet propped up on top.

"This library contains all that has been and will ever be written," Nyx said, making a sweeping gesture of the area. "Have a look around."

The sudden and unexpected change in scenery was more than enough to momentarily stop Stheno's attack, though she still hated the goddess with every fiber of her being. "Everything ever written?"

"And to be written," Nyx said again. "Would you like to see what's to be said about your sister?"

Though the gorgon's muscles kept taut as she anticipated yet another trick, her curiosity couldn't be stopped. "I would," she said. "Where's the book?"

Nyx chuckled, taking far more amusement than Stheno would've ever wanted in her reply. "Book? No, sweet thing," she said. "Volumes. Volumes that will fill the ages, be studied and pored over until time itself is sick of existing."

"Enough theatrics. Where are they?"

Nyx flicked her index finger off to the side. Stheno turned to follow it. A bookcase as wide as the Aegean Sea and stretching farther into the air than she could tell stood twenty yards away, softly illuminated by magical white flames that neither gave off heat nor damaged any of the tomes or shelves they danced along.

"Those are not all hers," Stheno said, shaking her head.

"And why wouldn't they be?" Nyx asked. "She's the one who's loved out of the three of you, the one whose accomplishments will be sung through the generations, the one whose actions will make their eternal marks throughout history. Granted, Medusa has a touch of fame as well, but it's nothing compared to what Euryale will have."

Stheno clenched her jaw as she marched to the bookshelf. She grabbed a random tome. It happened to have a coral-blue leather case that was well worn and cracked near the corners. Her sister's name, Euryale, was the only word embossed across the front. The gorgon didn't think much of it when she paged through, other than noting that this book was indeed about her sister, detailing exploits she'd never heard of before. However, when she pulled more and more books, she quickly discovered that they, too, were focused on Euryale. Praised Euryale. Fawned over Euryale.

Stheno tossed the book she held to the side, the ninth one she'd pulled, and sneered. "And what of me?" she asked Nyx. "Where are the things written about what I've done? Or are you going to try and have me believe I'm given nothing."

"Oh, pet," the goddess replied, dropping her brow. "I wouldn't ever suggest such a thing. I believe you're in that one, third from the bottom on the left."

Stheno turned back around, and sure enough, where Nyx had mentioned, there was a tall, slim book illuminated by the same magical fires that danced on the bookshelf, only these flames glowed orange.

"Page fourteen," Nyx said as the gorgon plucked the book from its spot.

Stheno flipped through the pages, finding the section easily. But as she scanned the text, and then reread twice more, she found no mention of her name, only a brief sentence that referred to her. "Euryale," she said, reading aloud. "One of three gorgon sisters, was the daughter of Phorcys and Ceto." She paused when she noticed a tiny number one at the end of the sentence and then another at the bottom of the page. "Medusa and Stheno," she finished.

"You see?" Nyx said. "You're nothing more than a footnote. An afterthought. Barely worth mentioning."

The book fell from her hands, and Stheno snorted with disgust, disgust at Nyx for her actions and disgust at herself for letting the goddess dig under her skin. "It doesn't matter," she said, marching back to the table. "None of this is real."

Nyx stretched her arms upward, her face awash with delight, and then clasped her hands behind her head. Her inky black eyes locked on to Stheno, never blinking, and stayed focused for several uncomfortable moments before she finally spoke again. "Do you know why she fears you'll abandon her?"

"She said it herself," Stheno replied. "She's afraid of those who chase power at the expense of their family."

"That's half of it, yes," Nyx said with a nod. "And you insist that won't be you."

"It won't."

Nyx hummed, shifting in her seat and dropping her hands gently into her lap. "Indulge me in something," she said. "How does it feel to realize your own sister thinks you're that weak? I genuinely want to know."

Stheno felt her blood warm, and though she inadvertently clenched a fist, she regained control and forced herself to relax. Nyx would not get the better of her, especially when her lines of attack were so blatant. "She doesn't," Stheno said, glaring. "Stop trying to cause trouble."

"It was a basic observation, nothing more," Nyx said with a smirk. "She thinks your ego is so delicate it must always prove itself."

"You're wrong."

"Oh, I'm afraid I'm quite right on that," Nyx replied. "As is she. Why else would you continually try and pick a fight with Achlys? Or me, for that matter. As if a paltry little thing like you could cause me any worry."

"Quiet."

"I imagine had any of my children been as fragile as you are, I'd want nothing to do with them either. Do you suppose that's why your father abandoned you as well, wishing to the Fates he could forget that you were even born?"

"I said, quiet!"

Nyx ruffled the feathers to her raven wings before reaching across the table and stroking the side of Stheno's face. "You have very pretty eyes, pet," she said. "But they're far too easy to read. You want to show the world you're not to be ignored, that your life matters."

Stheno heaved the table sideways and lunged, stopping only when her face was a hair's breadth away from the goddess's. "Everyone's life should matter!"

Nyx didn't even bat an eye. "Should matter and does matter are entirely different things."

Stheno ran her tongue across her ever-sharpening fangs, dying to sink them into Nyx's creamy neck and to drive her claws straight through her gut. How she'd love to see the life fade from that condescending goddess's eyes and revel in the shock that would splay across her face as she drew her final breaths.

"But you can't, can you?" Nyx said, stroking the side of the gorgon's face once more.

Stheno snarled and took a swipe at her arm, but all she managed to cut through was the thick air around.

Nyx, who'd shifted away a few feet in the blink of an eye, laughed. "You try, pet. You try," she said. "But you'll never, ever be enough. That's why she'll be written about, and you will not."

"After we save Cassandra and topple Zeus, the world will bow before us," Stheno snarled. "I look forward to the day when you walk down my hall and beg a favor from me, and then you'll see who's remembered."

"I have entertained your juvenile manners long enough," she said as she made a slow approach. "I will not tolerate them any longer."

"And I've played your games long enough," Stheno retorted. "Give me the flower. That was the deal."

"If that's what you want," Nyx said with a shrug. The goddess snapped her fingers, and everything disappeared in a torrent of rain and wind. A large room in the shape of a perfect triangle spanning fifty yards across sprang into existence with Stheno and Nyx standing in the middle of its cobblestone floor.

Set in the middle of the wall on the left was an open archway that gave way to a small room. An oak pedestal stood in the center on a platform made of white marble, and floating a few inches above, a delicate flower with long, oval, black-and-white petals hung in the air. The wall to the right held a similar archway, only the room it led into housed a simple well made of rough stone.

"Is that hemalander?" Stheno asked, scarcely believing what her eyes took in from the first room.

"It is."

The gorgon started for it, but before she took more than a single step, Nyx struck her across the chest with the shaft of her very own spear. "Something you should know, pet, before you take it."

Stheno narrowed her eyes and snatched her weapon back from the goddess. "And that is?"

"There are ways you can alter the course of the future, be remembered and revered."

"And those ways would be?"

Nyx gave a knowing smile before replying. "Waters of Chaos are trapped in that well," she said, nodding to the room on the right. "Waters that can imbue your spear with powers that will rival any other borne by the gods. If you wanted the throne of Olympus, that would certainly grant it to you."

"But?"

An hourglass, half a foot in size, appeared in Nyx's hand. She flipped it over before setting it on a small marble table that had materialized next to her. The blue sand in the upper bulb flowed through the narrow neck, forming a small pile at the bottom.

"I'm sure you can figure that part out," Nyx said.

Stheno stood still for a moment, her mind reeling as she not only weighed her options, but desperately tried to understand where the trap had been placed. She didn't believe for one second that Nyx was going to give her either the plant she so desperately sought or the abilities she craved to be respected and feared by all.

"What's it going to be?" she asked. "Time is fleeting, and the only one that will stop you from having either is you. So, would you rather have a cure or respect? Salvation or importance?"

One...only one. That wasn't a hard choice to make. No matter what, Euryale was her sister whom she loved dearly, even if she wasted the opportunities the Fates gave her—actions which drove her insane. With the hemalander in hand, they could then focus on what else needed to be done once Cassandra was healed: namely, toppling the Olympians.

But the blue sand flowed slowly. She could dart across the room they were in at least five times before it ran out. Maybe even ten. Was Nyx counting on her indecision? Or just thought that little of her that the goddess figured she couldn't do both?

"I wonder what Euryale will say when she learns you failed at grabbing either," Nyx mused. "Or Zeus, for that matter, though he probably won't care all that much when he takes a liking to your pretty face. I hear he's on a quest for redheads."

Stheno's mouth twisted into a snarl as she made a mad dash for the well. Halfway to the door, she had the presence of mind to glance over her shoulder and check the hourglass. The sand kept falling, but as she'd predicted, the upper bulb had a long way to go before being empty.

Through the archway she raced. She reached the well with such speed, she couldn't stop in time and ended up having to leap over the top. Her feet touched the floor a second later, at which point she pivoted and looked at the sands again.

Not even a quarter finished. Plenty of time.

"I'll show you," she muttered to herself, taking a look down the well. Rough stone formed the inner walls, and far below, she could see still, dark water. There was no rope or bucket anywhere nearby, but that didn't matter. It couldn't have been more than seven or eight feet down.

Stheno flattened herself on top of the wall and lowered her spear. The tip came close to dipping in the water, but not quite. The gorgon, undaunted, huffed, and let her grip slip a few inches. The weapon slid downward, and this time, the adamantine tip pierced the surface.

The water bubbled, and wisps of acrid smoke floated into the air. Hairs rose on her arm as warmth spread up the limb and across her chest. The gorgon's eyes rolled up in her head as euphoria took over. The world awaited her command. The very fabric of creation would yield to her every desire.

The sensation, however, faded. Her eyes shot open, and while the tip of the spear remained in the water, glowing a fiery red, the bubbling had stopped. A heartbeat later, the light emanating from the point dimmed.

"No," Stheno grunted. "Not yet."

She lifted herself up and craned her head back the way she'd come, praying she had time to submerge the weapon further and absorb more of the energy contained within the well. Half of the sand remained. She'd try once more, a few seconds at most, before she'd run for the flower.

"Five seconds," she promised herself, flattening against the top once more. She stretched her arm, painfully so, but she couldn't get more than an extra inch. Again, the waters bubbled, but that didn't last.

The gorgon set her jaw with determination and quickly slid off the side, using her free hand to catch the lip and keep her from falling. The weapon sank another foot and a half, maybe even two.

Gouts of steam shot from the surface as the water turned to a rolling boil. Muscles in her body twitched as energy raced through them. Her grip above tightened, instantly crushing the portion of rock she held onto, and she was certain her strength now rivaled Ares, possibly Zeus's. Her senses heightened like never before. She could hear the expansion of Nyx's lungs as she drew a breath, and her eyes took in colors more vivid than she'd ever dreamed. She could feel the individual grains of wood on the shaft of her spear, and in the air, she could pick out a thousand thousand different tastes.

Stheno held her breath, images of all the wrongs she'd right flooding her mind. She'd chain Zeus like a dog at the foot of her throne and grind anyone foolish enough to come to his defense into kibble. She'd carve her name into the sky for all to see, and not a soul would dare set themselves against her or her sister.

Her eyes snapped open as panic struck her chest. "No," she whispered, scrambling up and out of the well. "No. No. No."

The final grains in the upper lobe slipped through the hourglass's neck right as the gorgon ended up in a low crouch. But they hadn't fallen all the way yet.

"No!" Stheno screaming, shooting forward faster than her heart could plummet.

Her legs pumped feverishly, taking strides she never thought possible. She covered half the ground between her and the archway in the blink of an eye, but it wasn't enough. She had another ten yards to go when the last grain of sand fell. The moment it struck the pile inside the bottom lobe, the air beneath the arch turned to stone.

"NO!" Stheno cried, ramming into the wall as hard as she could. She stuck the barrier with her shoulder, sending chunks of stone and fine powder in all directions.

The gorgon ignored the blood flowing down her arm, took a few steps back, and rammed it once more. Though she produced similar results, she feared it wasn't enough, so when she stepped back a third time, she used her spear instead.

The adamantine point sank three feet into the rock with ease. The wall cracked and then split before chunks blasted everywhere. Despite the damage caused, more stone remained. And even more, and more, and more, when Stheno struck time and again.

"There's nothing there, pet," Nyx said after Stheno had carved a tunnel ten feet deep. "You had your chance. It's gone."

"No, it's not," Stheno said, clenching her jaw and hammering away. Her blows came faster and harder than before. The spear hummed with energy and exploding everything it touched with every strike. She didn't slow until she'd dug another half dozen feet and didn't stop until she doubled that.

"As I said, before," Nyx said. "It's gone."

Stheno screamed in frustration before pivoting on the balls of her feet and charging the goddess. With ten paces to go, she leaped into the air, using both of her hands to guide the spear, eager to drive it through the goddess's heart.

Nyx arched an eyebrow and casually raised her hand. The gorgon froze in midair, her face contorted in rage.

"Manners, pet. Manners," said Nyx.

"You tricked me!"

"I told you before, all I would do was let you be you," she said. "If you're going to blame anyone, blame yourself. Besides, trickery is only done by the desperate and uncouth. As you can see, I am neither."

Stheno's eyes burned with a vengeance like no other, and though she still couldn't move, she vowed she'd have Nyx's head the moment she could.

"Cheer up, pet," Nyx said. "You got what you wanted, after all. Isn't that the most important thing? Strength to topple Olympus? I'm sure your sister will understand."

"I hate you."

"I don't care," Nyx replied.

The goddess faded away, leaving Stheno paralyzed and hanging in the air, with nothing to keep her company but cold stone and her own thoughts.

Chapter At the Vault

Alex shared every bit of what happened to Euryale; at least, the parts he knew. There were a lot of questions Aphrodite and Ares had, questions he hadn't an inkling as to what the answers might be. But he knew the important parts: Cassandra was in dire straits, and Zeus's treachery was not one Euryale would ever forget—or him, for that matter. He left out his dealings with Hera. That portion was easy enough to omit.

"I don't know what to say," Aphrodite said after a long, uncomfortable silence. I can't believe he'd do that."

"Of course he did it," Alex said, clenching a fist. "You think I'd make that up?"

The rise in Alex's tone drew a snarl from Ares, but the goddess took his hand. "It's okay," she said to him before turning back to Alex. "I believe you. I do. I'm speechless, is all."

"All you have to say is you'll help," Alex said. "And all I need from you is to get in that vault."

"You don't know what you ask," Aphrodite said, shaking her head. "I want to help, but...What's in there that you need, anyway? Maybe we can find something else."

"I need that ax," Alex said.

"His ax. *The* ax," Aphrodite said, laughing in disbelief. "The most powerful artifact ever created? What makes you think I'll ever hand that to you."

"I only need its power to save Cassandra," Alex said. "By the River Styx, I have no intention of keeping it. I'm only trying to save my daughter."

Ares stiffened at the unexpected oath, and then he clamped a heavy hand on Alex's shoulder. "You have a noble reason for war, little Alex," he said. "Not that you ever need a reason, but it's good to have one nevertheless. But what makes you think this is a war you can win?"

"Athena and Artemis have pledged themselves to our cause," Alex said. "They both seem convinced others would join, especially if the two of you do as well."

"And how do you plan on winning?"

"I think if my wife can survive and enlist the help of Achlys, she'll be able to defeat Zeus," Alex said. "Especially if he's without that ax."

"Yes, the ax," the God of War said with an approving nod. "I could wield it."

"Does this mean we can count on your support?"

Ares was about to answer with a resounding yes when Aphrodite interrupted. "What happens after?"

Alex dropped his brow. "What do you mean?"

"I mean, who gets the throne?"

"Whoever has the ax gets the throne," Ares rightly pointed out. "And since both you and I went to war against Typhon, we should be the ones to rule. What other couple is there? Hades and Persephone? He has the underworld to take care of already."

Aphrodite soured her disfigured face, and Alex could tell she still felt conflicted. "True, but still..."

"Still, what?" asked Alex.

Aphrodite sighed heavily and shook her head. "It's not a betrayal, is it? From me, I mean, if I topple his reign."

"No, it's not," Alex reassured. "He has to answer for his crimes."

"Then why do I feel like it is?"

"Because all of this sucks," Alex said.

"It will suck less when we have the throne," Ares said, his face bright with anticipation. "Think of it, love. The wars we could wage together would be legendary, and our children's children could conquer the stars in our name."

Aphrodite leaned her head against her lover. "Hades and Poseidon will stand with him, though," she said. "I'm not sure anyone can stand against those three working in concert."

"I wouldn't be so certain, especially if Athena sets herself against them," Ares said. The God of War glanced to Alex. "Fear not, little Alex, we will honor your wife and her glorious sister, Stheno."

Aphrodite tensed at the gorgon's name but didn't speak anything of it. "First things first," she said, pulling away and smoothing out her chiton. "We need to get that ax."

"No time like the present," Alex said with no small amount of relief.

"Quite." Aphrodite rose on her tiptoes and kissed Ares on the cheek. "Go find Dad. Keep him busy for a while."

With that, Ares kissed her back and headed out the door. Aphrodite found a nearby mirror, fixed her hair, her chiton, her hair (again), and led Alex out of her estate.

It took longer than Alex would've thought to get to the vault, mostly on account of how cautious Aphrodite was in being sure they weren't seen by anyone. As nerve-wracking as she made that trip to be, his anxieties increased tenfold when they reached the entrance to the vault.

"You're sure you can open them?" asked Alex, his eyes focused on the double doors which towered above. They seemed every bit as imposing as Alex remembered them, and the air crackled with three times the energy.

"Yes," she said.

"You hesitated."

"Yes, I'm sure, Alex. Would you like to try in my stead?"

"No, but you haven't even stepped a single foot forward," he replied. "I found that curious, is all. Not trying to tell you how to do your job. Merely pointing out a tiny little observation."

Aphrodite ignored his comment. She lightly clapped her hands together several times while nodding to herself, as if she were trying to win an argument that only she was privy to. "Okay, I can do this," she finally said, rolling her shoulders back. "I can do this."

She didn't.

She stood there, unmoving, as if even the slightest wayward breath would cast her into oblivion.

Alex tilted his head. "Aphrodite? Are you okay?"

When she didn't answer, Alex eased around the goddess so he could face her directly. Her eyes, the only things about her that remained perfect in a mass of scars and missing features, stared out to infinity.

"Hey," he whispered. "What's going on?"

Aphrodite's gaze darted over to him, and she glared. The façade, however, fell in an instant. "Is she pretty?" she asked, voice trembling.

"Is who pretty?"

"Stheno."

"Oh...*Oh*," Alex stammered, feeling stupid.

Aphrodite laughed and shook her head. "That's a yes."

Alex didn't know what to say. Should he lie? Should he simply say no? It would certainly be the truth for many. Did she want her feelings spared? Or would patronizing her only make her more upset? All this flashed through his mind in a couple of heartbeats before he realized saying nothing would be the worst choice of them all. "She's pretty."

Aphrodite dropped her shoulders. "Tell me what she looks like."

"I don't—"

"Tell me!"

Alex twisted his mouth to the side and rubbed his chin, trying to find the words. He opted for the most sterile approach he could, figuring it would be the safest. "She has red snakes, not green like Euryale's. Stands a little shorter, too, with long nails and—"

He stopped when she shot him a displeasing look. "Not like that."

"Like how?"

"How does this see her," she said, tapping Alex square in the chest. "If you didn't have your wife, if you saw her for the very first time and knew nothing about her, tell me, Alex, how your heart would see her."

"She..." Alex's voice drifted away, and he cursed twice under his breath. Gods, how was he going to do this? It wasn't that he couldn't, but even with the history he had with Aphrodite, the last thing he wanted to do was cut her as deeply as this was going to. "She has a beauty that could send legions of men gladly to their deaths if they caught even a wisp of it."

Aphrodite swallowed and nodded. "Go on."

"Fiery red hair, or snakes if you will, cascades over slender shoulders that strike the perfect balance between power and grace," he said, closing his eyes and trying not to think about the consequences of what was being said. "Her eyes pierce a man's heart and make him forget to breathe, and her bronzed skin carries the aroma of countless nights spent making love."

"How does she walk?"

"Like she commands the world," Alex said without thought. "It wouldn't surprise me if one day that were true."

Alex stopped there, praying to the Fates he didn't have to go on. Aphrodite didn't make him, but when she spoke, he wished more than anything she had.

"And me?" she asked.

"Say again?" Alex said, even though he'd heard her perfectly.

"And. Me," she growled. "What do you see when you look at me?"

Alex inched back out of pure reflex and immediately regretted the action.

"Alex," she said, her voice intense and dominating. "If you don't tell me this instant what you see when you look at me, you will never—*ever*—get in this vault. Do you understand?"

Alex nodded. "I do."

"Then tell me."

"I see someone who paid the hefty price of war," he said, picking his words carefully. "I see someone who fought for those she once hated, who found strength she didn't know she had, who proved her doubters and naysayers wrong by her tenacity and bravery."

Aphrodite snorted. "But I'm not pretty."

"It's the in—"

"Don't you dare give me worthless platitudes," she snapped. "You know what I mean. You know it, and you still won't even say it. The very fact that you dance around how hideous I am only proves the truth to my words."

Alex nodded and sighed in resignation. "No," he finally said. "You're not pretty. Not like you were."

"Thank you for finally deciding to be honest." She then turned away and shooed a crippled hand at him. "You can stop gawking at me."

"Sorry," Alex said. "I wasn't trying to."

Aphrodite shook her head with a huff. Alex thought she was about to make her way to the vault doors when her whole body slumped. "I thought I was finally good enough and that I wouldn't care how scarred I was," she mourned. "You'd think I'd stop learning to delude myself by now."

Alex inched forward and carefully took her by the hand. Her skin felt leathery, and what bones remained in her stubby fingers seemed as if they'd crumble if he barely gave them a squeeze. Aphrodite stiffened at the unexpected contact, and he held his breath, expecting a rebuke or even a curse slung his way.

Neither came.

"This isn't you," he said, thumb gently massaging the back of her hand. "This is only a shell, a shell that will heal eventually, right?"

"I know, Alex," she replied. "That's my point. *I* am not good enough. Ares wants a shell. A pretty, sexy little shell to parade around."

"But he's been with you nonstop."

"Out of curiosity, nothing more," she said.

Alex shrugged. "Maybe you're wrong."

"I'm ugly, Alex," she spat. "I'm not stupid or blind. What the hell do you know what goes on between us anyway? Are you there in the bedroom? Have you written down all the things he once said to me and now no longer does? Did you even see the glint in his eyes when he talked about...about *her*?"

The fear and anger in Aphrodite's voice were palpable, and for the third time in this exchange, Alex was at a loss of words. He was beginning to think anything he said wouldn't solve a thing. And in truth, what could he say that would fix it all? Nothing.

He did notice, however, that she hadn't pulled away. Her hand still rested in his, despite the resentment etched in her face. "I'm sorry," he said, the void of silence finally getting to him.

"I don't want your pity."

"I know," he said. Cautiously and with as much care as he could manage, he pulled her hand. To his relief, and a little bit of shock as well, she inched forward. Alex slid his hands up her arms and across her shoulders—perhaps a little more sensually than he'd intended, but nothing came of it—and hugged her.

Aphrodite tensed before sinking into the embrace, resting her head against his chest. She trembled slightly, and then even more when he leaned his head on the top of hers. "I don't know what to do."

"Me either."

"That's not very hero-like of you, Alex," Aphrodite said with a pained laugh. "You need to work on that."

"No one's perfect. Not even me," he replied. He felt her relax some, and though he couldn't see her face, he imagined her smiling, too. As the room quieted and the moment stretched, he stood there with her in his arms and let her be.

Eventually, the goddess raised her head just enough so she could look in his eyes. "Is this real?" she asked him, voice barely a whisper.

"Is what real?"

"This," she said, not moving. "You being nice to me. Or are you using me to get what you want?"

"It's real."

"I don't understand that," she confessed, sinking back into his chest. "Everyone's always wanted something from me. Everyone."

"One day I hope you do."

Aphrodite found the sides of Alex's face with her hands, and the moment they did, she pressed her lips against his with unmatched fierceness and passion. An energy flowed from her into him that sent goosebumps racing across his skin and freezing his breath in his chest. Without thinking, Alex cupped her shoulders and squeezed, which in turn caused the goddess to press into him harder.

When they parted, she did so hesitantly and with a longing sigh. "I won't forget this," she said, before kissing him hard again. "Or that."

Alex, stupefied, didn't know what to say or do, even more so when the devastating weight of guilt crushed his soul. It had all happened so fast.

"I'll tell her," Aphrodite said, reading his mind like an open book.

"Say again?"

"I'll tell her," she repeated. "It'll clear that guilty conscience of yours." Alex tried to protest, feeling as if this was something he had to do, but she put a finger on his mouth.

"Shush," she said, now sounding like her old playful self again. "She'll listen. I promise. And if she ends up hating me, I don't care. It's not like she hasn't before."

"I still shouldn't have."

"We'll have to agree to disagree. Now come on, let's get into that vault," she said, starting toward the doors.

Alex ran his fingers over his head, fearing that this was the start of disaster. He hadn't planned on kissing her, and she kissed him, right? But he didn't exactly fight it off, either. Alex tossed the internal argument when he knew he had other things he had to focus on, namely getting inside the vault and getting that ax.

After a few quick steps, he caught up with Aphrodite and stood before the vault doors. She ran her hand across the purfled edges of gold and platinum before turning her attention to the handprint indentations on the side. After taking in one last breath and holding it a moment, she placed her palm on the print that was hers and spoke.

"*Phylathion gryallaros ionine myrmonia otephone.*"

Alex wasn't sure if anything was supposed to happen, but as wrinkles of worry formed across her brow, he had a feeling this wasn't going as planned.

Aphrodite shook her head and kept her palm pressed into the wall. "*Dadenor tygros thekate aryx tagamemnon.*"

Nothing.

The goddess blinked, pulled back, and cursed under her breath before trying again. Though she placed her hand in the same spot, this time it slipped a little, as she was no longer a perfect match. Aphrodite snarled at the realization and spoke all the words of power a second time. *"Phylathion gryallaros ionine myrmonia otephone. Dadenor tygros thekate aryx tagamemnon."*

Her tone was stronger, more confident, almost to the point of being brazen, but as before, the doors remained closed.

"Maybe he changed the password?" Alex offered. "Try adding a one at the end."

Aphrodite dropped her arms as what was left of her spirit plummeted. "That's not it," she said as she stared at her feet. "That's not it at all."

"Then?"

Aphrodite pressed her scarred lips into a tight line and held up her mutilated hand. "It doesn't fit, Alex."

"Right," he said. "I was kind of hoping you'd say something else."

The harshness in her face and voice faded away. "If only."

The ringing of an Olympi-phone ended the pity party. It rang with light, upbeat music that Alex realized was going to be stuck in his head for the next week. Aphrodite fumbled to pull it out of her chiton, and when she did, she ended up dropping it. It hit the marble steps with a quiet thud, ringing away, and the goddess scrambled to pick it up.

Her attempts weren't successful, thanks to her stubby, rigid fingers being unable to get a good grip on the device.

Alex dove for the phone, scooping it up, praying to the Fates she wouldn't be insulted, and pushing the answer button before slapping into her palm.

"I'm such a cripple," Aphrodite muttered before her face drained of color. Alex could see Zeus on the screen, ax resting across his shoulder. Aphrodite jumped in fright and mashed the screen, turning off her camera.

"Aphrodite?" his voice called out through the speaker. "What's wrong?"

"Nothing."

"Where are you?" he asked, sounding impatient. "And why is your camera off?"

"I don't want it on, that's why."

"You will turn that camera on right now, or Fates help me…"

Aphrodite's face flushed, and her nostrils flared. "No, I will not turn it on," she shot back. "I'm sick of people looking at me!"

"What are you talking about?"

"You know exactly what I'm talking about!" she spat. "I'm grotesque. I don't need you, or anyone else, giving me those looks. So, you can shut your damn mouth on this and deal with it, Dad, because I'm not turning this camera back on."

"Fine," Zeus said reluctantly, "but I expect you to be in the Great Hall at the top of the hour."

Aphrodite glanced to Alex, who could only shrug. "Why?" she asked. "What's happening?"

"Euryale has declared war on Olympus," he said.

Aphrodite's eyes went wide. "What?"

"She is in league with Cronus," he said, slowly and full of ire. "She's gone to Achlys for something terrible to wield against us all."

Aphrodite's jaw dropped. "This has to be a mistake," she said. "Why would she do that?"

"This is no mistake!" he roared with such intensity that Alex jumped back a couple of feet. "She sent a letter! She signed it! She's out to burn the city to the ground!"

Aphrodite glanced to Alex, who could only shake his head and mouth 'that's not true.' The goddess snarled. "I knew it," she spat. "That lying bitch. I knew it!"

"Knew what?"

"I took her to Nyx," she explained. "She said there would be a price for bringing Euryale back, but I swear, she never said it would be anything like this. I was trying to stop Typhon. You know I'd never, *ever*, do anything to threaten our home."

Zeus growled, sounding like a legion of thoroughly pissed off dragons. "I know," he said. "An unfortunate, but honest, mistake."

Aphrodite exhaled. "What now?"

"You meet us in the Great Hall so we can hunt the gorgon down swiftly," Zeus replied. "And needless to say, if you cross paths with her husband, Alex, I want him in chains the second you see him."

"He'll be lucky if that's all I put him in," she said with a snort. "I'm sure he has something to do with all of this, too."

"Likely," Zeus said, "but we'll see."

"And Aison?"

"The same," he said. "We'll give them a chance to prove their innocence."

"Fine." Then thankfully for the sake of Alex's sanity, Aphrodite shot Alex a reassuring look.

"What about Athena?" Aphrodite asked. "What's she said after all of this? Euryale is, after all, her pet project."

"Your sister is...indisposed at the moment."

Aphrodite cocked her head. "Indisposed?"

"Yes. For her own good."

All went quiet for a few beats. "Good," Aphrodite huffed. "I wouldn't be like this if it weren't for her anyway."

Zeus chuckled. "Thought you might see it that way. Now do what you need to do to be presentable and join us."

The call ended, and Alex blew out a huge puff of air. He ran his fingers over his head before balling both of them into fists. "Great," he said. "He's got the ax already."

"Alex—"

"I mean, damn it to hell and back," he went on. "How am I supposed to get it now?"

"Alex!" she barked. Once she had his undivided attention, she spoke more softly, but no less commanding. "Is it true? Is Euryale looking to raze Olympus?"

"No, of course not."

"Don't lie to me, Alex."

"I'm not," he said, throwing his hands up. "She's only after Zeus, I swear."

Aphrodite raised what used to be her eyebrows and threw him a skeptical look.

"She's not," Alex said. He then quickly amended. "Okay, correction, but it's still the same point. She's hellbent on destroying Zeus and anyone who stands with him. But Aphrodite, on the souls of my children, she's not after you or anyone else who helps us. I'm not lying about that, and I'm not lying about Athena and Artemis pledging themselves to her cause, either. They've had it with him."

Aphrodite spent a moment mulling to herself before she started back down the stairs. "Well, come on," she said, glancing over her shoulder. "You've got a goddess to find."

"Athena?"

"The same."

"Where is she?"

"I've got a good idea where Dad is keeping her," she said. "But you'll have to go alone. And for Fates' sake, don't you dare get caught. Dad will do far, far more than put you in chains if he finds you there."

"If he only knew the half of it," Alex muttered.

"Knew half of what?"

Alex shook his head. "Nothing," he lied. "I only meant that this situation is a total mess."

"It's only getting started, Alex," she said, picking up the pace. "It's only getting started."

CHAPTER THE FINAL COUNCIL

A somber mood filled the Great Hall as nine Olympians gathered in a half circle, with Zeus standing in front of them all.

Of the eleven seats in the throne room, Hephaestus's and Hera's having been already removed, ten stood intact. Euryale's throne of stone lay spit in two. A recent casualty of Zeus's thunderous speech.

Artemis listened quietly as her father heaped curse upon curse, vow after vow, all the while trying to judge who truly sided with Zeus and against the gorgon, and who was only playing along out of necessity. Sadly, to the latter, she suspected she was the only one in that circle. Maybe Aphrodite and Ares, but as she hadn't had the opportunity to talk to either in private yet, she wasn't about to stake her life on it.

Still, there were ways, she knew, she could draw out the allegiance of others. Ways her father wouldn't pick up on if she were subtle enough. So, when there was a distinct lull in what was going on, and no one else dared question any of it, Artemis seized the moment.

"Are you sure she's traveling to Chaos?" she asked.

"I'm sure," Zeus harshly replied. "You think Apollo doesn't know how to scry or I'd lie about such things?"

Artemis, having expected him to be critical at anything that might cast a shadow on what he'd said, didn't bat an eye. "I think the future is hard to see, Father," she said. "Even for Apollo. And even if that was her intention before, is it now? And most important of all, are we certain she hasn't already gone there?"

Zeus grumbled, and while it looked at first as if he were going to argue against her, not only did he not, but the sternness in his face softened ever so slightly. "We aren't," he admitted. "But we ignore Apollo's wisdom at our own peril. Yes, she could be merely going for a flower, but with Nyx and Achlys involved, they might have given her a way to tap into Chaos itself. If that's the case, she will spell our ruin once she returns. I see no reason not to hunt the gorgon down at the shores of Chaos immediately."

"Perhaps Athena would have a reason," Artemis said. "I suggest we consult her."

The tension in the air grew a hundredfold as the other gods shied away from her—and not without good reason. Zeus had made it clear that Athena was not part of this discussion (as he called it), and they'd be acting without her guidance. End of discussion.

"I thought I already spoke on such things," Zeus said, tiny sparks of lightning popping from the tips of his fingers.

"Given the stakes, given the importance of this hunt, perhaps we should reconsider," Artemis replied. "There's more that we need to take account of than an overly ambitious gorgon."

"Such as?"

"Such as Typhon," she said. "Such as Cronus. Such as Nyx and Achlys. Such as any other threat to Olympus we might not have yet considered. If we all chase Euryale, we leave this city defenseless."

"Chaos is not a land for the fainthearted," Zeus said. "None of you have been there and for a good cause. I tell you the truth, this is not a place I desire to go, but it is also not a place anyone should travel to alone. We must go. As many of us that are able. And when we find her, we destroy her before Chaos destroys us."

"Or we wait until she returns," Artemis calmly replied. "Or we trap her in any number of other places that are less dangerous, something Athena would be adept at planning."

"I told you, Athena—"

"I don't care what you said!" Artemis snapped. "You want us all to risk utter destruction by heading into Chaos? Then you better tell us why Athena isn't here to help with the planning. Because I, for one, have had enough of the secrets amongst us."

Zeus groaned and spun in frustration, which was precisely the reaction she'd hoped to draw out. In that brief moment when she had him distracted, she made eye contact with Aphrodite, crossed her arms over her chest, and rested her left pinky at a slightly crooked angle against her side.

It was a code the three sisters had developed a long, long time ago, mostly for fun, but it had had its uses in more serious times. Times such as these. It was a simple question the three had sworn to always answer honestly. And the question was this:

Are you with us?

"Athena has sided with Euryale, saying I was wrong to extract a confession from her in the manner that I did," Zeus growled as he came back around.

"Given the gorgon's intent, I'd count Euryale lucky that that's all that befell her," Poseidon tacked on.

"Agreed," Zeus replied with a curt nod. "As for my daughter, I have her locked away until we've finished the matter."

Aphrodite snorted and crossed her arms. "She needs to stay there. Part of the blame should lie with her."

Before the goddess finished, Artemis caught sight of Aphrodite's pinky, like her own, resting on her side, ever so crooked.

I'm with you.

With that reply, Artemis relaxed and backed off her objection. "That's regrettable," she said with a frown. "Then I have to admit, we have nothing left to do but hunt the gorgon down while we can. I can only pray to the Fates that after we do, Athena will come to her senses. Who shall go?"

"As I said, we all go, save Aphrodite and Ares," he said. "There is wisdom to your words, Artemis. The city should be defended, if for nothing more than defense against Typhon's spies."

"We should consider another matter Artemis brought up," Poseidon interjected.

Zeus dropped his brow and turned. "What would that be?"

"Nyx," he said. "If seven of us enter her domain, she will notice. More importantly, she won't tolerate such a blatant trespass. I fear the tempest she'll bring will be so swift and terrible, none of us will have a hope of surviving."

Zeus grumbled again as his fingers tapped on the handle to his double-bitted ax. "How many of us do you think she'd tolerate?"

Poseidon thought a moment, leaning against his trident with one hand and toying with his flowing gray beard with the other. "Two if we're lucky," he replied. "Three at the very most."

"Then you and I shall go," Zeus said with a short nod.

"I'll go as well," Artemis said, stepping forward. "You'll need me to track."

"No, you stay," he replied. "My brother is right. We try Nyx's patience enough with two of us treading on her realm."

"Father, please—"

"I said no, and I meant it," he snapped. He then drew in a deep breath and exhaled, his shoulders falling in the process. "My daughters have suffered enough due to my missteps. I'll not have you risk your very existence in such a reckless fashion."

"Without my company, how do you plan on tracking her?"

"We won't," Zeus replied. "Nor do we need to."

Artemis tilted her head. "We don't?"

"We don't," Zeus answered. He drew the corner of his mouth back and rested an index finger against his temple. "There is but one pass between Nyx's world and Chaos, and I know exactly where it is."

It felt like cheating.

Not that Alex hadn't already had lots of practice dodging one-eyed giants who couldn't see him. He had. And though he'd evaded capture by Polyphemus, stolen his mandrake, and escaped the cyclops's island intact, he never wanted to try that little stunt again. Blind one-eyed giants, as he'd quickly learned, even the old, decrepit ones, were still plenty strong, plenty fast, and plenty accurate when it came to slinging boulders.

The cloak Alex wore, still on loan to him from Artemis, felt like a godsend, no pun intended. Not only did it shield him from the cyclopes guards Zeus had roaming both in his estate and near the jail where Athena was likely being held, but it apparently did a fantastic job at dampening the sounds he made and hiding any scent he might leave lingering in the air.

Hence, slipping by the guards time after time ended up being simple, as long as Alex had the patience to move at the right time. And after learning a great deal of patience in dealing with Mister Lion a year ago, this was child's play.

Now he waited next to a stone cherub in Zeus's garden, his breathing slow and even, waiting for an opportunity to get through the door that led into the jail. Unfortunately for him, a pair of giants stood outside, giant clubs in giant hands. Worse, for the last twenty minutes, they hadn't said a word to each other, and they didn't look like they had any plans of being bored, distracted, or relieved of duty in the near future.

Alex was about to skirt around the building for the third time to see if he could find another way in when all that changed. The cyclops on the right cleared his throat and nodded to the wineskin that hung off his cohort's belt. "That ambrosia?"

The one on the left shied away a few inches. "What makes you think it's ambrosia?"

"Gar said you got some," he replied. "Said it was a little something extra from Dionysus."

The other cyclops soured his face and snarled, showing a mouth filled with broken yellow teeth. "Knew he couldn't keep his fat lips shut," he growled.

"What'd you do for it?"

The giant glanced around before dropping his voice to a whisper. "Got him a copy of Zeus's address book of mortals."

"What'd he want that for?"

"Wanted to look up a girl he saw Zeus flirting with the other week," he said. "Right before Hera caught him, that is."

"He's probably going to look up more than one," the first cyclops said with a snicker.

"Probably."

A few seconds passed between the two, and then the first one spoke again. "Can I have a sip?"

"No."

"Come on. A sip!"

"No," he said, harsher this time. "There's not a lot left, and trust me, if all you take is a sip, you're going to go crazy when you can't get more."

The first dropped his eyebrow. "You just want it for yourself."

"I do, but believe me, I'm sparing you on this one," he replied with a snort.

"Fine. Be that way."

Again, the two went quiet, but this time, not only was the tension between them palpable, but their argument also gave Alex an idea, one he'd need to capitalize on quickly if it was going to work.

Alex slipped from his hiding spot and quietly made his way to the two. As he drew within a few feet, he held his breath, and after making sure neither was looking directly at the other, he reached out and gently lifted the wineskin. Not enough to unhook it from the giant's belt, but enough that the shift in weight would be noticeable.

He was rewarded with the desired result immediately.

"Hey! Hands off!" Cyclops Number Two yelled, twisting and stepping back.

Cyclops Number One, predictably, looked at his partner like he'd been stricken mad. "What in Hades's name are you talking about?"

"You know exactly what I'm talking about," said Number Two.

"You're a loon."

Number Two looked like he was about to say something else when the clear signs of doubt overcame him. Alex could practically hear the giant's thoughts, wondering if maybe he'd imagined it all.

That was something Alex could fix.

The guard settled back down and eyed his partner a couple of times over the next few minutes. Once he seemed satisfied, or at least, not as paranoid, Alex lifted the wineskin again.

Number Two spun around once more, this time with his club ready to swing. "I'm going to knock your bloody head right off if you try that one more time."

"Look here, you stupid sod—"

"Sod? You calling me a sod?"

"You don't even know what a sod is!"

"I don't care what it is. I'm not warning you again. You even think about my ambrosia from this point on, and I'm going to fump you right through that wall."

The argument died, and Alex nearly let a groan of frustration slip. Still, he told himself, they weren't but a hair away from going nuclear on each other. They only needed that final spark to set them off.

One. Last. Spark.

Alex raised the wineskin a half inch. Number Two's back-handed club was so disgustingly fast, it nearly took Alex's head, and that was with him even being ready for the swing. Surprisingly, Number One caught the strike with his own club before it could connect.

The resulting melee turned into a brutal contest of who-could-rip-whose-arms-off-first in a matter of seconds. Between the kicks, blows, curses, and gouges, Alex managed to pop the door open and slip inside without them noticing.

Alex trotted down the circular staircase, trying to strike a balance between getting away from the warring cyclopes and being wary about alerting anyone who might be down below. Three hundred yards of descent later, he'd run into no one and found himself in front of a small prison cell, currently being occupied by one Goddess of Wisdom.

"Athena," Alex said, removing the hood of his cloak and coming into view. "Thank the Fates you're in here."

Athena, shackled at the ankles and wrists, perked. "Alex? Where did you get that cloak?"

"Artemis," he said. "She let me borrow it to get to Hera."

Athena nodded, though it looked reluctant as she eyed him with suspicion. "How do I know it's you?"

"Who else would I be?"

"Dad, for starters," she said. "Wouldn't be the first time, right?"

"Yeah, well, would your dad change into me simply to free you?" Alex asked, trying the door. Sadly, it was locked. It even stayed locked when he tried jiggling it a few times.

"You were saying?"

"Right," he said with a hefty sigh. "Guess that was stupid of me, huh? How do I get you out?"

"First, tell me something only Alex would say," she said.

"Um...you don't know the difference between Monet and Manet?"

Athena rolled her eyes and huffed. "Something everyone else already doesn't know you said."

Alex, drumming his fingers on his chest, drew a blank. And the more he tried to come up with such a simple request, the more his brain didn't want to cooperate. Eventually, he tossed out the only thing that came to him. "Could I maybe say something Zeus wouldn't say?"

"Such as?"

"Zeus doesn't know how to satisfy women," he said.

Athena arched an eyebrow.

"And Hera deserves better," he said. When Athena cocked her head, he threw in one last thing. "And he has a tiny penis."

Athena burst into laughter. "Okay, Alex. You can get me out now."

"I'd love to, but how?"

"Dad will have the key on him, I'm sure," she said. "Which means I hope you're a good pickpocket, because I don't think you'll get Hermes to help on that one."

"That's probably not happening anytime soon," Alex replied, shaking his head. "He's getting ready to leave and hunt Euryale down, and he's dying to put me in chains, too."

"Why? What's going on?"

Alex summed up his meeting with Aphrodite, including the phone call he'd overheard at the tail end of it over the next few minutes. When he finished, Athena looked exactly how he felt: at wit's end.

"You've got to go warn your wife," Athena said.

"I tried calling, like, twelve times," Alex said. "No answer."

"The phones won't reach into Nyx's world, and certainly not into Chaos," Athena replied. "Which is why you've got to go. Now."

"What about you?"

Athena put on a half grin and raised her arms as far as her chains would allow. "I've been here before," she said. "Recently, even. I'll be fine. Once you get that ax, you can cut me free."

"I need you to get it," Alex countered.

"No, you don't."

Alex laughed, but quickly caught himself, hoping he didn't sound mocking or argumentative. "Sorry, but we're talking about fighting your dad," he said. "I can't do that."

Athena shook her head. "You misunderstood me. I meant you don't have to fight him. At least, not alone. Euryale and Stheno will be there, and I'll put whatever wager you want that Artemis will join them on that trip. Between the three of you, perhaps you can set up some sort of ambush or trick that will rob him of it."

"That still doesn't seem like good odds," Alex admitted. "Better? Yes. Enough? Doubtful."

"Against my dad, I don't think you're going to find any odds are enough," she said. She straightened, and her subdued tone uplifted. "Do you want to know why I beat Ares time and again? It's not because I'm stronger than he is. I could never match his raw strength. I'm not even faster when you get right down to it. All I do is, I play to his weaknesses. I plan the battle before it starts, so it's already won by the time it matters, and most of all, I capitalize on surprise every chance I get."

"You're also a far better strategist than I'll ever be."

Athena smiled and nodded, conceding the point. "I am," she said. "But wishing for resources you can't get won't win the day. And right now, you've wasted enough time here. Go warn your wife and get that ax."

"Any chance you've got something I can borrow to help?"

"I do, in fact," Athena said. "Take my aegis. It's in my home, hanging in the study. It'll protect you from whatever Dad can possibly throw at you, like lightning."

"Okay, that sounds good."

"Also, tucked in a nearby chest, you'll find Hephaestus's net," she said. "You'll really, really want that."

"The one that's unbreakable?"

"The same. I went back to Mount Etna shortly after the Battle of Typhon and found it."

Alex felt hope take root in his soul. "That could come in handy," he said, rubbing his hands together and thinking back to how he'd once trapped Ares in it. "Really, really handy."

"Exactly," Athena said. "Tangle Dad in that, and you'll have no trouble getting the key, the ax, and me out of here."

"Then what?"

"Then I'll take the throne," she said. "We'll go from there."

Alex grimaced, something he immediately regretted as the reaction wasn't lost on her at all.

"Something the matter, Alex?"

"Everyone's going to want that ax and that throne," he said. "Aphrodite and Ares are expecting to claim it already, and I don't want to be caught in the middle of this power vacuum that's about to happen."

"Fair enough," she said. "I suggest, then, if you don't want to be at the epicenter, the first thing you do before anything else once you return is cut me free. I can deal with the others from that point."

Alex nervously bounced the top and bottom of his fists together in front of his chest for a few seconds before deciding the number of options he had were exactly one. "Right," he said. "Better get going. I'll be back soon."

Chapter A Choice

Euryale paced.

She'd long since given up waiting at the table, though she did try and sit until Stheno and Nyx returned for as long as she could bear. She'd passed the time nibbling on items here and there—the raspberries turning out to be her favorite, though the cheddar cheese was exceptional as well—and had even had a glass or five of wine. But as minutes turned to hours, and hours had to have turned to days or weeks even, Euryale tried easing her nerves by making slow circles of the dining hall.

Well past a thousand laps, with her imagination in overdrive at what was going on between Nyx and her sister, she finally dropped into her chair with a huff. She fell forward a moment later, her arms curled and head buried in the nook of her elbow.

"Apologies, pet, for keeping you waiting."

Euryale shot up as Nyx eased into the chair across from her. "Where's Stheno?"

"She's fine, I promise," the goddess said as she refilled her goblet. "A rude little thing, though, even when I gave her exactly what she wanted. Has she always been so impolite?"

A lump formed in Euryale's throat, one that she'd feared had been coming for a long time now. "She got what she wanted?"

"She did."

Silence fell between them, and Euryale felt her eyes go completely dry as she lost focus. Eventually, she snorted and laughed at herself for ever thinking otherwise. "Why do I even bother torturing myself?"

"Are you sad, pet?"

Euryale pressed her lips together into a fine line and spent a moment trying to decide how she should answer. "Why?" she finally asked. "Were you trying to hurt me?"

"Euryale, dear, do you think I'd need to go to such lengths if I wanted to cause you misery?" she replied. "All I did was take our conversation from the hypothetical to the actual. Now come, be honest, are you surprised she chose to empower herself rather than bring you back the flower you so desperately require?"

Euryale didn't need even a moment to answer. What surprised her, however, was that her reply was filled not with anger or hate, but pity. "No," she said, shaking her head. "I'm not surprised at all. I told you everyone is like that. Everyone."

"Including yourself."

"I'm not so foolish to think I'd be an exception," she said. "What makes me so special to think power wouldn't corrupt me given enough of it?"

"Hold on to that belief," Nyx said, smiling warmly. "It will serve you well and bring you riches you can't even begin to dream of. I promise."

"I don't care," Euryale said, trying not to choke up. "All I want is to save my daughter. So please, if you'd help me, I'll pay your price, whatever it is."

Nyx set her goblet aside, placed her elbows on the table as she leaned forward, and rested her chin on her hands. "Do you know why I find you so interesting?" she asked with a happy sigh.

"No," Euryale said.

Nyx cocked her head. "No?"

"I truly can't imagine that you do."

"Your honesty is so utterly refreshing," she said. "Those who dare come to my realm are filled with so much hubris, I want to gouge out my own eyes just looking at them. But you, my dear, sweet guest, genuinely don't know what you're capable of, and more importantly, you don't want to know, either."

"I don't know what to say."

"Then take my compliment and say nothing other than thank you."

Euryale bit on her lower lip, not sure what to make of what Nyx was saying. She wanted to argue with all that she'd said as she didn't believe a word of it, but at the same time, who was she to tell her she was wrong? In the end, she decided she needed to at least heed the goddess's request. "Thank you."

"Do you know what's really funny about you?" Nyx said, her face beaming as she cut herself a slice of bread and put some feta cheese on it. "I could offer you the entire world, and you'd refuse."

"Again, I don't know what to say, other than you're right. I don't want it."

"You're adorable. Simply adorable," Nyx replied. She took another sip of wine before leaning back in her chair. "Is there anything you'd like to talk about? I feel as if I've monopolized our time together."

Euryale wanted to say no, to end this encounter and find the flower, but she knew she couldn't. She'd promised Nyx conversation, a good one at that. Thus, she said the only thing that came to mind. "You'd mentioned earlier you wanted to know what it was like to be me."

"I did, didn't I?" Nyx said before nibbling on some cheese. "That might take us a while. Would you like to have that discussion here or somewhere else? I can always change the scenery."

"I'm fine with here."

"Are you sure? The stone might get boring after a few years," Nyx said while she gestured at the walls.

"I'm sure, but if you'd like a change of scenery for yourself, by all means, do so. We don't need to sit here on my account."

Nyx tapped her fingers on the table, and even though her eyes were still as black as a moonless night and as expressionless as those found on a shade long gone, Euryale sensed a storm brewing in them. "I'd like to adopt you, one day," she said. "What do you think of that?"

"I...I—"

"Have no idea what to say," Nyx cut in, laughing with a surprisingly light tone. "My children are all grown and talking with you has made me realize how much I miss raising little ones. And it's not as if we aren't related, albeit separated by a few generations."

Euryale's mind blanked, trying to wrap itself around what she was saying, and she felt her face do the same a moment later. "I don't deserve such honor," she finally said. "And I don't belong here."

"I said one day, not today," Nyx said. "When you're ready."

"What if I'm never ready?" she asked, more to herself than to Nyx. "I wasn't even ready to be in Olympus. Look what happened there. I'd surely disappoint you."

A few beats of silence formed between the two, and Euryale didn't know what to make of it. But as she was about to speak, to try and say something else for the topic at hand, Nyx pushed back her chair, took to her feet, and nodded her head to the side. "Follow me, if you would."

Euryale, flustered and hoping she hadn't committed some grave faux pas with the goddess, jumped up. "Is something wrong?"

"There are many things wrong, but none of them concern you right now," she said, starting to walk. "Now, come."

Euryale scrambled to get around the table and then joined Nyx at her side. They headed down a dimly lit hall that was filled with tension and a feeling of desperate wishes that could never come true. "Where are we going?"

"To gather something you want," Nyx said. "Or something you wish you didn't need, as the case may be."

"But our conversation?"

"Will wait, pet," Nyx said, smiling as she turned her face toward her. "I sincerely appreciate your willingness to entertain me, even at the cost of your family and sanity. But despite what stories and lies others tell of me out of fear and ignorance, I'm not without heart. Aphrodite will attest to that."

Euryale felt her mouth dry and her breath catch in her chest. Was Nyx bringing her to the flower she needed? She had to be, as Euryale couldn't possibly think what else the goddess would be referring to.

Nyx said nothing else until they'd traveled for what felt like miles, the route they traveled taking them down countless flights of stairs, through several hanging gardens, and even skirting along a path on the side of a steep mountain face with neither the top nor bottom in sight. Eventually, Nyx brought Euryale to a tall, heavy door made from ash, reinforced with bars of iron.

"Whatever is beyond this door you may take," she said, stepping to the side. "Some you may want. Some you may feel you need. And some will help you, while others may hinder you. Last, the door on the other side of the room will take you back to your chariot, where you are free to leave with my blessing."

"That's rather cryptic."

"I suspect once you enter, it will all be clear as a cloudless night sky," she replied. Nyx started back the way they'd come but soon stopped a few paces away. "Oh, Euryale," she said, turning to look over her shoulder. "One last thing."

"What would that be?"

"Do come again, when you can, and bring some more of that delightful discussion when you do. I'll be looking forward to it."

Euryale bowed graciously. "Of course. And thank you again for all that you've done."

Nyx had already disappeared by the time Euryale finished her sentence, leaving little more than a dark mist in her place that was rapidly fading away. Euryale wasn't sure if the goddess had heard her at the end. Probably. Most definitely. Euryale huffed and smirked at herself. Who was she kidding? Nyx probably knew everything that was going to transpire between the two before the gorgon was even born, being the mother to the Fates themselves and all.

The gorgon reached out and grabbed the handle on the door and gave it a turn. It took more effort than she'd anticipated, but after giving it an extra shove when it caught on a rough patch of stone floor, the door swung open with a loud groan.

Euryale stepped through the threshold and into a triangular room with another door set into the wall on the right. A long table stood near the center, and on it, a twilight-blue candle burned steadily, its flame flickering in the draft produced by Euryale's entrance. Next to the candle sat a couple of leather bags, one big enough to hold a chalice, the other big enough to hold a medicine ball or two.

Near the table, frozen in midair, was Stheno. Her body twisted to the side, arms held high and hands clutching a spear, clearly poised a moment before striking. Her vipers had their fangs bared, anxious to tear into a foe not there, while a mix of relief and utter shame marred her face.

"Thank the Moirae, you're here," Stheno said. She grimaced and then cursed a few times before sighing with disgust. "I still can't move."

Euryale slithered over as fast as her tail would carry her. "What happened?"

"Nyx happened," she spat. "What do you think?"

Euryale halted at Stheno's vehement reply, and everything that had transpired between Nyx and her came to the forefront of her mind.

"I don't have to ask, actually," Euryale said with sorrow. "Nyx told me. You took what you wanted and sacrificed my daughter to get it."

"That's not true," Stheno said, managing to shake her head.

"Then where's the flower?" Euryale asked, looking about. "Wasn't that the prize she offered you? A simple test you swore you'd pass?"

"It wasn't like that!"

"Then what was it like?" Euryale shouted, throwing her hands up in the air. She balled a fist and swatted the air before running both of her hands through her snakes and sighing. "You only had to do one little thing. Just one. That was it, and this all could've been over. The sad thing is, I wasn't surprised. I wasn't even mad when she told me, though maybe I should've been."

"Euryale, please listen," her sister said in soft tones. "It all happened so fast."

There was more to her speech after that, but Euryale didn't listen. For the sake of her own sanity, she tuned her out and instead focused on the items on the table again. There was something else there. Something she'd missed before. A folded card on heavy stock that stood a few inches away from the candle. It had a creamy texture with a beautiful watercolor of a raven in flight on the front.

The art alone would've caused Euryale to pick it up, but she also noticed a letter inside composed with elegant handwriting with sweeping curves and flowing lines.

The gorgon plucked the card from the table, still ignoring her sister, and looked inside. The letter read:

Nyx, Goddess of Night, First Born of all Creation, to my cherished Euryale, gracious bearer of conversation and humble Goddess of Stone. Below you will find a map to the flower you seek, as well as all pertinent instructions about gathering it. The bags on the table are handy little things, protecting whatever you desire during transport.

Your sister will remain where she is until the candle goes out, which will be in about ten thousand years, give or take a few decades. You're free to snuff the flame if you so choose.

- Nyx

P.S. Mind what dwells near Chaos, and whatever you do, don't touch the water.

Euryale turned the card over in her hands a few times before reading it again, after which, she looked at the map. Sure enough, Nyx had provided clear directions on how to get to the River of Chaos and presumably to the hemalander that grew there.

"Listen to me!" Stheno shouted, loud enough to grab the gorgon's attention.

"What?"

"I didn't choose power over your daughter," Stheno said, begging to be believed. "I thought I could take both. It was a mistake, I know. A dreadful, horrible mistake, but think if I'd succeeded, think of all we could've done."

"All you could've done, you mean."

"That's not fair," she said, sounding more angry than hurt. "You weren't there. You have no idea how simple it looked. Two rooms. One with the flower. One with a well. The two split by fifty paces. That was it. Fifty little paces."

Euryale folded her arms over her chest and ended up digging her claws into her side out of frustration. She wished she didn't have to hear any of it, because she knew it would only draw out her ire, her vengeance. But now she had a basic picture of what had taken place, and she couldn't ignore her need for details any longer. "Fifty paces? That's quite a way."

"Nyx set an hourglass," Stheno went on, snorting with disgust. "It had at least a minute to it. A minute! You're saying I didn't have reason to believe I couldn't run that far in a few seconds? There are men—MEN—who run that in five. I had plenty of time, but..." Stheno cut herself off as she turned her face to the heavens and groaned with frustration. "I was so close, Euryale. So close to finally becoming strong, ensuring that no one ever tormented us ever again, and saving Cassandra at the very same time."

"I don't care who torments us," Euryale said. "I'd suffer from here to eternity to save my daughter."

"I know you would," Stheno finally said, voice quiet. "I know. You've always wanted a family since you could first talk. For Fates' sake, you'd drive Medusa and me mad with your never-ending dreams of all the things you'd do with your daughter. The meals you'd make. The places you'd go. The stupid bedtime stories you'd tell her each night before kissing her on the head and sending her off to sleep."

"You're not helping your case," Euryale said.

"I'm sorry," Stheno laughed nervously. "I only meant that I know how important she is to you. But please, believe me, I did think about you in the few seconds I had to act. And what I ultimately realized was, what use is saving Cassandra if we can't keep her safe?"

"I told you—"

"I know, you'd suffer any torment to cure her," Stheno cut in. "But that still doesn't guarantee she'd have a life of freedom and joy, does it?"

Euryale shook her head as she started to gather everything up on the table, being sure to steer clear of the candle.

"You know I'm right!"

Euryale's tail rattled, and she had the urge to leave right then and there. But she wouldn't. Not before she had spoken her mind. "Tell me, then, Stheno," she said quietly. "Why did you run for the well first?"

"What do you mean?"

"You know exactly what I mean," Euryale said with disgust.

Stheno started to answer, but Euryale held up her hand and cut her off. "Don't bother," she said, heading for the exit. "I'm not interested in your excuses."

Chapter To Chaos

"You always had it easy."

Euryale whipped around, certain she'd heard her sister wrong. The look on Stheno's unyielding face, however, said the opposite. "I've had it easy? Me? Did the Fates strike you with madness?"

"You never once had to live up to Dad's expectations," Stheno said, not backing down in the least. "Never had to train incessantly to protect your siblings from all the enemies he'd made. Never had to heal in secret or spend countless sleepless nights terrified that if your sisters found out what stalked them each day, they'd bury themselves in a cave till the end of time. So yes, baby sister, you had it easy. You had it so damn easy. You can't even begin to understand what it's like to be me."

Euryale shook her head. "What are you talking about? Nothing ever came for us. Ever."

"Because I killed them first!" Stheno said, groaning with frustration. "While you and Medusa built pretend kingdoms and played with horses, where was I?"

"You played with us," Euryale said, slowly putting the memories together. "You were our loyal guard who always chased butterflies to far-off lands we couldn't see."

"Those weren't butterflies."

The pictures in Euryale's head of all those times were far too faded to grasp. On top of that, as they were thousands of years old, she couldn't be sure which were true and which were simply fanciful products of her imagination. She could picture Stheno standing post, never leaving the wall that encircled their play spot. She could picture her silhouette against the rising and setting sun, and sometimes against the moon, too, when Euryale would look out her window as she drifted off to sleep.

"Who?" she finally asked.

"Came after you?"

Euryale nodded.

Stheno laughed. "That candle will be gone long before I'm finished."

"Why didn't you tell us?"

"Because I wanted you to have a childhood I never had," Stheno said. "And I didn't want you to blame yourself for me watching over you."

"I wouldn't."

"Yes, you would," Stheno said, laughing again. "You've always blamed yourself. Do you remember when I came back from hunting and nearly lost an arm from a boar?"

Euryale shuddered as the image immediately flashed in her mind. It was one of the earliest memories she had of being truly scared. "It turned your arm to ribbons."

Stheno nodded. "You were convinced it was your fault because you'd borrowed my cloak and accidentally tore it when you used it as a makeshift swing."

"Oh, right."

"And it wasn't a boar I was fighting," she added. "It was a trio of wolves Gaia had sent against us after she and Dad had a falling out."

Stheno quieted for a moment, and Euryale didn't dare speak, as she knew her sister still had something else to say. She only needed the opportunity.

"I'm sorry I didn't go for the flower first," Stheno finally said. "All I've ever known is the duty to protect you, protect Medusa, and after I failed at both, I promised myself I wasn't ever going to let it happen again. After all, it's not as if anyone else ever cared about us. So, forgive me, please, for the choice I made. It was never as selfish as it might have seemed."

"I don't need you to protect me," Euryale said. "Not anymore."

"That's painfully obvious now," Stheno said. She forced a smile. "I guess that makes me the useless one of our little duo, doesn't it?"

Euryale wasn't sure what to say to that. Too much was going through her head.

Guilt. Sorrow. Pity. All of that weighed heavily on Euryale's shoulders. She felt remorseful at the fact that on some level, she thought she'd set her sister up for failure. As for the grief, she didn't need to scour the world to find the source of that, either. Euryale was about to lose her sister again, and quite possibly her daughter, too.

And pity? Euryale couldn't help but pity her.

Yet on top of it all, Euryale still wanted to leave. She wanted to take all of that hurt and betrayal Stheno had caused and use it to drive herself out of there so that she'd never have to see her again. Well, for a few eons, at least.

She wouldn't be able to hurt her again then, not any time soon.

But she couldn't. She couldn't leave Stheno to such a lonely fate, especially given all she'd recently confessed.

"I will not do this a second time," Euryale said slowly as she made her way back to the table. Her nails dug into her palms. The pain that stabbed through her hands became a welcome distraction from the misery that nearly overtook her. "Do you understand?"

"I understand."

"I mean it, Stheno," Euryale said. "If you sacrifice my children for your own gain, I'll bury you myself. I don't care how much of a grand picture you were looking at."

"I know," Stheno replied. "And I'll never put you in that position. I swear."

Euryale licked her fingers and pinched the candlewick. The flame disappeared in an instant with a hiss and a slight wisp of smoke. Stheno dropped at the same time, falling into a deep crouch but managing not to smack the unyielding floor.

"What now?" she tentatively asked.

"We head for Chaos, get the flower, go home. Same as it's always been."

Stheno nodded as her eyes nervously skirted everywhere in the room but where Euryale stood. "Can I get a hug?" she eventually asked. "If you're still not wanting to skin me alive, that is."

The gorgon wrapped her sister up in a tight embrace, lifting her off the ground.

"Ow!" Stheno said, laughing and feeling bones crack. "Ribs! Need the ribs!"

Euryale let her slip free but took Stheno's hands as soon as her feet graced the floor. "Thanks for watching over me."

"Thanks for not leaving me," she replied. She then glanced at the floor where her spear lay, lightly humming with energy. "You should take it."

Euryale shook her head. "No. You take it. It's yours."

"But—"

"I want you to have it," Euryale insisted.

"After all this?" she said, motioning to the room, dumbstruck. "Why?"

"Because in the end, you're still right," Euryale said. "There's enough out there that I want you to watch over me still."

———— ❧ ————

"Aw, come on. What's the worst that can happen?" Euryale teased.

The pair had halted a quarter mile from a narrow pass filled with shadows and flashes of light. On both sides of the pass, steep, jagged mountains stretched into thick clouds full of lightning. Rolling thunder filled the air, but coming from the pass ahead was a constant roar of what could only be the most enormous and frightening waterfall in existence.

"I'm quite certain I can't begin to come up with what's the worst that could happen," Stheno said with a nervous chuckle. "Are you sure this is the right place?"

Euryale took out the card and checked the map. "There's another way in off in that direction somewhere," the gorgon said, pointing to the side, "but this is definitely the route Nyx put down."

"Maybe we should give that place a look."

Euryale considered the suggestion but ultimately decided against it. "The horses are refusing to fly in this already," she said, gesturing at the low-lying clouds. "Who knows how long it will take for us to find that path. It's not like she drew this map to scale."

"Could be only a few hundred yards," Stheno said.

"Or a few thousand miles," Euryale said. "Or more."

Stheno groaned. "Fine. Let's go. I guess if Chaos starts tearing everything apart, the horses will go first."

"Exactly. It'll be easier than spearfishing in tide pools. You'll see."

One of the Akhal-Tekes turned his head back toward them, seemingly casting a glare at them both, before flicking his ears and snorting.

"Hush," Euryale said. "Don't be so dramatic. We'll be fine."

"Easy for you to say. You're not out in front," Stheno said as she bumped her with her hip.

Euryale stuck out her tongue before taking the reins and driving them forward. Despite her words, the gorgon second-guessed herself with every foot of ground they covered. What if Stheno was right? Maybe the other way was safer. Maybe it was closer, too, than she'd thought. What if something dreadful waited for them inside the pass?

There wasn't a lot of room to maneuver there, something the gorgon became acutely aware of as the chariot wheels had maybe a foot on either side once they'd entered. Her heartbeat quickened as one final thought dawned on her: Nyx had warned her about what dwelled in the area. That warning didn't come lightly.

Ahead, some forty or fifty yards, the air twisted and the ground rippled, as if reality couldn't make up its mind what it wanted to be. From the rocky floor rose an amorphous mass with a slick skin that pulsed and distorted for a few seconds before portions of it stretched into two distinct appendages, at which point it dragged its bulbous body toward them. A couple seconds after that, a fifth appendage grew, sporting a giant maw of jagged teeth.

"Fight or run?" Stheno asked, adjusting her grip on the spear.

Euryale glared at the approaching monster. Had it eyes, she'd have turned it to stone right then and there. Sadly, it didn't, and though petrification didn't seem an option, she wasn't about to turn tail, either, especially when she was so close to the flower.

"We're not running," she said. "I think it's time we see what this newly imbued spear of yours can do."

"If it does half of what it did back at Nyx's, get ready to pick your jaw up off the ground," Stheno replied as she nimbly vaulted over the front of the chariot, spear in hand.

Euryale watched her sister trot forward, spinning her weapon a few times in front of her, no doubt feeling its balance, while the creature ahead continued on. The closer the two drew, the faster and more eager it seemed to be to reach her, stretching its arms more and more.

When only a few paces separated the two, Stheno dropped into a slight crouch, her left leg bent and out in front, while her right trailed behind, ready to spring her forward or catch her backward, depending on what the situation called for.

"Come closer," Stheno said, amusement in her voice. "I won't bite...much."

Whether the creature could understand her, or even cared if it could, Euryale had no idea. Nor did it end up mattering.

Stheno lunged forward, driving the tip of her spear at the monster's head. It ducked and then ended up arching back to avoid a short slash she made a moment later. Its right arm slashed at Stheno's chest, doubling in length as it flew through the air.

Euryale's sister didn't go on the defensive. Instead, she launched herself over the attack, and as she came down, she stuck the spear right into the middle of the creature's body.

Like a boulder hitting water, the spear shot through the monster with ease, sending its body flying in all directions with a deafening clap filling the air. Once Stheno hit the ground, she immediately yanked her weapon free from the ground and readied herself to continue the fight if need be.

"Well, I guess that answers that," Euryale said after a slow whistle. "I don't think there's anything left of the thing."

Stheno grinned before noticing a fleck of goo on her shoulder. Her mouth curled with disgust as she flicked it off. "Ugh. You don't want to know how this smells."

Euryale recoiled, catching the tiniest whiff that reminded her of when a dead and bloated siren had washed up on her island shore long ago, and Medusa had had the bright idea of poking it with a stick hard enough for it to burst. "You're right," she said, covering her mouth. "I don't. Why don't you keep walking ahead? Way, way ahead."

"I'm old and can't walk for long," she replied as she trotted back to the chariot and climbed in. "But you're welcome to lead if you like."

"I'll pass, but thanks for the offer."

"Thought as much," Stheno replied. "Any idea what in the Fates that thing was?"

Euryale shook her head, but she took a stab at the question anyway. "No," she said. "But since we're nearing the literal source of all creation, I'd say another spawn of Chaos."

Stheno's mouth turned downward into a slight frown as creases of worry formed in her brow. "Let's hope any other spawns we encounter remain as weak."

"Agreed."

With that, Euryale snapped the reins, and off they went. The pass continued for what felt like miles upon miles, twisting and turning. The roar of water steadily built, drowning out all conversation unless the two yelled into each other's ears.

Eventually, the path split into three, and Euryale took the branch on the left in accordance with Nyx's map. From there, they rode on, following a dozen more branches—not to mention, dispatching a few more creatures—until the portion of the pass they were in suddenly opened up to a chasm wider than comprehension that was filled with deafening falls. Oceans' worth of water cascaded over a crest that was likely miles above the pair before plunging into a basin only Nyx knew the depths of somewhere down below.

Scalding mist billowed upward and filled the air with a smell that reminded Euryale of rotten cabbage. The deluge, like the clouds that had covered the mountains they'd come through, were rife with sheet lightning, setting the hairs on Euryale's skin on end, and for a few moments, all she could do was stand there and watch it in complete awe.

"What do you suppose is on the other side of that?" Stheno asked, sounding as completely overwhelmed as Euryale felt.

"Infinity."

"Yeah," Stheno said. "Yeah..." The gorgon grinned and bumped Euryale with her shoulder. "Too bad we can't harness that."

"I wonder how many have tried," Euryale said.

"What do you mean?"

"There are so many stories of so many gods and demigods—heroes, too, when you get down to it—that simply end abruptly," Euryale explained. "I wonder if any of them came here and never returned."

Stheno shuddered. "More than I'd care to know, I suspect."

"Exactly," Euryale said. "We should get moving."

Euryale checked the map one last time. Sadly, there wasn't a lot more to it, merely a cute little drawing of a flower next to where they were, circled, with a dash and the word "here" written nearby. To make matters more complicated, Euryale quickly realized that the path they were on not only skirted along the face of a cliff that dropped into oblivion, but the path narrowed so much, there wasn't a prayer that they could bring the chariot. If they were lucky, they could walk, but the gorgon had the dreadful feeling they'd be forced to scale the mountainside at some point.

"We should've brought rope," Stheno said. "I've got a feeling this isn't going to be anything like what we had to do back at Hera's place."

"No kidding," Euryale said, tucking away the note and sliding off the chariot. "I only hope it's not very far."

"Same."

The two carefully made their way down the ever-narrowing path. When it shrank to about three feet in width, Euryale's hands picked up an uncontrolled tremor. At two, her heart seemed to skip every third beat. And when the path tapered down to less than a foot, it was all she could do not to drop to her belly and scrape her way across, especially since the rock wall they were up against leaned out at a slight angle, threatening to push them off with every step.

"We really should've gotten you some rope," Stheno said, who thankfully had taken the lead. "Do you want to go back for the bridles?"

As much as Euryale would've killed for a tether to something, *anything*, the last thing she needed was to give up now. "No, if we did, I don't think I could work myself up to go through this again."

"When this is all over, you'll look back and laugh."

"Only if it's because I've finally had my nervous breakdown."

Stheno flashed a bright smile. "Still a laugh. That counts."

Her sister's joke put enough of a balm on her spirit that Euryale found pushing on a little more bearable, and it wasn't long after that when Stheno came to a full stop. She was pressed up against the rock, her back facing the roar of Chaos. The moment she halted, she glanced over her shoulder with an ecstatic look.

"I see it!" she said, beckoning Euryale close with a wave of her hand. "I actually see it!"

Thoughts of seeing her daughter alive, smiling, and most of all, free of sickness and the threat of death, spurred Euryale forward to such a degree that she nearly toppled both her and her sister off the cliff.

"Where? Please tell me it's right there."

Stheno ducked as much as the cliff would allow so Euryale could get a better view, and as she did, she grimaced. "Not exactly," she said, pointing.

Euryale followed her sister's finger. Far above, dozens and dozens of small caves could be seen in the mountainside—some no more than the size of the burrow of a badger or den of a fox, others looking as if they could swallow Leviathan with ease. On a ledge outside one of the larger ones, maybe a hundred feet up, grew a small flower with a long stem and slightly curled black-and-white petals.

"Thank the Moirae," Euryale said with a stress-relieving sigh. "Any idea how to get up there?"

"Climb?"

Euryale muttered a few curses before steeling herself for what she had to do. "I knew you were going to say that."

"Then why'd you ask?"

"Because I like to delude myself from time to time," she replied. "Now, let's go before I realize what I'm doing and drop dead in fright."

"You'll be fine. You'll see," Stheno encouraged. "Just don't look down. Or—"

A monstrous roar, one that drowned out even the rolling thunder from the falls, cut her off. Each one froze, eyes wide, and when a beast three times the size of a blue whale flew by, Euryale was sure she'd never see anyone ever again.

Chapter The Flower

Euryale and her sister flattened themselves against the cliff, each praying to the Fates that the monster would continue on its way.

Two sets of wings kept it aloft, much like those of a dragonfly, extending from its back with colorful cells throughout their entirety. At least two dozen pairs of long, thin legs curled underneath a hairy, segmented body, and two heads jutted from wide shoulders, each having a wolflike appearance, if one discounted the giant compound eyes, while a barbed tail trailed behind the thing and looked as if it could encircle all of Olympus with ease.

For a few tense moments, it flew by, seemingly uninterested in them both, trailing gale force winds in its wake. That changed when it made a wide circle out over the chaotic waters and headed straight for them.

"Go!" Euryale shouted, scrambling upward.

Stheno obeyed immediately, and the two raced up the cliff face, hands, feet, and tail using any scant purchase they could find with reckless abandon, desperate to reach one of the caves above.

Euryale reached the nearest cavern entrance first. The moment she dragged herself up and over the ledge, she twisted around, took her sister by the wrist, and pulled her up.

"Keep going!" Stheno yelled, pushing Euryale to the back of the cave.

The two flew from the entrance, avoiding being pulverized by only a fraction of a second when the monster slammed into the cliff. It furiously dug at the cliff with one of its feet before backing off slightly and dropping one head in front of the cavern mouth to take a look at its quarry.

"Petrify it!" Stheno shouted.

Her sister's orders, however, were unneeded, as Euryale was already hoping she'd be presented with the opportunity to do just such a thing. She met the creature's gaze with her own and felt her body warm. Her vision saturated with green as her curse built inside her soul, eager to be unleashed.

Her powers flew unabated, but to the gorgons' utter dismay, the creature only recoiled a few yards and briefly slung its head from side to side before howling like a banshee and going right back to digging.

"You can stop playing with it now," Stheno said. "Because I'm completely fine with you turning it to stone right this instant."

"I wish I could," Euryale replied, backing as much as she could before she hit solid rock. The cave they were in wasn't very deep, perhaps a couple of dozen yards, and though that was enough for the moment, it was clear it wouldn't be for much longer.

The creature suddenly switched appendages. Instead of a thick, clawed foot trying to get to them, a much slimmer leg with multiple joints and a mud-brown exoskeleton attacked.

Each gorgon dove sideways to avoid the strike. The foot buried itself two feet into the rock and sent chunks and dust flying before pulling back and trying twice more. Each strike found nothing but cavern wall, and on its third attempt, it lingered a little too long, and Stheno's panic had morphed into anger.

"Dig on this," she snarled, driving her spear into an exposed joint.

The head of the weapon sliced into the dark flesh with a violent hiss and a billowing of smoke. The monster shrieked and yanked back its limb so fast, Stheno barely kept a grip on her spear.

Euryale kept her focus on trying to find a way out, and with the newly carved chunks out of the back wall, it didn't take her but a moment to find an exit. A crack, half a hand in width, gave a view of empty space beyond.

"There's a tunnel here," she said, pulling on Stheno's shoulder and pointing to a crack. "Look!"

Stheno spun, and relief washed over her face. "Move. I can get us through."

Euryale jumped sideways as Stheno drove her spear into the rock. Her weapon hummed, and the broad head glowed fiercely before the wall exploded, revealing a low but passable tunnel.

"Thank the Fates," Euryale said, dashing for the exit.

"Or me," Stheno said as she followed right behind. They left the cave not a moment too soon. The creature stabbed at them both, pulverizing the area they'd been in not even a second before.

Initially, Euryale had simply darted through the tunnel, hunched over and trying not to strike her head on any of the rocky outcroppings. Once they'd gone several dozen yards and were relatively safe, however, she slowed to a stop after they hit a three-way branch.

"Thoughts?"

Stheno shrugged. "The one on the right goes up. At least that's the direction we want."

Euryale nodded in agreement. "Sounds good. Maybe our friend will have wandered off by the time we get out of here."

"You know, that might be something to consider," she said as they hurried through the tunnel once again.

"What?"

"Making him a friend."

Euryale laughed with disbelief and for far longer than she intended. "Are you serious?"

"Absolutely," she replied. "Imagine the look on Zeus's face when you come riding into battle on that."

"And I suppose you know how to tame it?"

Stheno shook her head but grinned at the same time. "No, but I know how to dream."

The wall shattered next to them as an armor-plated limb tore into the tunnel, missing Euryale's head by a few inches. It disappeared as fast as it had come, and both gorgons took off as fast as they could.

"Gods, that's a persistent thing," Stheno griped. "You'd think it'd learn after I stabbed it the first time."

"Or you only made it more determined," Euryale said.

They continued up the tunnel, the creature managing to burst through a couple more times before the passageway rose sharply. Euryale ended up having to use her claws to help find enough holds to keep herself moving. The rise lasted a couple of dozen yards, and when they reached the top, they found themselves in a cave wide enough to hold a small town. Small holes dotted the ceiling, each no bigger than a few feet across, and each showing nothing more than thunder clouds looming overhead. Though Euryale didn't care much for them, she did take note of a larger opening on the far side of the cave that overlooked Chaos.

"I'll see where we are," Euryale said. "Stay here."

"Are you sure? That thing could be right there, waiting to pluck you out."

"I know, but we need to get to that flower, and the only way to do that without blindly wandering the tunnels is to take a peek."

"Right. Be fast."

Euryale nodded and quietly slipped across the cavern floor, approaching the opening from the side. When she finally reached the entrance, she could only see the infinite waters of Chaos raging below.

"I think it's gone," she said after nearly a minute. She then cautiously leaned out. Above, nothing. When she looked below, however, her heart nearly burst from her chest with joy. The flower was there on a ledge, maybe eight feet beneath them.

"Stheno! It's here! I can practically touch it from where I'm at!"

Stheno hadn't a prayer of hearing her thanks to the constant roar of Chaos, but she clearly saw the look of elation on Euryale's face and sprinted toward her. About halfway through the cave, something grabbed her attention from above. Her head snapped up just in time to see the ceiling above her collapse.

Stheno dashed sideways, narrowly avoiding being crushed as the monster came crashing down. It caught itself on a dozen feet and shook its twin wolf heads for a split second before directing each one at one of the gorgon sisters.

"Run for the tunnel!" Euryale said, backing. But she didn't get far, as there was nowhere for her to go, save jumping out the small mouth of the cave. "I'll be fine."

Stheno kept her focus on the creature and brought her spear up. "I'm not leaving you."

The monster cut the conversation short as it whipped its tail at Euryale, forcing her to dive across the ground to avoid being impaled by its barb. At the same time, the creature twisted around and pounced on Stheno.

Like her sister, Stheno's reflexes kept her alive. Unlike her sister, however, the gorgon opted to take the fight to the creature instead of using a more defensive strategy. Her legs launched her forward with speed that surprised even her, and before the monster smashed its claws into the ground, Stheno had already darted between its limbs and used her spear to slash a deep wound across its flank.

A thick, tar-like substance spewed out of the thing, sizzling through every inch of rock it touched.

"Mind the blood!" Stheno yelled, spinning to avoid being scorched and stabbing the monster yet again.

The creature thrashed wildly before simply falling in a heap, trying to crush its tormentor. Stheno bolted out of the way with ease, but when it snapped its tail around, she never saw it coming. The blow struck her across the back of the head, sending her tumbling across the cavern floor in one direction and her spear scattering in the other.

Euryale bellowed and charged. With the monster's back to her, she easily reached it without trouble and launched herself up his side, clawing her way up the thick fur that covered its neck.

The monster snapped its head to the side and tried biting her, but she'd already climbed enough that it couldn't reach. It snarled and violently thrashed about, but the gorgon held on, even managed to climb a few feet more.

It may have been big, but it had nothing on Typhon.

The creature bucked and spun. When it stopped to see if its attempts at throwing Euryale were successful, the gorgon made her next move. She scrambled up one of the thing's faces, and before it could react, she stabbed it in the eye with a clawed hand.

A blood-curdling howl came from its mouths as it staggered sideways. More viscous, steaming goo burst from the wound. Most of it flew onto the walls and floor, but a fist-sized portion hit Euryale in the arm.

Euryale screamed as waves of agony shot through her. Flesh turned black and hardened. She instinctively let go, and when she hit the ground, she had the presence of mind to roll before the monster trampled her.

"Euryale, get up," her sister said. "We've got to go."

Euryale shook the pain off as best she could. Stheno's voice sounded far more panicked than she'd ever heard before, and when she regained her focus, she immediately saw why.

The monster, though it had staggered off a couple of dozen yards, was healing before their very eyes. New tissue quickly knitted the gaping wounds closed and reformed the eye Euryale had taken, and in a matter of seconds, the creature hadn't even the slightest hint of a scar upon it.

"We can't fight that," Euryale said, backing.

"No kidding," Stheno replied, following. She then shot a half grin and chuckled. "All the more reason we really need to make him our pet."

The creature dropped its heads and crouched. It drew back its lips into a pair of bloodthirsty snarls as rust-colored saliva dripped from its mouths.

"You run back to the tunnel, and I'll lead it away," Stheno whispered. "You can grab the flower when we're gone. I'll meet you back at the chariot."

Euryale shook her head. "You'll never make it."

"I will," she said.

Euryale shook her head again, knowing she was lying. It didn't matter what spear she carried or how much faster she'd become thanks to it, that thing that stood before them would need at least another Olympian to take down, if not two or three. Even then...

"Go. Now!" Stheno said, shoving her sister to the rear.

Euryale had yet to regain her balance when four arrows zipped through the air from above, two striking each head at the base of the skull. A split second later, a guttural cry filled the air, and Ares, God of War, flew out of the hole above them, spear held firmly overhead with both hands.

"How long can you last, foul beast?" Ares shouted as he drove his spear right through the creature's spine.

Three more arrows zipped in, two striking the monster in separate eyes, and the third blasting straight through its chest. The creature howled and stumbled under the onslaught of Artemis's arrows and Ares's relentless pounding. Though its scalding, sticky blood coated rock and god alike, Ares didn't seem to care. If anything, the smoke that rose from his skin only enraged the deity further.

"Yes!" Stheno cried, snapping out of her trance and rushing to rejoin the fight. By the time Euryale attacked as well, her sister had already scooped up her spear and was tearing into the monster's innards with repeated strikes of her spear.

"Ha! Look at you, gorgon!" Ares shouted, face beaming with pride. "Hacking away with all the vengeance of the Furies! I love it!"

Stheno didn't reply, verbally at least, but the smile that grew on her face went from ear to ear, and she struck harder and faster, spilling the tar-like blood by the gallon while staying clear of its burning effects.

Euryale, knowing the monster would heal in short order, was working on a way to hopefully finish the thing once and for all. She raced up the creature's side as it threw itself into the walls and whipped its tail through the air, desperate to fend off its attackers. When she reached its upper back where its wings attached, she shredded the webbing between the bones in each one.

"A potter from Athens fights stronger than you!" Ares laughed as he tore through one of the monster's snouts.

In response, the other head snapped at the god, managing to bite down on his legs and toss him through the air.

Ares hit the back wall with a thud. Though grievous wounds covered his legs, he wasn't slowed. Not in the least. At least, not until the damage he'd inflicted started to heal. The god skidded to a stop, eyes wide, and jaw dropped. "What insanity is this?"

"It can heal!" Euryale shouted, still tearing into the monster's wings. By now they were torn to ribbons, and while she feared it wouldn't be enough, she also knew she didn't have much time before they'd come back together as well. "Ares, I need you to toss him!"

"Toss him?"

"Out the cave!" she shouted, nodding at the entrance. "Into Chaos!"

"Yes! Into Chaos you go," he growled.

The God of War bolted forward, and within a few strides, he was back in the fray. Stheno kept cutting into the creature's legs, maiming each with a strike or two, and Artemis let loose arrow after arrow with deadly precision, taking eyes and striking vitals.

Though Stheno backed off when Ares took hold of the monster, grabbing it by one of its ruined legs, Euryale kept ravaging the wings, even when he started to drag it forward.

The creature shrieked and barked, all the while trying to fight off its assailants. And though its bones knitted and its tissue re-formed, it couldn't undo the damage faster than it came. Its body weakened and collapsed right as Ares reached the mouth of the cave.

"You'd best jump, gorgon," he said with a hearty laugh. "Lest you want to make Alex a widower."

Euryale took one last swipe with her claws at the wings, carving a two-foot gash in what was already nothing but tatters, and leaped off the monster's back right as Ares gave it a heave. He threw it with such force that even though it was too large for the exit, it flew out the mouth of the cave, taking a massive amount of rock along with it.

The gorgon raced to the exit in time to see the creature fall into the raging waters of Chaos. Other than a brief flash of light and a few extra strikes of lightning, nothing else happened once it disappeared.

"Is it gone?" Stheno asked as she leaned on her spear and caught her breath. "I mean, for good this time."

Euryale, still keeping watch, nodded after a few seconds. "It's gone."

"Smile, gorgon," Ares said, clapping her heartily on the back. "You're far too glum for such a decisive victory."

Chapter Botanical Extractions

Zeus pulled his chariot to a stop and eyed the narrow pass to Chaos. He'd only been here twice before, but the foreboding image of it that had burned into his mind thousands of years ago hadn't changed.

"Is something the matter?" asked Poseidon, standing at his side, trident gripped firmly in hand. "You've said little this entire trip."

"I fear we're about to cross a point of no return," Zeus admitted, eyes gazing out to infinity.

"In what way?"

"In that nothing will ever be the same," he said. "For reasons beyond my comprehension, not only has Achlys aided the gorgon but Nyx as well. Neither acts without purpose or measured steps."

Poseidon set his jaw and hummed to himself. "Agreed, but we've spoken on all of this already. This is the best choice we have."

Zeus drummed his fingers on the handle of his ax, smirking at himself. His brother's insight was far beyond such simple deflection. "Have I ruled unjustly?" he asked, eyes still staring far away.

"I think this is a test of your rule like no other you've faced," he said. "A wife in chains. A daughter in prison. An armorer petrified. Any king would have doubts, and it's only the one who would not doubt that would see his kingdom stripped away, for he would never find his faults and correct them."

"Then what faults do I have that led to this?"

Poseidon clapped his brother on the back of his shoulder. "Honestly, each of them are right to a certain degree," he said, much to Zeus's shock.

Despite his brother's sincerity and the fact that he had asked the question in the first place, fires of indignation lit his soul. "A certain degree?"

Poseidon nodded, not faltering or backing away. "Your affairs took their toll on your wife. There's no denying that," he said. "And all of us cast Hephaestus out of the city, and no matter how right that was, we were all fools to think that would snuff out his ambitions."

Zeus went to speak, but Poseidon held up his hand and continued. "None of that, however, means they were right in what they did," he said. "The same goes for Athena and Euryale. The gorgon had her chance to tell us what we needed to know, as you pointed out, and she paid the consequence. That, in turn, showed us her true character, her true loyalties."

"And you'd say Athena's as well?"

"Your daughter is young still, though she'd like to think otherwise," Poseidon said, shaking his head. "I suspect she feels guilty and indebted to the gorgon after what she suffered at the hands of Arachne and Typhon. No doubt, the encounter has left her second-guessing herself as well. What she needs is time."

The anger that had built in Zeus's heart faded as he mulled his brother's words. "And the gorgon?" he finally asked. "Does she need time as well?"

"Perhaps," Poseidon said. "But that might not be something she's able to be given any longer."

"What do you mean?"

"She declared war on Olympus and all who stand with you," he said. "Will you continue to give her a chance to repent right up until she takes your head from your shoulders?"

That was a question Zeus didn't have to think on for very long to answer. "No," he said, clenching a fist. "I won't. As you said, she had her chance, and if it's a war she wants, it's a war she'll get. Swift and terrible."

"Then we should set our trap while we still can."

"No."

"No?"

"Not here," Zeus said, driving the chariot forward. "I have a much better spot in mind."

The God of the Sea held fast and pointed at the entrance to the path with his trident. "An ambush favors us at this spot," he said. "You said so yourself back at Olympus."

"I know."

"Then..." Poseidon's voice trailed. "There's another way out of Chaos?"

Zeus nodded.

"You suspect another traitor?"

Zeus nodded again.

"Who?"

"That's what we're about to find out."

"How?" Euryale managed to get that out relatively quickly. But it wasn't until Artemis dropped from the ceiling and was halfway to the gorgon that she managed to get out the rest. "I mean...how? How did you find us?"

"Zeus found you," Artemis said. When Stheno's face went from shock to rage in the blink of an eye, she was quick to explain. "He and Apollo went scrying with the letter you sent. They know everything and turned Olympus against you—or rather, most of

Olympus. We're here to help, obviously, as are Athena and Aphrodite."

Euryale cursed before forcing herself to calm. She certainly knew her declaration of war wouldn't have led to anything else, but still, she hadn't dreamed he'd find her here in Chaos. She'd still been operating under the delusion that she could save her daughter before any of this came to a head. "Where is he?"

"Setting up an ambush for you at the start of the pass," she said. "He's with Poseidon."

"How exactly do you know all this?" Stheno asked, eyeing the goddess with suspicion.

"Zeus called a council telling everyone of your treachery shortly before he left," she explained. "Ares and I were supposed to stay behind. Obviously, we didn't."

Euryale's stomach knotted with worry, and her tail rattled with unease. "Where's Alex? Is he safe?"

"He's right—"

"Up here," Alex finished, looking down from the hole in the ceiling with spear and aegis in hand. He then dropped down as Artemis and Ares had, though much more winded than either of them had been.

"Sorry I'm late," he said. "Have you ever tried to keep up with an Olympian before in a foot race? In the mountains to Chaos no less?"

Euryale shot across the cave and pounced her husband, wrapping him in arms and tail, and smothering him with kisses until Stheno cleared her throat.

"Zeus?" she said. "Maybe we should get back to discussing that little dilemma."

"As I said, he's setting up an ambush at the entrance to the pass as we speak," Artemis said. "I can get us around that without him knowing, once you've gotten what you've risked so much to get."

Euryale slowly let go of Alex and motioned toward the mouth of the cave. "It's right out there," she said. "But that's only half of it. We still need a way to restore Cassandra."

"I've got that handled," Alex said.

"You got Hera to help?" Euryale said before wrapping him up once again and squeezing him tight. "What did she want?"

"Practically everything," Alex said with a snort. "But hey, I talked Ares down to paintball, remember? Trust me. I talked her down, too."

"What does she want, Alex?" Euryale pressed.

Alex sighed. "I can't say to anyone. It's part of the deal."

"Alex, she can't be trusted."

"I know," he replied. "But I have her oaths, and they're as binding as any others." Alex paused to glance over his wife's shoulder and looked to Ares, who was only somewhat paying attention to their conversation. Most of his attention was on Stheno, even if most of hers was not on him. "I promise it will work out in the end," he said.

Alex sighed heavily and slumped when she continued to give him a wary look. "Okay, I can probably be vague without the Moirae obliterating me. Let's just say a certain queen wants a certain king to feel emasculated when his prized possession ends up stolen and effectively destroyed, but not before its power is drained to say, help someone else," he said. "And a certain queen might want to raze someone else's house as well. And on a completely unrelated subject, how would you feel about living somewhere a little more tropical? I hear the Virgin Islands are nice."

Euryale sucked in a breath through clenched teeth. "Oh, this is going to get messy."

Alex frowned but said no more.

"How are we supposed to get that from him, anyway?"

Alex hitched a thumb. "I have Hephaestus's net back at the chariot. I was thinking we could ambush his ambush and take it."

"And then ruin it," Stheno said. Her face soured, and she turned to Euryale. "No, we can't do that. There has to be another way. Think of all we could do with a weapon that powerful."

"I don't care about that stupid thing. All I want is our daughter back."

"But—"

Euryale shot her a glare. "*We* don't need it."

"Alright, alright," Stheno said, laughing. "You're right. We don't *need* it. But at least let me be the one to destroy it. That's only fair."

"Why?"

"Because I want to gloat. Why else?"

"Consider your wish granted, then," Euryale said, smiling.

"Now that that's settled," Alex cut in. "Where's the flower?"

"Right over here," she said, leading him to the mouth of the cavern.

Alex laughed once he peered over the edge. "Damn. It is right here. That was easy."

"Says the husband who showed up at the end," Euryale teased. She then carefully started to make her descent. "Be right back."

"Watch yourself. That's a long way down."

"Believe me, I know," Euryale said. Though she still could feel her incessant fear of heights clawing at her soul, with Alex there, with a way to restore Cassandra in hand, it didn't feel as dreadful as it had before, and in no time, she reached the small ledge, taking care not to actually touch the plant, per Nyx's instructions.

"How about that?" she said, huffing with pride. "I did it."

"Never doubted you for a second."

Stheno appeared next to Alex and called down to her. "Mind the roots!"

Euryale nodded, though she'd already replayed Nyx's instructions a dozen times in her head. Petals were lethal. The stem was forever paralytic, and even the slightest damage to the roots would greatly hasten how fast it would wilt—which wasn't very long to begin with and was something that, if it happened in its entirety, would render the plant useless.

"I will. Give me a moment," Euryale said. When she crouched down for a better look and her hands grew a nervous twitch, she muttered under her breath. "Or twenty."

The gorgon took in a long, slow breath and thought of Cassandra, of her bright smile, her melodic laugh, all the dreams she'd shared with her, and all the dreams she had yet to realize. All of that steadied Euryale's nerves, and she began to carefully use a claw to scrape around the mountain soil.

The work proved tedious and slow. Though Euryale had tried to give as much of a wide berth to the root system as possible, the ledge was narrow, and the soil shallow. Time and again, she'd scrape away a few grains of dirt to find she'd almost nicked a root cap or split a hair. Each time, her heart skipped a beat.

Finally, after the Fates knew how long, Euryale eased back with a cautious smile on her face. "I think I got it," she said as she pulled one of the leather sacks that Nyx had given her off her waist. "Wish me luck."

"Good luck," Alex said. "And may the Force be with you."

Euryale paused and shot him an inquisitive look. "The what?"

Alex laughed and shook his head. "Never mind. Just a movie quote."

"Right, then here goes nothing," Euryale said, returning to the task at hand.

Carefully, she slipped the leather bag over the plant, being sure she didn't inadvertently brush any of it with her fingers. Once it was completely inside, she grasped the plant with the pouch and gently lifted it out of the soil.

The flower came free without protest, and then it was simply a turn right-side-up to get it all the way in.

"I did it," Euryale said, sinking against the wall and exhaling sharply. "I actually did it."

"Of course, you did," Stheno said. "Stop acting surprised and get up here."

Euryale was about to look for her first handhold when her eye caught the glint of something white near her tail. She squinted at first, unsure what it was, but when she drew near, her breath left her.

The tiniest sliver of a root remained in the soil, and when Euryale frantically opened the bag she carried, she could already see that one of the petals of the hemalander was turning brown.

Chapter An Inevitable Meeting

"Damn it!" Euryale cried, feeling her throat tighten. She fought off the tears and scrambled up the rock to rejoin the others. "I broke a tip!"

"That's bad?" asked Alex.

"That's bad," Stheno replied before directing her question to Euryale. "How long do we have?"

"I don't know," she admitted. "Not long. It's dying already."

"Then we'd best hurry," Artemis interjected. "Can you make it back to your chariot?"

Euryale nodded. "The tunnels are straightforward enough."

"Good. Then make haste. Ares and I will bring our chariots and meet you there. We can then all leave together." With that, the goddess broke into a trot before bounding out of the hole in the ceiling, Ares following right behind.

Euryale didn't waste any time leaving, either. She raced across the cave, sped through the tunnels, and at the end, descended the cliff with a speed that would raise an eyebrow of Hermes himself. She flew down the pass and reached her chariot even faster. There, next to hers, stood Alex's with his pair of ponies at the yoke, and on the other side, was a massive war chariot made of steel and bronze, complete with spiked wheels, armored sides, and four warhorses, six feet at the shoulder, with fiery manes and giant hooves that could probably shatter boulders with ease. Inside that chariot, Artemis and Ares were patiently waiting.

Euryale's spirits lifted seeing the two, thankful she wouldn't need to wait. And as she climbed into her own chariot and scrambled for the reins, only then did she look back to see if Stheno and Alex were following.

They were.

"You weren't going to leave without us, were you?" Alex chuckled as he hopped into his own.

Euryale's face held no amusement. "Maybe."

"You were?"

"Just you," Stheno said, taking her place at Euryale's side.

"Okay, Artemis," Euryale said, not wanting to delay any longer. "Lead the way."

The goddess nodded, and with her instruction on where to go, Ares sped off. His horses blazed a familiar path through the mountains, their hooves beating on the rock so hard and fast, had the gorgon not been there to see it firsthand, by the sound alone she'd have sworn a stampede of a thousand heads thundered through the pass.

After only a few minutes of racing back the way they'd originally come, Ares veered to the side, taking a winding path with a half dozen switchbacks. It ran alongside the lower mountain pass for about a mile before shooting off to the side and into territory they'd not seen before.

This path felt similar to the original at first, but quickly became more treacherous with numerous drops and a layer of thunderheads hanging above it that felt as if they were practically within arm's reach. Inside the clouds, flashes could be seen, and thunder could be heard. How deadly those clouds would be had yet to be seen, but Euryale was certain every second they spent under them was one too many.

This little fact was accentuated when bolts of lightning exploded the ground next to them, spooking the horses and sending Euryale's already stressed nerves into overdrive.

The three chariots rounded another corner when the path suddenly took a sharp dive, taxing all of Euryale's skill at the reins not to end her travels in disaster. Down they went, hammering over rock and crack, bouncing in their chariots and off one another, in what was little more than a controlled crash to the bottom.

Her chariot skipped off the ground once they reached the end of the steep slope, Stheno clutching the rails to stay onboard and nearly losing her spear in the process.

"Let's not—"

A colossal bolt of lightning cut Stheno off. It streaked through the air, striking the lead pair of horses on Ares's chariot, before jumping to the back two and finally passing through Artemis herself. As the animals collapsed in a smoldering heap, overturning the chariot and throwing its occupants, a second, smaller bolt ripped by.

This next one missed Ares by a foot but found its mark when it grazed one of Alex's ponies in the shoulder. The animal jumped and reared, toppling the cart and throwing Alex, and before he could recover, his ponies ran off in the opposite direction, taking the chariot with them.

"To the right!" Stheno yelled, grabbing Euryale's arms and yanking down on the reins for all she was worth.

The chariot veered to the side, smashing into a small alcove into the mountainous wall right as a third streak of lightning shot by. For a few tense seconds, Euryale kept absolutely still, unsure what was going on, but then a thunderous voice called out to her— a thunderous voice she knew and abhorred.

"Gorgon!" Zeus yelled. "At least have the decency to face justice with your head held high!"

Euryale growled and dared a peek. The path they were on opened up onto a wide plateau with a few house-sized boulders scattered across it. Standing on one of the boulders to the left was Poseidon, trident in hand, eyes full of determination, while Zeus stood off to the right on another. The Ruler of Olympus held the ax with one hand, keeping it resting on his shoulder, while his other gripped another bolt of lightning.

"There's nowhere for you to run, Euryale," he said. "Don't make your friends pay for your treachery more than they already have."

Instead of answering, Euryale surveyed the others. Ares had scrambled behind a rock, spear ready, face hardened, muscles taut. Artemis, on the other hand, lay unmoving several yards away, her clothes scorched black and smoke drifting off her skin. Alex, thankfully, hadn't shared her fate. He took cover behind another boulder, and while he didn't look quite as eager to square off against Zeus and Poseidon, he did have his shield and spear in hand.

"I'm not going to tell you again," Zeus yelled. "Surrender and spare the others your fate."

"I'm going to rip your head off and stick it on a pike!" Stheno shouted back.

Zeus replied with a bolt of lightning, but it wasn't aimed near any of them. It struck the mountain high above their position, sending chunks of rock raining down. A particularly hefty chunk landed near Ares, who promptly scooped it up and hurtled it at Zeus's head. The rock failed to connect, but his aim was true enough, and the missile flew fast enough, that it sent Zeus ducking for cover.

"Ha! Scared of a little rock, are you?" Ares taunted. "It's a wonder your rule wasn't challenged sooner!"

"When I'm done with the gorgon, you're going to be the next example I make," Zeus shouted back. "For the next thousand thousand eons, there won't be a soul alive who won't hear of your terrible end."

"Bold promises for an old and feeble god," Ares went on. "Come down off your pillar and toss your weapon. Let's see who's the strongest."

Zeus, to his credit, didn't take the bait. He answered by blasting the mountain again, and as rocks fell and cracks formed in the ground, it was clear it wouldn't take many more before he triggered an avalanche.

"He's going to bury us all," Euryale muttered.

"Then we'd better act," Stheno said. "Tell me what to do."

Euryale scanned the area one last time, trying to formulate a plan that didn't end in utter failure. Even if this was to be her last day, she wasn't about to let Cassandra die, and once she spied Artemis's bow and quiver near Ares, she had an idea.

"Ares," she called out. "Can you get that to me?"

"If it means a fight instead of pointless talk, I most certainly can!" the God of War called out. He darted from his spot and scooped the items up before dashing over to the two gorgons, lightning sizzling at his heels the entire time.

"I can't wait to see you in glorious battle, gorgon," Ares said as he handed the items over. His words, however, were not directed to Euryale, but Stheno.

After briefly weighing the bow in her hands, she strapped the quiver across her back—a quiver, she noted, which seemed ever full. Euryale then plucked two arrows free and turned her attention to her husband.

"Alex, you've got to get this pouch to Apollo," Euryale said, holding it up briefly before setting it down into the chariot. "Take our horses and go the moment you can."

"No, I'm staying with you."

"No, you aren't," she shouted back. "Now, toss your net!"

"But—"

"Do it!"

Alex swore up and down and shook head his before obeying. The net sailed through the air, and Ares snatched it with his meaty hands. The moment the god did, Euryale gave him and her sister the rest of the plan.

"Zeus wants me, so I'll go first," Euryale said. "The two of you charge Poseidon and wrap him in that net as fast as you can. That should clear a path for Alex. Once Poseidon is taken care of, the three of us take down Zeus. Any questions?"

"Only one, little gorgon," Ares said, eyes glinting with anticipation. "When do we attack?"

"Right now."

Stheno bolted free from their temporary hiding spot the second Euryale popped out and let loose two arrows. They zipped through the air, leaving bright silvery trails in their wake. The first arrow grazed Zeus's cheek, while the second bit into his chest, a little below his left collarbone.

"You're next, Poseidon!" Stheno taunted, bounding across the broken landscape.

The God of the Sea looked down from his perch without worry or seemingly even the need for haste, despite how quickly Stheno and Ares approached. He calmly leveled his trident at the ground in front of them and spoke words she couldn't hear.

A tight beam of water shot out of each point of his weapon, drilling into the rock. Reflexively, Stheno darted sideways, hoping to dodge whatever explosion was about to take place.

Instead of a blast, a serpentine creature formed from the water, three times as tall as Stheno, eyes glowing a fierce blue and maw filled with long needlelike teeth. It dashed forward on a thin layer of saltwater, hissing and snapping at the air.

Ares leaped over them both, clearly eager to engage his uncle, leaving Stheno to fend for herself. The gorgon narrowed her eyes at her fast-approaching adversary and readied her spear. She didn't need the god to take this thing apart. Hell, she'd trained on more fearsome things when she wasn't even a century old.

The sea serpent covered the last twenty yards between it and her like a rogue wave, an explosion of speed and power that seemingly came from nowhere. Stheno sidestepped the attack, slashing across its body with her spear as she did. The blade of the weapon sizzled through the creature.

The monster recoiled and reared back like a cobra, hissing. In that time, Stheno readjusted her footing a split second before it attacked again. The gorgon ducked under its strike but caught a tail slap in the process. She tumbled sideways, ears ringing and world spinning, and crashed into some rock.

Disoriented but far from helpless, Stheno had the wits to keep hold of her spear and tuck her legs beneath her, thereby enabling her to charge forward the moment she could. Water splashed across her face as the serpent tried to finish her off, but it failed to connect.

When her head cleared a second later, she found herself presented with the perfect opportunity to strike at its center.

"Maybe next time, snake," she muttered, driving her spear into its body. The tip easily pierced the monster, and the weapon sank deep.

Stheno tightened her grip as she could feel energy building in the shaft. The creature shuddered and thrashed for a second or two, trying to rid itself of its tormentor, and then exploded.

Stheno turned her attention to Poseidon who was locked in a furious duel with Ares. Though the God of War still held the magical net, it was clear that the two were in a stalemate.

But that wasn't something Stheno couldn't change. The gorgon grinned, eager to taste the blood of the god, and charged forward to join the fray.

CHAPTER A DIVINE CONFLICT

Euryale ducked behind her cover as rock exploded all around, and the scent of ozone filled the air. Right as she was about to duck back out, she shouted at her husband who was awaiting her command.

"Go, Alex!"

At the same time he did, Euryale shot free of her hiding spot to draw Zeus's ire. The moment she could, she sent a well-aimed arrow straight for his heart. The god held his ground, twisting sideways as it came, so it flew harmlessly by.

Alex dashed across the battlefield with his shield high, hoping to use the distraction to his fullest advantage. Lightning flew from Zeus's hands again but struck the aegis Alex carried, and the magical artifact easily deflected the strike.

Euryale sent three more arrows through the air, and though none of them found their mark, Zeus had to fall back enough so that once Alex jumped on the chariot, he was in the clear. In the span of a few heartbeats, the Akhal-Tekes that drove it blew across the battlefield and disappeared.

The day, no matter what else happened from here on out as far as Euryale was concerned, was won.

"That was a mistake, gorgon," Zeus said from behind his cover.

"Making you scramble?" Euryale called back. "Do tell."

"I don't have to worry about your husband," he said. "I was trying not to hurt him unless I had to."

Zeus appeared on top of his boulder once more, arms raised to the heavens. Euryale looked skyward right as the clouds above her lit up with an array of flashes and thunderclaps. The gorgon dove sideways as a foot-wide lightning strike obliterated the ground where she stood.

A second bolt, equally large and devastating, sent her scrambling again while carving out a sizable crater as well. Euryale kept moving, kept praying, as strike after strike thundered, each one drawing nearer and nearer.

The gorgon knew her life was measured in seconds if she didn't do something. Hell, it probably wasn't much longer either way. Still, she had to try. On her next scramble, instead of making another dive or cutback, she brought up her bow and let loose another arrow, not bothering in the least to worry about herself.

The arrow flew as if it had been launched by Artemis herself. The head bit into Zeus's chest, slightly left of his breastbone. The god hunched once it struck, bright-red blood spraying everywhere, but he didn't fall, and he didn't relent.

Another blast came from above, striking the ground only a few inches away. Though Euryale didn't suffer a direct hit, it branched out the moment it struck the ground, finding the gorgon with ease.

Stheno spun, a half dozen yards from Poseidon, when she heard her sister scream in agony.

Euryale had her back arched, arms rigid, as the lightning shot through her. A second later, she fell to the ground, smoking and twitching.

Stheno felt her heart stop at the sight of Euryale falling. But instead of being paralyzed with shock, she let go of what few restraints she had when it came to self-control.

"You're dead! You're all dead!" she screamed. "Do you hear me?"

The gorgon leaped through the air at Poseidon, howling with primal rage, eager to sink her spear into the god's back.

Before she could reach him, however, the god deflected a thrust by Ares and twisted around in time to parry her attack. Stheno landed heavily on the ledge on which they fought and thrust her spear again and again, and each time the weapon surged with power more and more.

However, each strike was deflected by the god, and Poseidon parried each one by Ares as well.

"Pathetic," Poseidon scoffed. "How you ever thought you'd win this battle is beyond me."

Stheno growled and launched herself forward yet again. She knocked his trident aside as she came, intent on closing the distance so fang and viper could do the rest. Poseidon, however, spun in place and whipped his trident around, catching her in the stomach and then the side with the butt of the weapon. The gorgon tumbled to the ground as the breath flew from her lungs.

Ares, seizing the opportunity, drove a strike home of his own. His own spear cut across the back of Poseidon's shoulders, spilling blood and causing him to stumble.

"You're even slower than your brother!" the God of War boasted, stabbing at him yet again.

Poseidon sneered as he turned to avoid the attack. As the spear flew harmlessly by, he wrapped his arm around Ares's and issued a wicked headbutt to the god that sent him reeling backward.

Stheno, finding air once again, gave no warning to her next attack. She simply sprang forward, spear tip leading the way. Though her balance had yet to return fully, she had enough to end the fight. The head of the spear bit into Poseidon's hip, cleaving through flesh and shattering bone.

The God of the Sea fell sideways, only managing to stay on his feet by planting his trident into the ground and using it to catch himself. Stheno was about to finish him off when he unexpectantly dropped and spun, twisting his trident free of the ground and hitting her with a blast of pure energy.

Stheno flew through the air, striking the unyielding mountain rock. As she slid down, breathless, agony coursing through her body, she managed to call out to Ares. "Finish him!"

The God of War, dazed and a few paces away, shook his head and growled. "Gladly."

With a heave, he launched the net. As it flew through the air, it opened wide and fully engulfed the Lord of the Sea. Poseidon reflexively tried to catch it with his hands, but it was too late. Hephaestus's infamous net wrapped him completely.

The god lost his balance and toppled to the ground. His muscles strained as he tried to break the net apart, but it held. Not only did it hold, but with every moment he struggled, it grew tighter and tighter, and within a few seconds, Poseidon was curled in a ball, laying on the ground, unable to move.

"All too easy," Ares boasted, standing tall. He strode over toward Stheno, intending to offer her a hand up, but he never made it there. The God of War went rigid, and lightning shot through him, jumping to her and knocking her senseless.

Euryale groaned and winced as a stabbing pain shot through her head. Her limbs continued to twitch, but with effort, she managed to get control of them and pushed herself up and onto her tail.

Each breath felt excruciating, and it wasn't until she rubbed her temples a few times that she realized where she was and what was going on. That happened to be at the exact moment Zeus struck Ares down.

The thunderous clap that reverberated through the air snapped her attention to the Ruler of Olympus. He stood on shaky legs with an arrow protruding from his chest.

"You gave a fight. I'll grant you that," he muttered as he reached up and broke off the arrow. "But not one that was enough."

Euryale's eyes darted to the ground where Artemis's bow lay a few paces away. Immediately, she dove for the weapon, scooping it up and notching an arrow. The shot flew off the string far slower than she'd have liked, and by the time it reached Zeus, he simply batted it away with his ax.

"What now, gorgon?" he asked as he hopped off his boulder and began marching toward her, ax ready.

Euryale notched another arrow, faster this time, and let it fly. Again, Zeus batted it away, unflinching and undeterred.

"What now, gorgon?" he repeated. "I've ruled this world for thousands of years. Defeated horrors you can't even dream of! Kept Typhon in chains and Cronus at bay! And you dare think you can oppose my reign?"

"I don't dare," she said, retreating and drawing yet again. "I will."

Zeus paused, twenty yards away, and crouched. A moment passed between them as the two narrowed their eyes, each trying to anticipate what the other was going to do.

Zeus moved first.

He leaped at the gorgon, covering the distance between with a madness in his eyes. As he flew, Euryale released her hold on the arrow. The moment the tail cleared the weapon, she dashed sideways and whipped the bow through the air, desperate to deflect the overhead chop Zeus was trying for.

Midflight, Zeus knocked the arrow aside with the flat of the ax, and keeping with its momentum, spun it back around in an effort to take Euryale's head from her shoulders.

The bow was the only thing that saved her life. The ax bit into the weapon, and thanks to its divine origin and as a testimony to Hephaestus's exquisite craftsmanship, the bow held together long enough to parry the attack before shattering.

Euryale, anticipating such a thing, didn't bother holding on to the weapon. Instead, she dashed forward, and before Zeus could swing a second time, she wrapped herself around him, her tail finding his legs, and her claws finding his face.

Zeus turned with the blow, and as blood sprayed from the deep gouges she carved in his face, he snapped his head back around and laughed maniacally. "I like it rough, gorgon," he said. "But then again, I know you do, too."

"Shut up!" Euryale yelled, ripping into him again, only this time, she used fang and viper. She bit into the forearm that carried the ax, and each of the snakes on her head did the same. Together, they dumped enough venom into his blood to fell the entire world ten times over.

Zeus ripped his arm free, howling with rage before smashing a fist into the soft center of her face. As her head snapped back, he then struck her in the gut with a fist and then an elbow across the cheek.

Despite the brutal assault, Euryale, incensed, did not relent. Each strike fueled her hatred for the god even more and more, and the two traded a dozen blows in a matter of seconds. And while the wounds Euryale inflicted were terrible, the ones he gave back felt three times more so.

"Should I tell Alex how much you begged for more?" he taunted. "It's a shame you chose to betray us. You and I could have had such passionate nights together."

"The only one who'll be begging is you," she spat, digging her claws into his cheek, desperately trying to work their way up to his eyes and rip them out.

Another elbow, this one the most forceful yet. Euryale's world spun and darkened, but she refused to let go. Zeus then hit her with an open palm before grabbing her by the throat. "You were saying?"

Euryale coughed, and as he turned her face to his, she let her curse flow from her body. Her eyes radiated a blinding flash of green, and the effects were immediate. Sadly, they weren't lasting.

Zeus's skin turned gray for a moment, even hardened in a few places, but the god grit his teeth and the deep magic he called upon, magic that Hera had used once before and that had likely been prepared long ahead of time, kept him safe.

"Remember this, Euryale," he said, drawing her close. "You didn't defeat Typhon. I did. Twice. Had I not been there to pummel him into submission, he'd have torn you apart."

Zeus's eyes shot wide, and he let her go. His chest heaved forward as the tip of a spear jutted out of his right breast. Stheno, standing behind him, grinned with delight.

Zeus roared, and clutching the spear with his left hand, he used his right to reach out to the thunderheads one last time. The air tingled around them all, and Euryale grabbed his head and forced him to face her one last time.

The curse she bore became a lethal weapon again, and in the instant it struck the God of Thunder, Ruler of Olympus, one more bolt of lightning fell from the heavens.

Chapter The Cost

Smoky, light tendrils curled in the air, wafting from every inch of Euryale's body. She shed some tears as her chest expanded, and another wave of agony ripped through her body.

"Can you move?" Stheno asked.

Euryale exhaled slowly, nodded, and uncoiled from the petrified Zeus. His body, forever frozen in time, stood twisted to the side, one hand raised and vainly trying to shield his face from the gorgon's power. The other hand was outstretched and open from the moment when he had drilled his last bolt of lightning into Euryale's chest.

"Are you okay?" she asked her sister.

Stheno laughed as she planted her foot into the ass of the statue, and with one enormous shove, yanked her spear out of its back. The weapon tore free with such ease that the elder gorgon went toppling. Her shoulder blades struck the inky and yielding ground a second before her feet flew over her head. Though her landing was ungainly, her recovery was anything but. Stheno rolled with the momentum and popped back onto her feet, spear in hand. At that point, she strode over to the statue, letting her hips sway from side to side as a diabolical smile spread across her face and crackles of deep-red energy formed in her eyes.

"I told you we'd kill you," she said, spitting on Zeus's face. "Not so damn tough now, are you? What are you going to do? What are you going to do!" The gorgon smacked him across the face and spat once more before sidling up next to him and draping her arm across his shoulders. "Where should we put him?"

"Nowhere," Euryale said as she slithered a few yards and scooped up the ax. "I don't ever want to see his disgusting face again."

"Come on," Stheno said with a playful begging. "He'd look so good in the throne room. Oh! Oh! Or even better, the acropolis, so every time anyone does anything in Olympus, they have to see what a pathetic wretch he's become."

"Tempting, but no," Euryale said.

"Please?"

"No."

Stheno fell to her knees and clasped her hands in front of her. "PLEASE!"

Euryale sighed heavily and rolled her eyes at her sister's overly theatric performance. "How would we carry him back, anyway? He probably weighs twenty tons."

The gorgon grunted and frowned as reality smacked her in the face. But as quick as that came, her eyes lit up. "Easy. We dismember him, load him in the chariot, glue him all back together once we get home."

"That doesn't sound easy."

"It'll be fun," she countered. "Like a puzzle. A glorious puzzle we can all enjoy."

Euryale shook her head. "Nothing about him will ever be enjoyable."

A groan drew the attention of both. Artemis sat up stiffly. Her eyes found her father's statue, and she arched her eyebrows. "He ambushed us, didn't he?"

"To his end," said Stheno.

"Still, I should've seen it coming." The goddess picked herself up with a grimace. "Where's Ares?"

Euryale pointed to the other side of the battlefield. "He fell on that ledge," she said. "Zeus hit him with lightning."

Artemis dashed over as fast as her smoldering body would allow. When she reached her half-brother, she knelt, and then with a grunt, she rolled him over and rested her head on his chest for a moment. "He lives," she said with a laugh. "Out of stubbornness and a lust for more battle if for no other reason." Artemis paused and scanned the area for his chariot. It still lay toppled, but at least one animal attached to it was trying to get up. "Go," she said. "I can bring back Ares and Poseidon on my own. You have a daughter to save."

Relieved but still concerned, Euryale couldn't help but check to see how true that was. "Are you sure?" she asked. "It's a long walk."

Artemis nodded. "One horse is enough," she said, eyes on the chariot and the creatures that pulled it. "With the Fates' blessing, I may be able to save another. Now go. Please, before all of this is for naught. Just keep following the path that way. We'll see you back in Olympus."

The gorgon nodded and quickly started for Alex's chariot, some hundred yards away. She stopped, however, when another thought came to her. "Take his head," she said to Stheno. "We might need it."

Her sister stopped dead in her tracks. "Seriously?"

"Yes, seriously."

Stheno glowed brighter than any star in the heavens. She bolted over to Zeus and twirled her spear in a full circle over her head before slicing the weapon's blade through the statue's neck. The head fell off cleanly, landing on the ground with a thud.

"Did that hurt?" she said, gleefully scooping it up and looking it in the eyes. "That looked like that hurt."

"Stheno…"

"Yes?" she said, throwing a grin to Euryale.

"Can you please stop playing with your kill?"

"Why? Do you want a turn?"

"No. I want to go."

The two made their way back to the chariot where Stheno stuffed the head into the other sack Nyx had provided. Euryale picked up the reins, and with a sharp snap, she sent the two ponies racing forward.

It didn't take them long to break free of the mountains, and once the rocky peaks had disappeared in the gloom behind them, the ponies shot into the air before crossing into Nyx's domain once again.

They sped over dark waters, carving a wake that stretched into the heavens. Though they'd enjoyed a brief respite once the battle was over, now that they raced back to Olympus, Euryale realized they'd yet to win the day. Cassandra's very existence still teetered on the edge of oblivion, and even if—nay, even with Alex reaching the city with the flower, Euryale had no idea how long the antidote Apollo would concoct would last. Would it deteriorate as fast as the flower wilted?

She prayed harder than she ever had that that would not be the case.

"Hang on, sweetheart," she whispered. "We're coming."

Stheno slid her arm over her sister's shoulders and squeezed gently. "She's going to be fine."

"I know," Euryale said, though the tremor in her voice belied the certainty she tried to show.

"We didn't come this far to fail," Stheno said. "*You* didn't come this far to fail."

Euryale smiled as she felt the tension in her body melt. Her sister was right. She hadn't gone through all of this just to be met with disaster in the final moments. Her daughter would be made whole, and before anyone knew it, this would all be a distant memory. Of course, there was still the matter of hunting down the one who'd poisoned her daughter in the first place—Typhon, no doubt, but that would come in time.

"Thank you for protecting me," she said, turning to Stheno.

"As if I'd do anything else. I'm not sure if I should be insulted at the insinuation or not."

Euryale nodded and didn't reply for a few minutes, instead just letting her thoughts churn as they flew. Nyx's island appeared off in the distance, and thoughts of their encounter with her resurfaced. When they did, Euryale couldn't help but ask her sister something. "Do you still want power?"

"What do you think?"

"Honestly?" she replied, keeping her eyes focused on what was ahead. "Yes, I think you do. Am I right?"

Stheno smiled and nudged her with her hip. "Does Atlas hold up the world? Do the Fates control destiny? Is Zeus a pretty little ornament I can't wait to place somewhere?"

Euryale laughed at the last remark, but in the end, she couldn't help but feel her shoulders slump. "I figured as much."

Stheno leaned her head against her sister's shoulder and gave her another hug. "Not at the expense of you, though," she said. "On this, I will always swear."

Euryale leaned playfully away. "Even if Nyx tempts you?"

Stheno burst into laughter. "Especially if Nyx tempts me."

The speed of their flight increased more and more. The cold air and dreamlike nature surrounding Nyx's home soon gave way to an open sea shimmering with a gorgeous sunrise. Euryale took a moment to enjoy it all, letting the salty air tantalize her senses and the warmth of sunlight strike her face. The relief she felt being back in the world she lived in and knew helped bolster her spirits.

Eventually, Euryale pulled on the reins, sending the chariot rocketing into the sky, and after plowing through a number of thick clouds the size of small countries, they found Olympus. Within a couple of minutes, they made one circle of Apollo's temple before landing at the foot of the steps leading inside.

"Alex? Apollo?" Euryale called out, jumping off the chariot and racing inside. "We're here!"

No one replied, but that didn't faze the gorgon in the least. She plowed through the god's home, racing through the halls and barreling through closed doors, ax in hand. When she reached the asclepeion, she burst through the door with such force, it was only by the intervention of the Fates that the door didn't disintegrate.

Alex, waiting in a chair next to their daughter, jumped from his seat. "You made it!" he shouted, bounding over and scooping her up. "You actually made it."

Euryale, still held high, looked down at her husband and smiled. "Yes, I made it," she said, eyes watering. Her hands caressed the sides of his face for a moment before she planted a kiss on his lips.

She kept pressing into him for an eternity, heart overflowing, body shaking, until her sister cleared her throat.

"Daughter?" she said. "I'm merely throwing it out there. Maybe you two love birds could ravish each other once we're finished protecting the bloodline?"

Euryale pulled back, feeling a little stupid and thoroughly overwhelmed. "Please tell me Apollo made a cure."

"I did," the Olympian said. The god stood on the opposite side of Cassandra's petrified form, holding a small glass with glowing, scarlet liquid. "Restoring her flesh, however, is still beyond my ability."

"But we have that taken care of, too, right?" Euryale said, looking at her husband as she eased out of his arms. "You said you did. You promised."

Alex nodded. "It is taken care of," he replied. He reached up and stroked the side of her face before running his fingers through her snakes. "You think I'd lie about that?"

A gnawing pit took hold of her stomach, and icy fingers gripped her heart. This, she knew, should be a moment of inexplicable joy and relief, but the sorrow in his eyes said this was anything but. "What?"

Alex smiled, clearly forced. "Nothing."

"This isn't nothing," Euryale said. She could feel her heart quicken in her chest. Her breaths never seemed to take in enough air, and even Stheno had picked up on his behavior, and she'd barely known him.

"I'll tell you in a minute. I promise," he said, outstretching his hand. "But let's save our daughter first. Give me the ax."

Euryale shied away at first, turning her head and eyeing him with suspicion. Despite her apprehension, she handed the weapon over.

"Exactly how does this work again?" Stheno asked.

Alex didn't answer. He walked around the table that held Cassandra and turned briefly to slip by Apollo. Right as he neared the door to a storeroom, it opened and out stepped Hera.

Euryale's jaw dropped, and then it practically hit the floor when Alex placed the weapon in her waiting hands.

"Hello, Euryale," the Queen of Olympus said with a snicker. "Seeing the look on your face almost makes up for what you did to me. Almost."

The gorgon barely heard her words. She recoiled, nearly losing her balance in the process, eyes fixated on her husband. "Alex," she gasped. "What have you done?"

"Saved our daughter," he replied.

"And you? You knew?" she said to Apollo, heart cracking as much as her voice did.

The God of the Sun and Medicine, Giver of Prophecy, merely nodded.

Hera casually made her way to Cassandra. She dropped her free hand on the child's forehead and stroked the cold stone a few times, all the while wearing a smirk upon her face. "Funny what the

Fates have done, isn't it?" she asked. "After all you did, all my plans you ruined, nothing's changed, has it?"

"More has changed than you'll ever realize," Euryale growled. She felt the heat of battle rise in her heart and power build behind her eyes. She had taken the goddess down once. She could do it again—*would* do it again.

The gorgon shook her head. No, she couldn't. Not while Cassandra was the way she was.

"Ah, good girl," Hera said, her words dripping with condescension. "I had my doubts when your husband promised me that you'd control yourself."

"You made your point," Alex said. "I've done my part. Now you do yours. That's the deal."

"Yes, I suppose my oaths are as binding as yours, aren't they?" She then placed her hand back on Cassandra's head and began to chant softly. The words that passed her lips had a slow rhythm to them, ones that put goosebumps across Euryale's skin and sent her vipers into a nervous state. As Hera went on, her hand glowed a soft orange, and that glow quickly spread across Cassandra's body and along both the shaft and the head of the ax.

A moment later, Euryale's daughter gasped, clutching her chest with one hand and using the other to keep from falling off the table.

Apollo darted to Cassandra's side, supporting her body with an arm below her back and using his free hand to bring the antidote to her lips. "Drink."

Cassandra took a sip but stopped as her face shriveled like she'd tasted something putrid. "It's gross."

"I know, but you must," he said, offering it again.

"Daddy?"

Alex patted her shoulder. "It'll make you better," he said. "Go on. I'll get you some candy cotton later."

"Cotton candy, Daddy," she said, coughing.

"Right, that too."

Cassandra eyed the concoction with a frown. Then, with a deep breath and a pinch of the nose, she took it all with a single gulp. Her face immediately soured even more, making her look a thousand years old with all the wrinkles it produced. Her snakes thrashed wildly, some even striking at each other, but after a few seconds, they calmed, and she relaxed. The black lines that marred her body shrank and quickly faded away.

"Do you feel better?" Alex asked.

"Yeah, but that was really gross," she said, trying to spit the taste out of her mouth. When she couldn't, she opted for licking her arm, which apparently didn't help either. "Like really, really gross. Like almost as bad when you tried making moussaka that one time."

Euryale couldn't help but laugh at the remark, and it was Cassandra enough that she snapped back into the moment and raced to her side.

Cassandra bolted off the bed in the opposite direction, darting behind her father and clutching him tightly.

"Sweetie," Euryale choked. "I'm not going to hurt you."

"Mmm, I bet you would've said that before, too," Hera gloated.

Euryale lunged; the only thing keeping her from tearing into the goddess before she reacted was the fact that there was still a table between the two. Hera instantly had the ax at the ready, its double blades glowing bright and humming with energy, causing Euryale to freeze in place.

"You teeter on destruction, gorgon," Hera said with a glare. "I suppose I'm obligated to tell you that as part of my arrangement with your husband, I'm to let you go. But don't for one second think that means I can't and won't defend myself. That's not a fight you're going to win."

"Zeus thought the same," Stheno said.

"Yes, I imagine he did," Hera said, unimpressed. "Turned him to stone, did you? He might look good as a statue for a while. But you'll find I'm a little more resilient when it comes to such things."

Stheno's only reply was slinging the sack she'd been carrying over her shoulder so that Zeus's petrified head contained within rolled out.

"Fates' end," Apollo muttered, eyes wide as he backed away.

Hera tightened her grip on the ax. Veins bulged in her neck and along the side of her head. "Get out of my city," she said in a slow, harsh voice. "Now."

"Your city?" Stheno replied, readying her spear. "I think you'll find it's ours, bitch."

Hera narrowed her eyes, and her fingers twitched, something Euryale knew was a prelude to a cascade of spells being slung their way, spells that no doubt would hit Alex and Cassandra in the process. And while the Queen of Olympus no doubt had a lot of anger for her former husband, it was clear that she hadn't wanted him to be decapitated. She longed for a fight, and the only thing keeping her from entering one was whatever oaths she'd made with Alex.

"I'll not ask again," Hera said. "Leave."

Stheno didn't budge.

Euryale gently took the gorgon by the elbow and tugged. "Not here," she said. "Not now."

"Yes, here, and yes, now!"

"Not while my child is in the middle of it," Euryale said.

"Come now, Stheno," Hera purred. "Are you afraid of me? That weak and insignificant, you're going to run with your tail tucked after an old crone shoos you away?"

"I'm not the one shaking," Stheno said. "You are."

"Am I?" Hera chuckled. "Then I guess you've nothing to fear. Come, strike me down. Take my place as Queen of Olympus, if you like. Who am I to stop you?"

Stheno tensed, and for a moment, Euryale thought she might strike, but the gorgon simply pointed the tip of her spear at Hera's head and spoke. "I'll be back for you," she promised. "This isn't over."

Hera grinned. "I'll be looking forward to it."

With a tentative moment of peace now at hand, Alex turned and knelt in front of Cassandra. "Go on," he said, tousling her vipers. "Go see Mommy. You'll be fine."

"I don't want to."

"I know she was scary before, but all that's over now," he said. "Don't you want to see your brother? And Tickles?"

Cassandra nodded and eased toward Euryale with trepidation. Euryale, in turn, patiently waited for her daughter to come, and when the girl didn't protest at taking her hand, Euryale scooped her up and hugged her tight. A few beats passed between them before she looked at her husband and gestured toward the door. "Let's go, Alex," she said. "We're done here."

"I...I can't."

"What do you mean, you can't?"

"Oh, did that little caveat to my help not get brought up yet?" Hera said with mock surprise. "How careless I am, but allow me a moment to clear up any misunderstandings. Your dear, sweet husband is now my loyal servant."

"Euryale, I—"

Hera shot her hand up, cutting Alex off. "Did I say you could speak?"

Alex shook his head.

"See? He knows his place already," Hera went on. "It'll give you something to think about on your way out."

Chapter Fin

"Mommy? Why isn't Daddy coming?"

It was at least the third time Cassandra had asked the question. Euryale wasn't sure of the total number since she was doing all she could to hold it together as they left. She knew Cassandra deserved an answer—*needed* an answer—but she had none to give, at least, none that didn't involve the foulest language and the most gruesome vows that the Fates would no doubt hold her to.

Stheno seemed to share the same sentiments. "Hera can't get away with this," she said as they cleared the entrance to Apollo's temple. "I thought—"

"She won't," Euryale said. "As you said, we'll be back. But I have to ensure the safety of my children first."

"Promise?"

"Absolutely," Euryale replied.

The trio soon exited Apollo's temple. Initially, Euryale headed for her own chariot with its adorable and loyal ponies waiting for her return, but when she spied Apollo's, the one Alex had used to escape the ambush with, she shifted course. Those horses were faster than any other she could hope to obtain. And that was something that she might need to rely on in the near future.

"Grab my chariot, if you would," Euryale said, nodding toward her own. "I'll take this one."

"Anything else you want to get before we go?"

"Only Aison," Euryale replied as she grabbed her phone to call Artemis. Right as she was about to get in touch with her, she noticed a small envelope tucked away in the chariot's carriage.

Unsure of its significance, Euryale picked it up and gave it a look. On the front, scrawled in her husband's messy handwriting, was her name. On the back sat a simple seal of emerald-green wax with "A&E" stamped in its center, perfectly round and unbroken.

"What is it?" Stheno asked.

"A letter from Alex," she replied after her heart skipped three beats.

With the care of a world-class surgeon, Euryale broke the seal and opened the envelope before gently removing the letter contained within. It was folded in half, written on heavy, rough paper. For a long time, all she did was stare at it, scared to death what it might say, for without having yet seen it, she already knew why it was there.

"Aren't you going to read it, Mommy?"

Euryale mouthed a yes, or at least, she thought she did.

"Come here, my vicious little niece," Stheno said, snatching her up. "Help me check the horseshoes."

"They don't have shoes, silly."

"Well, we better check anyway. You never know."

Euryale placed a pair of fingers to her lips and slowly opened the note. Her vision blurred the moment she saw Alex's chicken scratch, but she forced herself to focus on what the letter had to say.

It read:

To my dearest Euryale, the light of my life, keeper of my heart and soul, the woman I breathe for, and the perfect mother to our perfect children,

It's strange to pen this letter to you. I'm about to go find Hera, and if you've found this, that means things have gone, well, about as well I expected them to. You know, Hera and all.

At the very least, you should have Cassandra back. Let her know every day I love her with all my heart, just as I love you with everything I have and am. Tell her I think about her with every breath I take, and when she's grown, be sure to let her know how honored I am to be her father.

Aison, too. Tell him how he's so much stronger and braver than his dad ever was, and that I'm in awe of all that he does and all that he'll be. But most of all, make sure he knows there's not a father out there that's prouder of his son than I am of him.

And tell yourself...Oh, I could write countless books on that. I'm not sure where even to begin.

Do you remember when we first met? I mean after I jumped in fright and knocked myself silly on that boulder. When I stirred, thoroughly dazed, I called you an angel as you loomed over me. You laughed, that sweet, melodic laugh that warms my heart every time I think about it, and said, 'I'm no angel.'

Oh, how you're wrong.

So very, very wrong.

You're my angel. You're the woman who rescued me from an eternity of solitude, a woman who's shown more strength than Ares, more courage than all the heroes of Elysium, and who has proven herself the most capable, patient, and loving mother and spouse the world has ever seen.

If that's not what makes an angel, I don't know what does.

I'm sure our children will have questions. I'm sure you do, too. And if all of you are mad at me for what I've done, I understand. I would only pray that at some point in time before the stars burn out and this world grows cold, you don't hold my choice against me.

All that said, I don't know what the future holds for me. I will forever long to be at your side again, to see that beautiful smile of yours once more, to feel the soft caress of your hands and see that twinkle in your eyes when you look at me.

But if there's one thing I don't ever want out of all of this, it's that you suffer on my account. So, if the Fates have other plans that do not include our reuniting, I want you to find someone else. You shouldn't be alone, and you deserve to have someone love you as much as I did. I'm sure he's out there, somewhere, and I'm sure he'll take wonderful care of you—and you, him.

I love you. Always. Forever.
- Alex

Euryale carefully folded the letter closed, and sometime later, Stheno returned while Cassandra kept inspecting the ponies. She didn't know what sort of expression she wore on her face, but her sister embraced her fully the moment she looked at her.

"I'm here," Stheno whispered, hugging her tight.

Euryale furrowed her brow, digging her nails into Stheno's back. And as blood ran freely down bronzed skin, Euryale's eyes darkened, and her pupils went to slits. "I'm going to make her wish she were never born," she growled. "By the River Styx, I'll have her head on display for the world to see."

"That's dark," Stheno grinned, not at all taken aback by the utter seriousness of the oath. "I don't suppose you have a plan brewing in that delightfully vengeful mind of yours? Because I think she's going to command all of Olympus against us."

Euryale knew what to do, though up until a few minutes ago, she'd never have considered it. The Fates had set a path for her—a path offered not even a half day ago. "We go back to Nyx and do whatever it takes to become her adopted daughters," she said, slowly watching this future unfold in her mind.

Stheno chuckled. "You're serious?"

"More than I have ever been before."

"But she hates me."

"We'll have to find a way to change that," Euryale replied. "Because when we return, I want us both to be so dreadful, Hera could never fathom what we're capable of."

Stheno flashed a wicked smile. "Oh, I like the sound of that," she purred. "I like the sound of that a lot."

EPILOGUE

Athena wearily raised her head. Chains still bound her wrists behind her and kept her ankles pinned together, each link enchanted ten times over to nullify any magic she might employ to escape. When her gray eyes focused on her latest visitor who stood outside her jail, the Goddess of Wisdom sighed heavily.

"Athena, my dear, sweet child," Hera said, her voice teetering a strange line between contempt and elation. "What have you done to find yourself in such a predicament?"

"I'm sure you know already," Athena replied. "I take it Alex gave you the ax?"

Hera smirked. "I'm surprised you ever thought he wouldn't."

"Knowing he would and hoping he wouldn't aren't mutually exclusive."

"And yet you said nothing. Why?"

"Because it was the right thing to do," Athena said. "Cassandra had to be saved, and if she weren't, I still shudder to think what desperate measures her parents would resort to."

Hera folded her arms over her chest and drummed her immaculate fingernails on her side. For several tense moments, the Queen of Olympus stared at Athena, scrutinizing every inch of her

322

body. Eventually, the sharpness in her features softened, as did the tone in her voice. "Tell me, Athena, do you think I was wrong to seize the throne?"

"Why? Are you still looking for loyal subjects?"

"Is that a yes or a no?" When Athena didn't immediately reply, Hera, surprisingly, kept her calm. "I wasn't lying when I told Aphrodite I'd gone to great lengths trying to ensure no one was hurt when I tried the first time. And as it were, I'd love to put the past behind us and release you this very moment."

"If I pledge my fidelity to you," Athena finished.

"That and find your troublesome sisters as a show of good faith to me," Hera said.

Athena cocked her head. "Sisters?"

"Sisters," Hera said, nodding. "It would seem that Artemis and Aphrodite have fled Olympus. Being close to them both, you should have no trouble finding and bringing them back."

Athena snorted and shook her head. "To face your wrath?"

"Only if they don't bend the knee," Hera said. "I'm not so brutish to realize it would be a terrible waste to destroy either. You have my word they'll both be afforded the opportunity to repent so we can all live under a unified house once again."

Athena spent a few moments genuinely considering the offer, not because it was anywhere close to ideal, but because the threat of Typhon still loomed, and if he were able to regain his strength during an Olympian civil war, he could very well destroy whoever was left when the dust settled. That said, another matter—a more personal one—came to mind. "And what of Euryale? Are you going to let her be as well?"

Hera growled, and her features hardened at the gorgon's name. "With her husband as my loyal subject, I think we both know how that will eventually play out."

Athena nodded, her body slumping in the chains. "Then no," she said. "I will not help you."

The Queen of Olympus narrowed her eyes and drew in a long, slow breath. "You will rot here for the next ten thousand years if that's the path you want," she said. "Are you sure?"

"Dad was wrong to set himself against her," Athena replied. "Both in terms of underestimating her ability and in terms of refusing to believe he wronged her. Don't make the same mistake he did."

"And she killed him!" Hera roared, her hands grabbing the bars that separated the two. "She didn't just turn him to stone—something I could reverse. She took his head and cast it in front of us all to see. Did you know that, *child*?"

Athena jerked, body straightening, breath catching in her chest. "He's...he's dead?"

"Yes," Hera calmly replied and backing a half step. "Your father is dead by the gorgon's hand."

Athena shook her head as her gaze drifted to the stone floor at her feet. "I don't believe it."

Hera chuckled sickeningly. She didn't care one bit, no doubt, that her wayward husband had met his end, other than perhaps she found it a tremendous insult that a monster dared lay a finger on an Olympian. But she also knew how close Athena and Zeus had been, and no doubt was using his death to try and manipulate her. "Tell you what, dear child," Hera said. "I'll bring you his head, set it here for you to look at. And then in a week, we'll see where your heart is."

Athena managed a feeble nod for a reply. She said nothing, did nothing, until Hera had left. A solid two or three minutes passed before anything happened. Then, a portion of wall near the far corner of the room shimmered. Artemis dropped her arm and flipped her magical cloak over her shoulder, revealing not only herself, but Aphrodite as well, huddled against her.

"That was close," Aphrodite said, exhaling sharply.

"I told you I could beat a false path she'd take to," Artemis said, chest puffing with pride.

Aphrodite grinned as much as her disfigured face would allow. "I'm sorry I ever doubted you."

Athena cleared her throat. "Perhaps less chatting and more freeing should be in order."

Artemis gave a slight bow and whipped out a tiny copper key from the folds of her robe. "Of course. I'll have you out of there before you can say *logolepsy*."

"*Logolepsy*," Athena said.

Artemis froze for a moment with the key in the lock. "Maybe you should count to ten first." She then grinned and added. "Slowly."

Acknowledgements

I feel like I have to thank the Greeks at this point for giving me such a wonderful world to play in and explore, especially whoever first thought up Euryale and Nyx (who was surprisingly fun to write).

Thanks to all the fans of the series as well. Without you, it would never be.

And then of course, Crystal, my fantastic editor who's helped guide this series from the start, as well as Natasha, the best narrator an author could ever hope for, hands down.

Last, and never least, I'll always be eternally grateful to both the Mrs. and the Littles for providing motivation and inspiration as I work on all the stories in my head.

About the Author

When not writing, Galen Surlak-Ramsey has been known to throw himself out of an airplane, teach others how to throw themselves out of an airplane, take pictures of the deep space, and wrangle his four children somewhere in Southwest Florida.

He's also recently taken up murder yoga, and thus discovered a passion for choking friends out.

Drop by his website https://galensurlak.com/ to see what other books he has out, what's coming soon, and check out the newsletter. (Well, sign up for the newsletter and get access to awesome goodies, contests, exclusive content, etc.)

About the Publisher

Tiny Fox Press LLC
5020 Kingsley Road
North Port, FL 34287

www.tinyfoxpress.com